12/23/19

HUCKLEBERRY LAKE

Titles by Catherine Anderson

HUCKLEBERRY LAKE

A MYSTIC CREEK NOVEL

Catherine Anderson

BERKLEY
NEW YORK

BERKLEY
An imprint of Penguin Random House LLC
penguinrandomhouse.com

Copyright © 2019 by Adeline Catherine Anderson
Excerpt from *Spring Forward* by Catherine Anderson copyright ©
2018 by Adeline Catherine Anderson

Library of Congress Cataloging-in-Publication Data

Names: Anderson, Catherine (Adeline Catherine), author.
Title: Huckleberry lake : a Mystic Creek novel / Catherine Anderson.
Description: First Edition. | New York : Berkley, 2019. | Series: Mystic creek
Identifiers: LCCN 2019033794 (print) | LCCN 2019033795 (ebook) |
ISBN 9780593198032 (hardcover) | ISBN 9780399586392 (ebook)
Subjects: GSAFD: Love stories.
Classification: LCC PS3551.N34557 H83 2019 (print) |
LCC PS3551.N34557 (ebook) | DDC 813/.54—dc23
LC record available at https://lccn.loc.gov/2019033794
LC ebook record available at https://lccn.loc.gov/2019033795

Berkley hardcover edition / December 2019
Jove mass-market edition / December 2019

Printed in the United States of America
1 3 5 7 9 10 8 6 4 2

Jacket design and photo composition by Colleen Reinhart
Book design by George Towne

HUCKLEBERRY LAKE

CHAPTER ONE

Erin De Laney's hands were already shaking when her old Honda decided to get a bad case of mechanical indigestion. Just as she maneuvered the car around a sharp curve, it belched like a locomotive suddenly out of steam, lurched three times, and stopped on the gravel road with a shudder. The ensuing silence was punctuated by popping sounds from the cooling engine. She released a pent-up breath and let her shoulders go limp against the back of the driver's seat. A local mechanic had warned her the Honda's fuel pump was about to cock up its toes, but she'd taken a gamble that it would keep working until payday. Since Lady Luck had never been her friend, she was tempted to thump herself on the head. Now, here she sat, miles from home, in a vehicle that wouldn't move until a tow truck transported it into town.

Erin gazed out the dusty windshield dappled with afternoon sunlight that slanted through the needle-laden boughs of countless ponderosa pines. At least she would have a pleasing view while she waited for help. She loved her new hometown of Mystic Creek, Oregon, and the beautiful, mountainous terrain that surrounded the small valley where it rested. No matter where she was, she could find something lovely to admire. Unfortunately, that was the only plus in her otherwise dead-end life. Maybe Mary Poppins or Pollyanna would look on the bright side, but Erin's inner sunshine had blinked out.

Normally she didn't embrace gloomy thoughts, but having just attended her uncle Slade's wedding and witnessing so much love and hard-won happiness, she felt depression riding her shoulders like an oxbow. *True love, a reason for being.* She was glad that her uncle had finally found that. In fact, she was pleased for everyone involved that all had come right for Slade and his new wife, Vickie, in the end. But seeing so many faces aglow with joy had filled her with yearning for a taste of the same, and it was such an unlikely scenario that it made her feel empty and alone. She hated her job as a county deputy. Her social life consisted mostly of chatting with old ladies about their cats. She couldn't get a guy to give her a second look. She wasn't even sure anyone gave her a *first* look. And now her only form of transportation had petered out on her. Where in all of that was a silver lining?

She drew her cell phone from the pocket of her floral-pattern skirt to call for a tow truck, but before she dialed, it struck her that she should probably at least get out and lift the hood of her car. Otherwise she'd look like a helpless female, and that wasn't and never would be her MO. Other wedding guests would be traveling this road soon as they drove back to town. It was one thing for Erin to know she was pathetic; it was quite another to allow herself to *look* pathetic.

After releasing her seat belt and gathering the folds of her skirt, she pushed open the driver's door and stepped onto the gravel road. Sharp-edged rocks rolled under the soles of her pink heels, reminding her of how sore her feet were from wearing impractical footwear on a lumpy lawn all afternoon. Given her druthers, she chose to wear boots, county-issue riding boots when she was on duty and black commando boots when she wasn't. They never pinched her toes, and she didn't wobble like a tightrope walker when she wore them.

Tottering and wincing, she circled the front bumper of her car and popped up the hood. One thing her father had never insisted that she learn was how to do mechanic work. She peered into the greasy abyss and acknowledged that she recognized three things: the battery, the oil cap, and the windshield-cleaner reservoir. The unpleasant smell of gasoline wafted to her nose, verifying that the fuel pump had indeed malfunctioned. She deserved a gold star just for figuring out that much. Automobiles mystified her. Half the time, she wasn't sure what a warning light meant.

She wanted a life partner, not just someone to cheer her on when her confidence flagged, but a companion to watch movies with, dine out with her, and believe in her. She was lonely, damn it. Oh, sure, she had her best friend, Julie Price, to keep her company, but that was different. And, of course, she had Uncle Slade, who loved her dearly and was always there if she needed him. With his marriage to his lifelong sweetheart today, Erin had accumulated a heap of new relatives as well: her first cousin, Brody; his wife, Marissa; and their three sons, plus a gaggle of cousins and second cousins by marriage. Raised as an only child by parents who didn't socialize much with relatives, Erin appreciated having extended family for the first time in her memory. But having friends and relations wasn't the same as having one special person she could call her own.

Just then, she heard the rumble of a diesel engine. She quickly got a little grease on her hands so it would appear that she'd been tinkering with the engine. Then she straightened and peered around the uplifted hood. When she saw a late-model, silver Dodge pickup, she almost groaned. *Not Wyatt Fitzgerald. Please, God, not now.* Only it was Wyatt, of course. After being the recipient of his disdain all afternoon, she wanted to grind her teeth.

The driver's door opened. His dog, Domino, leaped out and raced toward Erin. A beautiful border collie mix, he had long, silky black fur splashed with white.

"Hello, sweet boy." Erin didn't want to pet him with greasy hands, but Domino reared up, planted his paws on her chest, and bathed her chin with doggy kisses, which gave her no choice. "Yes, I'm glad to see you, too."

She wished she could say the same for his owner, who strode toward her with a well-oiled shift of his narrow hips. She had just seen Wyatt a few minutes ago at the reception, and there was no reason for her to drink in every detail of his appearance again, but he'd changed out of a

Western-cut suit into work clothes, and he looked as sexy as a guy could get. Tall, well-muscled, and lean, he had the broad shoulders and deep chest of a man who pitted his strength against the elements every day. Beneath his tan Stetson, hair the color of an August wheat field fell as straight as a bullet to the yoke of his red shirt. His eyes, as blue as laser beams, struck a startling contrast to his sun-burnished face.

She forced her attention back to the dog before Wyatt could chastise him for jumping up and said, "It's been at least twenty minutes since we saw each other, which is seven times longer for a dog than it is for people, so I understand his excitement. Please don't scold him."

The last person Wyatt Fitzgerald wanted to see was Erin De Laney. For a man like him, she meant nothing but trouble. For starters, she was pretty, with her wealth of dark hair, dainty features, and expressive blue eyes. And she obviously felt as attracted to him as he was to her. *Not happening.* He'd sworn off women six years ago, and that was one promise to himself that he meant to keep. He'd be especially cautious with Erin, a county deputy. If he messed up with her, she wouldn't have to call the law on him; she *was* the law.

"Most people try to coast over to the side of the road when their cars break down," he called out. "When I came around that curve, I had to lock up the brakes to keep from turning that car into a Honda pancake."

She continued to pet his ill-mannered dog. "You're assuming that all cars continue to roll after the engine dies. My Honda did a three-count burp and stopped dead in its tracks."

"You should have recognized trouble with the first burp and steered toward the ditch on burps two and three. A stalled car in the middle of a curvy road is a hazard."

She gave him a syrupy-sweet smile that didn't reach her beautiful blue eyes. "How remiss of me. I'm sure you would have kept a much clearer head if you'd been behind the wheel. Unfortunately, not all of us are superior beings."

Wyatt knew he was being a jerk, but he had no experience with women who had romantic notions about him. He didn't know how to discourage Erin and be nice to her at the same time. So he was being a jackass. That worked. She didn't flirt with him when she was pissed off.

He shifted his attention to his dog, who was not aiding his cause. For reasons beyond him, Domino had fallen in love with Erin at first sight last September and remained besotted ever since. "Domino, *off*!" Wyatt ordered, disregarding Erin's plea for leniency. It wasn't her dog, and Wyatt didn't want Domino to develop bad manners. "Off, I said!"

Erin dimpled a cheek and said, "He's fine, Wyatt." Then she resumed ruffling the animal's fur. "Yes, you're wonderful," she told the dog. "It's good to know that at least somebody likes me."

Reading her lips to determine each word she uttered, Wyatt found himself wishing he could hear the intonations of her voice. Why, he didn't know, because he felt sure every syllable dripped with sarcasm. During the wedding reception, she'd attempted to chat with him, and he'd shut her down. So now she was all butt-hurt about it. A part of him felt bad about that, but he couldn't afford concern over her. For him, holding her at arm's length was a matter of self-preservation. Today, he found her even more tempting than usual. The silky blouse and flowery skirt displayed her body in a way that a shirt and trousers didn't, making him acutely aware of her physically. Not a good thing. Because of this woman, he'd recently awakened in the middle of the night from the first wet dream he'd had in at least fifteen years. Talk about embarrassing. He'd been surrounded by other men in the bunkhouse, and when he woke up, every other guy in the room had been sitting straight up in bed. Now, whenever Wyatt thought about that night, his stomach felt as if it shriveled up like a rotten walnut. *Dear God.* In his dream, he'd been making love to Erin, no holds barred. And although he hadn't asked, he knew all the other men had guessed what was going on. *Just our foreman, getting his rocks off. Poor, deaf bastard.*

"What?" Erin demanded. "You're glaring at me like I just popped your last birthday balloon."

He hadn't meant to scowl at her. Trying to smooth the wrinkles from his brow, he curved his lips in what he hoped resembled a smile.

It wasn't that he disliked Erin. Far from it. She just resurrected yearnings and feelings that he couldn't allow himself to have. He wished he knew how to distance himself from her without making her feel rejected. Only how could a guy do that? He guessed he could explain, but in order to do that, he'd have to tell her things about himself she had no need to know. His checkered past was his business and only his business.

Deciding to ignore her comment, he said, "What seems to be the issue with the car?"

She gave Domino a final pat and gently pushed him down. "The fuel pump bit the dust." She held up greasy hands. "There's nothing for it but to get a new pump. That means my car will be at the repair shop for a few days."

Wyatt dragged his gaze from her full lips to the exposed engine. He'd never met a woman with so many talents. He wasn't really surprised to learn that they included shade-tree mechanics. She could make a guy feel inadequate without half trying. "Any way to jerry-rig it so you can make it into town?"

She shook her head. "Nope. Replacing the pump is my only option. I was about to call for a tow truck."

Wyatt's boss, Slade Wilder, was Erin's uncle, so Wyatt knew she didn't make much money as a junior deputy. Towing services didn't come cheap, and the expense would put a dent in her budget. "No coverage for roadside services, I take it."

"I canceled it last month. Doesn't that figure? I paid the premiums for fifteen years and never needed to use it. Then, right after I drop the coverage, bang. Call it bad karma, I guess."

Wyatt preferred to think of it as plain old bad luck, at least for him. She needed help, and he was elected. His pickup was capable of towing her car into town, and he couldn't in good conscience allow her to call for assistance she couldn't afford when he was already on-site.

"I can tow it in for you."

She shook her head. "I appreciate the offer, but I don't want to bother you."

She bothered him more than she could possibly know. "I carry everything I ever need in my toolbox, including a heavy tow chain.

Unfortunately, I don't have a tow bar, but that only means you'll have to steer the vehicle and tap the brake when necessary so you don't rear-end me. Think you can do that?"

She folded her arms at her waist. And a very slender waist it was. When she wore a uniform, which was most of the time, her attractive figure was buried under loose-fitting clothing, and her waistline was bulked up by a belt loaded with cop paraphernalia. Today, dressed in feminine attire suitable for a backyard wedding and reception, she looked good enough to make a man's mouth go dry. And that was his whole problem with her. He couldn't be around her without wanting to taste that kissable mouth of hers—and other parts of her as well.

"I can do that, yes. But, like I just said, I don't want to be a bother." She rested a slender hand on Domino's head, her fingertips absently stroking his silken fur.

"No bother. I'm making a grocery run for the bunkhouse, so I'm going into town anyway. I'll drop your car off at the Timing Light and then give you a lift home."

"It's Sunday," she said. "Buck won't be there."

"He has a drop box for car keys. You can just lock up the Honda, drop your keys through the slot, and then give him a call in the morning to get an estimate."

"An estimate won't be necessary. That's the only auto repair shop in town. Taking the car into Crystal Falls for competitive bids would cost so much that any money I saved would be wiped out by towing fees."

Wyatt couldn't argue the point. He placed a hand on the side of the truck box and vaulted into the bed, landing on his feet. Without glancing back at Erin, he opened the lid of his diamond-plate toolbox, grabbed the tow chain, which lay at the top because he used it often on the ranch, and then leaped back onto the roadway. "I'll pull around and get in front," he told her.

"I really don't need a tow. I've got this."

Wyatt was reminded of the first time he met Erin. She'd been just as stubborn about accepting his help then as she was now, and he responded with almost the same answer. "The boss won't be happy if I leave you stranded out here."

Her chin came up a notch. "It's not exactly remote here. Dozens of cars will be returning to town on this road in a matter of minutes."

"Exactly. And every single driver will see that I drove right past you."

"I'll tell them you offered to help and I declined."

"Why not just accept the tow?" he pressed. "It's a favor between friends."

"We aren't friends. You make no secret of the fact that you don't like me. Now that I've made friends with Doreen at dispatch and get time off, I can finally visit the ranch more often, and whenever I do, you vanish as if I have a contagious disease."

Wyatt knew he was guilty as charged. But he didn't steer clear of her because he disliked her. The truth was that he liked her too much. "Whenever you visit, I'm on the clock. On any given day, I have a list of stuff to get done that's as long as my arm. I don't deliberately avoid you. I'm just busy."

Her expression told him she wasn't buying that. "Look," he went on. "Whether I like you or whether you like me isn't the point. Your uncle is my employer, and he'll be pissed at me if I don't lend you a hand. I need to keep my job, if it's all the same to you."

A subtle slump of her shoulders told him he'd won this round. "Oh, all right," she said with a flap of her wrist. "I'll let you tow the car into town, but only because I don't want to cause any trouble between you and Uncle Slade."

Wyatt didn't care what her reasons were, only that she'd finally accepted his help.

Erin had taken high-speed driving courses as a law enforcement officer, which had led her to believe she could handle a car in almost any situation. But getting behind the wheel of a broken-down vehicle was a whole different kettle of fish. The power steering didn't work with the engine dead, making the wheel difficult to turn. The brakes were also spongy, requiring more pressure on the pedal to engage them. On top of that, dust billowed up from the back of Wyatt's rig, making her range of visibility about a foot in front of her nose. The interior of the Honda grew uncomfortably warm. Even if she'd been able to roll down the windows, which she couldn't without power, she would have been breathing in dirt. As glad as she was not to be riding with Wyatt, she was exhausted and sweating by the time they reached the Timing Light.

Eager to escape the stuffy car, Erin opened her door and climbed out, fanning her face with one hand.

"You okay?" Wyatt asked.

"Just a little too warm. It's not really that hot today, but when you're inside a black car with the windows rolled up, it gets uncomfortable pretty fast."

"Ah. I'm sorry. I'll turn on the AC when I drive you home."

Erin locked her car, located Buck's drop box, slipped her keys inside, and turned to face Wyatt again, wanting to get this over with as quickly as possible. "I'm ready."

"Where's your purse?" he asked.

Erin clenched her teeth. "*Darn* it! I forgot it in the car." Frustration welled within her. She'd started carrying a handbag only months ago, and it hadn't become an ingrained habit yet. She thought she saw Wyatt struggling to hold back a smile. "It's *not* funny."

"Anything important in it that you can't do without until morning?"

"My cell phone. I have to have it with me at all times in case there's an emergency at the sheriff's department."

He shifted his weight onto one booted foot and rested his hands on his narrow hips. The stance made him look every inch a cowboy. Until meeting him, Erin hadn't found western attire attractive on a man, but now she did. That was just one more reason for her to resent Wyatt Fitzgerald. He messed with her head, making her look at things differently and analyze her reactions.

"Well," he said in that slow, thoughtful way of his. "I can probably jimmy a door lock if you won't make me your prime suspect the next time a car is broken into on Main."

Erin rolled her eyes. In Mystic Creek, a car was robbed only about once a year, and the most likely suspect would be a teenage boy. "Of course I won't."

He jumped back into the bed of his pickup, which sent a shiver up her spine. He emanated strength and masculinity in everything he did. Plus, he was too handsome for words. Only a blind woman would fail to find him attractive. If she polled all the adult females in Mystic Creek, she'd probably learn that more than half of them felt flutters in their stomachs when they encountered him on the street.

When he jumped back to the ground, he held a flat piece of metal in his hand. There was a similar device in each of the county vehicles that Erin drove. She'd used one more than once to unlock cars for people who'd accidentally locked their keys inside.

Within seconds, Wyatt had her car opened. He grabbed her purse, relocked the door, and strode toward his truck. "Let's roll out," he called to her.

Domino greeted Erin with a face wash as she climbed into the cab of the pickup. She sputtered but didn't scold the dog. As she settled on the seat and struggled to fasten her safety belt, she endured an ear wash as well. Wyatt glanced over to see if she was buckled up and collared the dog.

"Stop that, Domino!"

When the animal sat between them and faced forward, Wyatt pressed the ignition button. The diesel engine rumbled to life. He shifted into drive, stepped on the accelerator, and the next instant, Erin heard a loud thump followed by a lurch of the truck as it jerked to a sudden stop. She was thrown forward. All that stopped her from colliding with the dash was the strap across her chest, which flattened her left breast with crushing force and sent pain lancing over her rib cage.

"Damn it!" Wyatt shifted back into park, jerked out of his seat belt, and threw open his door. "I forgot to disconnect the chain from your car." He swung out of the cab, strode to the back of his truck, and let loose with more curses. Erin had a bad feeling and got out of the vehicle. The front of her Honda was crunched like tinfoil. "Son of a bitch!" he said. "You left it in neutral?"

Erin bristled. "Oh, so it's all *my* fault?"

He swept off his hat, raked his fingers through his blond hair, and then slapped the Stetson back on his head. "I'm not saying it's your fault. I take full responsibility. It's just that the car wouldn't have rolled forward if you'd put it in park and set the brake."

"No, it wouldn't have," she agreed. "Instead of the front end getting crunched, you could have just jerked the subframe out from under it and twisted it into a pretzel shape."

He sighed. "I'm sorry, Erin. I'll pay to get it fixed."

Erin didn't know why, but she started to laugh. It really wasn't funny. Repairing the damage would probably cost five or six grand. But the expression on his face, a mixture of incredulity and frustration, was priceless. She placed a hand over her chest, which still hurt.

"I don't get the joke," he said. "I just ruined your car."

"I think Buck does body work" was all she could think to say. "And he advertises on the radio that he offers payment plans. I'll get it fixed and make monthly installments."

"I can't let you pay for the damage. I'm the one who did it."

"While trying to help me. And, as you pointed out, I was at fault for not remembering to put it back into park. I can't let you take the financial hit."

"We'll share the cost, then."

Erin decided that was an argument that could take place later. "We'll talk about it. Okay? For right now, I'd like to get home and make some phone calls. Maybe Sheriff Adams will lend me a county vehicle for a week or so. Otherwise I'll have to rent a car. I live too far out to walk back and forth to work if the weather turns bad."

"In spring, that's a given. And now, thanks to me, you'll probably be without wheels for longer than a week. Maybe closer to two." He spun on his heel and strode toward the front of his truck. "Okay. Let's get you home."

"Wyatt?" Even as she said his name, Erin wanted to groan. The man was profoundly deaf and couldn't hear her even if she screamed. Running along the opposite side of the truck bed and waving her arms to get his attention, she got him to stop just before he reached the driver's door. His gaze became riveted to her face. "The chain, Wyatt? You still haven't unhooked it."

Wyatt could not believe that he'd forgotten to detach the chain from Erin's car, not once, but twice. Being around the woman screwed with his brain. He never made stupid mistakes like that. If he had, Slade would have fired him years ago. But around Erin, he became a dimwit, so aware of her on a physical level that his thoughts bounced around inside his head like lottery balls in a blower machine. He needed to deliver her to her cottage, tell her goodbye, and get away from her before he did something else stupid. As it was, she probably thought his IQ was lower than the winter room temperature of a poor man's house.

Disgusted with himself and unable to talk while he drove, he turned on the sound system, which he never used. She gave a violent start, and Domino started to bark, which Wyatt knew only because the dog's front feet parted company with the leather seat each time he emitted a woof. Wyatt quickly turned off the stereo.

"What?" he asked as he fixed his gaze on Erin.

"The volume is way up," she said. "So loud it almost burst my eardrums."

"You turn it on then," he suggested.

She shook her head. "I'm good. Not in the mood for music."

Wyatt wasn't in a mood for small talk. "I can't read your lips while I'm driving." He flicked his gaze back to the road. "It'd be just as dangerous as texting." He didn't know if she agreed, disagreed, or said nothing, and he wasn't about to pay less attention to the road in order to watch her lips. After messing up her car by making a stupid mistake, all the day needed was for him to have a wreck. "I thought music might compensate for the lack of conversation."

He stared straight ahead. It seemed to him that tension electrified the air. He mostly drove with only his brother as a passenger. With Erin, it was different.

He felt relieved when they passed the city limits and entered Mystic Creek. He drove to the town center and took the roundabout. He saw Blackie, the pawnshop owner, and Ma Thomas, who owned Simply Sensational, standing by the water feature, chatting up a storm.

When he reached the turnoff for Mystic Creek Lane, he took a sharp right. He'd never been to Erin's rental cottage, but Slade had told him where she lived, in a small, white cottage that backed up to the creek. He figured he could find it easily enough, and just following his nose would be far less trouble than asking Erin for directions. He'd have to pull over in order to know what she was saying.

She lived about halfway up the lane. The cottage sat well back from the road, a smallish structure with a picket fence. No garage. It was smaller than all the other houses they'd passed, and it was sorely in need of fresh paint. It did have a nice, covered veranda out front, though, and would have been cute with a few improvements and some landscaping. He knew firsthand that Erin hadn't gotten much time off until a few months ago, and by then, the inclement weather and deep snow had prevented even a die-hard gardener from working outside.

He pulled into the driveway and turned off the ignition. "Right place?"

She looked over at him. "Yes, and I'm wondering how you drove straight to it."

"Your uncle told me where you live."

"When?"

Wyatt frowned. "I don't know. A while back."

"Amazing. Directions to my house are engraved on your brain, but you forgot to unhook the tow chain twice."

He bit down hard on his back teeth. She'd already given him a pass on the car debacle, so he knew she wasn't pissed at him about that. If she was still upset because he hadn't given her his undivided attention at the wedding reception, then she would just have to get over it. A man was either attracted to a woman or he wasn't, and he owed Erin no further explanation. That was it, in a nutshell, at least on the surface, and as far as he was concerned, she could put her own spin on it.

"Thank you for the ride home," she said. "I really appreciate it."

"Smashed-up car and all?"

She shrugged, grabbed her purse, and opened the passenger door. "It was an accident." She turned to scratch Domino between the ears. "Goodbye, sweet boy."

After jumping from the truck, she slammed the door behind her with such force that Wyatt almost believed he heard the bang upon impact. He didn't, of course. With the AC running to keep her comfortable, he'd rolled up all the windows, and he'd only felt a push of air pressure and vibration. She walked straight to her porch, up the steps, and to her front door without looking back at him. He sat there until she was safely inside. Then he reversed his truck out of her drive and headed toward town. He purposely didn't look back, either. He did allow himself one glance into his rearview mirror, but if she was watching, she'd never know he had.

He released a taut breath and tried to relax. But his encounter with Erin had his nerves rubbed raw. She wasn't an easy person to figure out. He'd given her every opportunity to be a complete shrew when he tore up the front of her car, and she had given him a bit of a hard time, but she'd drawn the line at his offer to pay for all the damage. *Damn it.* How could he continue to give her the brush-off when she could be bitchy only to a certain point before her inherent sense of fair play took over?

"Don't look at me like that," he told his dog. "I know you really like her. So do I! But here's the thing, Domino. We guys can't let our dicks overrule our brains."

Erin's little house smelled of the potato salad and deviled eggs she'd made last night for the wedding reception. One whiff reminded her that she'd left what remained of the food in the trunk of her car. By the time she could return to get it, the Honda might stink to high heaven. She cut through the living area to the kitchen, which boasted a cute bay window that overlooked the creek. That alcove and the recently renovated master suite were her favorite features of the house. After plopping her handbag on the oak tabletop, she struggled against an urge to cry. Instead of giving in to it, she went to the adjoining guest bathroom to stare at herself in the vanity mirror. She took in her dark hair, her blue eyes, her facial features, and what she could see of her upper body.

"What's so *wrong* with me?" she asked her image. "Am I *that* unattractive? And even if that's true, am I such an awful person that he can't even be friendly?"

Erin knew it was silly to be so hurt, but she was. She felt like a teenage girl who'd crushed on a boy and been rejected. Well, she didn't really know how that felt, she supposed. Growing up under her father's thumb, she'd never had time to notice boys in that way. She'd been too busy trying to compete with them in sports in order to please her dad.

Erin pushed all of that from her mind, squeezed her eyes closed, and burst into tears. When she'd cried herself out, she fished her phone out of her purse and speed-dialed her best friend, Julie.

"Hello. I'm barely in the door from the wedding, girlfriend, and wearing only one shoe. After walking around on that grass in high heels, my feet are killing me and I can't get the torture devices off fast enough."

Erin bypassed a greeting and asked, "What's so objectionable about me that he isn't even interested in being my friend?"

"Have you been crying? Oh, God, you have. You sound all stuffed up. That isn't like you."

"Oh, that's right. I'm so tough and masculine, I never cry like a normal woman."

Julie sighed. "Erin, you need to listen to me. Are you listening? There's nothing objectionable about you. And you aren't tough and masculine. You looked absolutely beautiful today."

"He ignored me all afternoon. Then my car broke down on the way home. Right in the middle of the road, of course. He barely managed to stop without hitting me. And he did *not* look happy when he realized it was my car." Erin felt that pressure in her chest again, and this time the tears were so close to the surface that they erupted in a fresh flood. "If he isn't attracted to me, *fine*. But why can't he at least be friendly? What is it about me that turns men off?"

"Okay, okay. You're talking about Wyatt, right?"

Erin blinked and wiped under one eye. "Of *course* I'm talking about Wyatt. Who else?"

Julie sighed. "All right. I'm coming over with chocolate and wine, a surefire cure for whatever ails you, even PMS."

"Chocolate and wine?" Erin laughed through her tears. "It *is* Sunday afternoon. I'm off duty. A girls night sounds like just what the doctor ordered."

"Awesome. While you're waiting for me to get there, run a hot bath, strip off your clothes, and sink down in the water until it's up to your chin. It'll relax you and make you feel a little better. I promise."

Erin ended the call and went to her bedroom. After adjusting the water temperature on the garden tub, she rummaged in her pajama drawer for something besides an oversize T-shirt and sweatpants. When she found nothing, not even a top and bottom that matched, she almost started to cry again. Most women had at least a few lingerie items. The fact that she didn't pretty much said it all. She wasn't sexy. She did love lacy underthings, but that was mainly because nobody ever saw them.

She decided on a green-and-yellow University of Oregon T-shirt and a pair of athletic pants. Then, as Julie had suggested, she shucked off her clothes, caught her hair up in a band at the top of her head, and slipped into the water. As liquid heat surrounded her body, she sighed and decided Julie was right. She already felt better. She closed her eyes, forced her muscles to relax, and just breathed deeply for a minute before she turned the faucet off. Then she gave herself a pep talk.

"Why do you care if Wyatt detests you?" she asked herself. "Like he's the be-all and end-all of your existence or something? Don't be juvenile. You don't *need* a man in your life. It was probably a woman like you who invented vibrators."

She was still talking herself down when she heard the front door open. Julie yelled, "Hi, honey! I'm home!"

Erin called back, "I'm still in the tub! Pour us each a glass of wine. I'll be right out."

After giving herself a quick wash, Erin rinsed and vacated the tub. She toweled dry, slipped on her pathetic excuse for pajamas, and walked barefoot through the house. Just outside the kitchen archway, Julie had dumped her purse and an overnight case on the floor. She now stood at the counter, unloading her purchases from paper shopping bags.

"I'm staying the night," she said, flipping back her long, dark hair with a jerk of her head. "If I'm going to get hammered, which I definitely plan on doing, I shouldn't drive home. So I brought a change of clothes so I can go straight from here to my shop in the morning." Then her gaze sharpened on Erin's face. "Oh, boy. You aren't a pretty crier. Your face is so red and puffy, you look like you're having an allergic reaction."

"I don't cry very often. Doing it pretty must come only with practice."

Julie drew out a bottle of wine and unearthed Erin's corkscrew from the flatware drawer. "Just hang on, sweetie. A glass of vino and all the chocolate you can eat will make you feel better. I also got rocky road ice cream and takeout from Chopstick Suey. Your favorites: sesame chicken, orange chicken, spring rolls, and fried rice. Not a vegetable in sight. Well, little vegetable bits in the spring rolls, maybe, but otherwise dinner will be a heart attack waiting to happen. Just the way you like it when you blow your diet."

With a hollow plunk, she popped the cork out of the wine bottle, grabbed two goblets from a shelf above her head, and poured their wine without ceremony. After handing Erin a glass, she said, "Bottoms up. I've never met a bottle of wine yet that can't cure all my problems, at least temporarily."

Erin clinked her glass against Julie's. "To good friends who come running with chocolate and wine." Forcing a smile, she lifted her goblet. "Here's to you, and here's to me. Best of friends we'll always be."

"I've heard that toast. Don't say the rest, or I'll take my goodies and go home."

With a laugh, Erin helped put place settings on the table. Normally, she didn't bother, but Julie was a stickler for proper food presentation. They sat across from each other and began opening takeout cartons. Afternoon sunlight slanted through the bay window to splash gold over the tabletop.

"Yum." Erin knew her voice sounded flat, but she couldn't help it. "Give me a few minutes. If I talk about it now, I'll cry in my orange chicken."

Julie took a big swallow of wine. "Do *not* cry just yet. I want to have my mouth full of melting milk chocolate before you start. I can handle almost anything then."

That drew a genuine laugh from Erin. "Before I cry, I want a full tummy. I was too upset at the reception to eat. I didn't even try my potato salad, and it's my favorite recipe."

"I tried it." Julie gave her a thumbs-up. "Phenomenal."

"I left it in the trunk of my car," Erin said.

"Oh, no! It'll get warm and ruin!" Julie shot up from the chair. "I'll go get it."

"You can't. My car is at the Timing Light. The fuel pump cocked up its toes after I left the ranch. Then, thanks to Wyatt, the whole front end got smashed, so now it'll need body work, too. Buck offers payment plans, thank God."

Julie slowly resumed her seat. "Smashed? How did that happen?"

Erin held up a hand. "I'll tell you about it as soon as I can blubber on a full stomach."

When they finished eating, they adjourned to the living room and sat in two recliners turned slightly toward each other with an end table between them. Julie had brought the wine, Erin the goblets, and they were all set for a hen session.

"Now that it's time to talk about it, I don't know where to begin," Erin said. "It's been an awful day from start to finish." She recounted to Julie how carefully she had dressed for the wedding. "I spent a whole hour on my makeup and hair alone. I wanted to knock his socks off. You know? But instead, he took one look at me and got as far away from me as he could."

"Oh, sweetie. It may have seemed that way to you, but Wyatt isn't normally rude. Maybe he was just—I don't know—preoccupied."

"He was preoccupied, all right. Thinking of ways to get away from me. Most of the time, I can just shrug it off. He's been avoiding me for a while. But today . . . I don't know. With all that happily-ever-after talk. Seeing the absolute joy on Uncle Slade's and Vickie's faces. Thinking about true love and wishing it could happen for me. Watching my cousin Brody, who didn't even know Uncle Slade was his father a few months ago, standing beside his dad as his best man. It was all so perfect and romantic."

"It really was," Julie agreed. "And watching Brody and Slade together. Wow. They are so much alike, not only in looks, but in character and temperament as well. It's sad to think of all the wasted years when they should have been father and son, but that only made today all the more meaningful and wondrous. It was about as perfect as a wedding can be." Julie's expression grew thoughtful as she swirled her wine and stared into its burgundy depths. "Watching all that made me feel sad, too. Attending weddings can do that to single women." She took a sip of her drink and swallowed. "Did you know that single people who attend weddings tend to go off half-cocked and get married just to feel better?"

"Really?" Erin hadn't been aware of that fact. "I can see it happening, though. If some guy proposed to me right now, I might say yes."

"Me, too!" Julie exclaimed. "I've never loved someone the way Vickie clearly loves Slade, and I'd really like to experience that before I'm old and gray."

"What about Derek? You said you loved him."

"I thought so," Julie mused aloud. "But as time passes to separate me from the pain of his betrayal, I realize that I was more in love with the whole idea of marriage and raising a family." She shrugged. "Vickie and Slade have found the real thing."

"I felt awful for envying them," Erin confessed. "If any two people deserve to be together and happy for the rest of their lives, it's Slade and Vickie. How selfish of me to feel sad for myself instead of being happy for them."

Julie shook her head. "Stop! It wasn't selfish of you, Erin. Today put me in a romantic frame of mind, too. How could it not? Who doesn't wish for happily ever after?"

"It just made me realize how empty my own life is, and I felt so alone," Erin confessed. "And hopeless. I wish I could meet someone wonderful, and the only guy I really, *really* like won't give me the time of day."

Julie reached for a chocolate kiss and popped it into her mouth. "It's my opinion that your job as a deputy intimidates men. Most of the time when you meet guys, you're in uniform with a loaded gun, a Taser, and handcuffs on your belt. Definitely not a sexy look. Well, maybe if a guy is into kinky stuff."

"My job again," Erin said with a huff. "I wish I'd never listened to my father. I should have chased my own dream to become a speech therapist. But if I start over fresh in that field, I'll have to go back to school. I'll be paying off student loans until I'm old enough to draw Social Security benefits."

"Oh, you won't be *that* old."

"I'll be over forty," Erin interjected. "And the thought is daunting. How will I ever afford to buy a small house and get a new car if I spend half my life either in the wrong profession or paying for college tuition? And what about having babies? My thirty-fifth birthday is three years away. I can't seem to get a guy to give me a second look."

"Namely Wyatt Fitzgerald?" Julie twisted onto her knees in the recliner and poured each of them more wine. "I've said it before, and I'll say it again: Nothing about him adds up for me. He's young, handsome, and physically fit. Yet as far as I know, he never dates. In my opinion there's only one explanation for that, Erin. Women don't do it for him." She held up a staying hand. "Don't say that I think every man I meet may be gay because of my ex. That isn't true. Take Blackie, for instance. He's attractive and doesn't seem to keep company with women, but I don't think he's gay."

Erin squinted at her friend to read her expression. Then she gasped. "Oh, my God, you're crushing on Fred Black! What are you thinking? Blackie's fifty if he's a day."

Julie's cheeks turned pink. "It's just—well, he comes into the Morning Grind almost daily for pastry and coffee. He sits at one of the inside tables, and we chat. He's a really nice guy. And so what if I have a crush on him? The age difference is irrelevant. I'm no longer all soft in the head about having babies. I'm more interested in finding a mature and stable man whose company I enjoy. Blackie is mature and thoughtful and interesting."

Erin held her tongue and sipped her wine, because until this moment, she had never heard Julie sing any man's praises. Something was up, and even though Erin was tipsy, she realized that teasing Julie wasn't appropriate. She finally said, "I really like Blackie. Practically everyone does. I've never heard anyone say a bad word about him. If you're into him, I can't think of a single reason you shouldn't act on it."

Julie got back into a comfortable reclining position. "I'm nervous about it." She waved her hand as if to clear the air. "And I didn't come over here to talk about my issues. We need to stay focused on yours. The way I see it, Erin, you've come a long way since you moved to Mystic Creek. You've broken so many bad habits that were drilled into you by your dad. I truly believe it's the deputy uniform that's preventing the single guys in town from asking you out."

"Okay, I have to confess. I've looked into returning to college, and I found out that Crystal Falls University offers a degree in speech pathology."

"Oh, Erin, that's *fabulous!*"

Erin shook her head. "I'm pretty sure I can stay with Uncle Slade and Aunt Vickie while I do my coursework. Brody and Marissa's new home on the ranch is almost turnkey now, and they'll be moving into it soon, leaving Uncle Slade and Vickie with plenty of spare rooms in the main house. Only there would be so many hoops for me to jump through. I already have my bachelor's degree, but I'll need my master's as well in communication disorders and sciences, and then I'll probably have to do an internship and other stuff to get my license to practice. And once I do, I may have to travel in order to work unless I luck out and find a position in a clinic, which most likely wouldn't be in Mystic Creek. And I've come to love it here. I really don't know how I feel about living somewhere else. Maybe, if I had a partner I adored, and he needed to live elsewhere. But to take off and try to put down roots in a strange place all by myself, and leave everyone here that I love? It all just seems overwhelming."

"I don't like the thought of you leaving here, either," Julie admitted. "But I also want you to be happy, and you aren't in your present profession."

Erin released a weary sigh. "I know, and thanks for understanding how I feel. A whole lot of people will think I'm nuts for wanting to leave the job I have now. I just feel—I don't know how to explain it, Julie— trapped, I guess. So I know I need to make a change."

Julie got tears in her eyes. "It's hard for me to think of you leaving. No more girls nights. No more having you walk into my shop several times a day to get coffee you never have time to drink."

Erin reached over to touch her friend's hand. "No matter what I decide to do, nothing is going to happen quickly. I'll get my parents paid back over the coming winter. Then, and only then, will I feel free to pursue an education in another field. Then I'll be doing coursework for at least two years at the university in Crystal Falls and living in Mystic Creek during that time. I'll be so tight on money that I'll be visiting the Morning Grind every day to eat your stale pastry."

They both burst out laughing at the thought, because Erin was always watching her weight and rarely indulged in bakery items.

CHAPTER TWO

The next afternoon, Erin drove out to her uncle's ranch. As she parked near the main house in a county truck the sheriff had allowed her to borrow for two weeks, she searched for Wyatt, saw no sign of him, and was glad of it. From now on, she planned to avoid him just as he did her. He'd made it clear that he wasn't interested in her, and she needed to respect that. It still bothered her that he didn't at least want to be friends. But, oh, well. When they bumped into each other, they'd both be polite. Nothing more was required.

She rolled down the window for a breath of fresh air, delightfully laced with scents she'd come to associate with only the ranch. As was the case everywhere in Mystic Creek, the predominant scent was of ponderosa pines, but on her uncle's land, the piney sharpness competed with the perfume of new-growth alfalfa and grass, manzanita, wildflowers, the mist that rose from the creek, and the slight but ever-present hint of livestock manure, which, oddly enough, wasn't unpleasant.

After exiting the truck, she paused to let the sunlight warm her face and shoulders. She likened the sensation to having melted butter drizzled over her skin. After a harsh winter, the arrival of spring, no matter how fickle the weather, felt absolutely divine. She panned her gaze over the yard, taking in Slade's late-model pickup, so layered with mud that she could see only patches of red paint. Then she widened her focus on the outbuildings that composed the ranch proper and the fenced pastureland behind them that stretched in seemingly endless folds of green to the tree-studded foothills of the Cascades.

Raised by a mother who detested every aspect of country living, Erin had been slow to appreciate the simple pleasures that came with it, but now she was finally starting to understand why her uncle and Vickie loved this place so much. Out here, time seemed to slow down. The sound of a mountain breeze whispering through the pine boughs soothed her. In the distance, she could hear cattle lowing. Occasionally the soft drone of their cries was interrupted by the whinnying of a horse. If she listened closely, she could hear men's voices drifting on the air, not loud enough to disrupt the peacefulness, but only a reminder that this was an industrious place despite the slow, lazy beat of its pulse. It was like a sanctuary to Erin now, much like the inside of a church, where she felt compelled to breathe deeply, exhale fully, and let go of her problems. If she returned to school and was fortunate enough to call this home for a couple of years, she would have all the quiet she needed to study and pull good grades.

The thought made her stomach muscles bunch with anxiety again. It felt all wrong to be here to ask for help when she already had a good education and a wonderful job. Slade and Vickie might think she was nuts for even considering a career change. And maybe she was. She only knew she wasn't happy, and whether anyone else could understand that or not, it was her reality.

Her gaze came to rest on the house, which loomed two stories high, its natural wood and log exterior weathered to umber. Evidence of Vickie's presence was everywhere, from the spring flower beds that had appeared along the front edge of the veranda to the layer of fresh, forest-green paint on Adirondack chairs grouped to the right of the front door. Even the multi-paned windows glistened. Not that Uncle Slade had been a slacker when it came to maintaining his home. He'd always kept it clean, organized, and in good repair. But most men didn't think about the little things that added touches of hominess. Now, with Vickie in charge, a posy of flowers in a canning jar adorned a small deck table, and colorful pillows and throws invited the weary to relax in the sitting area. *Feminine touches.* Erin wished she had a talent for them. The front porch of her rental cottage looked shabby by comparison.

As she ascended the steps onto the wide, wraparound veranda, she noted that a pair of muddy galoshes sat near the welcome mat. Judging by their small size, she guessed them to be Vickie's. The woman was diminutive in stature, but what she lacked in bulk, she made up for with boundless energy. It was good to know she was sparing time to work outdoors with her husband. If any man deserved to have a loving woman at his side, it was Slade Wilder.

Her boots thumping against the wood planks, Erin crossed to the door and knocked. An instant later she heard footsteps approaching from inside and the faint hum of voices. When the portal swung open, Erin was treated to a waft of wonderful smells emanating from the kitchen.

"Erin!" As trim as a woman half her age, Vickie looked adorable in faded jeans, an emerald-green knit top that matched her eyes, and an overlong, checkered bib apron that she'd folded and tied at her waist to accommodate her small frame. Her red hair lay over her narrow shoulders in a riot of burnished curls. "Slade, you'll never guess who's here!" She threw her arms wide and stepped forward to dole out a hug, which Erin returned with genuine affection. "We were just wishing for company, and who should appear but one of our favorite people!"

Erin laughed and stepped into what had once been an entryway without adornment. Now professional photographs of Slade's horses were displayed on one wall, a rustic console table sported an antique gold pan that served as a catchall bowl, wildflowers spilled in haphazard profusion from the mouth of a copper vase, and a log bench held court over doffed footwear lined up beneath it like soldiers at muster. There was even an umbrella stand by the door.

Erin's uncle came around the corner just then. He wore wash-worn Wrangler jeans, a blue chambray shirt, and riding boots. His hair, originally a dark sable like her own, was now silvered at the temples. His eyes, a compelling gray, twinkled with pleasure as his sun-burnished countenance creased into a broad smile. With one long stride, he stepped forward to encircle her in his arms. "Our first official visitor since we tied the knot!" he said, his deep voice laced with welcome. "Come in, Erin, come in."

Erin wiped her boots clean on the entry rug. "Do I get a special door prize for being your first guest?"

"You do!" Vickie confirmed. "I just finished pulling cookies from the oven and I made lemon meringue pies as well. I've been beating Kennedy away with a bat. Lemon meringue is his favorite, and he kept trying to sneak pieces before the filling cooled." Vickie's green eyes sparkled with laughter. "Messing with my pies before they set is a shooting offense."

Erin couldn't help but grin. The couple's love for each other and their excitement about finally being together was wonderful to behold. "I think I'm gaining weight just by sniffing the air."

Vickie led the way to the kitchen, which, in a house designed for simple living, was in a direct line from the front door. A rancher came and went dozens of times each day, and all manner of dirt accompanied him. The kitchen was the heart of any home, but that was particularly true on a farmstead. Thirsty and hungry from hard work, people gravitated indoors for tall glasses of water and frequent snacks. The utilitarian floorplan diminished repetitive foot traffic in the more formal rooms of the house.

Erin locked arms with Uncle Slade before following her new aunt. "Are you two regretting that you didn't go on a honeymoon yet?"

Vickie swung around to walk backward. "No. Never. Now that I'm finally back in Mystic Creek, I don't want to leave!" She dimpled her cheek in a grin. "Well, I'll return to Coos Bay to see my parents and kids, of course, but otherwise Slade will have to drag me out of here."

Slade laughed. "I'm not dragging you anywhere. Other guys can look stupid in shorts and get sunburned legs on exotic beaches while they sip umbrella drinks. I'm happy with a Jimmy Buffett island song and a snort from my whiskey flask. If I can take my bride for walks in the moonlight and kiss her under a pine tree, I'm a happy man."

Cheeks turning a pretty pink, Vickie pushed at her hair. "And I'm so glad he feels that way. We talked about escaping to Fiji for a couple of weeks, but we couldn't take Pistol. And I'd have missed Four Toes and the horses, too."

Pistol was technically Uncle Slade's dog, but he had fallen in love with Vickie at first meet and now had two adoring humans to spoil him. Vickie had even crocheted a throw for the foot of their bed that had Pistol's name on it. Four Toes was a blond black bear that Uncle Slade had rescued as a tiny cub and that now, by benefit of special permit, was able to call the ranch his forever home. Erin hadn't spent time with any of the horses, but she knew how her uncle loved them. It was good that Vickie felt the same way.

Erin took a seat at the round oak table while Vickie filled a floral-pattern serving platter with cookies and Slade poured coffee. When they sat down, Erin felt nervous. She didn't know how to start this conversation.

Cupping her warm mug in her hands, she said, "I'll get right to the point and not take too much of your time. Whether you escaped to a tropical island or not, it's still officially your honeymoon."

Vickie flapped her hand. "Don't be silly. You're welcome here anytime. And this house is like Grand Central now that I'm here. The men love baked goods still warm from the oven, so we don't get a lot of alone time. That doesn't bother us. We go for long horseback rides. We're alone in the evening. For people our age, that works."

Slade winked at Erin. "What she's trying to say is that I'm not as good as I once was, but I'm still as good once as I ever was. The keyword in that assessment is *once*. We have plenty of spare time for socializing."

Erin nearly choked on her coffee. "You stole those words straight from a song."

Slade laughed. "At my age, I'm not very original, either."

Erin turned her cup in her hands. "I dropped by to tell you that I'm thinking about returning to college." She launched into a long and probably unnecessary explanation for that decision. "I'm just not happy in law enforcement. Some people love it, but I feel frustrated and disappointed." She shrugged. "I thought I could make a difference in the world as a cop, and I suppose in some ways, I have. But when I finish a shift, I can't see that I've made a measurable difference. Does that make any sense?"

Vickie nodded. "You talked with me about this last fall. Remember?"

Erin recalled how upset she'd been that night. "I do."

"I advised you then to consider a career change. You're young. If law enforcement doesn't fulfill you, you should change course and find something that does."

Slade nodded. "I completely agree, Erin. Maybe I'm wrong, but I got the feeling as you were growing up that your father pushed you to be a cop. I know he loves his job, but I don't think it was ever your dream."

"I tried to make it my dream," Erin confessed. "I worked as an aide in speech therapy for a couple of years, and that became my real passion. After working with deaf children, I walked away from every session with a feeling of accomplishment. I don't get that from police work."

Vickie took a cookie from the platter. "It takes all different kinds of people to make the world go round," she observed. "Some are born to be cops, and thank God they are, but not everyone is. I'm just glad you've realized that you made a mistake and that your life will be better spent doing something you really love."

Slade stirred his coffee and then tapped the spoon on the mug's edge. The sound of metal striking porcelain created a musical ping. "Have you considered a different aspect of law enforcement? Investigative, possibly? Or forensics? Maybe some other focus would suit you better."

Erin heard someone come in the front door, and a moment later, Kennedy, Wyatt's younger brother, entered the kitchen. "Hi, Erin!" To Vickie, he said, "Are the pies cool yet?"

Vickie hooked a thumb over her shoulder. "Under the tea towels on the counter. You'll have to cut one. Eight evenly proportioned slices per pie, no hogging."

"Eight?" Kennedy sounded appalled. "Can I have two pieces, then?"

Vickie rolled her eyes. "Of course, but only one serving at a time, use a plate, and no shoveling allowed. If you drop filling on my clean floor, I'll skin you alive."

While Kennedy rummaged in a cupboard for a dessert plate, Erin responded to her uncle's question. "I've considered other forms of police work. But in the end, it's all linked together, and I'm afraid I'd end up just as unhappy and dissatisfied as I am now." She plucked a pine needle off the front of her white blouse and smiled. "I'm also ready to start dating, and that isn't happening for me in law enforcement. My friend Julie thinks the uniform is part of the problem. I'm more inclined to believe it's the circumstances under which I meet most single guys in town. For some reason, none of them are inclined to ask me out when I'm issuing them traffic citations."

Vickie laughed. "I can see how that might dampen the ardor of most men."

Kennedy turned to rest his hips against the counter's edge. Erin met his gaze and felt a moment of embarrassment. Then she shrugged it off. Right now her career change was only in the discussion stage, but eventually everyone would hear some version of her reasons for no longer wanting to be a cop. At least this way, Kennedy was getting the real story.

As the conversation continued, Kennedy devoured two pieces of pie, then rinsed his eating implements and put them in the dishwasher before thanking Vickie and leaving the house to resume work. Slade watched him leave and then leveled his gaze on Erin. "I think you know you don't need our approval if you want to change careers, so as glad as I am of the visit, I wonder why you're actually here."

Erin sighed. Her uncle could always be trusted to cut right to the chase. "In order to return to school, I'll need a little help. I feel really icky about asking. I'm a grown woman, after all. But I'll be tight on money if I work only part-time while I'm going to college, and I don't think I'll be able to make my income stretch to cover the rent on my cottage." She held up a hand. "I'll be able to pay some rent. Don't get me wrong. But having my own house will become a luxury I can no longer afford."

"Say no more," Vickie interjected. "Of *course* you're welcome to stay here. Brody and Marissa are almost moved into the new house. Until they get their kitchen organized, they'll still have meals with us, but they're sleeping over there already."

Slade nodded. "I second that, and I won't hear of you paying us rent.

Maybe you're all grown up, but to me, you'll always be my baby girl. Anything we can do to help you return to school will be a privilege, not a burden."

Erin released a breath and with it went all her nervousness. "I *knew* you'd be supportive. Please don't think I doubted that. It just feels so weird to be thinking about quitting a good job and being broke all the time again. I thought I'd left those days behind me, and it's humiliating to find myself with my hand out."

"You haven't asked for money," he said.

"No, and I don't plan to, but I am asking for low-cost room and board. That's pretty much the same thing."

Vickie dunked the cookie in her coffee. "Staying with family when times are rough isn't the same at all. And it's not as if you'll be lollygagging. You'll have some kind of job, plus your coursework at the university. Students often need a helping hand. Look at Kennedy. He works here only part-time now, but he still gets room and board as one of his benefits."

"I know. But I won't be on Uncle Slade's payroll and earning the right to live here."

"It's your birthright," Slade countered. "You're my flesh and blood."

Erin wanted to hug both of them. "Nothing will happen right away. I have to keep working at the department until I get my folks paid back for my first round of education. I'll be settled up with them next winter. Then, no matter how upset they get, I'll tell them that law enforcement just isn't for me."

Slade's jaw muscle started to tic. "I think it's inexcusable that they expect to be repaid for what they spent on their own daughter's education."

"Slade," Vickie said softly, a note of caution lacing her tone.

He held up a hand. "I *know*. I shouldn't criticize her parents, but damned if I can keep my mouth shut. It'd be different if Gordon was a blue-collar worker living from payday to payday. But he's done well for himself. They've saved and invested. Their home is a showplace in a classy area of a town populated by mostly wealthy people. I just don't get it."

Vickie laid her hand on her husband's wrist. "I know it bothers you, but we don't know the whole story, and Erin's financial arrangements with them aren't any of our business."

Slade patted Vickie's fingers and reached for a cookie. "You're right. Sorry, Erin. I just don't understand people who make their daughter feel guilty for the help they gave her. Especially not when they go on elaborate vacations every single year."

Erin couldn't help but laugh. "You're right, and I completely agree. But that's just how they are. And in all fairness to them, paying them back was my idea. Even if I remain a cop, I'll never feel truly independent as long as I owe them a dime. And if I quit law enforcement while still in their debt, my father will go ballistic. It's a strange dynamic, but essentially he feels that he has a right to interfere in my life as long as I'm indebted to him."

"That's sad," Slade observed. "Granted, I'm new to being a dad, but if Brody ends up owing me a few bucks here and there, I'll never hold it over his head. I'll just feel blessed to help him in any way I can."

Erin knew her relationship with her parents was a mess. "I'm glad they take fabulous vacations every year. It was due to one of those trips that they left me on your doorstep, and when I look back on my childhood, that month with you is my favorite memory. I'm so glad I had that time with you." She angled a look at Vickie. "And you needn't worry that anything Uncle Slade says about my parents is going to offend me. They're unusual, to say the least. When I was little, I wished that Uncle Slade was my dad. I still do, even now."

Vickie nodded. "Way back when, I knew your mother pretty well. When I called to invite them to our wedding, she said she couldn't possibly attend because of her allergies."

Erin rocked back on her chair and laughed. "Allergies? To what?"

"Animals, grass, pine trees." Vickie chuckled, too. "*Dirt* of any kind, I imagine. She always hated being on a ranch and couldn't wait to turn eighteen so she could escape to the city."

Just thinking about her mom gave Erin a slight headache. But she hadn't come here to bash her parents, as much as they might deserve it. "I really appreciate your support. It's crazy to think about throwing away the life I've built and starting over, but I'm truly unhappy as things stand, so I think I'll do it, insane though it may be. Thank you so much for the offer of lodging. It's a relief to know that option will be available to me."

"Follow your heart," Slade said.

They chatted for several more minutes, which Erin greatly enjoyed. But she cut the visit short, even so. No matter how much they insisted that they wanted her to stay for dinner, they were still newlyweds, and she didn't want to be a pest. She even protested when her uncle tried to walk her to the car, so, to humor her, he hugged her goodbye at the door.

As she started to get in the truck, she heard someone call her name and turned to see who it was. Kennedy strode from a cluster of small pines next to the south paddocks and angled across the gravel parking area near the house. Tall, sturdy, and blond, he looked so much like his older brother, Wyatt, that her heart squeezed. Shoving aside her bruised feelings over Wyatt's cold manner toward her yesterday, she smiled and waited for the younger man to reach her.

"Hey, Erin. If you're in a hurry, I understand, but if you have a few minutes, I was wondering if we could talk."

Kennedy had started college winter term, and Erin had heard at the wedding reception that his spring finals were coming up soon. She hoped he wasn't having problems at school. "Sure. What's up? If you've got a class that's kicking your butt, you're not the first person and won't be the last. My first year, I thought for sure I was going to flunk out."

"No. It's not about school." Kennedy glanced over his shoulder. "It's—um—well, kind of personal. Do you have time to walk down to the creek? Nobody will overhear us there."

Erin liked Kennedy, but they weren't what she would call close friends. If he wasn't having issues with his studies, what on earth did he want to talk to her about? "A walk to the creek sounds great."

Kennedy led Erin to a quiet spot down by Mystic Creek, which flowed from the mountains to traverse the entire length of the Wilder Ranch. She guessed the young man came here often. A fallen tree, long since debarked and limbed by winter storms, provided a place for them to sit. She joined him on the log, keeping her distance but sitting close enough for them to converse over the babble of the stream.

"Oh, this is lovely," she said, gazing up through the canopy of pine boughs above them to glimpse patches of powder-blue sky. "It's like a grotto, designed by Mother Nature."

Kennedy nodded. "When it's warm in the afternoon, I like to brace my back against this log and crack the books. It's a great place to study. At the bunkhouse, I get interrupted a lot."

Erin took a breath of the air. Deep in a wooded area, the moldy scent of a forest floor lent the light breeze a scent of timelessness. "It centers you, I bet. I think it would me."

"Yeah." His Adam's apple bobbed as he swallowed. He tugged at the limp collar of his plaid work shirt. "When I'm stressed-out about something, this place reminds me that the day-to-day shit in our lives doesn't really matter in the end."

Erin couldn't help but smile. "As you just heard in the kitchen, guys don't have a corner on angst. Now that I know about this place, I might come here to unwind myself."

Kennedy pushed a hand through his straight, blond hair. Unlike Wyatt, he wore his short, but he was no less handsome. At thirty-two, Erin felt no physical attraction to him, but she imagined females a decade her junior probably had heart palpitations when he grinned at them. "I, um—" He broke off and tugged at his collar again. "Speaking of what I overhead at the house, there's something I feel obligated to tell you, and there's no way to say it except straight out."

Curiosity welled within her. "I'm listening."

Kennedy straightened his legs and studied the toes of his upturned riding boots. "I know you've got the hots for my brother."

Erin's first reaction was to cringe with humiliation. Had she been *that* obvious? The thought that everyone on the ranch might have noted her interest in Wyatt was embarrassing. For an instant, she considered denying the charge, but that was silly. Kennedy's brother was a very good-looking man, and there was no question in her mind that a lot of local women had the hots for him.

"I realize now that the feeling isn't mutual," she settled for saying. "If you brought me down here to ask me to back off, it's unnecessary."

A flush crept up his neck. "*No!* No. Nothing like that. I just—well, I can't stand aside and keep quiet when I know you're about to make a huge career change partly because you think your job turns men off. I've seen how Wyatt responds to you, and I can't let you go on thinking it has anything to do with you personally. He's that way with all women. He's never been interested, if you know what I mean."

The nape of Erin's neck tingled. "What are you saying, Kennedy?"

He took a deep breath and expelled it with a puff of his lean cheeks. "This can't ever be repeated. You need to promise me that."

"I promise."

He raked the heel of one boot over a gold carpet of last year's pine needles. "I, um—please, understand that I'm only guessing. Okay? Wyatt's never said one way or the other, but I have every reason to think he's gay."

Erin gaped at him. "Wyatt? What on earth makes you think that?"

"Apart from the fact that he's thirty-three years old and has never dated, you mean?" Kennedy held her gaze. "*Never*, Erin. Not once in high school, and as far as I know, never as an adult, either."

Erin averted her gaze to stare off at nothing. Kennedy's revelation was startling. "Being deaf from birth isn't easy. I'm sure you're more aware than I am of all the social difficulties your brother has faced. Imagine struggling to find the words to ask a girl out, only to have her laugh or turn you down cold. Maybe striking out with girls was so unpleasant that he just stopped trying."

Kennedy fixed his gaze on the creek. The blush on his cheeks faded. "I thought of all that, and for a long time, I believed Wyatt never approached women because they wanted no part of him. He used to talk weird. He didn't have a bunch of guy friends like I did, either. He hated school and couldn't wait to get home every day. Then he spent every afternoon and evening with the horses." He turned an imploring gaze to Erin. "I understood that, even as young as I was. He was different than me. He felt more comfortable with animals than he did with people. But you can hardly tell he's deaf when he talks now. Very few people figure out that he can't hear unless he tells them. I've seen a lot of women flirt with him." He gestured limply with one hand. "He could have his pick. But he walks away and never looks back. He has *zero* interest."

Erin throat constricted, making her voice sound thin as she asked, "Are you homophobic, Kennedy?"

He looked startled by the question. "No. Heck, no. Why do you ask?" He arched an eyebrow at her.

"I just wonder why you've never come right out and asked Wyatt. If you're correct about Wyatt's sexual orientation, and I think you probably are, it isn't a bad thing unless you or others in your family could never accept it."

Kennedy leaned his head back and closed his eyes. As his lashes fluttered back up, he said, "I can't speak for my parents or my grandpa. But if Wyatt's gay, I'll be fine with it."

"Do you think your parents and grandfather may come unglued?"

He straightened and crossed his legs. "I honestly don't know. As for never getting in Wyatt's face about it—well, it's not an easy subject to broach. You know? I've almost asked him a few times, but I lost my nerve."

Erin remembered thinking her friend Julie was out of her mind for suggesting that Wyatt wasn't attracted to women. It wasn't as easy to discount the possibility with Kennedy. He was Wyatt's brother and knew him better than anyone else. "I really appreciate your telling me this. Whether you're right or wrong, it helps to know that Wyatt avoids all women, not only me."

Kennedy's shoulders relaxed. "I wanted you to know so you won't let his lack of interest push you into changing your profession."

Erin couldn't help but chuckle, albeit without much humor. "So where does that leave me? I've been here over a year now, and not one guy has asked me out."

"Ouch."

"Yes, a big ouch."

Kennedy pushed to his feet. "Thanks for lending me an ear, and please keep what I've told you to yourself. I feel like I've betrayed my brother by talking to you."

Erin rose from the log and wrapped her arms around her waist. "You're a good guy, Kennedy. The way Wyatt treated me yesterday did do a number on my self-confidence. And it hurt my feelings. Now I feel better about all that." She wrinkled her nose. "Wow. I never would have hit on him if I had known."

"Well," he warned, "we don't really *know* anything for sure."

"True, but just being aware that it's a probability is a Band-Aid for my wounded ego. Thank you for the heads-up."

Kennedy gestured upstream. "I'm taking the long way back. I'd rather Wyatt doesn't see us walking out of the woods together. He'll wonder what we were doing down here."

"Good thinking." She lifted a hand. "Bye for now, and thanks again."

Normally Erin enjoyed the drive from the ranch back into town. She watched for deer that might bound out onto the road. She tried to remember the common names of the flora that encroached on the drainage ditches. If it was fair weather and there wasn't much traffic dust, she liked to roll down the windows and breathe in all the wonderful smells. But this afternoon she had other things to think about. In so many ways, Kennedy's theory about Wyatt made sense. Except for the day they first met, when he'd felt obligated to nurse her injuries and transport her back to the trailhead, he'd tried to keep his distance from her. It was almost as if something about her set off all his internal alarms. She'd tried to camouflage her attraction to him with mere friendliness, but if Kennedy had noticed, it stood to reason that Wyatt had as well. Little wonder that he avoided her. He was probably afraid she would abandon subtlety. That would have been embarrassing for both of them.

She just wished that he'd come right out with it. Something along the lines of, *I'm flattered, but I date men.* At least then she would have understood his coolness toward her and wouldn't have taken it personally. Most people were pretty open about their lifestyle choices unless, like Julie's ex-husband, Derek, they had reasons for secrecy. Maybe Wyatt's parents or grandfather would flip out if he told them the truth. Erin had never been judgmental and found it difficult to understand others who were, but she was also realistic enough to know that not everyone saw the world through the same lens she did. Her heart would hurt for Wyatt if he believed his parents would refuse to accept him for who he was. She knew firsthand how horrible that felt. Her father had withheld his approval of her since the day of her birth simply because she'd been born a girl and he would have preferred a boy.

Once at the cottage, Erin heated soup for dinner, ate while checking the latest news updates on her phone, and then adjourned to her bedroom to get her uniform laid out for work the next day. She drew comfort from rituals, a trait her mother had drilled into her since childhood, and she always slept better when she knew she'd have no surprises in the morning to make her late. Boots, polished and by the dresser. *Check.* Shirt and trousers, both freshly laundered, starched, and pressed. *Check.* Clean underwear. *Check.* When she finished, she wandered back to the kitchen, located the bottle of wine that she and Julie hadn't finished last night, and filled a clean goblet. Then she drew a hot bath.

As she undressed, she studied her body in a full-length mirror on the interior side of the bathroom door. She doubted that any woman loved everything about her body. It was normal to wish for perkier breasts, a flatter stomach, and narrower hips. But Erin wanted none of those things. Instead she wished for softer lines. Given that she exercised daily to maintain her well-defined musculature, her dissatisfaction with the results made no sense at all. But there it was in a nutshell. She hated how she'd made herself look, but she couldn't stop pushing herself to maintain every ounce of strength she possessed. It was a compulsion, one that she hadn't yet brought up during her counseling sessions with Jonas Sterling, not because she didn't think it was a problem, but because it would sound so weird to say it aloud. *I bust my ass every day to have a body like a man's.* What woman in her right mind did that? But Erin couldn't deny the evidence of her own eyes. Her trapezius, deltoid, and triceps muscles were overdeveloped. And she'd worked so hard on her pectoralis majors that her breasts capped the mounds like an extension of the muscles, no longer pointy and softly shaped, but far firmer than was considered feminine. She knew there were women who liked the look, but Erin no longer did and she had no idea what to do about it except to stop working out and lifting weights.

Tears gathered in her eyes. Refusing to let them spill down her cheeks, she struggled not to blink as she climbed into the tub. She would enjoy a glass of wine and focus on positive things, first and foremost that Wyatt had indeed been shunning her, that it wasn't all in her head, and that she should be relieved to know his distaste for her had nothing to do with her looks or how she came off to men. She could be the most beautiful and feminine woman in the world, and Wyatt would still have no interest.

Wyatt struggled to fall asleep, hoping that his tossing and turning wasn't keeping the other men in the bunkhouse awake. He couldn't tell if his cot squeaked or if bunching up his pillow made an annoying sound. In addition to Kennedy and Tex, two newly hired guys now slept in the room. If he kept all of them from getting their rest, they would be as cranky as old ladies tomorrow. Not that he hadn't been short-tempered himself today. Busting his ass from dawn until almost dark and then not being able to sleep at night had him running on pure adrenaline and foul moods.

He carefully released a pent-up breath, wondering if expelling air from the lungs made a sound that bothered others. What he needed to do was get out of this stuffy building and away from everyone else. Where he would go, he had no clue. He only knew he needed some alone time. Even sleeping in the hay-storage building would be better than this. At least there he wouldn't have to worry about making noise and disturbing his men.

Clad in only boxers, he sat up on the edge of his cot, jerked on his jeans, and then stood to button and zip them. Not bothering with socks, he shoved his bare feet into his boots and grabbed only his discarded T-shirt, which he carried balled up in his fist until he escaped outdoors. The chilly night air licked at his chest and made his skin pebble, but he wasn't worried about getting cold. He kept a jacket in his truck, and he could collect it if necessary. For now he just needed to work up a good sweat, and the best way he knew to do that was at the business end of a shovel. He struck off for the horse barn. On a ranch this size, there was never a shortage of work to be done, so he'd just muck out stalls until physical exertion drove the tension from his body. If shoveling didn't do the trick, maybe a dip in the creek would give him some relief.

Tugging on his shirt as he strode to the barn, Wyatt silently lectured himself for suddenly feeling dissatisfied with his life. Well, he guessed it wasn't sudden, not really. It had started last fall after he met Erin De Laney and had grown progressively worse over the last several months. Now he was so strung out with sexual frustration that he couldn't sleep for fear that he'd dream of her again and ejaculate in his sleep.

He wasn't what he considered to be a horny guy, constantly thinking about sex and panting after women. Hell, no. He'd tapped into that side of his nature for a few months while he worked in Medford, Oregon. It had ended in disaster, and he'd sworn never to have sex again. And he'd been just fine for six years, never feeling frustrated or overcome with yearnings when he was around a woman. He'd been content with his work, happy to spend most of his time tending to animals. Slade Wilder was a great employer, fair, levelheaded, and always willing to do anything he asked his men to do. The bunkhouse wasn't exactly the Taj Mahal, but it wasn't a bad place to live. The kitchen was fairly large and well equipped with appliances. They had only one full bath, but there was a second sink and toilet for urgent use. In the living area, they had a state-of-the-art flat-screen television with surround sound, Dish Network, and a Netflix account that Slade provided free of charge. Wyatt couldn't enjoy the sound system, but he greatly appreciated the closed captions at the bottom of the screen when he watched the news or a film. Life was good. It was *great*. So what was he bellyaching about?

When he reached the barn, he didn't go inside, choosing instead to walk around the building and adjoining paddock to head for the creek. He knew the water would be cold, but right at the moment, freezing his nuts off sounded like a stellar plan.

When he reached the creek bank where he knew the water was

deep, he took off his boots and clothes. Then he dived in. The shock that came with plunging into the icy water was worse than he expected. For a moment, he couldn't breathe, and his heart felt as if it might stop. Not a risk taker by nature, he almost scrambled back out, but his common sense forestalled him. The cold wouldn't kill him, and maybe if he stayed in long enough, it would shrink his aching balls. He'd read about men doing this to control their sexual urges. If it had worked for them, maybe it would work for him.

Before he got out of the water, he paddled to keep his head above the surface until his body began to feel numb. Then he stood on the rocky bank shivering and feeling like an idiot because he hadn't thought to bring a towel. A night breeze blew along the creek corridor. He hadn't noticed it when he was dry, but now it felt like an arctic blast. He tried squeegeeing water from his skin with his hands, but that didn't work. He finally opted to use his T-shirt to rub himself halfway dry and then just pulled on his shorts and jeans. After donning his boots, he headed back to the ranch proper to get his coat.

He still wasn't warm when he entered the hay barn, and he hadn't stopped to consider that the huge, round bales wouldn't provide him with a flat surface to lie on. He found a couple of horse blankets to pad the crevice between two bales and settled in for the night. The moment he started to feel halfway warm again, he heaved a sigh of relief. With any luck, maybe now he could sleep.

Only he wasn't lucky. When his body temp got back to normal, the throbbing ache in his groin resumed. He lay on his back in the dark, staring stupidly upward into what seemed like absolute blackness. He'd been unable to hear all his life, but the addition of sudden blindness made him feel claustrophobic. He scrambled to escape, got his boot stuck between the massive bales, and panicked until all his tugging finally jerked his foot from the shoe. *Shit.* Now what was he going to do? He had spare boots in the bunkhouse, but he wasn't about to go in there to get them. He'd wake everyone and have to explain what he was doing up in the middle of the night.

Heart still pounding from the panic attack, Wyatt talked himself down. This was a gigantic building, nothing confining about it, and he'd just let his imagination get the better of him. The darkness couldn't hurt him, even though it blinded him. He flopped back down and stared into the blackness again. Errant thoughts of Erin De Laney slipped into his mind. How her pretty blue eyes went dark when her feelings got hurt, more precisely when *he* hurt her feelings. How she would catch herself in a masculine stance, quickly correct her posture, and then flush with embarrassment. How, when she donned civilian clothes, she always wore a top that covered her shoulders and arms because she felt compelled to hide her torso. When in her presence, he found himself wanting to tell her how beautiful he thought she was and that she needed to stop trying so hard to be feminine. *Hello.* God had taken care of that for her. She could stand with her feet spread and her arms akimbo until hell froze over, and she'd never look manly.

Only he could tell her none of those things, because she'd know he was attracted to her the second he opened his mouth. That could *not* happen. He just needed to get his head on straight and stop thinking about her. So instead he fell back on a game that he'd played with himself since childhood. He asked himself, *What does the chirp of a bird sound like? When cattle bawl, what does the lowing sound like? What does the wind in the trees sound like? What does a rifle shot sound like? What does a belch or fart sound like?* It was a stupid game. How could he liken any sound to another one when he'd never heard anything at all?

He closed his eyes to prove to himself that the blinding darkness was nothing more than a matter of perception, a simple absence of light. Then he focused on his senses that were still in fine working order. *Smell.* The predominant scent was of the alfalfa hay stacked high all around him. To him, it smelled green, retaining some of the freshness of new grass. It also coated his nostrils with dust, which transported him, via his imagination, onto a field in summer, where the earth, still damp from irrigation, embraced the crops that absorbed its nutrients as well as its pungent odor.

And then, in his mind's eye, he saw Erin walking through the swaying clumps of alfalfa. She wore a filmy, almost see-through dress that clung to the angles and curves of her slender body, giving him tantalizing glimpses of her taut nipples, the slender dip of her waist, and the fullness of her hips. And, just like that, the fly of his jeans was bulging. He didn't need his sight to know that. His shaft, turned steely by desire, felt as if it were bent double within the confines of denim.

He sat straight up on the hay, which made the discomfort even worse. *What the hell?* Erin never wore sexy garments, so why had he imagined her in a dress that was the equivalent of daytime lingerie? *I'm in big trouble,* he decided. He couldn't go on like this. Was it possible for a man to get a testicular infection from lack of sex? He'd never been told of such a thing, but his nuts felt as if somebody had been whacking them with a Ping-Pong paddle. If he didn't start getting some physical release, he'd wake up surrounded by other men, his body in the throes of another wet dream, and he'd want to die of humiliation.

After six years of celibacy, he'd hit a brick wall. Or maybe it was more accurate to say that he'd waded into dangerous waters by wanting a woman he absolutely couldn't have. If this kept up, his resolve to stay away from Erin might weaken. Was he really willing to risk so much just to slake his physical needs? He knew from hard experience that a profoundly deaf man could get into huge trouble if he sought release with a woman who, for whatever reason, had second thoughts at the last second. Another rape charge could land him in the pen. Or even worse, what if, because he couldn't hear, he ended up doing Erin harm? A woman had a right to say no, and when she did, no matter what her reasons, a man should respect her wishes. Only there was a chance that Wyatt wouldn't stop, not because he was a selfish, forceful bastard, but because he couldn't hear that one, small word—*no*—even if a woman screamed it.

So exhausted it hurt to move, he maneuvered his way down from the tower of hay to ground level where there was at least faint moonlight coming in through the windows. With a deliberate stride, he headed for the personnel door and exited the building. After reaching a stand of trees just south of the creek, he stopped, tipped his head back to stare at the star-studded sky, and unzipped his pants.

A man didn't need a woman to take care of his business. Desperate situations called for desperate measures, and though he'd never made a habit of it, he knew how to play Five-Fingered Stud. He just hoped there was no truth to the old wives' tale that this activity could make a person go blind.

CHAPTER THREE

Late on Tuesday afternoon, Erin drove out to the Wilder Ranch. It had been overcast all morning, but now the clouds had moved out on a brisk breeze to make way for sunlight. Recent rain had rinsed the forests clean, settled the dust, and given the ferns and clumps of wildflowers a drink. Everywhere she looked, she saw the promise of summer warmth and new growth. In two months' time, everyone she encountered on the sidewalks of Mystic Creek would be complaining of the heat. Personally, Erin enjoyed toasty weather. Blessed with skin that tolerated the sun, she loved lying on a lounge chair in her backyard in a string bikini that she'd never be caught dead wearing in public. Last summer, due to a personal problem with a dispatcher, she'd gotten very little time off for sunbathing or anything else, so she was looking forward to indulging herself during the forthcoming good weather.

As she turned left to pass under the huge log archway that supported a sign reading WILDER RANCH, she anticipated a lovely visit with her uncle and aunt. She'd skipped lunch to save calories for Vickie's fabulous baked goods, which she apparently produced nearly every day. But before Erin went to the main house, she had an unpleasant chore to take care of that she shouldn't put off any longer. That was straightening things out with Wyatt. Whenever she visited the ranch, which had happened twice last week, she rarely saw him, and she was pretty sure he was going to great lengths to avoid her. In only a matter of months, she could end up living at the ranch, possibly for as long as two years. With the present state of affairs between her and Wyatt, how on earth would that work over a long period of time? Without betraying Kennedy's confidence, she needed to let Wyatt know that she understood his situation and that she no longer entertained any notions that the two of them might get together. Maybe then Wyatt would be able to relax around her and they could develop a friendship of sorts. Barring that, at least he would no longer feel that he needed to hide from her.

Just as Erin started to get out of the truck, a flash of blue caught her attention, and when she homed in with her gaze, she saw Wyatt vault over a perimeter fence and stride off into the forest. She suspected that he was walking down to the creek, somewhere near where she and Kennedy had gone the other day to talk in private. She also felt fairly certain that Wyatt was doing another disappearing act to avoid an encounter with her. *Great.* Just then her aunt Vickie emerged from the main house and waved at Erin to come inside.

Erin got out of the pickup. "I'll be along in just a few minutes, Aunt Vickie! First I need to talk to Wyatt for a second."

Vickie, dressed today in her usual jeans and knit top, had changed up her appearance by gathering her curly hair into what looked like a red pompom perched atop her head. She smiled and nodded, her expression conveying that she knew Erin had a thing for the young foreman. "See you in a bit, then. The coffee will be fresh!"

Erin grappled with an urge to grumble with dismay. Did everyone on the ranch know she had been crushing on Wyatt? Kennedy had certainly picked up on it. Apparently Vickie had as well. It disturbed Erin to think she had been so transparent. Embarrassment made her cheeks burn as she walked along the paddock fence through spring field grass that was already ankle deep. As she entered the forest, the carpet of green thinned out to reveal earth gone spongy from countless layers of ponderosa pine needles that had composted over the years into rich organic humus.

She took a deep breath in an attempt to calm down. Speaking to

Wyatt needed to go smoothly so their future encounters wouldn't be uncomfortable. She should keep the conversation simple and to the point without alluding in any way to her talk with Kennedy.

She found Wyatt sitting on the same log that she and Kennedy had sat on to talk. Approaching from behind allowed her to study him. He'd doffed his Stetson to let the light breeze ruffle his golden hair, which drifted over his muscular shoulders like strands of silk. Sunlight filtered through the pine boughs above him, dappling the cloth of his blue work shirt to make it look tie-dyed. He had leaned forward to brace his arms on his knees. Head slightly bent, he studied the movement of the creek with its eddying currents dotted with white froth. Erin wished there were some way to alert him to her presence and thought about lobbing a pebble at his back, but the way her luck seemed to run with him, she'd probably hit him on the head.

As she circled the craggy end of the fallen log, he jumped with a start and his laser-blue gaze cut into her like a sharp blade. "You are the only person on God's green earth who can sneak up on me like that."

Erin wondered how that could be true. He couldn't hear footsteps approaching him from behind, and she surely couldn't be the only person who ever startled him. Keeping her distance, she sank onto the log. Her brain kicked into overdrive, composing sentences and then discarding them just as quickly.

She couldn't think how to start this conversation and was starting to panic when Wyatt saved her the trouble by saying, "Erin, please don't take this personally, but you need to back off. I'm really not interested. I've tried to be polite about it, but you don't seem to be getting the message."

Erin nodded. "I know. That you aren't interested, I mean. And I'm really sorry for putting you in such an uncomfortable position. I grew up in the city. I understand that all of us don't march to the same drumbeat. It just never occurred to me that you're—well, you know. I followed you down here to set your mind at ease. I won't be bothering you again with my misguided notion that we could be anything more than friends." Embarrassment made her chest feel hot and tingly. "I just didn't pick up on the signals, I guess. Nothing about you suggested to me that you might be playing for the other team."

His chiseled features, burnished from daily exposure to the elements, suddenly went ruddy red with what appeared to be outrage. "Are you implying that I'm gay?"

The question set her back. Wasn't his sexual orientation the crux of their entire problem? "Wyatt, I'm not passing judgment. I only came down here to let you know I finally get it and won't be troubling you any further."

His face turned even redder, and his jaw muscle began to tic. "Your conceit has no equal. *Really?* If I'm not interested in what you have to offer, I must be gay? Well, I've got a news flash for you, sweetheart. I'm as straight as they come. I just don't find anything about you to be the least bit attractive. I'm drawn to women who aren't fixated on outdoing me physically at every turn. You're the kind of gal who not only wants to wear the pants, but you honestly believe you can fill them out better than a man can."

Erin felt as if he'd slugged her in the stomach. Never in her life had she felt so humiliated. She hadn't meant for this conversation to get ugly. Now he was saying things that cut her to the quick. And the worst part was that every word was the truth—or at least used to be. As Julie had pointed out during their girls night, Erin had come a long way. She couldn't say that it had been easy or that she didn't still have more changes to make, but it hurt to have all her faults thrown in her face.

Erin pushed up from the log. "I'm sorry if I've misread the situation," she pushed out. "Whether you're straight, gay, or playing for both teams, I wish you every happiness. In the future when I visit the ranch, you don't need to avoid me. I'll never try to hit on you again."

She spun on her heel and struck off the way she'd come, her vision so blurred by unshed tears that the forest floor resembled a Jackson Pollock abstract expressionist painting. She tripped on an exposed tree root and nearly fell. By the time she reached the paddock fence, cold droplets had slid off her chin, trickled down her chest, and collected in her cleavage. The main house swam into her line of sight, and she jerked to a halt. She couldn't go inside. She'd told Vickie she was going down to talk with Wyatt. It wouldn't be difficult for Vickie to figure out that the foreman had said something to upset her. Even though Erin felt

Wyatt had been out of line to get ugly and hurtful, she didn't want Uncle Slade to be pissed off at him. She'd just call Vickie on the way home and say something had come up at work to cut her visit short. *A white lie.* Erin didn't like lying, but sometimes, to protect others, she saw no way around it. Wyatt's livelihood could be at stake.

Still sitting by the creek, Wyatt held his head in his hands. He'd seen the hurt in Erin's eyes when he laced into her. Despite his initial outrage, he'd had no reason for lighting into her the way he had. *Damn it.* Normally he went out of his way not to hurt people's feelings. With Erin, he'd pressed a merciless attack on her femininity, and now he was furious with himself. In fact, when he considered all the angles, he'd be better off mentally and physically if he *were* playing for the other team. At least then he wouldn't be plagued with erotic dreams about a female deputy with handcuffs on her belt.

A tingling sensation suddenly washed over Wyatt's skin, and he snapped erect. Someone or something was approaching him. For a moment, he hoped it might be Erin returning, but he quickly discarded that possibility. She never set off his inner alarms, which was yet another thing about her that messed with his head. He could always sense it when another person or an animal got within a certain distance of him.

He glanced over his shoulder and saw Kennedy angling through the cinnamon trunks of the massive pines to reach the log where he was sitting. Wyatt knew it was no accident that his brother had sought him out. This spot along the creek was too far away from the ranch proper to draw passersby. The afternoon breeze suddenly picked up, stirring the pine boughs so briskly that splashes of sunlight danced over the forest floor.

"Hey," Wyatt said by way of greeting.

Tall and lean like Wyatt, Kennedy sat next to him on the fallen tree, his bent knees forming bony squares under the snug denim of his pant legs. "Hey," he replied, his expression troubled. "What were you and Erin talking about? She looked upset when she left, and I've got a really bad feeling it's my fault."

Wyatt sharpened his gaze on Kennedy's face. "Why would you think that?"

Kennedy hung his head for a moment. Then he looked up so Wyatt could see his lips. "Because I'm the one who told her you're gay."

It took Wyatt a moment to assimilate that. "You did *what?*"

"I'm sorry, bro. But it was all I could think to do!" As often occurred, Kennedy stopped communicating verbally and switched to American Sign Language, a habit that both he and Wyatt had developed during personal exchanges, because accurate lip reading took all of Wyatt's concentration and quickly exhausted him. Hands moving rapidly, Kennedy continued. "She was about to quit her job, all because she's gotten it into her head that men don't like women who wear uniforms. I overheard her talking to Slade and Vickie about it. How she was planning to go back to college and she'd no longer be able to afford the rent on her cottage. I had to do something. She was about to destroy her whole life! Since I knew your disinterest had nothing to do with her personally, I decided to tell her the truth."

Wyatt's brain froze. *The truth.* He felt as if he'd just awakened from a bad dream to discover that reality was even worse. Erin hadn't reached the conclusion that he was gay on her own. She'd been led to believe that by his brother. Which meant Wyatt had been completely off base in everything he'd said to her. *Oh, God.* He'd accused her of being conceited. Of being so stuck on herself that she couldn't wrap her mind around the fact that a heterosexual male could resist her.

A fresh flood of outrage swamped Wyatt. He stared at Kennedy, and for the first time in his life, he counted to ten in order to control his temper with his brother. "Exactly when did you determine that I'm gay, Kennedy?"

Kennedy's shoulders slumped. "I'm not sure. For a long time, I thought your lack of interest in dating women was somehow connected to your deafness. Only as I matured and started to—well, you know—I realized that a guy's ears are a long way from his equipment. His sense of hearing or the lack of it plays no part in his sexuality. Deaf, blind, mute. It doesn't matter. So I started thinking of other reasons you might not like girls. I wanted to talk to you about it, but every time I tried, I couldn't think how to broach the subject."

"Well, the moral of that story is that maybe you shouldn't think. I am *not* gay."

"You're not?" Kennedy shook his head. "But that's all that makes sense. My whole life, you've never liked girls. You didn't even go to your senior prom."

Wyatt resumed his former position, elbows planted on his knees, forehead resting on the heels of his hands. He didn't know if Kennedy continued to talk. It didn't matter. "I liked girls in high school, but they didn't like me. I was deaf and I talked weird. Any time I made a move on a girl, I got shot down." Wyatt straightened to look at his brother again. "That's one of the reasons I worked so hard back then to improve my speech. I hoped to be more like the other guys and get a girlfriend."

Kennedy's brow furrowed in a frown. "So you like women? I don't get it. You speak fine now. If you're interested, why don't you ever hook up with anybody?"

Wyatt ran a hand over his face and blinked. "There are things about me that you don't know. You were only fifteen when it happened, and Mom and Dad kept it from you. It was bad, really bad, but it didn't happen in our hometown and wasn't front-page news, so they were able to keep it a secret. Mostly, anyhow. Grandpa knew. Our minister and a couple of really close friends from church knew. And practically everyone in Medford must have known, because the paper followed my trial closely. But if the news ever reached Klamath Falls, it must have been buried on a back page."

"Trial? Damn, Wyatt, what'd you do?"

After expelling a ragged breath, Wyatt explained to his brother in detail what had happened and why he still avoided the opposite sex because of it.

When Kennedy had heard the story, he stared at the creek with a stricken expression on his face. Finally, he turned his gaze to Wyatt again. "You're deaf, Wyatt, not dead from the neck down. That's no way for a man to live his whole life. You're a great guy with a lot to offer. You should have a wife, raise a family. When Grandpa passes on, the ranch will go to you. Without kids, you'll have no one to take over when you get old, kind of like Slade before Vickie came back. He didn't know he had a son and believed he had nobody to leave the ranch to. *Nobody.* Remember how sad he was about that?"

Wyatt managed a weary smile. "You'll have kids. Maybe one of them will love ranching."

"And maybe one of them won't. Then what?"

"Even if I had kids, there'd be no guarantee that one of them would want the ranch. Look at Slade's sister. She hates this place. Besides, falling in love and getting married to raise a family isn't for everyone." Wyatt collected his hat, which he'd set on the log beside him. "And as sad as that may seem to you, I'm a guy who just isn't interested. You have to kiss a lot of girl frogs before you find a princess. Shopping around is too risky for someone like me. I could have done hard time, Kennedy. The only reasons I didn't were because I had a determined defense attorney and the victimized woman told the absolute truth when she was on the stand."

"Victimized? The way I see it, you were the victim!"

"No. I orchestrated the entire situation by deciding to pass as a hearing person so I could hook up with women. I didn't anticipate all the things that could go wrong, and I ended up hurting someone who did nothing to deserve it."

"You didn't intend to do anything wrong," Kennedy insisted.

"No, I didn't, but I didn't think of every possibility, either. For a guy like me, the term *responsible sex* takes on a whole different meaning."

"So what's your plan?" Kennedy asked. "To live like a monk all your life? To punish yourself for something you never meant to happen?"

Wyatt thought carefully before he answered. "Being celibate isn't so bad, really. And to be honest, hitting on women is an unpleasant experience for me." He gestured limply with one hand. "Dating is hard enough. For me, it's doubly complicated. I can't live my life pretending to be something I'm not in order to attract women. Do you agree with me on that?"

"Absolutely."

"And that leaves me where? Striking out isn't fun. It wears down the self-confidence. And like it or not, most women run the other way the moment they realize I'm deaf."

Kennedy slapped at a fly that landed on his leg. "Erin knows, and she isn't running. Why can't you just level with her and see what happens? She's a really pretty lady."

Wyatt couldn't argue those points. "True, but I'm a risky bet for almost anyone, even a woman who is interested in me despite my disability. Let's say I ask Erin out and she accepts. We hit it off, and one night, the situation heats up, so she asks me over to her place. The moment the lights go out, I can no longer read her lips. Even if she leaves the lights on, a guy can't always see a woman's face as he has sex with her. Can you see how that complicates things?"

Kennedy nodded. "So you're afraid she'll change her mind at the last second, and you won't hear what she says to you."

"Exactly." Wyatt settled the Stetson on his head and angled the brim to shade his eyes before he walked back to the ranch proper. "But that's not the only risk factor for me. Women like some things and don't like others, and no two women are the same. Erin couldn't communicate to me what she wants me to do or doesn't want me to do. There's also the possibility during sex that something that usually doesn't bother a lady can suddenly be painful. If I can't read her lips or see her hands move, she would be unable to let me know."

Kennedy puffed air into his cheeks and rubbed the bridge of his nose. "There has to be a way around that. Other deaf men have significant others in their lives."

"True, but it's probably safe to say that there's still a huge communication problem when the lights go out."

"Will you at least consider talking with Erin about it?"

Wyatt wished his brother would just let it go. "Sure, I'll consider it. But my biggest concern right now is that I hurt her feelings. I said some pretty ugly things and owe her an apology. The sooner I take care of that, the better."

At a quarter after three the next afternoon, Wyatt got in his truck and drove into town. He knew through Slade and Vickie that Erin worked the day shift this week, so by the time he reached her house, she'd most likely be home. If she wasn't, he'd just sit on her porch and wait. It was perfect weather for that, sunny and warm for Mystic Creek in May. He'd had a busy morning, allowing him little time to think about how he should apologize to her. Maybe if he had a few minutes of downtime, he could come up with a brilliant approach to what would probably be a tension-packed conversation.

As he pulled into Erin's driveway, which was in sore need of grading and fresh gravel, he saw her on the front porch. She was bent over something big and black. Through the glare of sunlight on the dusty windshield, he squinted to see what she was doing. She appeared to be dumping potted plants into a garbage bag. She didn't glance up at the sound of his truck, which he thought was odd. According to Kennedy, diesel engines emitted a loud rumble. Wyatt had no clue what a rumble sounded like, but he figured Erin should have heard him pull up.

Throwing off his seat belt, he opened the door and swung out of the pickup. As he walked toward the steps, bypassing the county truck in the driveway, he kept his gaze riveted on Erin. She still didn't glance his way. *Okay. She's pissed at me*, he decided. *Not that I blame her.* When he'd closed the distance between them to about ten feet, he saw a glistening of tears on her cheeks, and his stomach clenched. He also saw her lips moving, but he wasn't at the right angle to determine what she was saying. Was she talking to herself? Wyatt knew hearing people sometimes did that, but it wasn't an activity that he normally engaged in. He couldn't decide if she was ignoring him or just didn't know he was there.

"It looks like you're on a mission," he called out to her.

Still holding a small flowerpot in her right hand, she startled and whirled to face him. Her eyes were puffy from crying, and her nose was as red as Rudolph's. She dropped the container at her feet and clamped a palm over the center of her chest. "What on earth are you doing here?"

"I have something I need to tell you."

"I have no interest in anything you have to say," she retorted. "As far as I'm concerned, you've said more than enough already."

Wyatt couldn't deny the charge. He'd totally messed up yesterday, and he needed to repair the damage if he possibly could. He climbed the steps and sat sideways on the landing with his back braced against the roof support post so he could still see her. How, he wondered, did a guy lead into a conversation like this? She was too upset for any small talk. But he decided to try, anyway. "Why are you throwing everything away?"

"I'm getting rid of all these stupid decorations." She gestured at a lineup of wind chimes that dangled from the overhang and then at what few plants remained. "Everything's going, and if you don't get your sorry ass off my porch, you'll be next."

Wyatt glanced at the large pots that flanked her front door. They held what looked like half-dead petunias, one of the few flowers he recognized by name because his mother loved them. "That seems hasty. They're a hardy species. You might be able to revive them."

"Me?" she asked, jabbing her chest with a grubby forefinger. "They were fine when I brought them home, and I've watered them every single day without fail! They're dying right and left."

"Maybe you're overwatering them. You need to moisten the soil around them daily, but you don't want to drown them. It's a balancing act."

"If you know so much about them, you take them and work your magic. I'm done!"

Wyatt had a really bad feeling that her attack on the flowers was somehow connected to what he'd said to her yesterday. Oh, how he wished he could go back and undo every word, but that was impossible. "Erin, I came to apologize for the things I said yesterday. I had no business ripping into you that way. Will you sit down for a moment and let me tell you how sorry I am?"

"No, I will not!" Fresh tears sprang to her eyes, making their depths resemble the blue of tropical lagoons that he'd seen in travel brochures. "And there's no need for you to apologize, because everything you said was true."

Wyatt's heart sank. He'd used words as weapons, and they had wounded her far more deeply than he'd ever intended. He had to think of some way he might get through to her. If he failed in that, she might carry the pain with her for a long time. Sudden inspiration struck him, but he hesitated. He'd be opening up a can of worms. Only he could think of no other way to make her listen to him.

"No, Erin, I lied to you. Nothing I said was true, including the bit about me not being attracted to you. I do find you attractive. *Too* attractive for my own good, actually, because feeling this way is dangerous for a guy like me."

That got her attention. She stared down at him with a mixed expression of incredulity and bewilderment. Then, saying nothing, she bent over to retrieve the dropped flowerpot and chucked it into the garbage bag. From there, she advanced on the large containers that bracketed her door mat, upending them inside the plastic bag to dump out the soil and dying flowers.

"I still don't get why you're getting rid of everything," he said. "Petunia starts don't come cheap."

She rounded on him, allowing him to once again see her face. "I tried to make my porch look pretty like Julie's!" she cried. "She got petunias, so I got petunias. She got wind chimes, so I got wind chimes. But she has a knack for decorating that I lack. No big surprise! She's good at everything: picking out clothes, doing hair. There's very little she doesn't know about makeup. In short, she's ultra-feminine. Maybe you should hang out more at the Morning Grind!"

Wyatt winced. "Erin, I said some really shitty stuff. I wish now that I'd handled the conversation differently. That's why I came to talk with you—to hopefully set things straight. My pride got the better of me when you implied I was gay." He held up a hand. "I have nothing against gay men or women. It's just that I'm straight, and no straight guy likes having his sexual orientation questioned." He paused to gather his thoughts. "Well, I didn't like it, anyway. Maybe I'm oversensitive because I'm deaf, but my first reaction was anger. I'm sorry about that. I struck back at you, and I shouldn't have."

The stiffness left her shoulders, and she came to sit on the step. He didn't miss the fact that she kept some distance between them. Looking directly at him, she said, "Okay. I get it. I just misread the situation, I guess. But you don't have to lie and say you're attracted to me in order to apologize. Let's keep this honest, at least."

Wyatt realized that she was trying to protect Kennedy. "You didn't misread my signals, Erin. Kennedy came down to the creek after you left. He was worried, because you appeared to be upset, and he confessed that he told you I was gay."

"Oh, poor Kennedy." She squeezed her eyes closed. "I'm sure that went over like a lead balloon."

Wyatt allowed himself to relax slightly. "Actually, we had a pretty good talk once I got over my initial temper spike. And frankly, I can see why he thought that. As far as Kennedy knew, I'd never dated anyone. He just put two and two together and came up with five. I'm really not gay." He took a deep breath and slowly exhaled to give himself another moment to think. "And I'm not lying about the fact that I find you very attractive. It's just that I won't allow myself to act on it. I swore off women six years ago."

She gave him a long, measuring study. "Why on earth did you do that?"

Wyatt's original purpose in coming to Erin's cottage had been to apologize. He'd had no intention of baring his soul. Only how could he explain why he'd embraced a celibate lifestyle without telling her more? Thinking quickly, he decided that he could safely tell her at least a little of his story. "I had what you might call a difficult encounter with a woman. There was a lack of communication, and I had a brush with the law. It all got sorted out eventually, but when I came out on the other side of it, I promised myself that I'd never have anything to do with women again."

Wide-eyed, Erin listened without interrupting him.

"For reasons I don't feel I need to get into, that's a promise to myself that I feel obligated to keep," he went on. "No dating, no hooking up. That doesn't mean I have no desire. Take you, for instance. I find you very attractive, and I believe you might be interested in me as well, if I gave you any encouragement. But I just can't go there."

She let a long silence stretch between them before she said, "I think you're just saying that to make me feel better. And I appreciate that. Really, I do. But one of the reasons you hurt my feelings so badly is because every word you said was true. I am competitive with men. I'm going to counseling, and I've been working on that, but it's like trying to reprogram my brain. I know I'm not very feminine. My dad hated it when I got what he called 'girly notions' as I was growing up. He wanted me to think like a boy, act like a boy, and essentially *be* a boy. Changing all of that and developing different habits is a painfully slow process."

Studying her as she talked, Wyatt knew she spoke straight from the heart. She truly had no inkling just how feminine she actually was. How sad that she struggled so hard to change when she was beautiful and attractive just as she was. She wore overlarge jeans, a ratty, yellow T-shirt, not a trace of cosmetics, and had her long hair knotted in a turkey tail at the nape of her neck. But in his opinion, she was lovely without any embellishments. Her blue eyes dominated her oval face and were so expressive she could almost communicate her feelings to him without words. The bow of her mouth, slightly swollen from crying, was plump and perfectly shaped. She was slender yet well-rounded in all the right places. How could she look in a mirror and not see that? He guessed that nobody saw themselves the same way others did.

"Is that why you tried to copy Julie?" he asked.

"For me, she's a great person to emulate. You've seen her window displays at the shop. Her house is even more delightful. I'd love for mine to look even half as nice." She lifted her hands and shrugged. "I'm just no good at things like this." She gestured at the wind chimes. "I don't have an eye for what works and what doesn't. I got too many, and they look junky. Plus they make so much noise that they keep me awake at night."

"It seems a shame to just throw them away."

"Yes, well, I doubt that they're a hot yard sale item. Maybe so, though. I could try to sell them this summer, I guess."

Wyatt had done what he'd come there to do, only he still felt as if there was unfinished business between them. He guessed that stemmed from the fact that she clearly didn't believe that he found her attractive, which meant she probably didn't think any other man would, either. He wished he knew how to convince her otherwise. Of all the people he might have attacked verbally, he shouldn't have done it to her.

"May I ask you a question, Wyatt?"

He met her gaze. "Sure. Fire away."

"I understand your reluctance to get involved with anyone again, but don't you think it could behoove both of us to at least try to be friends? We're going to bump into each other all the time. It would be more comfortable for everyone if we feel no need to avoid each other when I'm visiting the ranch." Her cheeks went pink. "I promise not to hit on you. To be perfectly honest with you and also with myself, I probably need a good friend far more than I need a lover. Right now, I'm way too messed up to get involved romantically with anyone. But being friends is harmless."

Wyatt's first reaction was to say no. How much worse would his attraction to her become if he agreed to be her friend? A horny man could be around a woman he wanted only so much before his self-control snapped. Only something he saw in Erin's eyes tugged at his heart. She truly did need a friend. And whether he liked it or not, they'd both be a lot better off if running into each other at the ranch was no big deal. So, instead of rejecting the idea, he asked, "Can friends share a casual meal out? It'll be my treat if you can spare the time."

She planted a hand atop her head. "My hair is a complete mess!"

Her eyes were also red and swollen from crying, but he wasn't going to point that out when she already thought she looked awful. "Well, I'm not really dressed for dinner out, either. When I knocked off work for the day, all I did was shower and throw on clean clothes. But it'll take you only a couple of minutes to freshen up, and the Cauldron has no dress code. Sissy and Ben keep the downstairs ambience pretty casual."

She closed a fist over the front of her shirt, frowned slightly, and then smiled. "You're right, and I can change in a jiff." She stood up, met his gaze, and asked, "Are you sure?"

"I'm positive," he replied with more confidence than he actually felt. "Go get ready."

As she disappeared into the house, Wyatt wondered what he'd been thinking to ask her out on what she might construe to be a date. If she resumed flirting with him every time they bumped into each other, he'd be so screwed. He was already plagued with erotic dreams about her that awakened him from a sound sleep and kept him wound up for the rest of the night.

CHAPTER FOUR

Fifteen minutes later, Erin emerged from the house onto the porch. For an instant, Wyatt gaped at her in startled wonderment. She'd changed into a simple denim skirt and a pink knit top, which were dressy enough for where they planned to eat, but she wore black commando boots on her feet and had a brown leather bomber jacket draped over her arm. *What the hell?* But as unconventional as her choices in accessories were, she looked adorable in spite of herself, and the fact that she hadn't aimed for a sexier look eased his mind.

Once they were inside his truck, Wyatt said, "Unlike most people, I can't safely converse while I drive. If you'd like to listen to music, I won't mind if you turn on the stereo."

She smiled and shrugged. "You forget that I spend most of my shifts inside a truck with a police radio blabbering at me. I appreciate silence inside a vehicle. It gives me a chance to clear my mind and let my thoughts wander."

Wyatt couldn't imagine what it might be like to hear people talking nonstop over the airwaves all day. He was pretty sure it would give him a bitch of a headache. "All I get is silence. That would drive me crazy."

He said nothing more until they reached West Main and he nosed his pickup into a parking spot. As he turned off the ignition, he glanced over at her and grinned. "How's that for luck? We're only a few feet from the door."

She gave him a thumbs-up. "That's one of the many reasons I love living in Mystic Creek. In the Seattle area where I grew up, there are so many people that parking spaces are normally at a premium."

She didn't wait for him to walk around to open her door. Instead she exited the vehicle when he did, and they met on the sidewalk. The Cauldron had gotten a recent facelift. Sissy and her mother, Doreen, had done extensive remodeling inside but hadn't been able to afford to have the exterior brick sandblasted and revitalized right away.

"This place is starting to look pretty uptown," he said, mostly because he was nervous and could think of little else to say.

Erin nodded. "I love what they've done with the interior, too. I hadn't moved here yet when the renovations were done, but Sissy had the foresight to take before pictures. The difference is amazing."

Wyatt pushed open the door and stepped aside so she could enter first. A wave of delicious smells wafted to his nostrils, and his stomach growled. He hoped it hadn't been a loud sound. "Sorry," he said. "I'm hungrier than I thought."

She laughed and said, "That makes two of us. I can't wait to see the specials she's offering this evening."

The café was busy, with local people lined up on stools at the bar and most of the tables already taken. Wyatt hung his Stetson on the rack near the front door and led Erin to a corner table where they could enjoy the fire without sitting so close that they grew too warm. Surrounded by skillfully mortared river rock, the firebox held a crisscross of burning logs, the flames licking up over the wood, a brilliant blue at their base and then turning from orange to yellow. The stones, which rose to the ceiling, were divided midway up by a log mantel that displayed antique cooking utensils. Above them hung a gorgeous painting of Mystic Creek and the natural bridge near the town center.

"Sissy struck just the right note with her choices of décor," Erin said as she laid her coat on an extra chair at their table. "I envy her that ability."

Wyatt stepped around to the back of her chair, which prompted her to look over her shoulder at him and say, "You don't have to help me. I've got this."

"I insist. A gentleman always seats a lady before he sits down himself."

She rolled her eyes and allowed him to assist her. As he leaned over her, he got a whiff of her hair, which she'd loosened from the band she'd worn earlier and brushed to lay over her shoulders in a silky cloud of dark chestnut. The scent of vanilla wafted to his nose. Given that the other aromas in the building had already spiked his appetite, he wished she didn't smell like something good to eat.

The moment they had taken their seats, Sissy's husband, Ben Sterling, advanced on their table with menus. The couple's infant son was cradled against Ben's chest in a baby sling. He was a cute little guy with his daddy's tawny hair and whiskey-colored eyes flecked with green.

"Oh, how darling!" Erin exclaimed. "He's grown since I last saw him." She reached up to touch one of the baby's chubby fists. "How old is he now?"

"Just turned six months," Ben said, his face glowing with pride. "We wanted to name him Jeremiah Paul after my pop, but Jeb's son was already named after him. Sissy's a big fan of *To Kill a Mockingbird*, so we settled for naming him Jem, my dad's nickname when he was a kid." Just then his daughter, Katie, appeared. Well, her face appeared. She peeked through the inverted V of her father's slightly spread legs and peered up at Wyatt as if he had a third eye in the middle of his forehead. He grinned and mouthed the word *hello* to her. Her chubby cheeks dimpled in a quick smile that revealed tiny baby teeth, and then she hid her face against her daddy's denim pants leg. Ben leaned slightly sideways to see around his infant son to locate his daughter. "Katie, here, just turned two. Sissy says our next one better be a girl, because her mom's nose is out of joint. She wants a granddaughter to be named after her, too."

"My goodness!" Erin exclaimed. "You and Sissy must already be the busiest couple in town with two little ones, a restaurant, and a ranch to run. I can't believe you're thinking about another child."

Ben's burnished face creased in a broad grin. "Oh, yeah, we're pretty busy, all right. But we wouldn't have it any other way. I grew up in a large family, so I always wanted at least three kids. Sissy has no siblings, and she resented that growing up, so she wants a large family, too." He shrugged and cupped a protective hand over the back of his son's head. "And honestly, it's not so bad when we bring the kids with us to the café. All our customers know them, so somebody's always ready to lend us a hand." He inclined his head at Erin's menu and then made eye contact with Wyatt. "When you're ready to order, just wave me down. I'll be back in a second to take your drink orders."

As Ben walked away, leading his daughter along beside him, Wyatt wished the guy would have stayed. Erin seemed nervous now that it was just the two of them, and he shared the feeling. Two people didn't instantly feel comfortable with each other merely because they had agreed to be friends.

Wyatt read all the menu choices. He was a huge fan of Sissy's beef bourguignon, but he'd had that the last time he was in, so he decided on the spaghetti and meatballs. Sissy simmered the sauce for twenty-four hours, and her meatballs were homemade delicacies. A person couldn't go wrong.

Ben returned for their drink orders. Erin asked Ben to select a nice red wine for her. Wyatt thought maybe a goblet or two of vino would take the edge off his nerves, so he asked Ben to make it a full bottle with two glasses. Then he said, "And I'm ready to order my meal." He directed a glance at Erin. "Have you decided, or am I rushing you?"

She shook her head. "No, no, I've decided on the spaghetti."

Wyatt smiled. "Great minds think alike." To Ben, he said, "Make that two spaghetti dinners."

As he settled his gaze on Erin again, he immediately regretted his choice of entrée. Eating spaghetti was almost always messy. He didn't want to end up with spaghetti sauce on his chin.

"Spaghetti is messy," he said. "Maybe I should have gotten the beef bourguignon so I won't embarrass you."

Erin's blue eyes widened. "Oh, dear. You're right. It probably will be messy."

Wyatt winked at her. "Which must mean you don't possess talent for rolling noodles around a fork with a spoon."

"No. I shouldn't have ordered spaghetti. I don't know what I was thinking."

"It's fabulous spaghetti. Let's just both agree not to watch each other eat."

She nodded. "Agreed!"

Ben returned with their wine. Wyatt tasted a small sample, approved the selection, and the restauranteur poured a measure of the merlot into each of their goblets. Erin took a sip of hers, swallowed, and waited for Ben to leave before saying, "I'm so glad you got a whole bottle. When I suggested that we try to be friends, I didn't think I'd feel this nervous."

Wyatt wondered if she'd picked up on his tension and was only trying to help him relax. But when he searched her expression, two realizations struck him. Erin truly did feel on edge, and there wasn't a trace of guile in her eyes to suggest she was given to artifice. He felt some of the tension ease from his neck and shoulders.

"I didn't think I would, either," he confessed. "But except for that one time months ago when we met for dinner at the Straw Hat, we've never been around each other very much."

"No. Out at the ranch, you always run the minute you see me."

Wyatt chuckled. "I'm sorry. I guess that is how it must have looked, but believe me when I say that it was nothing personal."

She took another taste of her wine. "I was flirting with you back then. I promise not to do that anymore."

Wyatt hoped that she wouldn't. He considered himself to be a strong-willed man, but his sense of purpose faltered when this woman came on to him. He lifted his glass in a toast. "To friendship. *Only* friendship."

She pressed the edge of her goblet against his and agreed by saying, "Only friendship." Then she smiled and said, "That's going to be so much easier. When you sent me a text last autumn to meet you for dinner, I thought you meant it as a date and almost had a heart attack."

Wyatt frowned slightly, trying to remember why he had felt it was necessary to dine with her that evening. Then he registered what she'd said and focused his gaze on hers. "A heart attack? Why?"

"I was in uniform, and I didn't want to meet you looking that way. I raced over to the Morning Grind, and Julie switched clothes with me. Then she did my hair and makeup."

"Wow. I had no idea." Wyatt did remember how different Erin had looked that evening, though, and he also recalled feeling relieved, because he preferred women who didn't fuss very much over their appearance. He liked certain perfumes as long as the application was light. He was okay with a touch of makeup. But he wasn't into bedhead hairstyles, false eyelashes, too much mascara, or bright red lipstick. In short, he had been more attracted to the Erin in uniform than he had been to the dolled-up version of her that evening, and to him, that had been a good thing. "You looked great," he said, which he told himself wasn't really a lie. Most guys would have been salivating. It was just that Wyatt had a lot more trouble resisting Erin when she didn't put so much effort into it. "I can't for the life of me remember what it was I needed to talk to you about that night."

She dimpled one cheek in a saucy grin and settled a twinkling gaze on him. "I think you wanted to give me a quick course on camping basics. I got you an electric coffee grinder as a gesture of apology for the way I behaved when we first met, and I thought you could use it at base camp."

Wyatt laughed and said, "Oh, yeah. I remember now. I was afraid you'd show up with a hair dryer, a curling iron, and an electric blanket."

She leaned slightly forward. "I wasn't *that* clueless."

"You were pretty clueless," he insisted, thinking as he spoke that she had an almost magical ability to convey by expression when she was emphasizing a word. When she talked, her whole face went into action. It made conversing with her really enjoyable for him, which was a rare occurrence. *Perfect for me,* he thought, and then he slammed the door on that nonsense, because, as he had explained in detail to Kennedy, no woman would ever be perfect for him. "And you did good up on the mountain," he added. "You packed light. You got the things I told you to buy, but other than that, you brought only the bare necessities."

"And I nearly had a meltdown about feeling obligated to arrest Uncle Slade for making a pet out of a black bear."

"Oh. I didn't know about that. Well, I did know Slade could get into huge trouble if you saw Four Toes, and I knew the bear scared you out of ten years' growth in the cook shack, but I heard nothing about a meltdown."

The animated expression on her face vanished, and he thought her eyes darkened with what he believed was sadness. He hoped it was only an illusion created by the flickering amber from the fireplace. "That was the night I realized how much I hate being in law enforcement."

"Ah." He could think of nothing else to say.

"Vickie was the only person who saw me during my meltdown." The genuineness of her smile had vanished with the light he usually saw in her eyes. "She gave me good advice."

"And what was that?"

"To quit law enforcement and go back to school for another degree."

"Ouch. That's costly, isn't it?"

"And life altering. I'm thirty-two, and I'd really like to have children. If I go back to school, I'll be hard at it with classes for at least two years, and afterward I'll be saddled with paying off student loans while I travel around to find clinical work. By the time my life is back to normal, I'll be too old to safely bear a child."

"A lot of women are having kids when they're older now," Wyatt pointed out. "And who knows? You might meet the right guy at the university."

"Not likely. Granted, there are a few older people who return to college in their thirties and forties, but they aren't the norm."

Ben arrived just then with their meals. Carrying a fold-out serving table in one hand and balancing a large tray on his shoulder, he grinned and said, "She outdid herself on the marinara, folks. It's always good, but my mouth waters when she takes wonderful and inches it up to extraordinary."

In that moment, Wyatt realized that he no longer felt nervous, and he couldn't attribute the change to the wine, because he'd barely touched it yet. It was due to Erin and her ability to dispense with airs and pretense. He leaned back in his chair as Ben set an individual platter on the table in front of him. As Ben served Erin, he inquired about the wine. Wyatt had a side view of his face and couldn't see the motion of his lips, but he could see Erin's mouth and was able to determine from her responses what Ben was saying.

After they were served and Ben departed once again, Erin plunged her fork into a meatball, trimmed off a bite with her knife, and then rolled her eyes as she tasted it. "Oh, wow! Messy or not, Wyatt, I'm so glad we ordered this. Most times when I come here, I can't eat all that I'm served. It's always great the next day for lunch or dinner. But I *never* have leftovers with Sissy's spaghetti. I shamelessly devour the *whole* meal."

"It's one of my favorites, too," he admitted. "My mom makes fabulous spaghetti. Like Sissy, she simmers the marinara a full twenty-four hours."

She arched her finely drawn brows. "My mother doesn't, and hers isn't very good. Or maybe it was the tension at the table that interfered with my appetite. She was always after me during meals about my manners and worried that I'd soil her tablecloth."

"My mom doesn't get bent out of shape about spills on her table-cloth. She's pretty relaxed."

As he spoke of his mother, he found himself wishing that Erin had been raised by someone just like her. She was a loving and patient woman who would have made sure Erin had a happy and normal childhood. Only that would have made Erin his sister. How in the hell could that ever work?

With a start, Wyatt realized that this cozy dinner for two had all kinds of crazy thoughts about Erin forming in his mind. *Not good.* He needed to keep his head on straight and remember that they were friends, *only* friends, and could never be anything more.

Determined to relax and enjoy her company, he did what he did best and encouraged her to talk. Producing words himself had become a lot easier over the years, but combined with lip reading over the course of an evening, it wore him out. He would say something here and there, he decided, but only enough to make her feel that they were having a normal conversation. The rest of the time, he would just take in what she had to say and watch her. He *really* enjoyed watching her, especially when she laughed. He liked the way she tipped her head back and let the sounds flow up her throat. Since he couldn't *hear* laughter, he gauged the sincerity of it by watching the person. A lot of women flashed a demure smile and allowed their shoulders to jerk only three times. In his estimation, that wasn't real. It was a practiced social gesture and gave no visible measure of how amused someone actually was. Erin just went with it, and he lost track of how many times her shoulders jerked because her breasts jiggled each time and distracted him. She clearly didn't emit a dainty laugh. Hers came from the gut, and he knew it was a warm, natural expression of mirth.

"So, there, you see? My uniform is a man deterrent."

With a start, Wyatt realized he'd stopped reading her lips to admire her breasts and had missed a large portion of what she'd said. "Oh, well. A man who can't see beyond the uniform probably isn't worth having, anyway."

Judging by the way her chest rose and fell, he thought she sighed with discouragement. Or possibly defeat. He wished he could think of something to say that might boost her self-confidence and reassure her. "When the right man comes along," he added, "he won't even see the uniform. He'll see only you." He took a moment to refill their wine-glasses and realized that they each still had yet another glass to go before they could call the bottle a dead soldier. "You're lovely, Erin. A guy would have to be blind not to notice that."

Her cheeks went pink. "Thank you. That's very sweet."

Just then, Ben Sterling came to remove their plates and the bread basket, which was almost empty. Wyatt remembered taking the first bite of his spaghetti, but from that point forward, he'd been so engaged in their exchanges that the remainder of the meal had passed in a blur. It wasn't often that he could relax and enjoy a woman's company so much.

Ben returned with dessert menus. "You can't leave without trying one of Sissy's offerings. Her mom makes some of them. Sissy, the others. My personal favorite is Sissy's cheesecake. She adds caramel sauce, and the crust is caramel as well. It's like taking a bite of pure heaven."

Erin placed a hand over her midriff. "Oh, I shouldn't. Do you know how many calories are in cheesecake?"

As far as Wyatt could see, she didn't have an ounce of fat on her anywhere. "Come on. We don't get to splurge on Sissy's special cheesecake every day."

She studied him with unnerving solemnity. "I really shouldn't."

"You can go for an extra couple of runs over the next few days," Wyatt suggested. "That should settle the calorie score."

She sighed again and then grinned. "Oh, heck, why not? I really don't indulge often."

It seemed to Wyatt that their desserts arrived in a flash. He found himself not wanting the evening to end. They had arrived early, and the first wave of diners had long since left, only to be replaced by people who liked to eat a little later. He wondered how long he and Erin had been lost in conversation. He guessed that they'd been talking for at least two hours. That was a record for him, and he didn't feel exhausted.

Erin so enjoyed every morsel of the cheesecake that she threatened to lick her plate. Wyatt rarely laughed without trying to modulate the sounds that he produced. He always controlled his mirth so as not to embarrass himself. Only Erin had a way of making him forget that, and her threat to lick up what was left of her caramel sauce tickled his funny bone. The instant he forgot himself and let loose with a guffaw, he checked Erin's reaction. She only seemed to be laughing with him, and none of the other diners had looked oddly at him. He guessed maybe his laughter wasn't too off the charts.

As Erin enjoyed what was left of her wine, she smiled slightly. "I hope you don't mind, but I have a question I just have to ask. How did you manage to perfect your speech to such a degree that most people can't even tell you're deaf?"

Wyatt topped off his glass and hers with what little was left in the wine bottle. He felt nicely relaxed, but not even a little tipsy. He guessed they had been at the table for so long that enough time had passed to offset their consumption rate. "I learned how to speak properly by using programs that teach people how to speak a foreign language. For me, that language was English. And the only feature in all the programs

I purchased that I could actually use was the repeat-after-me feature. I could see the word, and as I tried to say it, the program would kick it back at me if I didn't pronounce it right."

"That must have been grueling. And the time you had to invest must have been huge."

He shrugged. "I spent hours in front of a computer every night. And when you're deaf, saying a word correctly once doesn't mean you have it down. You forget how you said it, and you have to say it again and again." He pressed a fingertip to the rim of his glass and circled, thinking of how Kennedy loved to make crystal sing. "It took me forever and hundreds of dollars to find an application that truly worked for me, one that focused mainly on pronunciation and wouldn't let me move forward to another word until I said it right."

"How old were you when you started practicing?"

"A teenager. Up until then, there weren't many programs that could help me, and in the end, the one that helped me the most was the cheapest, wasn't touted to be the best available, and probably wouldn't have pleased hearing learners at all, because it mainly focused on correct pronunciation. That was key for me. I needed a program that wouldn't let me skate by, saying a word slightly wrong. It was exacting. It frustrated me. Sometimes I wanted to throw the computer out the window. It didn't tell me how I was saying the word wrong. It just repeated the word with proper pronunciation, but I couldn't hear the example given. I just had to keep saying it until I got it right."

"And you ended up speaking almost perfectly."

"I'm not sure how perfect my diction is. What matters to me is that nobody has laughed at me for the way I talk for a long time."

A suspicious glimmer of moisture shone in her eyes, and she caught her bottom lip between her teeth. He had a feeling she was battling tears. "Oh, Wyatt. I'm so sorry that ever happened to you. People can be such idiots."

Wyatt almost told her that truer words had never been spoken, because he was working his way toward idiocy himself. All he could think about was how lovely she was and how badly he wanted to kiss her. Big problem. He wouldn't want to stop with only a kiss, and anything more would be as risky for her as it would be for him. He needed to drive her home, walk her to her door, and then put as much distance as possible between them before he did something he might regret.

Only how did a guy walk away from an almost perfect evening with a woman when he'd never experienced perfect? The firelight warmed the whole room, and being a visual person, Wyatt was acutely aware of every flicker of amber. How it shimmered and danced on Erin's dark hair, making her look as if she wore an animated halo. How it shifted in energetic and unpredictable patterns over the rustic wood walls. How it lent an effervescent glow to the lighting globes in the chandeliers. And the feelings he had from being here with her filled him with expectation, as if an invisible hand had just opened an equally invisible door to show him a plethora of pleasurable things that he'd been too blind to see until now.

"If anyone ever laughs at you again, I'll punch their lights out." She leaned closer as she said those words, and Wyatt suspected that she'd only mouthed them. Her sparkling gaze held his, and her expressions were so vibrant, evocative, and fleeting that he could almost believe he heard the inflections of her voice. "I know how it feels to be the odd one out. To be ridiculed and laughed at. To want so badly to be like everyone else that you'll do almost anything."

He sensed there was a story behind her last words, and he wished she would reveal it. He saw old but lingering pain in her eyes.

"Who made fun of you?" he asked.

"Why do you want to know?"

"So I can find them and kick some ass."

She treated him to another laugh. "I've never had anybody want to fight a battle for me. It's so *nice*. It makes me want to revise our agreement about being only friends. I've never had a big brother—or any brother at all, for that matter."

Wyatt didn't want to be her brother. He'd already bumped into that imaginary wall when he'd found himself wishing that his mother had raised her. "Tell me about the very worst time that someone made fun of you," he said.

The merriment and rosy color drained from her face, and for a mo-

ment, Wyatt thought she might not share the memory. "I stole something as a teenager."

It was hard for Wyatt to imagine her doing anything illegal, but
maybe it was because he'd mostly seen her only in a law enforcement
uniform. "What did you take?"

"Clothing, one of the hardest things to steal. And it wasn't that I
needed any clothes. I did it on a dare."

"You stole something you didn't need," he mused aloud. "Why? Not
being judgmental. Really, I'm not. Did you *want* the clothes? Were they
special somehow, something your parents wouldn't buy for you?"

"Nothing special about the clothes. I didn't even care if I wore them
again." Judging by the pensive frown that pleated her forehead, he
thought she took a quick mental trip back in time. "I was seventeen and
had no girlfriends." Flushing again, this time with what appeared to be
embarrassment, she shrugged and wrinkled her nose. "I know this
sounds lame, but I was a teenager, so go figure. I wanted more than
anything to be part of this certain group of girls. Looking back, I could
have chosen more wisely. They were pretty wild. Wore a lot of makeup,
hid out on campus to smoke cigarettes, sometimes pot. And they had
turned shoplifting into a fine art. But all of that was what drew me in
and excited me." She offered him a smile. "Cop's kid, looking for thrills.
Wanting to be bad, just because. Breaking the law simply because I resented my father, and it was his life's goal to uphold it."

He grinned as he took another sip of his wine. "Like the child of a
minister embracing a life of sin?"

"Exactly. Some kids want to rebel against everything a parent stands
for. I think that's particularly true when the parent is a domineering ass,
which my father definitely was. *Is*, actually. He's never changed. For a
brief while, his way and my way were poles apart."

"So one of the girls dared you to steal clothing."

"It wasn't just one girl. All of them were in on it. In order to belong
to their group, I had to go through an initiation and do something so
bad I'd be in huge trouble if anyone ever found out. In my seventeen-
year-old brain, it made perfect sense, a loyalty-among-thieves kind of
thing. Everyone in the group had done something risky, and none of

them would ever really trust me until they had something bad to hold over my head."

"But you got caught."

Ben arrived just then with a discreet black folder that concealed the bill for their meals and drinks. Erin almost offered to pay her half. She doubted Wyatt made more money than she did. But she'd glimpsed pride and stubbornness in his expression as he'd told her how he had perfected his speech. He wasn't a man who'd offer to treat a woman to dinner and then worry about the drain on his bank account. He had invited her. She had accepted. She needed to leave it at that. Maybe the next time they met for dinner, she could pay. If there was ever a next time.

Erin finished off her wine, thinking that Wyatt would want to leave as soon as he'd signed the credit card receipt. Instead he took care of the bill, put his card back in his wallet, and rested his folded arms on the table's edge. "You were saying?"

"It's late. You need to get back to the ranch. Morning for you will come early."

"I'll decide when I stay and when I go. You got caught stealing. Now tell me the rest."

She laughed. "It's really not that exciting a story. I had to steal three outfits, and I couldn't carry a bag or backpack to hide anything. I had to walk out wearing all three ensembles. That takes some thought."

"I guess it would."

"My plan was to do it by wearing clothes in three different sizes, the smallest next to my skin, the largest as the top layer." She shook her head. "I probably looked like a polar bear as I tried to leave the store. Three layers of clothing bind up on one another. They also make you look a lot fatter. I'm sure I waddled out of the dressing room, and I was apprehended the instant I stepped outside the store. It took a while for the cops to come. I was handcuffed and escorted from the building by an officer. As he was putting me into the back of the car, I heard snickering."

"Oh, damn. It was the girls that dared you to do it."

Erin searched his gaze and finally nodded. "Exactly. I'd been set up. They didn't want me as a friend. And they thought it was funny that I'd been dumb enough to think they'd accept me into their group, no matter what I did to earn the privilege. So you weren't the only kid to be laughed at. End of story."

He shook his head. "No, Erin. I think that's only the beginning of your story."

She placed her napkin on the table. "No, actually. My story ends there. From that moment forward, I put everything I had into pleasing my father, and it became his story, his dream, and I was only an actor on the stage. I knew what I wanted, but it was never the same thing he wanted. I wasn't as strong-minded as you, though. You were determined and never gave up. I wasn't determined enough, and after my one brush with the law, I caved. My dad got the offense expunged from my record. I'm not sure how, but I think he must have greased palms and called in some favors. And from that point forward, I lived to accomplish the dreams he had for me. I wanted to be a speech therapist. He wanted me to become a state cop. I rebelled by becoming a county cop instead, but as good as it made me feel to do it *my* way, it didn't last, because in the end I realized that I was still doing what he wanted and only changing it up a little."

"And you're angry."

She spent a moment thinking about that. "Not angry, really. I made my own decisions, and even though he pressured me to make the choices he wanted me to make, I could have stood up for myself. Somewhere along the way, it became all-important to make him proud of me. I craved words of praise from him, which didn't come often, but that only made me want his approval all the more. Jonas says we can all fall victim to that when we don't fit in as kids. We find one thing that we believe will make us feel better and doggedly pursue it. For me, that one thing was hearing my dad say, 'Good job.'"

"And for me, it was learning to talk so well that I could pass as a hearing person."

"Yeah, I guess. I hadn't thought of the similarity."

"It's very similar, actually, except that achieving my goal has made me feel better, and I'm not so sure you do."

"Not really, no. Mostly I just feel lost. I was never passionate about law enforcement. Instead I wanted to help people. When my father kept pushing me, I told myself I could do a lot of good as a cop." The color in her cheeks deepened, a telltale sign that it embarrassed her to speak of something so personal. "I pretty much pictured myself as Mother Teresa in uniform. Someone on the streets who helped runaway teens and drug addicts, the homeless, and abused children. Only that isn't what law enforcement is about. Officers don't *stop* crime. We just discourage it with our presence or do follow-up. We don't save children from abuse. Most of the time, we're called in after the fact, and our only job is to get the child to a safe place and try to make the person responsible pay. We're not always successful. Children get returned to the war zone. The abuser gets his hand slapped. Sometimes it all happens again and again to the same child. I got a rush at first. I thought we were winning the battle. But over time, I came to understand that I was only doing cleanup. I stopped nothing bad from happening. Very little, anyway. And before long I felt so disillusioned."

"It doesn't sound like a very fulfilling profession."

"For some people, it is. My dad is one of them. But for me, not really. I loved working in speech therapy, because I could see improvement and hope. In law enforcement, I don't get that sense of satisfaction. Others do. They feel that they're taking a small bite out of crime in their little corner of the world. They can take pride in those moments, and it's enough for them."

"In other words, you were never geared for this profession."

"Nope, and now I may be stuck with it."

He slid back his chair and rose to his feet. Whether he wanted this evening to end or not, she'd been right to point out that morning came early on a large ranch. "As much as I hate to call it an evening, I really should get back so I can get some sleep."

She stood and grabbed her bomber jacket from the seat of the extra chair. Prompted by childhood training, Wyatt stepped over to grab it from her hand and then moved behind her to line up the sleeves as she reached backward with her slender arms to find the openings. As he drew the heavy garment over her shoulders, the collar clamped down on her long hair. Using a scooping motion, he plunged his fingers beneath the drape of silky strands to tug them free. And that was his mistake. His knuckles grazed the velvety nape of her neck, and he felt her shiver. His own body reacted as if he'd just touched a live wire that put out 220 volts.

The blue-gray of twilight hovered between the tall buildings that lined each side of the street when they exited the restaurant. Even as Erin noticed the encroaching dusk, the quaint lantern lights that lined the sidewalks began coming on, their globes glowing a cheerful yellow. The cool night air cut through her clothing and made her shiver, a sensation that wasn't nearly as pleasant as the one she had experienced when Wyatt's fingers caressed her neck. He cupped her elbow as they walked to his truck. When they reached the front bumper, she expected each of them to go their separate ways, but he strode beside her to open the passenger door and help her get in. Logistically, his attempt to help only complicated the process. She was accustomed to jumping in and out of high-clearance vehicles dozens of times a day and had her moves down pat. He interfered with her rhythm and the swing of her body weight. He grasped her at the waist to give her a boost up, which made her feel foolish. And feminine. She refused to allow those feelings to get her hackles up. Instead she needed to think about how nice it felt to have a man look after her.

As he climbed in from the driver's side a moment later, he said, "We're entering the no-speak zone again. I'm sorry I can't chat while I drive."

Within the confines of her seat belt, Erin shifted to face him. "If I sit in the middle, will you promise not to think I'm hitting on you?"

His golden brows snapped together in a puzzled frown. "Why else would you want to sit right next to me?"

"Because I've got an idea!" She disengaged the seat belt hasp. "For chatting, I mean."

As he buckled up, Erin shoved back the center console and slid over to sit beside him. After engaging the center restraint across her lap, she smiled up at him and said, "Okay. Let's try it. You stare straight ahead like you're driving and ask me a question."

As dubious as he appeared to be, he did as she asked. "What's your favorite color?"

Erin extended her hands to speak in sign to the right of the steering wheel. "My favorite color is pink. Some of my signals will be out of your visual range, I guess, but maybe you can see enough to get the general gist."

"I got that you like pink."

"You see? It may work if we play this right."

As they drove home, Wyatt engaged with her verbally while she responded in ASL. At one point when she needed him to see all of her to get a point across, she unbuckled her belt, slid forward on the seat, and turned to face him. He immediately hit the brakes and pulled over onto the shoulder of the road.

"Erin, I'm a fuddy-duddy about seat belts. Please get yours back on."

Erin gestured at the windshield. "It's a country road, Wyatt! Hardly any traffic. It is Mystic Creek, remember. Do you know how many thousands of times I've buckled up and never once needed a safety restraint?"

His laser-blue eyes gleamed with determination. "So you're canceling your only insurance as a passenger? It didn't work out very well for you when you canceled your policy for roadside assistance. Look what happened to your Honda."

She couldn't help herself and giggled. "*You* happened to my Honda."

"Yeah, well? I'm driving. Don't give me an opportunity to happen to you."

It wasn't really that funny, but the next thing Erin knew, they were both laughing like fools, and she discovered that she loved the sounds of Wyatt's mirth. They were unpracticed and from the gut. It was as sexy as a man's laugh could get.

When the hilarity finally subsided, Wyatt sighed as if he were exhausted. "Oh, man. I haven't laughed like that in years. Maybe never."

"Why on earth not?"

"Because there's no language program that critiques the sound of laughter, and I know us deaf folks can have some really weird laughs." He glanced over at her. "Back to your own side, Erin. You promised not to hit on me."

"I wasn't hitting on you!" she protested.

"Tell that to my body. It doesn't register the difference between a friendly leg rub and a flirtatious one."

"Oh." Erin felt as if he'd just doused her with cold water. Her leg had been touching his. "Sorry." She slid back over to the passenger side. "I didn't think of that."

As he pulled back out onto the road, she considered the implications of what he'd just said. The dash of coldness suddenly turned tingly and warm, spreading over her body from head to toe. He'd told her earlier today that he found her very attractive, but she hadn't believed him. Guys said stuff like that to reassure a woman even when they didn't mean it. But Wyatt's reaction to leg rubbing? That had to be totally genuine. And he'd told her more than he probably knew by revealing his physical reaction to her. Even better, he'd warned her to keep her distance. It told her that he really was hot for her in a way that words could never convey.

When he pulled the truck into her driveway, the headlights cut through the deepening darkness to illuminate her front porch with a quick sweep of the high beams. She'd left a huge mess in front of the door, and now it was too late to clean it up. Like Wyatt, she had to get squared away for work tomorrow.

Leaning forward so the dash lights illuminated her, she signed to him with her hands. "This has been the nicest evening I've had in a long time. Thank you so much for inviting me."

He smiled, a slow transformation of his face that deepened the crow's-feet at the corners of his compelling eyes and elongated the creases in his lean cheeks. "It was my pleasure. I had a really great time."

Erin started to open her door and stopped mid-motion when she saw him unfastening his safety restraint. "What are you doing? I don't need you to escort me to the door, if that's what you're thinking."

"What you need me to do and what my father taught me to do may be two entirely different things, and if we're going to be friends, you need to stop hassling me about it."

"Do you make a habit of walking all your *friends* to their doors?"

"As much as this may shock your feminist sensibilities, Erin, I escort all *lady* friends to their doors. I realize you have two good legs. All right? That you don't really need me to play watchdog as you walk up your own driveway. But my dad wired me to be a gentleman in certain situations, and taking a woman out to dinner is one of them." He paused as if to give her a moment to assimilate that. "How is this friendship idea going to work if you get all sensitive over stupid things like me pushing your chair forward when you take a seat? Or when I open a door for you? Can't you think of it as practice for when the right guy comes along and starts treating you like a lady?"

Erin was more than willing to practice polite behavior, but she wouldn't be doing it in hope that the right man would eventually enter her life. She had a feeling he'd already arrived. But for reasons beyond her, Wyatt didn't see how perfect they were for each other.

"Okay, fine. Walk me to the door. I'm good with it."

He piled out on his side as she exited on hers. As he came around the front bumper to meet her, he said, "For the sake of proper practice sessions, a lady waits for a gentleman to open the car door for her and help her get out of the vehicle."

Light from the cab still illuminated the area where she stood. Erin grinned as he cupped her elbow in one big hand. Then the dome light blinked out. "I'll remember that, but please bear in mind that I'm a work in progress and didn't receive the same instruction as most girls when I was growing up."

No response. She peered up at him through the darkness and realized he couldn't see her lips clearly. Using ASL to communicate with him wouldn't work, either. For Wyatt, all conversation had to occur when he had a good visual of the person talking to him.

When they reached her porch, he stood off to one side so she could unlock the door. As it swung open under the press of her hand, she turned to smile up at him. Moonlight illuminated them, but it wasn't a strong enough light for him to read her lips. For a long moment, he just gazed down at her. Her experience with dating was minimal. She'd hooked up with two guys in brief but exclusive relationships, so she had stopped playing the dating game for long periods of time. But she did know how the goodnight kiss was supposed to go. Every girl who'd ever been walked to her door by a boy never forgot that part.

Only Wyatt just studied her. And then he asked, "Would you like me to go in with you to make sure there hasn't been a break-in?"

She reached around the door frame to flip on her living room lights so he could see her face. "That's thoughtful of you, but I think I'll be fine."

He touched the brim of his hat in that timeless way of all cowboys. "Goodnight, then. I hope you have a great rest of your evening."

She turned to watch him descend the steps in one long-legged leap. He was surefooted, even in the dark. She also noticed for the first time all evening that he wasn't wearing a jacket to ward off the chill of the night air. A sad feeling moved through her chest. It truly had been a fabulous evening, but he'd said nothing about them doing it again.

CHAPTER FIVE

As Wyatt drove away from Erin's cottage, he felt oddly empty. Or maybe *hollow* described it better. He'd had such a good time with her tonight, and he truly wished they could be friends. On the surface, it had gone so well, and when he'd been with her, he'd had fun. He didn't normally have much fun. He focused on his responsibilities at the ranch, tried to set a good example for Kennedy, practiced his word pronunciation every evening, and did his best to get a good night's rest when each day drew to a close. When he went into town, he shopped for groceries, bought himself small bags of specialty coffees, picked up parts to repair whatever needed fixing, and ran errands. He never went anywhere specifically to enjoy himself. On the rare occasions that he stopped someplace to eat, he did so because he was hungry, and he hurried through the meal because he always felt pressed for time. He also avoided conversations with the locals, not because they weren't nice, friendly people, but because he always got himself into what he'd come to think of as lip-reading events. Out and about in town, he rarely had an opportunity to talk with only one person. Someone else always wanted to put in his two cents' worth, and Wyatt ended up trying to read too many pairs of lips at once. On top of that, his brain was forced into high gear, trying to supply him with the words he needed to say. Afterward, he always felt exhausted and frustrated. So he had backed away from all of it and worked harder to accept himself for who and what he was, a nice enough guy who liked people but couldn't communicate well with them. And in the process of reaching that point of acceptance, he'd also had to embrace his disability and be glad of it.

With Erin this evening, he hadn't struggled in order to communicate with people, though, and that was a first for him. Recalling their meal together, he belatedly realized that she'd made a point of keeping her face visible to him as she'd conversed with Ben. That had allowed him a clear view of her lips whenever she spoke, so even when he couldn't see Ben's, he'd been able to get the general gist of what he'd said by reading her responses. *Wow.* It had been wonderful not to get that awful feeling of frustration and inadequacy that always flooded through him when more than one person was talking and he couldn't keep up.

And Erin had made that happen.

It boggled his mind. Not even Kennedy completely understood Wyatt's reasons for avoiding group interactions. Yet somehow, Erin not only understood, but she had made sure it wouldn't be unpleasant for him by striving to keep him in the loop. She'd told him that she had worked with deaf kids and had yearned to make a career of it before her father redirected her footsteps toward law enforcement. Apparently she had retained a lot of knowledge about hearing-impaired individuals. It wasn't only that Erin knew a lot about deafness. She actually understood the obstacles that a non-hearing person faced, she truly cared, and in a natural, low-key way that hadn't embarrassed him, she'd made sure he wasn't left out of the chitchat that transpired between her and Ben. Nobody had ever done that for him, not even his parents or Kennedy. Wyatt knew they loved him. He knew they had all three gone out of their way to accommodate his differences. But they just didn't get it, not in the same way Erin did.

Damn. She was the perfect friend for him. With her riding shotgun, he could even try to have a social life, which had always been so laborious for him that he'd given up on it. For years, he'd stripped all the social activities from his routine. No church events. No going to a night spot to hang out. He even avoided simple things like sidewalk markets, school festivals, and town hall meetings. Everywhere he went, people wanted to talk to him. He appreciated that and knew they accepted him as a member of their community, but they were pretty much clueless about *how* to talk with him. For him, going to a farmers market was like trying to shop where nobody spoke English. If he asked a question, people often turned their heads as they answered it. He didn't get angry about that, but it sure did thwart his efforts to be part of this town.

As his friend, Erin could open doors for him into the heart of Mystic Creek. Only how could he ever make a mere friendship with her work? Being around her made him want so many things, foremost in his mind right now a goodnight kiss. *And more.* If he were smart, he'd run like hell. Only he had all these feelings he didn't know what to do with. Tonight, she'd shown him how good life could be if he had the right person at his side, and he wouldn't be human if he didn't want more of that. He'd also seen the expressions on her face as she talked about her youth and her father and the mother who never intervened to make her childhood more tolerable. She truly did need a friend, and so did he. Only not just any old person would do for him. He needed someone just like Erin, a person who really understood what it was like to be deaf.

Troubled by his thoughts and overwhelming physical desires, he pulled off to park in the town center and strode across the one-lane circle to the artsy water feature. He stood with his knees pressed against the rough edge of the fountain bench and stared into the swirling water. A light mist touched his face. The bottom of the manmade pond was swimming-pool blue and carpeted with coins. Copper pennies shimmered among metallic nickels, dimes, and quarters. He even saw a few silver dollars, which led him to wonder who had been foolish enough to throw away good money to make a wish that would never come true. Someone like him, he guessed. Somebody who had wanted to move forward with his life and didn't know how. Someone who had not only come to accept his circumstances but had learned to feel happy about them, only to find himself suddenly feeling dissatisfied and yearning for things he might never be able to have.

Wishing for things was dangerous for Wyatt. He knew that. He couldn't spend his entire life railing at fate because he'd been born deaf. He couldn't let his heart be crowded with negative emotions simply because he'd been dealt a rotten hand of cards. Until tonight, he'd been pretty happy with the way things were. He'd learned to be thankful for his hearing loss. He'd stopped chasing after false hopes that the latest breakthroughs in ear surgery would cure his deafness. He'd also learned to count all the ways that his disability had made him a better person. More caring and compassionate. More thoughtful. More focused on what really mattered. And at the top of the list, more grateful for all his blessings: his parents and their gift to him of unflagging support; Kennedy, who'd stepped beyond merely being his brother to being his friend; Slade, who'd given him a job and then promoted him to the highest-paid position on the ranch. His life had been filled with gifts, beautiful gifts, and now he found himself wanting more. What did that make him? An ungrateful shithead? His future had been written in stone when he'd still been in his mother's womb. His auditory nerves had been affected by congenital rubella syndrome, and to date, nothing much could be done to correct that. Maybe someday scientists would be able to grow new auditory nerves for people in test tubes and implant them, but Wyatt wasn't going to hold his breath. He had to be content right where he was. It was the only way he could be happy and remain balanced.

He fished in his front pocket for his change. All of it. He'd stopped here with some foolish notion of tossing coins and wishing for things he could never have. But he wouldn't follow through on that impulse. Erin was a beautiful woman, both inside and out, but he didn't need or want her in his life. Some people went into relationships with a lot of heavy baggage, but he would go into a relationship with the propensity to do harm. He had allowed that propensity to manifest itself into a harsh experience for one woman. He couldn't let that happen again.

So he wouldn't wish for things he couldn't and shouldn't have. Instead he would throw all his change into the water at once and wish that he could return to being satisfied with his life the way it was.

The following afternoon, Julie closed her shop and locked the front door at five o'clock. Normally she had cleaning and shelf restocking to do after she counted out her register, but business had been slow that day, allowing her time to do all the after-closing chores between customers. As she strolled through the Mystic Creek Menagerie, an ancient, round building that had once been home to a sawmill, she waved hello to Tony Chavez, who owned and operated Dizzy's Roundtable, a restaurant that featured a round, revolving platform for unique formal dining. Luckily for Julie, Tony was open for only lunch and dinner, which enabled her to compete with him for customers. His prices were higher, and the food he offered was fancier. Julie had found her own niche with her talents as a barista and baker.

"Hello, Julie!" he called.

She stopped to smile at him. "I love what you do with your table settings."

"Thank you. I like what you do with your window displays. Even when shoppers aren't hungry, they stop to look, and they usually end up going inside to grab coffee and a cinnamon roll."

"I cheat by piping the aroma of fresh-baked goods into the concourse where everybody smells them. It gets their mouths to watering, and then they can't resist."

He laughed and winked at her. "Smart thinking. Maybe I'll try that."

"Oh, no. I patented the idea."

Julie waved as she walked away. She and Tony got along well, but she was careful not to get too chummy. When it came to neighbors, whether residential or business, she believed in the old saying, "Familiarity breeds contempt."

As she pushed out the double front doors to the sidewalk, she checked her watch and was pleased to see that it was only a few minutes after five, which gave her plenty of time to walk to Blackie's Pawnshop, located just beyond the town center on West Main. She'd been wanting to drop in for ages, but she hadn't wanted to practically run to get there before Blackie closed up for the day. This afternoon, everything had fallen into place for her to finally walk over at a leisurely pace. She knew Blackie called it a day at six o'clock sharp. He'd told her once that he kept his doors open an hour later than the bank for people who worked a nine-to-five. That gave them time to drop in and hock their rainy-day treasures or redeem something.

It was a lovely afternoon, still sunny and warm despite the breeze blowing along the street. Julie loved the smells that teased her nostrils. The aroma of freshly baked bread drifted across the street from the Jake 'n' Bake. Tantalizing scents wafted from Chopstick Suey, a Chinese restaurant owned by Hunter Chase. She even caught a whiff of permanent wave solution from the Silver Beach Salon, operated by Crystal Malloy Richards. But mostly what captivated Julie were the myriad perfumes of flowers that grew in window boxes along each side of the thoroughfare. Now that May had a firm foothold and the weather was warmer, the display of color was also a pleasure point, the pinks of petunias vying for center stage against yellow daffodils, heather, and daisies. Seeing the blossoms made Julie yearn to hurry home to her own gardens.

But that wasn't on her agenda for today. She needed to close a sad chapter of her life at Blackie's Pawnshop. A foolish part of her hoped against hope that she would get a happy ending, but her pragmatic side scoffed at her for even entertaining the notion. It had been two years since she'd hocked her deceased grandmother's engagement ring, and it was too beautiful a piece to have escaped the notice of bargain shoppers who drove from town to town to find great deals in pawnshops.

She almost stopped at the fountain to toss in a coin for good luck. But then she smiled at her own silliness and sprinted over the crosswalk onto the corner of West Main where Blackie's shop was first in line on the north side. Like all the businesses along Main, Blackie's had a quaint, two-level storefront, sporting sandblasted brick, arched windows, and a lunette above the wooden door. She stood outside for a moment, lecturing herself. *You know he doesn't still have that ring. Why are you letting yourself hope for something you know isn't possible?*

Straightening her shoulders, Julie grasped the doorknob and pushed inside to the raucous jingle of an overhead bell. Most pawnshops were musty and dark, but Blackie's place was just the opposite. Shimmering glass display cabinets formed an inverted U shape with walking lanes behind the top end and along both sides where the proprietor could move freely to assist customers. He had installed excellent lighting. His merchandise was showcased against spotless black or dark green velvet. Like many pawnshops, this one featured heaps of jewelry and time-pieces, but behind the front barrier of glass, more locked cases displayed handguns, rifles in wall racks, and miscellaneous items on tidy, polished shelves. He kept things so clean that it resembled a retail shop.

Standing with his back to the cash register, he turned at the sound of the bell and abandoned whatever he'd been doing. When he saw her, his eyes, incredibly blue and lined with sooty lashes, began to twinkle, and he smiled as if he'd been hoping all day to see her walk in. He had a way of making everyone feel special, she reminded herself. He would act just as pleased if his least-favorite person in town had just appeared.

"Julie," he said, drawing out the syllables in her name as if it were a word in a song. "To what do I owe this honor?"

Suddenly wishing that she'd fussed a bit more over her appearance, she pushed at her windblown hair and smoothed the front of her bur-gundy knit top, which wasn't one of her nicest and had been mostly hidden all day behind an apron that sported "Morning Grind" across the bib in large block letters. "I managed to escape early today, so I'm treating myself to a little window-shopping." That wasn't precisely true, but she needed to be a bit sneaky about seeing if her grandma's ring was still part of his inventory. Blackie had a kind heart, and he would feel awful if he'd already sold something she wished she could redeem. "Do you mind if I browse?"

"Heck, no. Look all you like."

Every time Julie saw this man, she marveled at how handsome he was for a man his age. Stocky of build, he was of medium height, yet he seemed to be much taller until she stood right beside him. He'd kept his muscular body trim with regular exercise and what she presumed were good eating habits. During his walks, he made it a habit to stop in at eateries, one of which was hers, and he always had coffee and some sort of treat, but his weight didn't seem to fluctuate as a result.

"Thank you," she murmured.

She descended on the display of necklaces first and pretended intense interest in gaudy designs that she wouldn't ever wear. Then she moved to the earrings. When she finally got to the rings, she looked at each one twice and then struggled to hide her disappointment. Her grandmother's diamond was nowhere in sight. Julie had been in desperate straits when she'd hocked it in order to finish the renovations of her shop. At the time, she'd believed she would soon be making good money and would be able to redeem the heirloom. Only that hadn't happened. It had taken a while for business at the Morning Grind to pick up, and she'd barely broken even that first year.

Blackie, who'd been watching her, asked, "Are you sure you're not looking for something in particular?"

She forced a smile. "Oh, no. I'm just dreaming."

He searched her gaze. They had become friends over time, because he often came to her shop in the afternoon after her lunch-hour rush, making it possible for her to visit with him, but she still hated it when he looked into her eyes. She felt as if he looked deeper and saw more than she would like. Since her divorce and all the gossip that followed, she'd become a person who valued her privacy.

His full mouth tipped into a slight smile. "I still remember that ring you sold me a couple of years ago. I knew then that it was special to you, so if you ever want to redeem it, I have it on hold in the back room."

Julie could scarcely believe her ears. "*What?* Why on earth didn't you sell it?"

He shrugged his broad shoulders. "Sometimes I can tell when people are forced to hock something that's precious to them. When that happens, I do my best to keep the item." He grinned in a self-deprecating way. "I'm no saint. Don't get me wrong. If I got hard up for cash, I'd sell a lock of my mother's hair. But I've done well here. I own my shop and upstairs apartment. No mortgage payment hanging over my head, and I live simply. The shop supports me in fine style."

He stepped into the back room and returned a moment later with a small, white box. When he stepped to the counter and lifted the lid to let Julie see inside, she felt tears gathering in her eyes. The diamond-and-emerald setting was just as beautiful as she remembered.

"Oh, my stars! I can't believe you kept it for so long." Her joy dimmed slightly as reality sank in. Blackie purchased items to make a profit, and it still remained to be seen if she could afford to buy the piece of jewelry back. "How much?"

"I never charge a redemption fee. I just ask to be reimbursed for what I paid for an item." He shrugged again. "Well, for something large, I might charge a nominal storage fee, but this ring took up very little space."

"Is that a common practice?"

"Oh, heck, no. Most pawnbrokers charge some kind of redemption fee, sort of like interest fees on a loan. And some bleed people when they want to redeem an item. We're not in business for the joy of it. I just happen to be a little more sentimental than most, and I don't feel right about robbing people when they're forced to hock something really special."

"How do you know when it's something really special?"

He narrowed an eye at her. "Your hands trembled when you brought this in to me. And your voice shook just a little. I'm not heartless. I pick up on stuff like that. Like I said, I would have put it up for sale if I got in a pinch, but I didn't."

He lifted out the ring holder, and Julie saw that he'd written the purchase price on the floor of the box. "Looks like it'll cost you a thousand. I can sell it back to you on a payment plan if you're tight on cash. The only catch is that you can't take the ring until you've paid it off."

Julie wasn't tight on cash. She wasn't rich, by any means. Unlike him, she did have a monthly payment on her house. But she'd managed to keep all her other expenses down, rarely hired help in her shop, and banked all the profits she possibly could.

"Can I just write you a check?" She laughingly added, "You know where to find me if it bounces."

"You're a straight shooter, Julie. Of course I'll accept a check."

She reached for her purse, which she'd set on the glass countertop. As she wrote the check, she said, "You'll never know how much this means to me. When I hocked the ring, I knew my grandmother would understand. My whole future in Mystic Creek depended upon me making it with my business, so I really needed that thousand. But it still half killed me to sell it."

"I understand." He rested his bent arms on the glass surface, which brought his suntanned face closer and made his shoulders look even wider. "I got a raw deal with a pawnbroker once. He didn't wait the customary thirty days to put my hocked possession up for sale, and when I walked in and found it in the display case, I was pretty steamed. I had my receipt, of course, but the bastard had written the wrong date on the original bill of sale to cover his ass. To add insult to injury, he charged me a small fortune to buy the damned thing back. It was my grandfather's pocket watch, a priceless family treasure."

Julie slid the check over to him, and he straightened to put it in his register. "So when you became a pawnbroker, you promised yourself that you'd deal fairly with people?"

He flashed her a grin, displaying nearly perfect white teeth. "Something like that. I was going through a rough time, and I sure didn't need to be kicked when I was already down."

As Julie slipped the ring box into her purse, she met his gaze. "Thank you so much for holding on to her ring for me. My ex-husband hated it and bought me a showy diamond, so I never got to wear this one during my marriage. You'll never know how much it means to get it back."

"Ah, but I do know. From personal experience."

"I won't offend you by trying to repay the favor," she said, "but I would love to have you over for dinner at my house some evening by way of a thank-you."

Blackie looked deeply into her eyes again. "Please don't think I'm a presumptuous old man by asking this, Julie, but exactly where do you think the two of us are going with this?"

Startled by the question as much as she was by his directness, she couldn't think what to say and stammered without managing a coherent reply.

His expression softened. "I'm too old to play games. We can continue to dance around the issue, but that seems kind of silly to me. We're both adults and know there's an attraction building between us. That happens. Only I'm a good deal older than you are. Twenty years, I think.

Not to say I'm pushing for anything serious, but in case that happens, how is the age difference going to work?"

Julie had barely wrapped her mind around the fact that she liked him. Well, okay, she thought he was really hot, and as Erin had so succinctly pointed out, Julie was crushing on him. But she hadn't considered the nuts and bolts of a relationship.

"I'd like to have a mature male friend," she blurted out. "But I'm not ready for a romantic relationship yet. I have some trust issues since my divorce."

He chuckled. She loved the sound of his laughter, so deep that it seemed to curl around her like warm smoke. "The first step toward healing after a divorce is admitting you have trust issues."

"Yes, well, my admission doesn't make the trust issues go away. Don't I wish?"

"I'd like to hear about that. What went wrong in your marriage, I mean."

She laughed. "It would be much easier to tell you what didn't go wrong."

He nodded as if that was everyone's standard answer, which made her feel a sense of camaraderie with him. He'd mentioned once that he was divorced, but he'd never hinted at how bad the marriage was. "I can close up a few minutes early. We can go upstairs and crack open a couple of beers while we share war stories."

Julie wanted to say yes, but her trust issues were real.

As if he read her mind, he winked at her. "Come on, Julie. When I stop by your shop, we're usually alone. If I wanted to make an inappropriate move on you, I would have already done it. That's not my style."

"Okay, but just so you know, I hold a black belt in karate."

He laughed again. "God save me. The only black belt I hold is for bending my elbow to eat your cinnamon rolls."

She found herself following him up the narrow staircase that led to his private quarters. In the downtown area of Mystic Creek, most of the shops had upstairs living areas or vast storage spaces. Being in the Menagerie, the Morning Grind had no second story. But over time Julie had seen many of the Main Street stairwells. Having been designed well over a century ago by smaller people, they tended to be dark, steep, and treacherous, but Blackie had dispensed with that feeling. He'd installed good overhead lighting, added sturdy handrails along both sides, and painted the walls and ceilings a pale banana yellow, which seemed to bring in sunlight.

As he opened and held ajar the door at the landing, she stepped over the threshold into his apartment with more a sense of curiosity than apprehension. She expected to see—well, she wasn't sure what she anticipated. A bachelor pad, she supposed. Most men didn't bother with color schemes and seemed to think a mismatch of outdated furniture looked fine. But Blackie had carried the illusion of buttery sunlight into his living area, and he had appointed the rooms that she could see with a sturdy, brown leather sofa and well-cushioned chairs, offset by a collection of honey-and-black Amish accessories, a theme that flowed flawlessly from the sitting area to embrace the dining room and kitchen.

"Oh, *wow*."

Stepping inside behind her, Blackie asked, "You like?"

She couldn't help but smile. "Fishing for compliments?"

He chuckled. "Don't all amateur decorators fish for them? Of course, I did more than just decorate. I gutted the entire apartment and started over from scratch."

To Julie's discerning eye, he'd done a fabulous job. The great room concept worked beautifully, each area flowing nicely into the next. Being a woman who loved to cook, she felt beckoned by his kitchen. She glimpsed a Sub-Zero side-by-side, chrome-and-black double ovens, a built-in microwave, a utilitarian work island that begged for a rolling pin and pie dough, and a wealth of cleverly designed storage.

"I think you performed a small miracle." The apartment wasn't that large, but he'd somehow made it seem spacious. "The kitchen is amazing."

"Grab a seat. I'll grab us each a brew. I keep a selection: IPA, ales, and darks. What's your pleasure? Don't be afraid to name a certain brewery. I may have it on hand."

Julie felt the last traces of tension ebb from her body. She'd liked Fred Black the first time she met him, they'd chatted at her shop almost daily over coffee for months, and this was really no different. He wouldn't suddenly transform into a lecherous jerk simply because he'd lured her into his private quarters. "I'm not an expert on beer," she confessed. "I always forget the names. But I love a dark with a hint of smoke and sweetness."

As he rifled through his fridge, Julie chose to sit on one of two recliners that angled toward each other near a gigantic flat-screen television. The sofa looked equally inviting, but the position of the chairs provided a perfect place for people to chitchat. It also lent itself well to viewing football games. Blackie was a self-proclaimed enthusiast who unabashedly admitted that he had purchased two external hard drives to save sporting events so he could watch them at his leisure all year long. She plopped her overfilled purse on the barnwood floor in front of an end table. As she sat down, the leather chair seemed to melt around her body. She resisted putting up the footrest. This was her first visit, and she didn't want to appear too relaxed, even though she suddenly was.

He walked back into the living area with an easy, fluid stride. Today he wore a rich brown plaid shirt and form-hugging black jeans that made him seem like another accessory to the room's color scheme. And in this setting, which reflected his simple tastes and down-to-earth personality, he seemed to emanate masculinity and strength. Here in his element, he seemed even sexier than he did at her shop, which was saying something. He'd poured their beers into tall, chilled tumblers.

As he bent forward to hand Julie her drink, he said, "Special, just for you, and I know you've never tasted it. You can't buy it here."

Julie accepted the beer and glanced into its dark depths. "What kind is it?"

He grinned, flashing his straight, white teeth. "A Scotch ale reputed to be a favorite with most ladies."

Subtle overhead lighting glistened on his black hair, bringing out the blue undertones and highlighting its curliness. He kept it short, and it waved over his crown like a rumpled cap, inviting her to run her fingers through it. The thought jarred her, and she pushed it away. She took a tentative sip of the ale, and it was so good that her eyes nearly closed.

"Oh, it's delicious."

He sat in the matching recliner, which she noticed now had been wallowed out by use to the shape of his sturdy frame. "You don't get off that easy. What flavors do you taste?"

She took another sip and rolled it over her tongue, savoring the faint sweetness. "I definitely taste a hint of smoke." Meeting his gaze, she added, "And I'd swear I taste chocolate and coffee, two of my favorite things ever."

"Very good! You nailed it. That's Cold Smoke, an award-winning brew made and sold in Montana. I have a pawnbroker friend who hits estate sales up there. Whenever he goes, he picks me up a few cases."

"So you like a ladies' beer?"

He winked at her. "I like everything about ladies, so why not? As for the flavors, who doesn't love a hunk of chocolate and a cup of hot coffee? Men like those things, too. Honestly, though, I'm all over the place with beer, which is why I keep a variety in my fridge. I allow myself only two a day, so I like to change it up and experience different blends."

She settled back, thinking that the recliner was like the man who sat near her, all-enveloping in a solid but gentle way. "I love it," she said after taking another swallow. "And now you've gone and done it! I'm turned on by a beer I can't get anywhere in the state!"

He laughed. "My buddy can get you more if you really like it."

"I really do!"

He smiled at her over the rim of his foggy tumbler. "Well, then, I'm your man."

Julie wanted to ask how expensive the beer was, but another thought dashed her enthusiasm. "In college, I loved going to pubs to sample different beers. It became something of a hobby, actually. I wasn't into getting looped, mind you. I just found all the different flavors fascinating and toyed with the idea of starting my own microbrewery."

"Really?" He chuckled. "I'm still thinking about it."

"About a microbrewery?"

"Yep. I also like wine, but the different types are pretty much established. With microbrews, it's open to the imagination."

"Exactly!" she replied with more enthusiasm than she had intended, which brought warmth to her cheeks. "Sorry. It's a passion I buried a long time ago, and tasting this Scotch ale has resurrected it."

His smile faded. "A passion for something should never be buried. What happened?"

"I got married." She tried to laugh, but the sound came out wobbly and faint. "Derek liked wine and expensive liqueurs, and he acted as if beers were an affront to his refined taste buds."

"Hmm. Sometimes there's no accounting for people's tastes, I guess. Some people love beer. Others detest it. But he must have been something of a prick to have forced his preferences on you."

Julie almost choked on the liquid chocolate and coffee flavor. "Yep, a real prick."

He laughed and reclined his chair another notch. "I'm settling in for this story. I've wanted to ask you about your marriage, but I always held back. I can tell by the way you behave that he did a real number on you. Speaking from experience, I know how awful a truly bad marriage can be, and it takes time before a person can talk about it. I didn't want to push then, and I don't now, if you still feel uncomfortable about sharing."

"I thought I loved him." Her voice came out squeaky, so she swallowed hard before she went on. "I'd just finished college and gotten a job. Accounting and bookkeeping, so I sat at a desk all day. I immediately realized I needed a gym membership, and that was how I met Derek. He was one of those hunky, handsome trainers at the facility. He asked me out, I accepted, and I went a little crazy, I think. It was all so exciting and seemed so wonderful."

He smiled and took a sip of his blond ale. "Unfortunately, those wonderful feelings don't last. Unless, of course, you find *true* love. I'm not saying it doesn't exist. I've known people who found that with each other, but I think a large percentage of people stumble into what they believe is the real deal, only to wonder a year or so later what on earth they were thinking."

"Exactly," Julie agreed. "Only it took me longer than that. In retrospect, I wonder if I wasn't more enamored with the idea of love—the perfect marriage, a house with a picket fence in a rural area, two children, and a minivan. You know? But the truth was much more grim.

Derek used me, as embarrassing as it is now for me to admit. I was an ornament in his life to conceal the truth about his sexual preferences. He never wanted his parents and siblings to know he's gay. I should have realized all wasn't right in our relationship, but it was my first go-around with marriage, and I thought maybe all husbands grew less amorous right off the bat. Derek did his husbandly duty once a week at first, then every two weeks, and I wasn't really suspicious when he backed off to once a month. Disappointed, yes. I was trying to get pregnant, and he wasn't giving me much opportunity. But he had flair when he made love to me that camouflaged his lack of desire. Once a month, he created a blissfully romantic setting, making a candlelight dinner, putting love songs on the stereo, telling me how wonderful I was. I really believed everything was good between us until I came home early one afternoon and caught him in bed with his true love, another male bodybuilder."

"Ah, Julie," he said softly, his voice low and gravelly.

"I'm okay now," she hurried to say. "But at the time, I was shocked, incredulous, and devastated all at once."

Julie expected Blackie to offer the usual platitudes, something like, *I'm so sorry that happened to you.* Instead he kicked down his footrest to sit forward on his chair, his beer precariously balanced in one hand as he rested his bent arms on his knees. "The son of a bitch!" He gestured with his free hand. "If you still have feelings for the asshole, I apologize, but any man who'll do that to a woman is a self-serving jackass. What he did was inexcusable, and you're lucky that you walked in on them that day. Otherwise you might have remained in the marriage and there could have been kids in the picture when it finally imploded."

Julie felt as if a weight had been lifted from her chest. While it was true that she would never trust easily again, there was something so genuine about Blackie that it reassured her. "I'm glad of it now, for sure. When I was yearning for a baby, I wasn't angling to be a single parent. Some people pull that off, but I worked long hours. I would have needed a full-time father on board to help me. Plus, how much worse would it have been to have had a child with him before I learned the truth?

"I felt stupid enough as it was. My family was awesome and very supportive, but even though they never judged me, my sisters did ask how I could have been with him—well, you know, *that* way—without realizing the truth. And I had no answers for them."

Blackie remained on the edge of his chair. "None of us on the receiving end of marital treachery ever have a reasonable explanation. When we fall in love, we wear blinders, I think, and when something happens to open our eyes, we squeeze them closed again rather than face a truth we don't want to accept."

She released a taut breath. "That's exactly what I did. Like the fancy dinners and music? It occurred to me once that it was as if he set a stage and then played a role. But I immediately clamped a lid down on those thoughts, and even if I hadn't, I would have believed he'd fallen for another woman, not some guy. That possibility never even entered my mind."

He took a slow sip of his drink. "What he did—hiding who he really was to keep up appearances to please his family—well, it tells me that he's a self-serving person who thought only of himself and never once about what his deceit might do to you. But it isn't only men who can be treacherous. I'm living proof of that."

Julie had only ever known Blackie as a happy bachelor. He'd mentioned once that he was divorced, but she'd never wondered overmuch about the particulars of his marriage. "What happened to you?"

He sighed. "When I suggested that we should share war stories, I didn't think of how ugly it would feel when it came to my turn. It's something I've never talked much about except with a counselor, and only then because I needed to vent and put the ugliness behind me."

"If it's too difficult, you don't have to talk about it."

He sighed. "Not difficult, exactly. It's more the unpleasantness of remembering and wondering where my head was at. Believe it or not, the day will come when you won't think about your ex-husband anymore, and all the pain will be entirely gone. That's where I am now. I've put it behind me." He shrugged. "My wife played me, too. I wonder now if she even loved me on our wedding day. I was twenty-six, a young stockbroker when I married her. She was twenty and going for an associate's degree. Wanted to become a legal secretary. She came from a broken family. Had an ornery, controlling stepfather who doled out money to her with conditions attached. Now, knowing how extravagant she could be with a credit card, I wonder if he was really all that bad. But she hated him, and I've wondered since then if I was only her ticket out. I made good money, even at that age." He hunched his shoulders and then rotated them as if to work out kinks. "I think all of us wake up one morning in a marriage and realize the pizzazz is gone. That definitely happened with me, anyway. Our relationship wasn't all that I'd hoped it would be, but I did care for her, so I settled. Looking back on it now, I can't even say she went out of her way to deceive me into thinking she loved me. What she failed to do, I made up for with excuses, because once you draw back the draperies to examine reality, it's too brutal and painful to face."

Julie nodded. "I get it. I did the same thing. He'd put on those big shows of love and devotion as if they were plays that were scheduled for one evening a month, and sometimes I wanted to scream that I didn't need grandiose gestures. What I needed was for my husband to cuddle with me on the sofa to watch a film or to turn to me during the night just to hold me close or to talk to me about his day. Only he didn't need those things from me. He'd already gotten them from someone else."

"It was basically the same for me. She got involved with a married man who was dragging his heels about getting a divorce. So she kept the home fires burning with me until she could make a smooth transition from one all-expenses-paid life to another. She redefined the word *lazy*, yet another fault of hers that I chose to overlook. The sofa was her throne, and television and books were her entertainment. I'd come home to a messy house and clean it up myself rather than quarrel with her. I honestly never saw the divorce coming. I won't say I was the most fabulous husband that ever walked, but I did my best. She had free rein with my earnings. Spent unthinkable amounts of money on clothing and salons to look like a million bucks. I was thirty-five when she dropped the bomb on me. And it wasn't enough for her to simply leave. She had to tear me apart before she walked out."

"I'm so sorry she did that to you." Julie realized she'd just spouted a canned line of sympathy and quickly added, "Any woman who uses a man like that is a complete witch."

He chuckled. "I'm over it now, but it took me a long time to get there. Through counseling, I learned that some people must feel justified when they destroy someone else, so they re-create reality and demonize the person they're leaving. She told me that she'd never had such boring sex in her life. In fact, everything about me was boring, and my faults were many. She even complained about my habit of organizing my underwear drawer." He slanted her a mischievous look. "It never occurred to me to tell her I might not have fallen into that habit if she'd ever once done the laundry and put it away." He swung his hand. "It's weird, because my underwear drawers are a mess now. I think I fell back on organization because living with someone so totally chaotic drove me nuts. She wanted no structure in her life. No planning ahead. She was like a five-year-old who wanted ice cream and cookies or takeout for dinner every night."

The notes of resignation and disgust in his voice made Julie laugh, and then she immediately hoped she hadn't offended him. But he chuckled, too, and shook his head.

"Trust me. It was bad." He swirled his beer and took a big gulp as if to fortify himself. "But, oh, well, water under the bridge. We live, we learn, and then we move on. It took me nearly five years to take a dip into the dating pond again. That was after I moved here, and when I wandered off the straight and narrow, I went to Crystal Falls. I met a few women and had delightfully boring sex."

"That's a long way to drive just to find companionship," she observed.

"Screwing around in Mystic Creek would be bad for business."

Julie got a sip of beer down the wrong pipe as an unexpected giggle erupted. Blackie held up his hand and grinned. "Laugh all you like, but a lothario in Mystic Creek gets boycotted by jealous husbands and faithful wives. I didn't want to have that reputation. Besides, going to Crystal Falls gave me a change of scenery. I lived in Portland before coming here. Crystal Falls is a larger town with a better selection of night spots. If I had a couple of drinks, I spent the night in a motel and checked out the pawnshops and galleries before I drove back. I don't go much anymore. It's been about three years, I think." He broke off and cleared his throat. Then he rolled the base of his tumbler between his palms. "One-night hookups served me well during that stage of my life, but at this point, I'm looking for something a little more meaningful."

Watching him, Julie wished she'd been more honest when he asked where they were headed. She'd made it sound as if she were looking for only friendship when she actually yearned for more than that. There was something inexplicably attractive to her about Blackie. He was sure of himself in a way that soothed her. There was no pretense with him. And he truly did seem to be content with his life as it was, which she found intriguing. He wasn't needy. He made her feel safe, she supposed, and yet there was a masculine edge to him that also excited her. What she really wanted was to be a little crazy just once and go to bed with him. She had a feeling he would be anything but boring. But she needed to think this through and be sure before she confessed that to him.

They sat in silence for a minute, and even the lack of conversation felt soothing. She felt no urge to fill up the quiet with words. With Blackie, she could just be.

After retrieving her purse, she got up and walked into his kitchen to put her glass in the sink. The space was tidy and polished, but he had a rack of pots and pans above the gas cooking range and appliances on the counter that told her he didn't always eat out. "I love your apartment," she told him. "It suits you."

He pushed to his feet and strode toward the island. "I'll have you up for dinner some night. I fix a pretty decent steak."

She met his gaze. "I'll hold you to that offer, but first I want to serve you a meal at my place to thank you for holding on to my grandmother's ring." She patted her handbag. "I can scarcely believe I actually have it back. Most pawnbrokers would have sold it and banked the profit without a second thought."

He nodded. "Yeah, well, I'm a sentimental old man, I guess. Work or business can't be all about making money. At least not for me. I'd rather sleep well at night, and I can't do that if I stop caring about the people who walk through my shop door."

Julie understood precisely what he meant. Every once in a while an older person on a fixed income would visit the Morning Grind and order only a cup of coffee. She liked to pretend she had a bargain hour, the time for which she changed as the situation dictated, and her cinnamon rolls or donuts were suddenly only a quarter apiece. It did her heart good to see an elderly woman or man order a treat to accompany a hot drink. And when she thought about her day as she fell asleep that night, she could smile because she'd brought a little joy into someone else's life.

"You're a good man, Blackie." She stepped around the counter and gave him a quick kiss on the cheek. "I'm going to enjoy wearing my grandma's ring now. On my right hand, of course, like a dinner ring."

He inclined his head. "It'll look beautiful on you."

CHAPTER SIX

After leaving Blackie's apartment, Julie went home and spent forty minutes watering all her deck and porch plants. Her automatic sprinkler system took care of her lawns and gardens. Having that chore programmed automatically allowed her to expend her energy on weeding, trimming, and mowing.

When she finished her chores outdoors, she entered the house, wondering as she crossed the living room/dining room combo and entered the kitchen what Blackie would think of her decorating efforts. Her home definitely sported a more feminine touch, but she'd tried not to overdo it. Stepping over to the fridge, which looked pathetically small compared to Blackie's, she grabbed another beer, poured it into a glass, and returned to the living area, where she kicked off her shoes and sprawled on a gray easy chair with her legs draped over one cushiony arm. After savoring only one sip of ale, which didn't taste as good as the special brew Blackie had served her, she plucked her cell phone from her pocket and speed-dialed Erin, who was working the day shift this week and got off at three.

"Erin's Whorehouse," her friend said when she answered. "How can I help you?"

Julie burst out laughing. "Last time I called this number, I got Joe's Bar and Grill."

"Yeah, well, Joe got really boring, so I'm changing it up. How did your day go? Since you didn't bug me while I was on duty, I'm assuming that the ovens didn't break down and the coffee machines behaved themselves."

"I had an uneventful day, and this afternoon was blessedly slow, so I got out of the salt mine right at the stroke of five. Then I finally did it."

"Oh, man. When you say that, I know I better brace myself. What, exactly, did you finally do?"

"I walked over to Blackie's Pawnshop."

"And did what? Please don't tell me you had monkey sex behind a glass display case. Very tacky."

"No." Julie smiled so big her face hurt. "I looked to see if, by some miracle, he still had Grandma's engagement ring."

"Oh, wow! And I'm guessing, because you sound so happy, that he did. Watch out for that guy, Jules. He's angling for something more than a cinnamon roll."

"Maybe so, because he kept it in his back room all this time and never even tried to sell it. I—could—not—believe—it. But he had it, and the very best part is that it didn't bankrupt me to buy it back."

"Uh-huh. What did he charge as a redemption fee?"

"Nothing. I got it back for exactly what I sold it to him for."

"Oh, boy. This is serious stuff, Jules. He's definitely buttering you up for something more than baked goods and fabulous coffee."

Julie waggled her feet and curled her toes. "I don't think so. Not that he isn't interested in more than my baked goods. He pretty much made that clear this afternoon."

She heard a rustling sound come over the air, and then Erin said, "Do tell. It sounds like your evening has been a lot more exciting than mine."

Julie filled her friend in on every nuance of her conversation with Blackie. "It was all I could do to walk out of there, because I lied when I told him I wasn't in the market for a romantic relationship. I think maybe I am."

Erin jerked her cell phone away from her ear to stare at it. Were her ears deceiving her, or had Julie just said she was ready to get serious about a guy again? And with Blackie, of all people. He was so much older. But Erin guessed age wasn't always a deciding factor in relationships. Sometimes, something clicked between two people and nothing else mattered all that much. Theoretically, she got that. It had just never happened for her.

"So . . ." She let that word hang there for a moment. "What is it that you're seeking in a relationship? I mean, I understand that physical satisfaction is pretty much a given after being single as long as you have, but is that all you're interested in, or does it go deeper than that?"

Julie sighed with frustration and blasted Erin's eardrum with a whoosh of air. "I don't know. Seriously, Erin, I'm not sure what I want at this point, which is why I collected my purse and got out of there. There's just something about Blackie that draws me."

"What is it about him that gets to you?" Erin asked. "I mean, he's definitely got it nailed in the looks department, but there's no shortage of handsome men in Mystic Creek, and you're pretty enough and nice enough to take your pick."

Julie sighed again, which made Erin grin. "Well, he's as solid as a rock, for one thing. He not only knows what he wants out of life, but he's already attained it. He's happy with his work and daily routine. And you know the instant you walk into his apartment that he enjoys his leisure hours. I saw heaps of books on his shelving. He's got a television almost big enough for Marcus Mariota to run the ball clear to the goal line on the screen. And I could tell, just by looking around, that he cooks, does laundry, and keeps his place spotlessly clean."

Erin frowned in bewilderment, because to her way of thinking, Julie was basically saying that the attractive things to her about Fred Black were pretty low on her own importance list. "Okay," she said. "Go on."

"Well, honestly?" She heard Julie shifting positions and could almost picture her with her legs dangling over the arm of her favorite chair. "I think one of the most attractive things to me about Blackie is that he isn't looking for anyone to fix his life. It's full just as it is. If I have a relationship with him, I'll be a fringe benefit, not something he actually needs."

It took Erin a moment, but she finally said, "Aha, I'm finally getting it. Derek *needed* you as camouflage, and you suffered greatly for that. Isn't it perfectly normal—and emotionally healthy—for you to feel strongly attracted to a man who needs nothing from you? That's how solid relationships should begin, anyway, I think, with an attraction that isn't fueled by desperation. With Blackie, you needn't worry about a hidden agenda."

"Exactly!" Julie exclaimed with a shrill note of excitement in her voice. "I find his transparency and honesty so incredibly *sexy.*"

Erin smiled in spite of herself. "Well, I see absolutely nothing wrong with that, Jules. So just go for it."

"Maybe I will," Julie shot back. "I just want to be sure. You know?"

"I do. Absolutely."

After the call ended, Erin contemplated her attraction to Wyatt and wished she could see her own situation with such clarity.

Kennedy sat at the long, rectangular table in the bunkhouse. The overhead light in the kitchen had dead houseflies in the glass globe, and their dehydrated corpses cast polka dot shadows on the pages of his textbook. He needed to climb up there and clean it, but between classes, studying, and working on the ranch taking up most of his time, he couldn't work up the energy. Besides, it didn't seem to bother anyone but him. His brother seemed to have a filter in his brain that allowed him to sift through all the things that needed to be done and focus on only the most urgent. Bugs in the light globe didn't rank high on that list.

Bugs didn't rank high on Kennedy's list, either. But that was what he had to study if he wanted to ace his final exam. *Bugs.* He guessed he was missing something, because he couldn't see how it was important for him to know that the common housefly's scientific name was *Musca domestica.* He wanted to be a game biologist, not an entomologist. And besides, who in his right mind would say, "Somebody needs to get those darned *Musca domestica* out of the ceiling lights?" Nobody, not even Wyatt, the self-made scholar, would know what he meant.

Kennedy closed the book with a little more force than necessary. He was tired of reading. He'd been at it for so many hours that his vision was blurring. His stomach was also rumbling with hunger, which wasn't unusual. He had a big appetite, and food didn't stick to his ribs very long. That was especially true tonight, because it had been Tex's turn to cook, and he'd made macaroni and cheese, one of Kennedy's favorites, but he'd ruined the whole pot by dumping in a bunch of canned tuna. *Yuck.* Kennedy liked tuna in a sandwich or creamy casserole, but he didn't want fish mixed into his cheesy comfort food. Even the lingering smells of their meal turned his stomach.

Abandoning his textbook, he pushed up from the chair and advanced on the cupboards, which Wyatt kept well stocked with snacks. Only Kennedy felt the need for something more substantial than cookies or chips, so he decided to make a peanut butter and jelly sandwich. That meant he'd need to make two. Four Toes, Slade's rescued black bear, dearly loved PB&Js, his favorite treat next to a squeeze bottle of ketchup. Kennedy laid paper towels out on the Formica counter, not because they didn't have cutting boards, but because he was lazy and hated washing the darned things. He saw no point in making a sandwich on a stupid board when he could do it this way, save himself work, and use the towels as a napkin as he ate.

After making a second sandwich for Four Toes, with extra jelly because that was the best part as far as the bear was concerned, Kennedy took a huge bite of his own. He expected a satisfying burst of flavor to fill his mouth, only it didn't taste all that great. What he really wanted was a big, juicy cheeseburger and a large order of fries. Normally he wouldn't consider driving clear into Mystic Creek for only that. Going back and forth to college in Crystal Falls already had his gasoline expenses skyrocketing, and he needed to watch his budget. But he also had to take into account that he hadn't treated himself to anything special in a while. Studying and working. Working and studying. Sometimes a guy just needed to say to hell with all of it and take an evening off. Besides, the Mystical Burger Shack had recently been remodeled into one of those old-fashioned drive-ins where people could pull into the parking lot, order over an intercom, and eat in their cars. Kennedy hadn't seen the renovations yet, let alone eaten there. That meant he hadn't gone out for a cheeseburger in months.

He wrapped both sandwiches up in the paper towels and left the bunkhouse, only to almost trip over Wyatt's dog, Domino, who was curled up on the porch. Kennedy stepped fancy to keep from falling or hurting the canine, who complicated the situation by leaping to his feet. When Kennedy reached down to pat the border collie mix, the animal caught a whiff of the peanut butter and emitted a mournful whine.

"Okay, okay," Kennedy said. "Four Toes will never know he missed out on a second sandwich."

Domino wolfed down his PB&J in two bites, then sat and looked up at Kennedy expectantly.

"You can't have both of them, Domino. You'll get fat. Besides, Four Toes wants one, too. His mouth is probably already watering. Bears can smell goodies from as far as a mile away."

As Kennedy descended the steps, Domino fell in beside him. "Okay, you can come," he conceded. "But you don't get to share. You had yours."

When Kennedy and the dog reached the hurricane fence enclosure where the bear was confined at night, Four Toes was nowhere in sight. Kennedy unlatched the gate, and Domino followed him inside. They found the bear curled up and asleep inside his cave, which had cost Slade a small fortune to have built. Even in the darkness, the animal's gold fur was visible. Kennedy waved the sandwich back and forth to awaken his furry friend. Four Toes let out a rumble and rolled to his feet when he smelled the peanut butter. Laughing, Kennedy handed the bear the treat, and Four Toes sat back on his haunches to enjoy it.

"See you in the morning, Four Toes," Kennedy called as he led Domino out of the enclosure and refastened the gate. "I'll bring you some ketchup tomorrow night." On the way to his pickup, Kennedy texted his brother. Craving a cheeseburger. Taking Domino with me to town.

Wyatt always carried his cell phone in his pocket so he'd feel the vibration when he received a message. He texted back: OK, bro. Thnx 4 letting me know.

Kennedy loved his new truck. Well, it was new to him, anyway. He'd bought it secondhand, but it served him well for driving back and forth to school and came in handy on the ranch when he needed to haul something. As he drew up to open the driver door, he gave it a fond pat.

Driving at night always soothed him, especially in spring, when the evening air felt almost balmy after a long, hard winter and he could roll down the windows. Domino shared his enjoyment of the fresh air by hooking his paws over the sill and poking out his head. The wind caught the dog's fluffy ears and flattened them against his skull, which made Kennedy grin.

A few minutes later Kennedy arrived at the Mystical Burger Shack, and the place was lighted up like a Christmas tree. Periwinkle Lane was still mostly undeveloped, so it was as dark as the other country roads around town. The sudden radiance as Kennedy came around the bend was startling. The last time he had driven by, the burger place had been little, basically a square building with the interior partitioned off in three sections for storage, a commercial kitchen, and a dining area. But now, with the long overhang built perpendicular to the main structure, it looked almost as big as a football field. Servers on roller skates rolled in and out of the building by a side door, carrying trays of food that hooked over the partially lowered windows of vehicles. There were so many cars that Kennedy decided half the population of Mystic Creek must have been craving a hamburger, too. He was amazed that there was so much business this late at night.

He found a parking place and raised the passenger window slightly so Domino could still poke his head through the opening for fresh air but wouldn't be encouraged to jump out. Working dogs leaped out of trucks all the time on a ranch, and Domino wouldn't understand the rules were different here in a public place. Kennedy studied the menu. Then he pressed the button to order a cheeseburger and fries for himself and a corn dog for Domino.

While waiting for his food, Kennedy observed other customers through their windshields, breathed deeply of all the delicious smells, and watched the teenage waitresses zoom back and forth on skates. *Wow.* Now that he was twenty-two, he shouldn't think girls under eighteen were sexy, but short, pleated skirts blowing in the wind around slender thighs had a way of snagging a guy's attention whether he intended to look or not. A couple of the teens were totally hot, but the little blonde eclipsed them even though she'd made no attempt to glam up with cosmetics. Her shoulder-length hair was overall golden with darker streaks the same color as the honey he drizzled over his flapjacks. *Yum.* She looked good enough to gobble up and still be hungry for seconds.

He was jazzed when he saw the petite blonde roll to a stop in front of his truck. He admired her skill on roller skates as she stepped off the curb and zoomed around to the driver's-side window. As she hooked the tray over the lowered pane, she parroted, "One cheeseburger with bacon, a large order of fries, a corn dog, and a Coke. Right?"

Kennedy hadn't asked for bacon, but the place was super busy, and he didn't want to quibble over a little mistake. He placed his credit card on the tray to cover his tab. She pulled a cell phone from her tiny apron pocket and ran his card through a fob attached to it. Then she handed her phone to Kennedy and chirped, "Signature, please."

He signed with his fingertip and returned her phone. "Thanks. Tell the owner I like the drive-in."

A dimple flashed in her cheek as she smiled. "Isn't it amazing? My grandparents say it's just like the olden days! Back in the sixties, drive-in hamburger joints were in almost every town."

"It's pretty awesome."

As she skated back toward the building to pick up another food order, Kennedy removed Domino's corn dog from the paper sheath and fed the dog first. He waited for Domino to bite down on the end and then pulled out the stick. "Bon appétit," he told the canine.

Kennedy's mouth watered as he unwrapped his burger, and he was glad they'd made a mistake on the bacon. After forcing down bites of Tex's awful supper, he was hungry enough to eat twice what he'd ordered. He settled back against the seat to eat, but Domino polished off his treat in three gulps and whined for some of Kennedy's.

"You *always* do this," Kennedy grumped. He heard cars starting up all around them and glanced out to see several vehicles backing out. By the time he'd given the dog one of his bacon strips, there were only two cars left under the overhang besides his truck. "Next time, we'll come earlier. Right?"

As Kennedy enjoyed his first bite of the burger, another car left and then the second one followed. He didn't mind sitting out there all alone, though. He got a lot of quiet time while working on the ranch, but he rarely had an opportunity to just sit, eat, and not talk to anybody. Meals in the bunkhouse were almost always noisy, with the guys chatting non-stop, the only exception being Wyatt, who'd given up on reading lips when people's mouths were full. On days when Kennedy had classes and ate at the cafeteria, the college union was jam-packed with students, who also talked nonstop. It was kind of nice to eat in silence, with the pine-scented night air drifting through the truck cab. Studying for final exams had drained him, and he was glad that he'd taken a break.

Just then, a '56 Chevy Bel Air Sport Coupe pulled in under the overhang and almost took out the intercom post. Kennedy startled so badly that his behind parted company with the bucket seat. *Holy hell.* That car was fully restored, with cherry-red and gleaming white paint, tail fins almost sharp enough to cut bread, and chrome polished to such a shine it glinted. *And that kid almost creamed the front fender.* He also recognized the raucous rumble of a glasspack muffler. *Sweet.* Kennedy would have given his right arm to own that vehicle. What father in his right mind allowed an addlebrained teenager to go joyriding in a classic? Kennedy guessed he shouldn't pass judgment. Some people had money to burn and others didn't. He also needed to remember that it hadn't been that long ago when he'd been a rowdy teen with more testosterone than brains, not to mention too many beers under his belt.

There were four boys in the car, all of them laughing and acting silly. Kennedy remembered those days, too. He smiled as he took another bite of his burger and stuffed in a couple of fries. The teenage driver pressed the intercom button and tried to place the orders, which involved a lot of arguing and revising before he finally got it right for his friends. Then all four kids settled down to wait.

Kennedy had finished half of his burger when the little blonde emerged from the building with a heavily laden tray balanced on her hands. She was all-over adorable in a red-plaid skirt barely long enough to cover her butt cheeks and a white knit top that showcased her small breasts. Again, he admired her skill on skates. He'd probably end up flat on his ass with hamburgers all over him, but she managed on those roller skates as if she'd been born wearing them. She hesitated when she saw the Chevy, but then she stepped off the curb and wheeled over to the driver's side. Just as she got close, the door flew open, knocking her almost off balance and sending the tray flying. Kennedy nearly dropped his sandwich.

What the hell? He forgot to swallow and just sat there with a glob of food in his mouth. The driver, a dark-haired kid with a jock's muscular build, leaped out and grabbed the blonde by both arms. One of the boys in the back pushed the driver's seat forward and leaned halfway out of the car. The jock jerked the girl toward his waiting friend. Watching on, Kennedy realized that they were going to force her inside the vehicle. *Crazy.* What were they thinking? If they succeeded in nabbing her, they'd be in more trouble than they could imagine.

The boys were about the girl's age, but the jock had a definite physical advantage over her. Kennedy tried to look away rather than interfere. Trouble between local-yokel kids was none of his business. But the driver was determined to get the waitress into the car, and she couldn't resist while wearing roller skates. When he pulled on her arms, her body followed, even though she tried to put on the brakes by twisting her feet sideways. It was all she could do to remain upright.

All four boys were now out of the car. They started pushing the girl back and forth between them, grabbing her in inappropriate places when they caught her and then shoving her over to the next guy so he could cop a feel. The girl began screaming, and the jock popped her on the mouth. A chill washed over Kennedy. He glanced toward the building, hoping to see someone race outside. Surely the owner had outdoor camera surveillance so the young waitresses weren't entirely on their own out here. But nobody emerged from the burger shack to intervene.

"Shit." Kennedy pushed open his door, which sent his Coke flying. He couldn't just sit in his truck while a girl was overpowered by four young men. As his boots connected with the asphalt, Kennedy shouted, "Hey, guys! Let's keep it friendly. Okay? Let the girl go!"

The jock spun around to glare at Kennedy. "You and whose army is gonna make us, jackass? You need to mind your own fucking business!"

One look at the terrified girl told Kennedy that he couldn't turn his back on this. The last thing he wanted was to get in a fracas with minors. Now that he was twenty-two, he could go to jail for that. For all he knew, striking a kid could be a felony, and if the charges stuck, he might never be able to work for the state. *Doesn't matter.* Nobody else was rushing from the building to help the girl, so it fell to him to do something.

He walked toward the Chevy. "I don't want any trouble, guys."

"Then back off," the jock demanded.

The smell of alcohol and weed wafted to Kennedy's nostrils. *Just great.* These boys were hammered and probably had the collective genius of a fruit fly. Kennedy really, *really* didn't want this to escalate into a fistfight. He pulled out his cell and dialed 911. When the dispatcher answered, he said loudly enough for the boys to hear, "Four male youths are accosting a teenage girl at the hamburger joint, and—"

The jock leaped onto the center walkway where the waitresses skated back and forth and slapped the cell phone from Kennedy's hand. Hoping the dispatcher could still hear him, Kennedy shouted out the license plate number on the car. Within seconds, all four boys were on Kennedy. He wasn't too worried. There was only one hamburger joint in town, so the authorities knew where to go even without a business name or address, and Kennedy could hold his own until they arrived.

"I don't want any trouble!" Kennedy yelled at the towheaded teen and backed up a couple of steps. "But be warned. If you start it, I'll finish it!" From the corner of his eye, he saw the girl slumped against the side of the car. "Run! Get inside the building!" he told her.

Kennedy hoped the girl could manage to get inside. She probably knew the boys' names to identify them when the cops arrived. If she could escape into the building, Kennedy wouldn't have to fight. He could just jump back in his truck and lock the doors. But he saw the girl try to push off on her skates and fall to the ground. As she struggled to get back up, the skates kept rolling out from under her.

Sometimes a guy had no choice but to fight.

Kennedy's instinct to survive kicked in. He glimpsed the flash of a knife blade and started swinging. He was no scrapper. He had always preferred to talk his way out of a confrontation. But his father had taught him how to throw a punch, and Wyatt had taken over from there. Kennedy had spent many hours wrestling and play-fighting with his older brother. All that training came to his aid now.

Kennedy took a few punches from the boys, but he returned them with more force. By the time a county sheriff's vehicle sped into the parking lot, the fight was almost over. The kid with the whitish-blond hair knelt on the concrete, holding his middle and puking. The jock was staggering around and holding his face, with blood dripping through his fingers. The other two boys saw the cop and ran.

More county vehicles pulled up. An older man, probably the new owner of the burger joint, emerged from the building. Two deputies took off into the woods after the runaways. The other boys were too banged up to attempt an escape and started saying that Kennedy had taken the first punch.

"That isn't true!" the young lady cried. With the help of a female deputy, she had gained her feet but leaned heavily against the law officer to keep her balance. "They jumped me! They put their hands on me!" Her voice began to shake, and she made a mewling sound. "They said they were going to take me into the woods and rape me!"

"That's a lie!" the jock yelled. "She's just pissed off because I broke up with her last week, and she's trying to get me in trouble."

The two deputies who had raced into the woods reemerged, each of them holding the arm of a runaway teen.

"I broke up with *you*, Rob!" the girl cried. "And you just tried to get even because it embarrassed you!" The girl turned to the deputy. "It's true. You have to believe me!" She pointed a shaky finger at Kennedy. "Ask him! He saw it all and stopped them from forcing me into the car!"

After saying that, the girl dissolved into tears and would have collapsed if not for the support of the deputy's arms around her. Kennedy was glad the girl wasn't badly hurt, but she was definitely shaken up. He was relieved when the female officer guided her to a county vehicle and got her safely tucked inside. The cops would call her parents now, and they'd probably take her to the emergency clinic after filing a police report.

Kennedy stayed to give his statement to Deputy Barney Sterling. Kennedy really liked Barney. He was a hometown boy and came from a well-respected family. He wasn't on his high horse about being a cop, either. Even so, the whole time Kennedy was being questioned, he kept expecting to be cuffed and stuffed for beating up four minors. Instead Deputy Sterling asked if he needed to see a doctor. Kennedy didn't hurt that much anywhere and refused medical attention, even though Sterling told him he was bleeding from a scalp wound. Kennedy's student insurance had a pricey deductible, and he really couldn't afford an emergency room charge right now, when none of his cuts and scrapes felt life-threatening.

When he walked back to his truck, he saw that Domino had eaten the rest of his hamburger and fries. Normally he might have scolded the dog. It wasn't okay for Domino to take human food unless it was offered to him. But the black-and-white collie hadn't jumped out the open driver's window, and Kennedy knew that had taken a lot of restraint. Things had gotten pretty exciting for a couple of minutes, and Domino was still young enough to want in on all the action. Kennedy was glad the dog had stayed put. To him, all of it would have seemed like a game, and he could have gotten hurt. Kennedy doubted that Domino had ever witnessed a serious fistfight, only scuffling when a bunch of ranch hands were playing around.

"Good boy, Domino. You stayed in the truck. Awesome job." Kennedy ruffled the dog's fur and then removed the tray from the slightly upraised window to set it on the concrete median. He figured someone who worked there could collect it. He sure wasn't going to carry it to the building. The jock had dealt Kennedy a kidney punch, and his flank ached. His head didn't feel all that great, either. He climbed back in the truck, started the engine, and backed out of the parking slot. "Mystic Creek, the town with no crime. Ha! Shit goes down almost everywhere," he told Domino. As he got the truck lined out on the road, he fondled the dog's ears. "You were a really good boy, Dom. I'm proud of you."

The drive home wasn't nearly as pleasurable for Kennedy as the trip into town had been. He was developing a bitch of a headache from a blow to the side of his head, and, damn it, his hands throbbed from ramming his fists against so many blockheads. *Stupid kids.* But, no, what they'd done went way beyond stupid. They'd meant to do that girl great harm, and Kennedy could only be thankful that he'd gone out late for a burger. Otherwise she might have been alone, and God only knew where she'd be right now. Maybe lying dead in the woods somewhere.

Minutes later when Kennedy entered the bunkhouse, Wyatt glanced up from where he sat at the table playing cards with Tex and then leaped to his feet, almost knocking over his chair. "Dear God, what happened?"

Tex looked over his shoulder. "What'd you do, son, tangle with a mountain lion?"

Kennedy hadn't bothered to look in a mirror before driving home. "I'm fine," he tried.

Wyatt grabbed his arm and guided him to a chair at the table. "No, you're *not* fine. You're bleeding like a stuck hog. Who did this to you?"

While Wyatt parted Kennedy's hair to examine the wound, Tex phoned the boss, and the next thing Kennedy knew, Slade and Vickie burst into the bunkhouse kitchen. Vickie carried a first aid kit, which she immediately set on the table and opened. But then she saw Kennedy's head.

"Uh-oh. We'll have to take him in. That's going to need stitches."

"How did this happen?" Wyatt demanded.

Kennedy answered, but Vickie had her hand clamped over his head and he couldn't lift his face so his brother could read his lips. He heard Tex repeat what he'd said so Wyatt would get the whole story.

"A knife? Dear God, Kennedy, what were you thinking?"

Kennedy told them about the girl and how she'd been overpowered by the boys. Whenever he stopped to take a breath, Tex said it all over again for Wyatt like they were playing a repeat-after-me game. When Kennedy refused to go to the emergency clinic, Vickie said, "This cut has to be stitched up, honey. It'll never heal like it is."

Kennedy had grown up watching old westerns on television. "Can't you just do it?"

Able to see Kennedy's lips now that his head was no longer bent, Wyatt said, "That will hurt like nothing you've ever felt. Why go through that when it'll barely sting if a doctor does it?"

Kennedy just wanted to get it over with and crawl into bed. As the minutes passed, more places on his body throbbed. "I'm a big boy," he reminded his brother. "And I can't afford the deductible on my insurance for something this little. It'll only be a few needle pricks. I can take it."

"I'll pay the deductible," Wyatt countered. Slade chimed in with, "So will I. This is flat crazy."

Tex interrupted. "I've done my fair share of stitchin' on horses. I reckon I can fix him up."

So it was decided that Tex would do the sewing. He disinfected the wound first, and Kennedy hissed through his teeth, which earned him a comment from Slade. "If the sting of alcohol has you sucking for air, son, it's not a positive indicator of how you'll hold up when he goes after you with one of those fishhooks."

Tex thrust one of the curved needles in front of Kennedy's nose. "There it is. You sure you want me usin' that on your head?"

By this point, Kennedy's pride was kicking in. He wasn't a baby, and he'd drawn a crowd. The newly hired cowhands had rolled out of their cots and stumbled into the kitchen. He'd bet money that any one of the men standing over him could get stitched up without whining. "I'm sure."

Tex said, "Well, okay, then. I wish I had me some of that Novocain stuff to numb you up, but we used all of it last week, and Wyatt ain't gone back into town for supplies yet."

As Tex went to work, Kennedy steeled himself for the first poke. But even so, he wasn't ready for the pain when it came. "Hold it! Hold it!" he yelled. Then he looked at Wyatt. "Can you give me something to bite down on? And some whiskey. I want some whiskey."

Vickie sighed. "You've watched too many cowboy movies."

Tex stood aside while Kennedy guzzled down some booze and said, "I don't reckon that's a smart idea, son. Alcohol thins the blood, and you're already bleedin' like a pig on slaughter day."

"I'll be fine." Kennedy looked around for Wyatt and saw him walking from the sleeping area with a sock in his hand. "What's that for?"

"For you to bite down on."

Kennedy swallowed more whiskey, and asked, "Is it clean?"

The following day Wyatt worked straight through until the sun reached its zenith, doing both his work and his little brother's. He'd spent the morning transferring round bales to various places on the ranch for easy feeding. The month of May definitely had a foothold in the Cascades, but even though the pastures were now brilliant green, the grass itself still needed more sunlight before it became nutritious enough to sustain the cattle. After making sure the critters were fed, Wyatt decided to get some grub himself and went to the bunkhouse. After slapping together three sandwiches, he sat at the table to wolf them down. While Wyatt ate, Kennedy rolled out of bed with a groan. Wyatt stopped chewing to watch him stand up. The kid walked hunched over slightly.

"You switch bodies with Tex during the night?"

Kennedy slanted him a dirty look. "Make fun. I may be walking like an old man, but I was up against four guys last night, and trust me, they looked worse than I do."

Wyatt nodded. "I'm sure they did, and with all the surgery taking place in here last night, I forgot to say how proud I am of you. I don't approve of fisticuffs, and neither do Mom and Dad, but sometimes a man has no choice."

"I was afraid I'd get arrested for beating up minors."

"Could have happened. But the possible consequences to you became a moot point. You saved that girl from a terrible fate, Kennedy, and at no small risk to yourself. You've become a man I'm proud to say is my brother. A little stupid, maybe. Getting your head stitched up by a retired jockey wasn't the smartest choice you could have made."

"I lived through it."

"My sock will never be the same."

Kennedy showed Wyatt his back as he bellied up to the counter to make sandwiches for himself. When he sat at the table with all three creations stacked on a paper towel, Wyatt asked, "Why the hell don't you ever use a plate?"

Kennedy swallowed before replying. "Because I don't want to wash it."

"It takes two seconds to rinse a plate and stick it in the dishwasher."

"That's two seconds wasted that I could spend doing something else, like studying."

Wyatt polished off his food, stuck his plate in the dishwasher, and headed for the door, where he stopped to don his Stetson. "Lie down for a while longer and sleep. Your body needs time to heal."

"I may study lying down." Kennedy lifted his brows. "And just so you know, Erin's here. I looked out the window as I got up and saw her deputy truck parked by the main house."

Wyatt froze with his hat not yet positioned on his head. "Great. We're working on being friends, but it was never my aim to be bosom buddies."

"Maybe she's not here to see you."

Wyatt stepped out the door, thinking, *Fat chance of that.* But as he crossed the dooryard, which sported more dirt than sprigs of grass because of constant foot traffic, he saw no sign of Erin. He guessed that her Honda still wasn't fixed, and he was reminded that he needed to call the Timing Light to pay for the repairs with his credit card.

Hours sped by, and it was three o'clock before Wyatt had time to notice that he still hadn't seen Erin. The county truck was still parked out front. He doubted she was still at the main house visiting with Vickie. So where the hell was she? If they were friends now, shouldn't she at least find him and say hello? Curiosity got the better of him and he finally went looking for her, feeling more than a little miffed. Some friend she was. Was *she* avoiding *him* now? Had he said or done something the other night to piss her off?

Without willing his feet to move, Wyatt found himself walking first one direction and then another. Why, he didn't know. Okay, he did know, but admitting to himself that he was searching for Erin De Laney stuck in his craw. She meant trouble for him with a capital *T*. But he kept walking anyway, and then he saw her out in one of the cow pastures with Slade. It looked as if they were mending a section of fence. He tipped his Stetson brim lower over his eyes so the slanting sun couldn't blind him while he enjoyed the view.

Watching Erin work was a pleasure. She had stripped off her shirt to reveal a tank top she had apparently worn underneath it, offering him a great view of her torso, which was sculpted with muscle from working out. She wasn't pumped up like a female bodybuilder, but she was definitely strong for a woman. He knew she hadn't developed that musculature behind the steering wheel of a county vehicle. Results like that took dedication and a lot of sweat.

An image circled through his mind of all that moist skin and sleek muscle pressed against his nude body. He shoved it from his mind. *Friends.* No flirting with each other. No hooking up. That was their agreement, and he wouldn't be the one to mess it up.

CHAPTER SEVEN

It was Erin's turn to man the posthole digger, a two-handled implement with shovel blades that worked like a pair of scissors. She opened the blades, plunged them into the earth, and closed them to pick up dirt to dump on the pile beside the new hole. It was a demanding job, but she was enjoying her afternoon with Uncle Slade. She'd traded shifts with Serena Paul today to give the other woman Sunday off to attend a family wedding, and even though Erin had a dozen other things she should be doing at home, she was glad that she'd chosen to come out to the ranch instead. She and Slade talked while they worked, and she was having a great time with him. He seemed so happy now that Vickie was back in his life, and that made her nearly as happy as he was.

"Howdy!" someone called out.

Erin glanced over her shoulder to see Wyatt walking across the pasture toward them. Embarrassed to be seen in only a skimpy tank top and jeans, she dropped the posthole digger to grab her shirt and put it on before she turned to wave at him. Except for being caught with her arms and shoulders showing, she was glad to see him. It proved that he would no longer avoid her when she came out to the ranch, and that was a good change. Even though the shirt stuck to her sweaty skin, she was relieved that she'd put it back on, because Wyatt's laser-blue gaze traveled slowly over her body as he closed the remaining distance.

"I didn't know this section was in need of repair," Wyatt said as he drew to a stop. "I could have taken care of it."

"Yeah, well, you stay pretty busy," Slade replied. "And I need to keep my stirring spoon in the pot. Otherwise I'll get out of shape and have a beer belly."

Erin decided to take a breather while the men discussed other sections of fence that needed repair. Working hard with a shirt on would be unpleasant. She would wait until Wyatt left and then strip it off again. She listened with only half an ear to what each man said about the west pasture. It was more fun just to watch them talk. They stood with their booted feet braced wide apart and gestured with their hands. When she'd lived in Seattle, she couldn't have imagined a scene like this, two cowboys wearing Stetsons, Wrangler jeans, and riding boots, cast against a spectacular backdrop of rolling green pastureland edged by dense forests with snowcapped peaks reaching toward the sky. She felt as if she'd stepped onto a film set for a western movie.

Wyatt was of particular interest to her. He was such a good-looking man, his body lean and hard from daily labor. Just studying him made her insides tingle, a feeling she must learn to ignore if she meant to keep her word and not flirt with him again.

Instead of admiring him, she tried to focus on how clean the air smelled and how nice the breeze felt when it touched her hot cheeks. She'd had fun today and wished she could do this more often. Out here under an open sky, she felt liberated. She could be herself, not worry overmuch about her appearance—unless Wyatt came along, of course—and could let her mind drift. That felt amazing to her. While on duty, she constantly had to be on her toes, watch what she said, and make sure her uniform looked perfect.

Brody rode up on a red quad and braked to a stop. Not for the first time, Erin marveled at the similarities between him and his father. Like Wyatt, they were both tall, lean, and well-muscled, but their hair was a dark sable brown, their eyes were gray, and their skin was a shade darker than the blond foreman's. Nobody would ever mistake Wyatt for a

Wilder, but anyone could instantly tell Brody was. He and Slade looked alike, talked alike, and even seemed to think alike.

"Marcus will be back home in about three weeks," Brody told his dad. "He and I can fix the fence in the west pasture. I checked on it the other day, and I'm pretty sure it'll hold firm until then. It'll be great to work with my boys again. As soon as school lets out, Blake and Hank can team up with us to get the work done, too. It'll be good for them."

Brody met Erin's gaze and grinned. "You look whupped, cousin. 'Bout time for you to knock off and carb up on Mama's caramel streusel bars. They're so good, your eyes will roll back in your head."

Erin wasn't quite ready to quit for the day, but she could tell Brody wanted to spend some time with his dad. On such a large ranch, they probably didn't get a lot of one-on-one moments together. She hugged her uncle goodbye. Then Brody caught her up in his arms for a hard squeeze, which caught her by surprise and made her laugh.

"We're family. Remember?" her older cousin told her. "You gotta stop being so standoffish."

Erin grinned up at him. "I wasn't being standoffish. It's just that I'm all sweaty."

As Brody released her, he pulled the brim of her cap down until it almost covered her eyes. "I'll be sweatier than you are in a couple, so a little extra salt on my shirt now won't matter a bit."

As Erin walked away, she hoped Wyatt might join her, but he remained with the men. *Friends, only friends.* He'd stressed that to her the other night, and she needed to remember it. No matter how attractive she found him to be, there could never be anything intimate between them.

Julie had a bad case of late-afternoon drowsiness, which was compounded by a lack of business in her shop. In the early days of being a shop owner, she'd always panicked when the flow of customers trickled down to almost nothing, but nowadays she knew from experience that it was only a lull. Flagg's Market was probably running a produce special or something. She decided to use the downtime to catch up on dusting and restocking shelves, polishing the oven fronts, and cleaning her beverage equipment.

She had just defeated a syrup spill when the bell above her entrance door jangled. She turned from her task, wearing her customer smile, which faded abruptly when she saw Erin entering the shop. Only this wasn't the Erin she had come to expect. Today the perfectly pressed deputy uniform had been replaced by faded jeans; a purple, wash-worn tank top; and a big blue shirt that was smeared with dirt. On her head, her friend wore a ball cap with her wealth of dark hair ponytailed out the back. Julie wasn't shocked, exactly. Whenever Erin was out of uniform, she was a loose cannon when it came to her clothing ensembles. True to form, her tank top clashed with the red hat.

"Well, my goodness, look what the cat dragged in," Julie called. "I thought you were on duty today. I guess not."

Erin sauntered over to the ordering counter, which was a red flag to Julie. Her friend had been in counseling for nearly a year to get rid of her masculine mannerisms, and Julie had become her chief advisor. Sauntering was not allowed. Neither was hip jutting, a posture Erin assumed the moment she drew to a stop in front of the cash register.

"Is business slow?" Erin asked. "I need an ear."

"Slow? The place has gone completely dead. I think Flagg's is running another produce special."

"Nope. There's an art festival at the town center. Kids from the high school are selling their paintings and crafts to raise money for the football team next year. All the proceeds will go to buy new uniforms and safety gear."

Julie's shoulders relaxed. "Ah. So I'm losing my ass today for a good cause." She went to make two coffees. "I'll take a break with you, then. You can choose our table." She angled her friend a searching look. "You dieting today? I have a new flavor I'm dying to try, caramel mocha with cinnamon, but I haven't purchased any sugar-free syrup yet. I gotta try the real deal before I invest in another case of the stuff."

"Hit me," Erin replied. "I burned off enough calories today to propel a Learjet from here to New York."

Julie quickly created their drinks, topping them off with whipped cream. She found Erin sprawled on a chair at what Julie called the lube table, featuring a spouted oil can that held a spray of daffodils and fern. She set down her friend's coffee and took a seat across from her, thinking that Erin's choice of table might be psychologically significant and could mean that she was slipping back down the slippery slope of behavioral change into her father's clutches. *Again.*

"What's up?" She studied Erin's expression. "First, you look worn out. But you also look happier and more relaxed than I've seen you in a while."

"I am happy and relaxed." Erin took a sip of her coffee and came away with a white mustache, which she squeegeed away with a sideways sweep of her tongue. "Yum. Just what the doctor ordered." She sighed, slumped on the chair, and spread her denim-clad legs in an unladylike manner. "I switched shifts with Serena to give her Sunday off. Kind of unexpected, so I had free time and went out to see Uncle Slade right after I grabbed lunch. He was fixing a section of fence, and I got to help."

Julie sensed something afoot. "And?"

Erin's blue eyes sparkled. "I had the *best* time. Working out in the field with him was *incredible*, Julie. I honestly think I could skip college and just do that for a living."

"You want to become a fence fixer?"

"No, ranching. I think I might love being a rancher."

A career in fence repair had sounded bad, but in Julie's estimation, ranching was even worse. "How long has it been since you had a counseling session with Jonas? He'd be a better sounding board."

Erin wrinkled her nose. "Are you hearing me? I see Jonas because I'm unhappy! Today I'm not unhappy. I'm actually excited for the first time in more years than I want to count. I *loved* being out there, Jules! It's like a different world, maybe *my* world. The elusive something I've been searching for practically all my life and could never find because I looked in all the wrong places."

Julie's heart squeezed. She'd known Erin for a year now, and she'd never seen her face glow with such enthusiasm. "You honestly think you've missed your calling to be a rancher?"

Erin leaned forward over her mug. "There are no *rules* out there. I don't need to worry about how I walk or how I talk or how I'm dressed. It's like—hell, I don't know—like I've been lost all my life, searching for home, and it was right under my nose the whole time. I feel as if I belong there."

Julie didn't wish to burst Erin's bubble, but she was in business for herself and had some experience. "I'm not dissing the idea, Erin. Please don't think that. But it isn't that simple. You can't just decide you want to be a rancher and *become* one. You need a piece of land. And buildings—the horse and cow kinds. And fences. Do you know how much that would cost?"

"My mom turned her back on her heritage," Erin retorted. "And by doing that, she denied me mine. I'm a *Wilder.* I have as much right to a share of that ranch as my cousin Brody does! And that was how it felt today, like I'd gone home. It was so fricking liberating to be out there, pitting my strength against the earth. You just don't get it."

Julie took a bracing sip of her coffee and plucked a napkin from the holder to blot her upper lip. "I *do* get it. I'm just saying that you must have a ranch in order to be a rancher, and as it stands, you don't. Are you honestly thinking about talking your mom into reinstating herself as half owner of the Wilder Ranch? Are you prepared to mess up your uncle's life after he's worked that place all alone for half a century? And what about Brody? He's got three boys who stand to inherit the place from him. What happens if you take half of the pie away from him?"

Erin slumped lower on the chair, but her posture was no longer relaxed. "You're right. I can't do that to Uncle Slade or Brody, and I sure don't have the money to buy my own place."

Julie felt awful for playing devil's advocate. "There's a bright spot. You'll always be welcome out there. No matter what you decide to do professionally, you can go *home* whenever you want."

Erin closed her eyes. Then she shoved up the bill of her cap and sat up straight. "I don't really *need* to own a place. People still go into ranching. Look at Wyatt, Tex, and Kennedy. They have no financial interest in the Wilder Ranch, but they still work there for fairly good wages, plus room and board."

"I suppose you could join them. I'm sure your uncle would give you a job. But do you really want to go into a new profession riding on his sense of familial obligation?"

Erin slumped again. "No, of course not. I'm such a rookie that he'd have to teach me everything from the ground up, and I'm sure there's a lot to learn. But there are other ranches that need hired hands. Maybe right around Mystic Creek. I could apply for jobs on my own merit and possibly land a position."

"Yes, you could do that," Julie conceded. "But I think you'd be wise to consider all the angles first. Maybe spend more time actually working on a ranch. Visit your uncle a lot. Get out there and grub around. This could be a life-altering decision, and you should be certain it's really right for you."

"I truly think it may be what I was meant to do," Erin said softly.

Studying her friend's dirt-smudged face, Julie felt concerned. She thought about just keeping her mouth shut, but she and Erin had bypassed the need to be cautious in their relationship. "It seems to me that your discontentment with your job must be weighing heavily on your mind for you to come up with this idea. Hiring on as a ranch hand? It came out of the blue."

Erin smiled and shook her head. "Come on, Julie. Not looking at my options and following my heart is what landed me in this mess. I understand your concern, though. I haven't been out at the ranch enough yet to say for sure, but I think I might really enjoy the lifestyle. It would upset my parents, of course, but when I leave law enforcement, they'll be furious no matter what."

Julie sipped her coffee. "If you spend time there and still feel you'd be happy doing ranch work, more power to you. Taking that direction in life would cost you a lot less than returning to school. Just be sure it's really what you want and that you're not going off the deep end simply because you're unhappy as a deputy."

Using a coffee stick, Erin stirred the whipped cream into her drink. "I'll think it over before I make a decision." She sighed and grinned. "Thanks for listening and keeping an open mind. I know it must sound a little crazy. So enough about me and my job debacle. What's happening with you?"

Julie heard Erin's stomach growl and got up to get them each a cinnamon roll. "Not much besides work," she replied from behind the display case.

"Where are you with Blackie? The last time we talked, you sounded as if you were ready for a relationship and he looked pretty appealing."

Carrying a tray laden with baked goods and two plates, Julie walked back to the table. "I'm still waffling." She set the food to one side of the floral arrangement and then chuckled at the look of distaste on Erin's face. "Come on. Forget dieting and live a little. You did say that you burned off a lot of calories working out there. Toil like a rancher, eat like a rancher. One or two goodies won't put weight on you."

Erin took a plate, plucked two napkins from the dispenser, and selected a roll. "You're right. And I'm famished. I may go wild and have three." She met and held Julie's gaze with a glint of curiosity in her blue eyes. "And you just changed the subject. What about Blackie?"

Julie filled a plate for herself. "Honestly? I like the man. A *lot*. And I'm definitely attracted to him. For me, that's saying something, because I haven't felt as much as a twinge of desire for another man since the divorce."

Still chewing a bite of cinnamon roll, Erin dabbed the napkin at the corners of her lips and swallowed. "If you're attracted to him, why not explore the possibilities?"

Julie chased a mouthful of glazed donut with a swallow of coffee. "Actually, I'm having him over for dinner tomorrow night. Not a date kind of thing. It's my way of thanking him for holding on to Grandma's ring." Julie raised her eyebrows and shrugged again. "Maybe I'll explore the possibilities then."

The remainder of Kennedy's week was tough. While recovering from the fight, he managed to keep up with his studies, but he wasn't his usual, energetic self. By Saturday, he felt a little better, and with the sense of normalcy, he began to worry about the little blonde at the burger joint. She'd been pretty shaken up on Wednesday night, and he wondered how she was doing. Since he had no classes on the weekend, he decided to return to the hamburger place after he finished his ranch chores and had studied for a while.

He was pleased to see the blonde waiting on customers in the drive-in section of the eatery, and he parked next to an intercom, hoping she might deliver his order. After a short wait, he saw her exit the building and held his breath as she skated along the median. She slowed in front of his truck. A rosy blush touched her cheeks as she approached his lowered driver's window, which made his stomach clench. He hoped she wasn't embarrassed about seeing him again.

"Hey," he said by way of greeting. "I didn't expect to see you back at work this soon. How are you doing? I hope you didn't get hurt the other night."

She propped the food tray on his window. "I'm okay. A few bruises, nothing more. It was scary coming back, but my dad says the only way for me to move beyond it is to climb back in the saddle."

Kennedy had heard that old cowboy adage all his life. "It has to be hard, though."

The color in her cheeks deepened. Kennedy spent a moment admiring her eyes, which were blue and defined by lashes a shade darker than her golden hair. He appreciated that she wore little, if any, makeup. She was pretty without it. "Yes. It has been hard. But facing stuff instead of running from it is always the wiser choice." She toyed with the collar of her white, short-sleeve blouse and cast a nervous glance over her shoulder as a car pulled in across from him. "I'm glad you stopped by, because I wanted to thank you for helping me. I don't even know your name, so I couldn't try to contact you."

"Kennedy Fitzgerald. But no thanks are necessary. It was no big deal."

She glanced at his head. Kennedy had tried to hide the shaved place with a comb-over, which Wyatt said made him look like Donald Trump.

"You were hurt. I'm so sorry."

"It's nothing much."

She fiddled with her collar again. "I'd like to talk some more, but I'm on the clock. Would you mind giving me your number? That way I can call and thank you properly. Maybe treat you to a movie or something."

Kennedy was charmed by her innocent overture of friendliness, but he was also alarmed by his reaction to her. She was way too young for him. "That would be fun."

As if she guessed his thoughts, she said, "I'm a senior, about to graduate, and almost eighteen."

Almost wasn't good enough for Kennedy. Even when she turned eighteen, he'd still be four, almost five, years older. And he'd learned the hard way that brushing elbows with trouble could rub off on a guy in unpleasant ways. Nevertheless, he gave her his number, pausing between digits as she entered each one into her phone.

"Thanks," she said as she skated back to the median. "My name's Jenette Johnson. I'll be in touch!"

Kennedy's appetite for the hamburger and fries was ruined. He couldn't get involved with her. *No way.* Then he realized she'd forgotten to make him pay for the food. "Hey, wait! What do I owe you?"

She waved him off. "It's my treat."

Before he could protest, she was zooming back to the building, her blond hair flowing in the wind behind her. He sat for a moment and then reached for the foil-wrapped sandwich and envelope of fries, which he set on the center console. After putting his capped soda in the cupholder, he rang the intercom buzzer for tray removal. He was relieved when Jenette's coworker, a brunette who wore a lot of makeup, came to collect it.

As Kennedy drove back to the ranch, he promised himself that he wouldn't see Jenette again. She was still just a kid. In a few more years, she'd probably be a complete knockout, but by then he would have his degree and be long gone. He hoped he would be lucky enough to get an assignment near his hometown of Klamath Falls, and that was a three-hour drive south, too far away for him to visit Mystic Creek often. *Who am I kidding?* he asked himself. *Jenette is already a knockout, and that's the whole problem. I need to stay away from her.*

Once back on the ranch, he'd just pulled into the parking area near the main house when his phone jangled a text notification. He didn't recognize the number, which meant it wasn't one of his contacts. Curious, he opened the message.

Hi. This is Jenette. I just wanted to tell you that the mouthiest guy, the one with the knife, is my ex-boyfriend. I broke up with him because he wanted to have sex and tried to force me one night. I think he's got a screw loose, and I want nothing more to do with him. I have plans for college. My older sister got pregnant in her senior year. She got married, had the baby, and got divorced. There went her plans for college. I can't let that happen to me. I want to be a vet and work in a wildlife shelter to rehabilitate rescued animals.

Kennedy groaned. In addition to being beautiful, Jenette had a lot in common with him. He was taking a different approach, but his goal was to work on behalf of the wildlife, too. *Damn.* She was perfect for him. And that made him angry for reasons he couldn't quite define. He left his hamburger on the console, not caring if it spoiled, and walked to the horse barn to muck out the stalls he hadn't gotten to earlier.

He'd been hard at work for about twenty minutes when Slade walked into the barn and caught him grumbling to himself.

"What put a bee in your bonnet?" Slade asked.

Kennedy wanted to tell the man it was none of his business, but that was no way to speak to his boss. "Nothing serious," he replied. "I just have the hots for that girl who got attacked the other night."

Slade came to lean against the stall gate. "Hmm. Why is that a problem?"

Irritation crept into Kennedy's voice. "She's seventeen."

"Uh-oh. Jailbait. Steer clear of that, son. It could spell trouble."

Kennedy forked another mound of straw and manure into the skidder bucket. "I know *that*. Do I have *stupid* engraved on my forehead?"

Slade crossed his arms. "Oh, boy. She's got your tail tied in a knot, judging by the temper you're in."

That comment aggravated Kennedy even more. "It isn't only about sex. Why is it that everybody always boils everything down to that?"

"Sex makes the world go 'round," Slade replied. "Not to mention that procreation keeps the globe populated."

"True. But it isn't only about that. She's pretty, yes, and I'd have to be dead not to notice. But I don't have scrambled eggs for brains. It's just that she's pretty *and* smart. She's planning to become a vet and work to rehabilitate wild animals so they can be returned to their natural habitat."

Slade said nothing, and Kennedy sent him a questioning look. "What?"

The older man crossed his ankles. "Just thinking. It sounds like the two of you have a lot in common."

"Exactly!" Kennedy jabbed the pitchfork tines into the earth and cupped his palms over the handle end. "She's got her sights set on college. She doesn't want to make any dumb mistakes that might ruin her plans. I don't know if she's saving her wages for college, but I think she is. She's perfect for me. You know? Only I'd have to be nuts to even take her out on a date, let alone get involved with her."

Slade scratched behind his ear. "Son, the age difference may seem gigantic to you right now, but in the end, relationships between men and women aren't based on birthdates. It sounds like you've found a young lady who's a good fit for you. As long as you keep your fly zipped, there's nothing wrong with you dating a girl that's younger. You have some lofty plans of your own, and you don't want anything to screw them up, either. It sounds as if you two could be good for each other."

Slade left the barn then to let Kennedy mull that over. As Kennedy finished the stall, he considered the possibility of dating Jenette. *Problem.* He hadn't dated much since coming to Mystic Creek, and he wasn't confident in his ability to keep his jeans zipped with a girl he found so attractive. He should probably just stay away from her. Only he kept remembering what she'd said in the text about her sister and how she didn't want to make the same mistake. Maybe when his willpower bit the dust, Jenette's would kick in. Or, if all else failed, he could use superglue on his zipper tab.

As Erin emptied the dishwasher that evening, she couldn't get Wyatt off her mind. His failure to leave the pasture with her that afternoon had been more eloquent than words. He truly meant to keep things platonic between them, which bothered her. *Okay, okay. I agreed to those terms, but if he's truly attracted to me, why isn't he willing to at least take a shot at romance?* She had no answers. But something he'd said kept circling in her mind. *"I had what you might call a difficult encounter with a woman. There was a lack of communication, and I had a brush with the law. It all got sorted out eventually, but when I came out on the other side of it, I promised myself that I'd never have anything to do with women again."* The story had been so vague that she hadn't stopped to think at the time that she had at her disposal a wealth of information. Brushes with the law normally remained on someone's record, and with her training and a law enforcement computer, there was very little information on the Internet she couldn't find if she dug deep enough.

Once the thought entered Erin's mind, she couldn't banish it. She didn't finish unloading the dishwasher. Instead, she went directly to her bedroom to grab a quick shower. Then she threw on clean civilian clothes, hopped into the county truck, and drove to the sheriff's department.

When Erin stepped inside the building, Noreen Garrison, one of the department's dispatchers, glanced up from her desk. When she recognized Erin, she beamed a smile and pushed at her red hair, which had recently been cut to frame her face in a pixie style. "Hey! You're the last person I expected to see this evening." She winked and dimpled a cheek. "If you're hungry, we've got warm pizza and I brought a batch of my chocolate chip cookies."

Erin had already caught a whiff of the pizza. Normally she would have been reminding herself that nothing ever tasted as wonderful as it smelled, but she was too preoccupied right then to worry about her calorie intake. "I pigged out over at the Morning Grind late this afternoon, so I'm not hungry. Not even pizza tempts me."

Noreen's blue eyes twinkled with amusement. "I quit dieting. Hank says I'm perfect just the way I am." She wrinkled her nose. "Not that he's seen me without clothes yet to be a good judge. But I don't feel so unhappy with myself now."

Erin was pleased to see the happy glow on her friend's face. Hank Bentley, a hefty man who reminded her of Hoss in the old *Bonanza* reruns, had given Noreen the cold shoulder for a while because of a department rule, instituted by the sheriff, that none of his staff could date one another. When Erin had learned of Noreen's attraction to Bentley, she'd gone behind the scenes to talk with other deputies, and they'd formed a committee to petition the sheriff for a change in department policy. Now a person could go to Sheriff Adams to ask for permission to date a colleague. She was glad Hank and Noreen had gotten special dispensation.

"You look fabulous," she told her friend. "And you shouldn't feel even a tiny bit unhappy with yourself. Hank is right. You *are* perfect just as you are."

Noreen blushed. "Well, nobody's perfect, I guess. I'm just glad Hank likes me back."

Erin felt as if she were talking to a teenage girl, but when she thought about it, she guessed Noreen probably wasn't much more experienced. Afflicted with dyslexia, she'd grown up feeling second-rate, married a man who preyed upon her insecurities, and then had divorced him for the sake of her children. She'd had little opportunity to interact with men. Not that Erin possessed a lot of knowledge about the opposite sex. She supposed many people felt out of their depth when it came to dating.

"What are you doing here so late?" Noreen asked. "I thought you'd be enjoying your unexpected day off and doing something fun tonight."

Erin had already devised a response to that question. "I just came in to catch up on paperwork." It wasn't uncommon for deputies to drop by the department at odd hours to file shift reports. "And I did spend the afternoon out at the ranch with Uncle Slade and had a wonderful time."

"Good! After what I did to you, it pleases me to see you enjoying life a little."

Erin gave her a warm smile. Not so very long ago, she and Noreen had been archenemies, with Noreen making sure Erin never had a moment to call her own. But Noreen had done her best to make up for that over the last few months, and Erin was now helping her memorize police codes despite her difficulty with reading. It was fun, and Noreen was amazingly receptive to alternative methods of learning. She'd even stopped chewing bubble gum at work.

Erin wagged her fingers at her friend and headed into the back room, which was partitioned off from the front by a wall of glass windows and a personnel door. Only two deputies had desk duty, and both of them were on the phone, either fielding questions or trying to mitigate a domestic dispute without dispatching another officer to the scene. Erin enjoyed desk duty. It was one of the few things about police work that she actually liked.

Her colleagues only nodded in greeting. She inclined her head to acknowledge the gestures and found a desk in a back corner where no one could look over her shoulder while she did some sleuthing on a department computer. In only minutes she was so immersed in her research that she barely heard the telephones ringing or the other deputies talking. Knowing Wyatt's name had made short work of finding information on him.

It took her an hour to read everything, and afterward she felt sick to her stomach. With shaky hands, she cleared her Internet history on the computer, then collected her purse and left the building with only one thought in her head. She needed to talk with Julie. It was almost eight thirty, a little late to knock on someone's front door, and Erin knew Julie was normally in bed by nine. But this was an emergency. What Erin had learned shocked her to the core. She also had no idea what she should do next. No two ways around it, she absolutely had to hash it out with Julie, who always kept a level head and thought of every possible consequence before she offered Erin advice.

Erin hoped the drive to Julie's house might clear her head, but twenty minutes later, she still hadn't calmed down. She hurried up the front steps of the Victorian-style home's front veranda and rapped her knuckles against the ornately carved door. Then she leaned on the doorbell, which sent out a muffled peal of musical notes. Moments later she heard the hollow thump of bare feet on the hardwood floor of the entryway, and the next instant, the door flew open to reveal Julie in silk pajamas and sporting a pillow-tossed mane. The blue streak, which she'd worn in her dark hair since her divorce, feathered over her hazel eyes like a bedraggled geisha fan.

"Erin?" she said, blinking owlishly. "What on earth? Has something awful happened?"

Erin moved over the threshold, forcing Julie back a few steps. "I just found out something *really* awful, and I need to talk."

Julie pushed the door closed. "Okay. I was asleep, but, yeah, that's what best friends are for. What did you find out that's so awful?"

Erin pushed at her wind-tousled hair. "Wyatt Fitzgerald raped a woman."

CHAPTER EIGHT

Julie looked as if her feet had put down roots through her wood floor. Her eyes went wide, and her face drained of color, making her smoky-rose pajamas look almost red next to her skin.

"What?" she whispered. "Say that again, because my brain just froze."

"He didn't do it intentionally," Erin hurried to say "Don't misunderstand."

The sleepy look left Julie's eyes. "How in the hell can a man rape a woman without meaning to do it?"

"I know, I know." Erin followed her friend through the beautifully decorated living room, which lay in shadow because no lights had been turned on. Julie had appointed the area with touches of Victorian stuff to offset her preference for comfortable furniture, creating a perfect blend that remained true to the style of the home without making it too fussy. "I'm still reeling, Jules. I've barely gotten my mind wrapped around it. And, oh, God, my heart just breaks for Wyatt."

As Julie entered the kitchen ahead of Erin, she pivoted on one bare foot to gape at her. "Your heart breaks for Wyatt? What about the poor woman?"

"Her, too," Erin said. "I'm sorry for her, too. Oh, Julie. It's so *awful.*"

Julie swept the drape of blue hair away from her face. "Okay. I thought about making herbal tea, but 'awful' calls for wine. White or red? Since you're the one upset, I'll let you pick."

Aware of Julie's preference, Erin said, "White will be perfect."

Julie went to her fridge, where she always had a bottle chilling. She kept reds in a rack on the counter. "White it is."

Erin went to sit at the round table Julie had found at a garage sale and refinished in white to go with her kitchen cabinets and countertops. She'd accented the room with touches of forest green, and once again, Erin wished she had the same knack for decorating.

Julie came to the table with two glasses of wine, one of which she passed to Erin before she sat across from her. "Okay. The first order of business is for you to calm down, so take a couple of big gulps before you tell me anything. Maybe then you can share what you just learned without making me hate Wyatt Fitzgerald's guts."

Erin took a sip of wine and followed it with a deep, calming breath. "You won't hate him when you hear the story. The poor guy. It's awful, Jules, but he really didn't mean to do it."

Julie followed her own advice and took two big gulps of wine. "Okay, if you say so, I believe you, but it's kind of hard to envision." She snapped her fingers. "I've got it. He was just walking around with a hard-on, the woman just happened to be naked and bent over, and he ran into her from behind."

Erin felt miffed with her friend. "That is *not* nice."

"Sorry, but like ninety-nine percent of our gender, I get bent out of shape when I hear the *R* word."

Erin nodded. "I understand, but it isn't only my opinion that the incident occurred accidentally. A judge and jury, eight of them female, felt the same way. Wyatt was as much a victim as the woman was."

"Go on."

Erin sighed. "Have you ever noticed how beautifully Wyatt speaks? For a deaf person, I mean. His pronunciation is almost flawless, and that is extraordinary for anyone profoundly deaf. I won't go into detail, but he got a language program and practiced his speech for hours and hours in order to talk like everyone else. The reason he did that is because he was shunned by other kids when he was in school. Can you imagine how that felt? To never fit in. To ask girls out and get laughed at. To be the outcast who couldn't even hang out with other boys because they wanted nothing to do with him?"

Julie's expression softened. "That's awful. Kids can be so cruel. And no, I can't imagine it."

"Well, that was Wyatt's life back then, and he hated school because of it. He couldn't wait to get home to spend time on his grandfather's ranch with the animals. I think that's how he became so amazing with horses, because they accepted him when everyone in the outside world wouldn't."

"That is so sad," Julie conceded, "but I still don't get how that landed him in court for rape."

"Long story. According to the court documents and all the testimonies, Wyatt got a job in Medford, Oregon, as a hired hand on a ranch. By then, he had fallen into a habit of passing himself off as a hearing individual. He made friends with another ranch hand who liked to cruise bars, looking to hook up with women, and Wyatt started going out with him, pretending he could hear."

"Okay." Julie nodded. "I would have, too. Who wants to be a pariah his whole life?"

"Exactly," Erin went on. "I can't blame him for not wanting to advertise his disability. It wasn't a crime to pretend he could hear, and on the surface, what harm could that do?"

"I can't see how it could harm anyone." Gripping the stem of her goblet between her index finger and thumb, Julie turned her glass back and forth in a slightly agitated manner. "And I definitely can't see how it could have led to rape."

"It couldn't unless the situation was exactly right. Let's say a woman comes on to a guy, so he goes with her back to her apartment, where she's still all over him and acting eager. Only she's recently divorced, hasn't been out with any guys since her husband, and she turns out the lights to undress because she feels suddenly shy. And then, after going to bed with the man and letting things escalate, she changes her mind."

The color drained from Julie's face. "Oh, my God."

"I know. Right?" Erin's stomach clenched. "Wyatt couldn't see her, and without a view of the person he's with, he can't communicate. I know that firsthand. When he walked me to my porch in the dark the other night, I said something to him without thinking, and he never replied. He hears *nothing*, Julie, so when there's no light, he's both blind and deaf. Well, not totally blind. He has excellent night vision, so far as I can tell, but he can't see another person's lips well enough to determine if they're even talking, let alone what they're saying, and unless there's some source of illumination, he can't accurately read sign language, either. And in this particular instance, the woman had a sudden change of heart when they were in bed together. We're talking when Wyatt was at point of entry, possibly with his chin hooked over her shoulder. He said in his testimony that he felt the vibration of her voice, but he had no clue what she was saying. He didn't know she'd changed her mind until she started scratching his back, and by then, he had already entered her."

Julie's face was now nearly as white as her cabinets. "Oh, dear God, poor Wyatt."

"He backed off instantly. Even the woman admitted that on the stand. But at the time, she believed he ignored her pleas for him to stop, and she called the cops. She accused him of rape, he was arrested and charged with the crime, and if not for her honesty on the witness stand, he could have been convicted."

"In other words, by pretending he could hear, Wyatt created the perfect storm."

"Yes," Erin agreed. "I forgot to say they were both intoxicated. Apparently the woman had consumed more alcohol than Wyatt had, because in her testimony, she said she suddenly realized how drunk she was and decided she was in no condition to make wise choices. Having sex with a stranger was something she'd never done."

"I can understand that," Julie said. "Look at me with Blackie. I'm still on the fence. It's important to be sure before you jump into the sack with a guy." Julie shrugged. "Well, that's not true for a one-night hookup, but when feelings are involved, I want to be sure nobody gets hurt."

"Exactly, but she was drunk. Unfortunately, she didn't start to have second thoughts soon enough to send up a red flag to Wyatt. Wyatt's attorney cross-examined the woman, and it was her answers then that saved Wyatt's ass. She said she thought Wyatt was a gentleman who would stop if she asked, and so she simply tried to tell him she'd changed her mind. She didn't want to panic and do anything stupid, like hit him or scratch him. So she asked him several times in a louder and louder voice to please stop. She believed he would do that, only he didn't. Finally, when she took her protests to a physical level and began scratching his back, he realized and did stop, but it was already too late."

"So she didn't struggle? Did nothing to let him know?"

"With a deaf man, even screaming at him that you've changed your mind isn't going to work. But she didn't know that and tried to be diplomatic about saying no."

"I would take the diplomatic approach myself. It's not smart to piss a guy off when he's that aroused. Man, Wyatt's so lucky he didn't get convicted."

Erin nodded. "Very lucky. Only was he really lucky, Jules? I think he blames himself for all of it and that's why he's sworn off women."

Julie got up to fetch the bottle of wine and refill their glasses. "Another impromptu girls' night, I guess. I'll have a headache in the morning and hate you, but what the hell?" As she sat back down, Julie said, "A number of people might not believe Wyatt's side of the story. Unless you weigh all the circumstances and understand the limitations of someone who's profoundly deaf, it's kind of incredible. I mean, how can a guy not realize when a woman is resisting?"

"Oh, but she didn't resist, not in time to convey her change of heart to Wyatt." Erin took a sip of her wine. "She only tried to tell him. Reading the testimonies was surreal. At the beginning of the trial, the prosecuting attorney wanted Wyatt's head on a platter. By the end, the judge, twelve jurors, and many onlookers who were interviewed afterward—I got that information from newspaper accounts—believed Wyatt was innocent. Even the woman—the victim—broke down on the stand crying and said she had no idea he was deaf. That she never would have accused him of rape had she known."

"Well, we can't blame her," Julie said. "I mean, hello, I'll bet thousands of guys have said they didn't know their partner had lost her enthusiasm for the activity. Some men get pissed if a woman leads them up to a certain pitch of arousal and then wants to stop at the last second."

"Yes, but they can hear and deliberately ignore a woman's wishes. Wyatt didn't ignore the woman's wishes. He couldn't *hear* what she was saying."

Julie closed her eyes. "That's one of the saddest stories I've ever heard. I mean, how awful. I'm sure the woman is still finding it difficult to trust men because of it, and Wyatt is undoubtedly afraid ever to be intimate with another woman for fear it could happen again."

Erin's heart twisted with pain for Wyatt and for the woman. She didn't know which of them had suffered more. Obviously it had been a horrible incident for either of them to put behind them. "Since I don't know the woman, it's easier to distance myself from what she must have gone through," she confessed. "But I do know Wyatt. I saw him work with a frightened horse last year. He was so patient and perceptive with that poor animal, and watching him soothe its fears was one of the most amazing things I've ever seen. He's a good man, Jules. A kind man. I don't think he would ever deliberately harm anyone or anything. And suddenly his determination to avoid any kind of romantic entanglement makes perfect sense to me."

Julie gazed thoughtfully into her wine for a long moment. "I feel bad for both of them. The woman didn't realize that Wyatt was deaf." She shrugged. "I've only ever been with three guys that way, and I never changed my mind at the last second, but if for some reason I had, I probably would have handled it pretty much the same way she did, simply by asking the man to stop. I mean, getting frantic and hurting him would be pretty stupid. You only go for the jugular when a guy *won't* stop. First, you try to just tell him you've changed your mind. It's only when he doesn't stop that you go bat-shit crazy on him."

Erin met Julie's gaze and maintained eye contact. "I'm really, *really* attracted to Wyatt."

Julie reached across the table to curl her fingers around Erin's hand. "Sweetie, I don't blame you. He's extremely easy on the eyes, but guys like Wyatt go way deeper than the skin. He's a genuinely good person, I think. I liked him from the start."

"Did you know he was deaf when you first met him?"

Julie shook her head, her mouth curving into a tremulous smile. "I'd heard about the deaf cowboy in Mystic Creek. In a town this small, information like that reaches a newcomer pretty fast. But I didn't recall the man's name, so I didn't know Wyatt was the deaf cowboy. In fact, if you'd told me he was deaf right after I first met him, I'd have laughed, because he doesn't appear to be even slightly hard of hearing. I finally figured it out when he left his wallet lying on my counter one day. I yelled at him to stop. He didn't. So I ran after him, and with his long legs, he was halfway across the concourse before I caught up with him. That was when I realized. Like you say, he speaks amazingly well for a deaf person. I never even suspected."

"His ability to speak so well didn't come easily to him. He spent hundreds of hours perfecting his pronunciation, and he says he still practices."

Julie's hold on Erin's hand tightened. "You have tears in your eyes."

Erin nodded. "This will sound crazy, but knowing what happened, I now understand Wyatt in ways that I couldn't before. And it bothers me that he holds himself entirely to blame. Yes, he did misrepresent himself to her in the bar, and, yes, he held fast to the act all evening. But I'm convinced he never anticipated that she might have a sudden attack of misgivings and want to bring a halt to everything. He was twenty-six years old and, like almost every guy that age, wanting to score. But it ended so disastrously for him that even now, nearly seven years later, he's never been with a woman again."

Julie's eyes went sparkly with tears, too. Her big heart was one of the things that made Erin value her so much as a friend. "That's amazing. For a guy to do that, he has to feel pretty awful about what happened. But I'm not quite getting why you're so upset that you woke me up to tell me about it. It's over and done. There's nothing you can do about it now."

"I'm into him, Jules. I want to *be* with him. And now I've ruined any chance of that ever happening, because I betrayed his trust and learned things he didn't choose to tell me. Not little things, either, but something so serious it changed his whole life. Going in, I had no idea I would find something *that* bad."

Julie released Erin's hand and sat back on her chair. "Just don't ever tell him you did it."

Erin shook her head. "Eventually I'll have to tell him, and he'll be angry with me in a way that I may never overcome."

"Then just don't."

Erin's heart felt as if it were breaking. "You don't understand. Wyatt is special. He's inherently honest. Not about his lack of hearing, obviously, because that awful night might never have happened if he hadn't fooled that woman into believing he could hear. But in every other way, he's probably the most direct and honest man I've ever met."

"Sometimes," Julie said softly, "being too honest can do more harm than good."

"And sometimes not being completely honest can destroy what might be absolutely perfect."

As Erin drove home, her thoughts were centered on Wyatt and how she had pressed him to be her friend. She hadn't really believed him when he said he was attracted to her. She'd thought he was just being nice. But now she was starting to wonder if he had been telling her the truth. As she'd tried to express to Julie, Wyatt seemed to be intrinsically honest. And if he was attracted to her, every moment he was around her might test his willpower.

Later, as she lay in bed, she wished with all her heart she hadn't dug into Wyatt's past. For one, it had been his secret to keep. And now that she knew what had happened, she wasn't sure how to proceed. Should she tell him she'd used her badge to invade his privacy? That she knew things about him he hadn't chosen for her or anyone else to know? She finally plunged into a troubled sleep and had nightmares about running after Wyatt as he walked away from her. She screamed his name and pled with him to forgive her, but he just kept walking. So she pulled out her only big gun and yelled that she loved him. When he just kept walking, she realized he couldn't hear her. That she was wasting her breath. The only way she could ever convince him of how sorry she was would be to make him look at her, and she didn't know if he'd ever willingly look at her again.

She jerked awake and sat straight up in bed. Sweat trickled down her sides and along the curvature of her spine. Her hair was soaking wet. She felt as if a clawlike hand was ripping her heart from her chest. As sleep moved away to make room for reality, she registered that it had been only a dream. She wasn't in love with Wyatt Fitzgerald. She'd only known him for a few months. Well, more than a few, but they hadn't been around each other all of that time. Falling in love with a man took time, lots and lots of time. But in her dream, the feelings had been so sharp and painful within her that she couldn't deny them now as she shook off the last vestiges of the nightmare.

They'd felt real, and they still did.

That brought her wide awake. She looped her arms around her upraised knees and stared into the shifting moonlight and shadows that cloaked her bedroom, willing herself to shove the absurd feelings away. She wasn't a teenager who imagined herself to be in love with every guy she crushed on. She was just letting her hormones get the better of her, she reasoned. Even worse, she was allowing her feelings of desperation to find the love of her life to mess with her head. She still had time to find her one and only. She was letting her age and her dissatisfaction with her job plant within her subconscious a need to find someone before it was too late. So she was just fabricating a great love story between her and Wyatt.

She slipped out of bed to pace her house, wearing only a T-shirt and panties. She always turned down the heat at night, and she was soon shivering. Not even that physical discomfort could chase her back to the warmth of her bed, because the dream terrified her. She absolutely could not allow herself to fall wildly in love with Wyatt Fitzgerald. At best, he was a bad bet, because he was determined never to be in an intimate relationship again. And it was entirely possible that he was as screwed up emotionally as she was. If she let herself fall in love with him, she felt pretty sure he would walk away from her, just as he had in her dream, and he'd never look back. If that ever happened, it would destroy her.

The days were getting longer, Blackie decided as he pushed the ignition switch of his Ford Edge to kill the engine. The driver's seat immediately moved back into what Blackie thought of as the escape position. Even so, he sat for a moment, staring at Julie's home, a Victorian reproduction that sat on the edge of the Bearberry Loop golf course. It was a pretty house and appeared to be large enough for an entire family, which gave him an uneasy feeling. Like him, Julie had been running away from a nasty divorce when she'd found a hidey-hole in Mystic Creek, only it looked as if she'd brought at least one of her unattained dreams with her: to one day have children. Why else would a single woman living on a shoestring budget buy a home large enough for the Partridge family?

Blackie almost pressed the ignition button again, his every instinct warning him to get away. He was fifty-three years old, and it would be nuts for him to start a relationship with a woman twenty years his junior. He could plead a last-minute illness, he guessed. A sudden stomach complaint would work. Or the beginnings of a sore throat. Only he wasn't big on polite lies. In fact, he wasn't into lying, period, not necessarily because he was morally superior, but because he had never been able to pull it off.

He sighed and studied the house. A flagstone path curved from the parking area to the Victorian's front veranda, bisecting a velvety green lawn interrupted only by blue spruce trees and well-tended flower beds that displayed a riot of color, lending credibility to the saying that "April showers bring May flowers." Only this was mountain country, where the nights could bring temperatures below freezing. It wasn't easy to grow things here until June had a good foothold.

With a sigh, Blackie forced himself to man up. Julie was fixing him dinner. He had accepted the invitation. If he backed out now, he'd hate himself for a week and feel guilty. It wasn't Julie's fault there was something about her that got to him as no other woman ever had. It also wasn't her fault she was two decades younger than he was and still had life goals that were the norm for people her age. He'd just enjoy dinner with her, be a gracious guest, and keep his eye on the end goal, going home as fast as his legs would carry him. Seeing her house told him things about her that he hadn't been able to detect in other settings.

She was still in the nesting stage of her life.

Blackie climbed out of the car. Without bothering to lock it, he strode along the curved path. Once on the porch, he noticed tasteful wind chimes hanging from the porch eaves. Large porcelain pots filled with Wave petunias accented the white safety railing around the veranda. There was even a sitting area, appointed with Adirondack chairs and a two-person swing. He had to give Julie credit; she knew how to make a house into a home.

With a sigh of resignation, he stepped onto the doormat and reached sideways to ring the doorbell. Almost instantly, the front door opened to reveal Julie, who was all smiles of welcome. As always, she looked beautiful, with glossy, dark hair spilling down her back. She wore a pink top the same color as some of the petunias, one of those silky-looking things that had cutouts at each shoulder, a style that mystified Blackie. When he bought a shirt, he wanted all its parts to be present. He sure as hell wouldn't let clothing manufacturers save money on fabric by convincing him it was the style to go around with sections of his arms naked.

"Blackie! I'm so pleased that you came!" As she stepped forward, her shin-length skirt shifted gracefully, the floral pattern sporting the same shade of pink as her half-there blouse. Her arms encircled his neck in what he was sure she intended to be a friendly hug, but when her slender body, so femininely soft in all the right places, pressed against his, he felt a lot more than friendship burgeoning between them, and he quickly put distance between their hips. "You're just in time for before-dinner drinks and appetizers."

She had already teased his appetite, only it wasn't for food. Blackie followed her into a foyer with barnwood flooring in muted tones of gray and brown. The satin, no-gloss finish would stand up well to the patter of little feet, he noted. The snow-white walls, however, were a bad choice for kids, which she would regret when and if her yearning for a family was ever fulfilled.

A curved staircase swept up from the foyer to a second floor, but she turned right and led him through a large living room, which he expected to be ornate and too fancy for practical use. But even though she'd added touches of Victorian fussiness, her sofa and recliners were big, cushiony, and upholstered in gray leather, picking up the color that streaked the floor. To his left, he saw a large, formal dining area, open to the living room, but they passed through another archway to reach a blazing-white kitchen with equally white appliances. More into earth tones, Blackie didn't immediately like it, but then the dark green accents caught his eye, and he decided he did, after all. It was a bright, welcoming kitchen with a large work island and a spacious bay that was home to a round table, also white, but adorned with a centerpiece that sported green foliage.

"Your home is lovely," he told her.

"Oh, thanks. I like it. Way too large for me, but I fell in love with the yards. I'm into gardening." Stepping over to the fridge, she opened the door and said, "I decided to be brave and serve dinner outside. It'll get a little nippy as the sun goes down." She grinned at him over her naked shoulder. He decided he could grow to like tops with some of their parts missing. They allowed a man to admire things about a woman that he wouldn't normally see, and Julie did have beautiful skin, creamy white and smooth. "I'm glad you wore a light jacket. I was prepared to drape an afghan over you if necessary. I hope you enjoy eating al fresco."

"I do." Blackie had added a balcony onto his upstairs apartment so he could barbecue and dine outdoors. He enjoyed the treehouse feeling it gave him, and food always tasted better to him when fresh air accompanied it. "As for the light jacket, I've lived here long enough to anticipate the chill that comes with sundown. It can get nippy even in July and August."

She drew a tray from a refrigerator shelf, turned, and bumped the door closed with her hip. "Don't you love that, though? Over on the west side of the Cascades, the summer nights can be so hot that you need air-conditioning in order to sleep. Here, Mother Nature cools things down. I replaced all my downstairs windows last year. Well, the ones that open, anyway. I wanted the kind that lock into position, no matter how wide they're opened. That way, I can raise them only slightly to enjoy the fresh air and not worry about a burglar gaining access to the house while I'm asleep."

Blackie almost warned her that most burglars knew how to disengage simple locking mechanisms like that, but since this was Mystic Creek, where a lot of people didn't even bother to lock their doors, he kept that information to himself. "I'm the same way. I open all my windows at night to enjoy the cool air. I have regular windows, though. I'm upstairs and don't need to worry unless a cat burglar comes to town."

She led the way through open French doors onto the deck. "I love your apartment. I've been to Jonas Sterling's place above the Straw Hat. Since Jonas doesn't own it, he's done no improvements, so the place is still partitioned off into too many rooms for the space. It's nice, but it sure doesn't have the open feeling that you've created."

Blackie felt the tension easing from his shoulders. As lovely as she looked and as naked as her shoulders might be, she hadn't staged a seduction scene. The outdoor table was set for casual dining. An ice bucket held two bottles of white wine and two bottles of beer. He didn't fail to note that she'd bought the same brand of ale that he'd drunk that evening when he'd taken her up to his apartment. She had a gift for helping people relax. She talked a lot, smiled even more, and didn't put on airs.

"I was going to cook something fancy," she told him, "but so often when I do that, something goes wrong and I have a kitchen disaster. Then I'm all nerved up and can't enjoy myself. So tonight I went for simple, a chicken enchilada casserole, a tossed salad, and a loaf of garlic bread I baked fresh today." She lifted the lid off the appetizer tray. "I made canapés, also easy. No fuss, no muss. That way we can focus on good wine and conversation."

Blackie removed his jacket as she filled two wineglasses from a chilled bottle. "Just as a starter," she told him. "You can enjoy the beer as well."

"I do have to drive home," he said with a laugh.

"Oh, but this is Mystic Creek, surrounded by country roads. The biggest danger is a deer bolting out in front of the car."

"And cops. Our sheriff's department is extremely well staffed because this is the official county seat."

"One beer, then," she conceded with a laugh.

Blackie draped his coat over the back of a chair and helped himself to a canapé before he even sat down. Julie grinned and followed suit as she took a seat across from him. The breeze picked up just then, molding her silky top to her upper body and lifting her dark hair to drape it over her slender shoulders. He wasn't sure he liked the blue streak, but on Julie it somehow worked. She sat back and crossed her legs. On her narrow feet, she wore burnished gold sandals that showed off dainty toenails painted the same color as her blouse.

"These are delicious!" he said after he swallowed the bite of food.

"My version of smoked salmon-and-pea vol-au-vents." She took a bite. "The recipe called for serving them warm, so I altered it a bit, made them ahead, and chilled them instead. I wanted to enjoy your visit. Too many last-minute things keep me in the kitchen."

Her pronunciation of the French words was almost perfect, telling Blackie she'd studied the language either in high school or college. Most of his classmates had taken Spanish, which was a more practical language to know in the States, but Blackie had always been a romantic. At one point in his life, he'd yearned to visit Paris. He'd fancied himself to be an artist at the time and had later discovered he couldn't paint worth a darn.

"You studied French."

She laughed. "Only enough to get myself into trouble if I ever make it to France. If I do, I'm renting a chalet at a vineyard and spending most of my time in the tasting room." She pointed a finger at him. "Never fear. I don't plan to take up wine making. As I told you, I'm way more interested in the complexity of beers. But in college, I fancied myself to be quite the sommelier and came to love wine."

Blackie tasted her selection and winked at her. "Nice choice."

Their conversation turned to the French language and places they yearned to visit in that country. With a glass of wine under his belt,

Blackie forgot to be nervous about Julie wanting babies and was able to simply enjoy being with her. As they savored the taste of the canapés and sipped chardonnay, they discussed business, beer making, and how best to go about starting a brewery. Blackie got so caught up in the conversation that he helped her carry things from the kitchen for their meal rather than allow a lull in their exchanges. Blackie couldn't help but think how perfect Julie was for him, but there was absolutely no way he wanted to start a family at his age, and he feared that she had her sights set on kids.

Over the enchilada casserole, which was delicious, Blackie ventured a leading sentence. "Well, if you're really into starting a brewing company, you'd better have your children soon. Starting another business won't leave you much time for burping babies and changing diapers."

She laughed and flapped her hand. "Bite your tongue. I'm all done with the baby idea. In my twenties, oh, yeah. I wanted children. But no longer. Maybe I've grown selfish, but since my divorce, I want it to be all about me—and maybe about a significant other. I love my life as it is. Well, I still dream of a brewery, to be honest, and trips to exotic locales. But mostly I'm happy right where I am, with the freedom to do whatever I want when the mood strikes. The shop holds me down, of course, but as time wears on, I hope to afford another baker and employees to work out front. That'll give me lots of time for traveling, and I won't have to worry about the business suffering while I'm gone."

Blackie liked the sound of that, and he also noted that she seemed willing to make room in her life for a man. Julie shivered and ran inside for a wrap while Blackie donned his jacket. She was laughing when she emerged from the house with an afghan draped over her shoulders. It made her look like a beautiful gypsy.

"I have a shawl, but it's crocheted and so holey it won't keep me warm!"

So was her blouse, but he refrained from saying so. "Despite the chill, I'm enjoying this. It feels good to eat outside. The fresh air, the fading sunlight, the sound of birds chirping as they settle on their roosts. Truth be told, I just plain love being outdoors. That's why I walk and hike instead of going to a gym."

"I'm the same way. Even when there's snow on the sidewalks and the going is icy, I prefer to walk for exercise."

"You ever hike?"

"No. I'm a little wary about going into the mountains alone."

"You should go with me sometime. My favorite walks are up the Strawberry Hill and Huckleberry Lake trails. Beautiful at all times of year. I even sneak in one last hike on each trail after the first snowfall. It's incredibly gorgeous in the mountains then."

"Oh, I'd love to go up with someone familiar with the area!" she exclaimed. "If I encountered a bear or cougar, I wouldn't know what to do."

Blackie laughed. "I know what to do if I come face-to-face with something that'll eat me, but I've never had that experience."

"You have the look of a man who can handle almost any situation."

Blackie appreciated the tip of her hat to his physical condition, but he chuckled nevertheless. "I'm a fast runner."

She rolled her eyes. "Aw, a humble man. I like that."

Blackie was feeling the same way about her. He liked almost everything about her. Gazing across the table at her, he couldn't help but think how perfect they were for each other. He wondered if the same thought had occurred to her. He needed to guard his heart, though. The age difference between them was an obstacle. He'd be an idiot to forget that. She was a young and beautiful woman. If she hung out her shingle, every unmarried man in town under forty would be pounding on her door. Why would she settle for a fifty-three-year-old guy who'd probably develop coronary disease over the next decade?

They moved on from the topic of hiking to talk a bit about their disastrous marriages again. Then they discussed life as single people. They shared their tastes in music, literature, and film. He was delighted to learn that she was also an art enthusiast.

Blackie said, "I wouldn't know a DiCaprio if it ran up and bit me on the ass."

As he'd hoped, her eyes widened in dismay. "It's Da Vinci who was the artist. DiCaprio is a film star."

Blackie gave her an *I gotcha* wink, and she burst out laughing.

The mood between them became so relaxed that Blackie dared to broach another topic: his expectations of a relationship. "I doubt that I'll ever want to marry again," he said. "And I absolutely don't want a kid at this point in my life. Back in my thirties—hell, even in my forties—I mourned the fact that I'd never have children. But I've moved beyond that now."

Her smile faded, and her expression grew solemn. "I can tell you're worried about that, but with me, you shouldn't be. There was a time when I thought of little else but having a baby. In retrospect I wonder if I wasn't searching for an easy fix to my troubled marriage. Whatever the reason, the last thing I want now is a child. Even if I were happily married again, I'd think twice. I enjoy my life the way it is. I like sleeping in on my days off, walking in the rain, and puttering in my gardens. Oh, and I'm a shopping fanatic as well. Have you ever seen a mother of young children enjoying a shopping excursion?"

She pretended to shudder, which made Blackie chuckle. "No, ma'am, I can't say I have. I like kids. Don't get me wrong. Even at my age, I'm still in good enough shape to be a competent parent for a while. But what about when I'm in my sixties?" He shook his head. "Nope. I missed my window of opportunity. It wouldn't be fair to a child to have an old man as a daddy."

After helping Julie tidy the kitchen, Blackie invited her for a moonlight walk. She donned a jacket. Since she lived on the golf course and it was after-hours, Blackie led her onto one of the cart paths. At some point, she slipped her hand into his, and when they came upon a water feature, Blackie gathered the courage to kiss her. She had the softest, most inviting lips he'd ever tasted. She opened sweetly for him and pressed her body close to his. Within seconds he was aroused and knew she was as well. Young stud antics were far behind him, though, meaning sex on a golf course was out. He drew back and cupped her face between his hands.

"You're too young and beautiful for me," he said softly.

"And you're too wonderful and mature for me," she retorted just as softly. "We can think this to death, Blackie. Most people would tell us we're nuts. But do we really care? This feels right to me."

"It feels right to me, too, honey. But I'll admit that frightens me. I got my heart walked on once, and it's taken me damned near twenty years to recover."

"Ditto," she said with a laugh. "Well, not for the twenty years of recovery, but for the rest. I got my heart broken, too. Maybe that's why it's so easy for us to connect, because we understand each other."

"So . . . ? Where are we going with this?" he asked.

"I have no idea," she confessed. "I kind of lied to you the last time you asked me that. I said I wasn't in the market for anything intimate, that I was looking for a male friend. The truth is, I was already attracted to you on many different levels, one of them physical, but I was too big a coward to tell you so."

He ran his thumbs up to her temples and felt the rapid thrum of her pulse. That turned him on as nothing she said ever could, but he forced himself to release her and take a step back. "When you reach a point where this no longer frightens you, just let me know."

"And then?"

Blackie wasn't going to pull the wool over this young woman's eyes. She was too honest for him to do her that disservice. "I'll decide if my courage is as great as yours is, I guess."

She burst into a fit of giggles and laughed so hard that Blackie grasped her arm to hold her upright. She leaned against him and rested her head on his shoulder. "Oh, Blackie, this is so dangerous. I could very easily fall madly in love with you."

His heart caught, because he was feeling the same way. "When terrain is dangerous, smart people tread cautiously."

She didn't pull away as he walked her home. Instead she snuggled closer within the circle of his arm.

And that felt so perfectly right that it scared him half to death.

CHAPTER NINE

Kennedy was having a serious problem with his cravings for hamburgers, not the kind he could make at home, but the ones he could buy only at the Mystical Burger Shack. He couldn't seem to let an evening go by without going to the burger joint to be served by a pretty blonde on roller skates. Had he gone crazy? But even when she was super busy, Jen found time to stand beside his truck and visit with him, and he enjoyed her company. She was witty and liked to laugh, but she was also serious about her plans for college. She vowed that she would never do anything stupid to screw up her future, and he really liked that about her.

Unlike so many kids at the university who seemed hell-bent on partying, Jen understood why Kennedy walked the straight and narrow. It was kind of weird, actually, that she had such a firm grasp of the situation Kennedy was in when she was still only in high school. But she'd been thinking about college ever since her freshman year, and she knew no money was likely to fall off a tree in her backyard. She said she would be in school for a long time in order to become a vet, and once she graduated, she'd have to work really long hours to pay off her student loans and make ends meet. That meant she'd have to wait to have a baby in her thirties.

Jen's dad had talked to her boss about his daughter working different hours. Because of what had happened with Jen's ex-boyfriend, he didn't want her to work until closing for a while. The new owner of the burger joint hadn't done a very good job of watching the camera monitor, which was in the kitchen. And, hello, the jock was still at large. Because Jen hadn't been seriously hurt, the kid had spent only one night in jail and then had gotten released into his father's custody. He was in big trouble, of course, and would have to go before a judge, but chances were good that he'd get only some probation and a slap on the wrist. That meant he was still a threat, and Jen's dad worried that he might come back to the burger shack to harass her. As a result, Jen got off before dark now, and Kennedy was glad of that. He doubted her jerk of an ex-boyfriend would dare to cause her any more grief, but he liked that her dad was being proactive.

The change in Jen's hours disrupted Kennedy's study times. He had to go in for a burger earlier in the evening, before it got dark. On the three days a week he had classes, he drove back to Mystic Creek to get his work done on the ranch, grabbed a quick shower, and then went back into town for dinner. He thought of his visits with Jen as his dessert. When he got back to the ranch, he still had KP duty in the bunkhouse, so he helped put away food and then did his part to clean up the kitchen. Wyatt said the rules remained the same even when Kennedy didn't eat with all the guys. Dining out was Kennedy's choice, but not being present for a meal didn't mean he was off the hook. On Kennedy's nights to cook, which only happened about one night a week with five guys on the payroll, Kennedy would have to stay home and throw a meal together. Kennedy didn't mind that, and he sure didn't mind doing his chores on the ranch. Slade had given him a sweet deal, free room and board, plus a little in wages. Kennedy knew he was way better off than a lot of college students who had to work to help pay their way.

One evening when Kennedy went to the burger shack, he noticed Jen was fidgety and kept looking over her shoulder at the cars pulling in. "Is the jock still pestering you?"

She shrugged her shoulders. "Not really. I blocked him on my phone, so he can't even text me now."

Kennedy didn't like the sound of that. "After getting into that much trouble, he still had the nerve to text you?"

Jen wrinkled her nose and tried to smile, but Kennedy could tell it was forced. "He's a spoiled brat. Has a rich daddy who never tells him no, and his mom's not around to change that."

"Where is she, always at a spa?"

Jen laughed. "Rob's folks are divorced, and Rob was old enough to choose which parent he wanted to live with. He hates his mom. At first, I thought she was a really bad person, but now I think she just had the guts to tell Rob no."

"Maybe he wouldn't be such a dick if she was still around."

Jen shrugged again. "Sorry if I'm acting nervous. I'd recognize the sound of his car if he pulled in, but last time I was inside when he came. When you're in the kitchen, you can't hear much of anything outside. People are yelling back and forth."

Kennedy wished she could quit working for a while. Eventually the jock would find some other girl to fixate on. "I don't blame you for being nervous. I was there, remember. I get it."

This time her smile was genuine. "And I'm glad you were there. If you hadn't stepped in, they would have gotten me into the car." Her lips thinned and she glanced over her shoulder again. "I shouldn't think about what might have happened. But I do. And it's always in the back of my mind that Rob might come in one of his friends' cars. You know? No glasspack muffler to warn me."

The outdoor buzzer went off, which was Jen's signal that another order was ready to be delivered. "Sorry. Gotta go."

Kennedy watched her skate away, wishing the jock would leave Mystic Creek and never bother her again. He couldn't believe the stupid jerk had dared to send her threatening text messages. And there was no doubt in Kennedy's mind that the messages had been threatening. There was something haywire about that kid. Maybe he was doing other drugs besides weed. Kennedy just hoped Jen would tell him if the dude was still giving her trouble.

The next evening when Kennedy pulled in at the burger shack, the place was hopping. All the parking spots were taken, and people were honking their horns for service. The owner, a stout guy in his fifties who wore an orange Burger Shack hat and shirt, was outside without any skates, trying to deliver orders, and he looked totally pissed off. Kennedy positioned his truck next to the building and got out to ask what was wrong. He didn't see Jen, which was odd, because she'd texted him earlier that she was working.

"What's wrong?" the owner cried. "What's *wrong*? Your girlfriend just walked out in the middle of her shift and left me shorthanded! That's what's wrong. No warning. Nothing. She just up and disappeared!"

Kennedy's stomach clenched. "Jen wouldn't just walk away. She's saving almost all her wages for tuition. Have you looked at the camera footage? Something must have happened."

"You hear all those horns blowing? I'm too damned busy to stand around with my thumb up my butt. You want to watch footage, you go right ahead. I have a business to run!"

Kennedy couldn't blame the guy. Being shorthanded during dinner hour, he was in a heck of a fix. But didn't the man care if Jen had gone missing? Kennedy strode into the building. Kids were all over the kitchen in their Mystical Burger Shack tops, which looked like prison scrubs with a logo on the front and back. Kennedy looked up at the monitor, which was essentially a flat-screen TV with a camera feed. *Problem*. Kennedy had no idea how to back up the recording.

"Hey," he said to a kid flipping burgers on the grill. "Do you know how to back this camera thing up?"

"Hell, no, man. The boss doesn't teach us that stuff. He watches us more than he does the customers. He thinks we'll give away food to our friends."

Kennedy stared up at the screen, which was divided into frames. *Shit*. Something had happened to Jen. He felt it in his bones. The different zones covered almost all the outdoor area where cars pulled in. He needed help to watch the footage.

Kennedy thought about calling the cops, but since he wasn't positive that Jen hadn't been irresponsible and just left, he was hesitant. He decided to call her folks instead to see if they knew where Jen had gone.

"Hey, buddy, do you have Jen's home phone number?" Kennedy asked the patty flipper.

The kid, who wore a net over his dark hair, jerked his head toward the commercial refrigerator, a silver monstrosity with papers taped all over the front. "Should be posted there. If not, the boss has it."

Kennedy advanced on the fridge, located Jen's home number, and punched it into his phone. When Jen's dad answered, Kennedy said, "My name's Kennedy Fitzgerald, and I—"

Mr. Johnson cut Kennedy off. "Well, hello, Kennedy. I've never had a chance to thank you for standing up for my girl that night. I really appreciate what you did for her."

Kennedy was in too big a panic for chitchat. "Look, Mr. Johnson, I appreciate that, but right now I'm worried about Jen. I'm at the burger shack. She texted me that she was working today, only when I got here, she wasn't anywhere around. Her boss is ticked off. He says she walked out in the middle of her shift."

"Jenette would never do that," her father said. "And she's supposed to be there. If something came up, she would have called us."

Kennedy didn't want to be an alarmist, but he was worried. "Mr. Johnson, I think you should call the cops. I don't think Jen would walk off the job like this, and if she didn't, something else went down."

"Oh, God. That damned kid, Rob Sorensen. He's big trouble. I'll call the cops, all right."

Kennedy's stomach was still tied in knots. He had a really bad feeling about this. If those kids had returned, they could have overpowered Jen and forced her into a car. "Hurry, Mr. Johnson. Tell them you think Rob Sorensen kidnapped her. It may not be true, but given what he did the other night, I don't think he deserves any benefit of the doubt."

"I agree."

Kennedy started to say something else but realized Jen's father had ended the call. At a loss as to what to do next, Kennedy decided that messing with the camera footage would be a wasted effort. The county deputies would arrive soon. They would know all about surveillance systems. Kennedy's time might be better spent looking around outside. He remembered how the food tray had been knocked from Jen's hands that night Rob shoved his driver door open. Was there a tray and cold food lying on the ground outside that the owner hadn't noticed?

Kennedy exited the building and scanned the parking area. There were so many vehicles under the overhang that he wouldn't see a tray lying on the asphalt. Kennedy walked along the concrete median that the servers skated on to deliver orders. He accidentally stepped into the path of a waitress and made her spill a soda.

"Damn it!" the owner yelled. "Get the hell off the runway! Can't you see how busy we are?"

What Kennedy saw was that Jen's boss was so angry at her for leaving him in the lurch that he didn't care what had happened to her. But Kennedy wasn't going to let that stop him from looking around. What was the guy going to do, kick his ass and throw him off the property? Kennedy didn't think so.

After walking the full length of the median, Kennedy cut a wide circle around the parking area, and as he finished the loop, which took him near the back of the building where a big green dumpster sat, he finally saw a tray. It lay on the ground with one of its legs broken, but no food was around it, only an empty hamburger wrapper, a smashed drink cup, and crumpled napkins. Kennedy closed the distance, anyway, just to get a better look. He saw nothing alarming. No blood or anything.

The thought of blood sent a weird feeling through his chest, not exactly a pain, but more like an ache. He'd come to care about Jen. She was a sweet girl, and he didn't know what he'd do if something bad had happened to her.

Just then he heard a shrill sound. For an instant, he thought it was a distant cop siren wailing, but he only heard it once. Sirens usually kept blowing. His feet suddenly felt as if they were stuck to the ground, and his heart started to pound.

"Jen?"

The shrill sound came again, and Kennedy's boots came unglued from the dirt quicker than a heartbeat. He ran around the dumpster, and there lay Jenette, her right arm and hand twisted and turned at unnatural angles. Her skirt had been ripped halfway off her, and the crotch of her leotard was unsnapped. Blood smeared her inner thighs.

"No!" Kennedy cried.

He knelt beside her, but he couldn't think what to do. She was hurt. She was hurt badly. *Sweet Jesus, show me what to do.* Only nothing came to Kennedy. He was afraid to even touch her. She didn't appear to be conscious. Her face was all red and puffy, like she'd been repeatedly struck by a fist. Anger roiled within him.

He leaped to his feet and raced back around the building. "I found Jen!" he yelled. "She's hurt! Somebody call an ambulance! Tell them to hurry! I think she's dying!"

And Kennedy truly believed that. The ground under her was soaked with blood, and he was afraid she was hemorrhaging internally from injuries he couldn't see. He'd been scared a few times in his life, but never like this.

Wyatt was lunging a horse in the round pen when his cell phone vibrated, his signal that someone had texted him. He almost didn't stop working to read it. Over time, he'd learned that texts could normally be ignored until he had time to look at them. But something, maybe a premonition, told him this message might be urgent. *Foolishness.* He didn't get premonitions. Well, he had gotten some doom-and-gloom feelings a few times, but they'd never amounted to anything. He'd just been anxious about nothing.

Even so, Wyatt brought the horse down from its lope and drew out his phone. He was surprised to see that it had been Erin who contacted him. He started reading her text.

I'm on duty and just responded to an emergency call.
Kennedy's friend at the burger joint has been raped and beaten.
Don't know if she'll pull through. Kennedy took off in his truck. I
think he's looking for the Sorensen kid, her ex-boyfriend. If he

finds him before we do, he may kill him, and right now, I'd consider helping him do it. Find your brother, ASAP.

Wyatt almost didn't answer Erin's missive, but after handing off the horse to Tex for a rubdown, he drew his phone back out of his pocket as he left the barn and texted her back. Thanks for the heads-up. Going to look for him. Wish me luck.

Wyatt's hands were shaking as he started his pickup. Kennedy was normally levelheaded, but when a guy cared about a girl and she got hurt by a jerk, all bets were off. Kennedy might do something totally idiotic if he found that boy.

It had been a long time since Wyatt had been a teenager. In fact, he guessed if he were honest, he'd never really been a normal teen. The boys his age hadn't wanted to hang out with him. But Wyatt did remember the things those youngsters had done for kicks, and alcohol had almost always been part of their repertoire. After raping and beating a girl within an inch of her life, the Sorensen boy had to be scared, and Wyatt was willing to bet money that alcohol would be his sedative of choice. He pulled his truck over to the curb on West Main and texted Erin again.

Where do kids go to get drunk in this town?

Erin wrote back: The creek. Drive out Mystic Creek Lane and take every road to the left. You can tell if it leads to a house. There'll be a mailbox. All other roads go to water. Kids go there to avoid being caught in possession.

Wyatt fastened his seat belt and felt his phone vibrate again. He got it out of his pocket and saw that Erin had added: We'll be combing the same area soon. Scrambling at moment. Arranged emergency transport for girl. Sending to Crystal Falls. Dealing with crime scene now and questioning all kids here.

Wyatt knew things were probably crazy at Erin's end, and he was glad to know the authorities would soon launch a full-blown search for the Sorensen kid, undoubtedly their prime suspect. Wyatt only hoped he could find Kennedy before he did something crazy that could land him in jail.

Instead of driving around town, which probably would be a waste of time, Wyatt headed toward the north side and turned onto Mystic Creek Lane. Erin had it right. This was an area where kids could hide. Pines so thick he couldn't see through them. Dirt roads that had been driven during the winter to create ruts that had now hardened like cement. Definitely not inviting, not even to cops.

The first road Wyatt drove down ended at the creek, but there were no vehicles parked near the water and he saw no sign of kids. So he went back out to the main road and took the next left without a mailbox. Again, he found nothing. He'd searched five creek-side spots and was starting to worry he wouldn't find Kennedy when he finally hit pay dirt. As he bumped his way down the sixth road, he glimpsed a blue vehicle through the trees. Kennedy's pickup was blue. A second later Wyatt saw a refurbished red-and-white Chevy. He floorboarded the accelerator, pushing his truck to such a high speed that it bounced and went airborne over the ruts. When he entered the clearing by the stream, he slammed on the brakes and put the vehicle into a sideways skid.

Kennedy and a kid built like a brick shithouse were squared off with their fists raised, but Wyatt's unexpected appearance and the cloud of dust sent up by the truck tires startled them both enough to make them look at Wyatt instead of each other.

Wyatt leaped out of the vehicle. "Kennedy, let the law handle this! It's not your place!"

Kennedy gave Wyatt a wild-eyed glare. "You didn't see what they did to her! By God, I'm going to kill the little fucker!"

Wyatt held up his phone and dialed 911. He watched the screen to see when the dispatcher answered the call. "My name is Wyatt Fitzgerald. I'm deaf and can hear nothing you say to me. The young man who raped and beat the Johnson girl is hiding out off of Mystic Creek Lane down by the creek. Send officers to the scene. Tell them it's the sixth road south of the north end."

Kennedy stomped over and grabbed Wyatt's phone. For an instant, Wyatt thought his brother truly had lost his good sense, but instead Kennedy put the phone to his ear. "The guy's name is Rob Sorensen. I know he did it, because he's got her blood on his hands and the fly of his jeans. Three other boys were in on it. Get here as fast as you can, be-cause the jerk has a knife."

Just then Rob Sorensen came tearing across the clearing. Wyatt saw that he was yelling something, but he couldn't make out the words. Wyatt stepped into the kid's path. If the boy jumped Kennedy, Kennedy would fight back, and at all costs, Wyatt hoped to keep his brother out of trouble. Kennedy had a bright future ahead of him, and Wyatt didn't want his plans to be ruined over a fight with a minor.

The impact of the youth's body sent Wyatt flying backward, and the kid landed on top of him. Wyatt rolled out from under him and sprang to his feet. "Stay out of it, Kennedy," he commanded. "Stand back and let me handle this."

Sorensen staggered erect and swung wildly at Wyatt with the open blade of a pocketknife. Wyatt swung up his arm to block the thrust and managed to knock the weapon out of the boy's hand. From that moment forward, all Wyatt did was block punches. He would do everything he could to avoid hitting the kid. A grown man could get in serious Dutch for assaulting a minor. Kennedy tried to come in on the scuffle once, but Wyatt threw out his arm and knocked him backward.

"I said stay out of it." Wyatt turned to face off with the boy again. "I may go to jail, Kennedy, but I'll still have a job when I get out. You might ruin your whole life."

Wyatt's arms were starting to ache from blocking the youth's wild swings, but he just kept circling and blocking until the three boys hud-dled together by the car ran over and tackled their friend. One of them, a teen with whitish-blond hair, extricated himself from the dogpile and turned to face Wyatt.

"We didn't do it!" he cried. "We thought he was just going to give her a scare. You know? And then he went all crazy, and we didn't know what to do! We kept telling him to stop, but he wouldn't! When she kicked him on the shin with her roller skate, he went totally berserk. Carried her to the dumpster. Threw her on the ground. That's when her arm got bro-ken. And then"—the kid's shoulders started to jerk—"he ra-aped h-her. R-right in fr-front of us. There was s-so much n-noise out front that nobody h-heard her scr-screaming. I swear, we n-never t-touched her."

Wyatt managed to read the kid's lips and understood most of what he'd said. "The cops are on their way. You need to tell them your story."

The kid's face twisted and tears spilled down his cheeks. "I don't w-want to g-go to j-jail. I had n-nothing to d-do with it!"

"Well, son," Wyatt said slowly. "I'm sure Jenette Johnson didn't wake up this morning wanting to be beaten and raped, either. And even if you didn't lay a hand on her, you did allow it to happen. A good man doesn't do that. He defends a woman with every ounce of his strength."

"I'm not a m-man yet."

"No, but you soon will be, and if you don't start choosing your friends more wisely, you'll be a poor excuse for one."

Wyatt made sure the other two youths still had Sorensen pinned to the ground and then turned to deal with his brother. He expected Kennedy to be fuming with anger, but instead the younger man's blue eyes were bright with unshed tears. "Thanks, Wyatt. I would have killed him."

Wyatt nodded. "I know, and I couldn't have blamed you. But a judge might not have seen it that way."

"You all right?" Kennedy asked.

"My arms will be sore for a few days. The jock throws one hell of a punch."

Just then Kennedy whirled at some sound Wyatt couldn't hear. "Sirens," Kennedy said, looking over his shoulder so Wyatt could see his face. "The cavalry is almost here."

Lights flashing, three county vehicles finally pulled into the clearing. Wyatt curled an arm around his brother's shoulders. "Our business here is finished, Kennedy," he said. "We'll only distract the deputies by hanging around. Now that the sun is about to dip behind the mountains, it'll be dark soon. If possible, we need to get your truck home. Are you okay to drive?"

Kennedy nodded. Then he met Wyatt's gaze. "What he did to her. I'll never get it out of my head. What if she dies?"

Wyatt's throat went tight. "Let's pray that doesn't happen. It's all we can do, Kennedy, just pray. She's in God's hands now."

"Just so you know, when I get back to the bunkhouse, I'm stealing one of your jugs of whiskey from under your bed."

Wyatt tightened his grip on Kennedy's shoulder. "Promise not to drive after you've had a drink?"

"You know I won't."

"Then you're welcome to my whiskey. Just buy me another jug if you drain it."

Kennedy started to walk away and then stopped to face Wyatt again. "What're you going to do?"

Wyatt shrugged. "First I'm going to collect my hat and try to clean it up. That little shit knocked it off my head, and it rolled in the dirt. Then I've got a couple of errands to run in town. When I'm finished, I'll head home."

Kennedy nodded. "Thanks again, Wyatt. I wouldn't have just blocked his blows."

"I know."

As Kennedy walked toward his truck, Wyatt searched the clearing for Erin and saw her over by the tricked-out Chevy, interviewing the three boys who had witnessed the attack on Jenette. He wanted to thank her for the text she had sent to warn him that Kennedy might be hunting down Sorensen. By contacting him, she had been instrumental in protecting Kennedy's future. If it hadn't been for her quick thinking, Wyatt wouldn't have found his brother in time to stop him from doing something stupid. He also hoped to get more information on Jenette's condition, mostly because he knew Kennedy would want to know how the girl was doing before the evening was over, and with all the patient privacy laws, Wyatt feared they would get no information through normal channels.

Watching Erin do her job, he decided he should wait before he tried to talk to her. She was busier right now than a one-legged cowboy trying to kick his own ass. Maybe he could grab a bite to eat and then catch her at the sheriff's department later.

The back parking lot at the sheriff's department was for law enforcement only, but Wyatt knew that was where he would most likely spot Erin as she came or went. He'd rarely seen so many police vehicles in one place, some of them two or three years old, others brand-new. All the bubble tops might have given Wyatt a nervous stomach if he'd been a criminal, but as it stood, he sat in his truck and ate two calzones from the Jake 'n' Bake for supper and drank a giant-size soda. He was feeling just a little sleepy by the time Erin walked out the rear door of the building. Wyatt climbed out of his truck. She hesitated midstride and then changed direction to come toward him. He liked the way she strode with brisk steps, her legs solid under her slender but toned body.

When she reached him, Wyatt had every intention of thanking her for calling him about Kennedy, but she spoke first. "I need a glass of wine. No. Correction. I need a whole gallon, straight into a vein."

The artificial daylight cast by the yard lights enabled Wyatt to read her lips, and he was initially startled by the vehemence he saw in her expression. He considered all that had happened and decided she truly had been through one hell of a day. "Are you off shift? I'd be happy to get you some wine to say thank you for helping me head Kennedy off at the pass. He had murder in his eyes."

"I almost wish he'd finished the deed before you got to the creek!" She leaned against the fender of his pickup. "That little punk is inside, whining like a baby because his father refuses to lawyer up and get him out on bail. I can barely stand to look at him." She fixed Wyatt with a tear-filled gaze. There was a look of utter defeat in her eyes. "I want to take him apart. A good cop doesn't allow himself to think that way. That's why this job isn't right for me. I can't compartmentalize my emotions. I'm either walking around feeling hollow or I'm upset. Most of the time, I just go for the hollow feeling."

Wyatt's heart hurt for her, and even worse, he had no answers. "I'm sorry, Erin. Feeling hollow all the time is no way to live."

The tears in her eyes slipped over her lower lashes. "I'm sorry for turning someone else's tragedy into being all about me and my stupid job. It's not right, I know, but I can't seem to focus on anything but the fact that I let Jenette Johnson fall through the cracks."

"Honey, what happened wasn't your fault." Wyatt immediately regretted the form of address. He had no business using terms of endearment with her, and yet it had popped out. They had agreed to be friends, and friends were supposed to care about each other, but the feeling inside him went deeper than mere friendship. He yearned to hold her in his arms and comfort her. "Please, don't blame yourself. You had no way of knowing he'd go clear over the edge and do something like this."

"Oh, but I did. That night at the burger joint when he tried to force Jenette into his car, she told us he threatened to take her into the woods and rape her. That was a red flag we shouldn't have ignored. Now Jenette is fighting for her life."

Wyatt moved in beside her to rest his arm against the pickup. "Are all the other deputies as upset as you are?"

"No. They're sad about what happened. But they think it's just one of those things nobody could prevent. I don't think they feel inadequate and"—she broke off and tipped her head back to stare at the sky, which, in the artificial light, appeared to be black and devoid of stars—"guilty for failing. They're cops. Their job is to deal with the criminals after the crimes are committed. Sure, they try to prevent bad things from happening. We cruise the streets. We give talks at the schools. We counsel parents. But when shit happens anyway, they don't feel the same way I do."

Wyatt had known for some time that Erin was disillusioned and frustrated with her job, but he hadn't understood how completely out of her comfort zone she actually was. "Not everyone is cut out to be a peace officer. That's no reflection on you. And just so you know, Kennedy suspects Rob Sorensen is into drugs. That means his behavior may be erratic, depending on what he's using."

"Meth, we think, mixed with alcohol. His choice for today, anyway. His car was impounded, and a bunch of stuff was found in the trunk. Meth, crack, sedatives, and pot. Meth can make people crazy, all right."

Wyatt grabbed ahold of her last sentence. "Crazy people are unpredictable. Not even cops can anticipate what they'll do."

She looked up at him. "But he told us what he meant to do. Don't you get it? Through Jenette, we knew what was on his mind, and we did nothing to stop him."

"What could you have done?"

"Nothing! Not legally, anyway! And that's the whole point! Don't you see?"

Wyatt was beginning to wish for a big glass of wine himself. He could see the pain in her eyes, but he couldn't think of a way to make her feel better. "I'm sorry you blame yourself."

A glassy look entered her eyes. "I looked at him through the bars of his cell. Sitting there on his cot, blubbering and cursing his father." She locked gazes with Wyatt. "I had an unholy urge to blow his head off. Even if Jenette survives, he's probably destroyed her life. If it's my job to clean up after a crime is committed, why shouldn't I start by obliterating that piece of crap in our jail? But, no. We have to turn him over to the courts and hope justice is done. Only justice is rarely dished out. His father will hire a fancy lawyer. They'll plead drug-induced insanity or something. And in the end, he'll probably do time in a rehab center where he can watch TV, eat popcorn, and bullshit a psychologist about how sorry he is."

Wyatt didn't have it within his power to fix the world. He wished he did—for her sake. "What are you going to do?"

She straightened away from the vehicle. "What I should have done in Washington before I ever came here. I've had it clear up to my eyebrows. Nobody who has thoughts like I did tonight should be wearing a badge."

She gave Wyatt no opportunity to say anything more. She pushed off into that brisk, surefooted stride of hers and retraced her path back into the department. He had a horrible feeling she was about to turn in her badge. He couldn't say that would be the wrong choice for her. In fact, he believed it was the right one. But that didn't negate the fact that she was going to be a basket case afterward.

He didn't know what to do. He'd never watched someone throw her life away. He only knew he couldn't leave and let her face the consequences of what she'd done alone.

CHAPTER TEN

Wyatt waited beside his truck with his gaze fixed on the rear door of the county building. He knew Erin would return to the parking lot sooner or later. As far as he knew, she was still driving a county vehicle while her Honda was being repaired. When Wyatt had dropped by the Timing Light to pay the bill, Buck Hannity told him he'd had to order most of the parts and it was taking longer than expected to get them in. If Erin actually quit her job tonight, would she even have a vehicle to drive? He guessed she wasn't thinking about everyday stuff right now. Not that he blamed her. A lot of worry had to be circling in her mind.

In only a few minutes, Erin emerged from the building. She paused on the back steps to search for him, making him feel glad that he'd stayed. Blue eyes sparkling with tears, she struck off toward him, her arms straightened and stiff at her sides. As she drew closer, Wyatt saw no badge gleaming on the front of her uniform shirt.

As she drew up about three feet away from him, she said, "For better or worse, I'm finished."

Wyatt's heart felt as if it had dropped to somewhere around his ankles. He'd been hoping that someone inside the building might have been able to talk her down. But, no, she'd made a snap decision that would affect the rest of her life. What if she woke up in the morning with a change of heart? He decided that maybe a big glass of wine was just what she needed, after all. It would help to calm her down, and talking things over might clear her head. He'd stop by Flagg's Market for a bottle of vino and meet her on her porch in twenty minutes.

"Can you still use the county truck?" he asked.

She nodded. "Sheriff Adams says I can keep it until I get my car back. Guess he's not too mad at me for quitting."

"You still wanting a gallon of wine straight into a vein?"

"Maybe even two gallons," she replied.

"I'll meet you at your place, then. With wine. My treat."

"You'd do that for me?"

"We're friends. That's what friends do at times like this."

En route to Flagg's Market, Wyatt asked himself what the hell he thought he was doing. Being around Erin kept him on edge and filled him with yearnings he shouldn't allow himself to have. But he had agreed to be her friend, and, damn it, she'd just quit her job. He couldn't quite wrap his mind around that. He'd known she was considering a change of profession, but he had expected her to prepare for that before she cut her losses. She had monthly bills, and they wouldn't stop coming just because she had no income. And how could she hope to attend college in Crystal Falls to pursue another career without a job to cover her expenses?

When he pulled into the driveway that led to her cottage, he saw Erin in the wash of the high beams, sitting on the porch. Wyatt's concern for her mounted when she didn't glance up at the sound of his truck. He grabbed the two bottles of wine that lay beside him on the seat and exited the vehicle. When she still didn't look up, he strode to the steps, scaled them in one leap, and went into her house in search of a corkscrew and glasses. He'd never been inside her place. It reminded him of her, with practical furnishings and very few doodads to clutter up surfaces. Even so, it felt homey and looked nice. Of course, his idea of decorating was to put a bootjack by the door, hang his hat on a hook, and thumbtack a calendar to the wall. And now that he had a cell phone, sometimes he didn't bother with the calendar.

Moments later when he joined her on the porch with two glasses of wine, he turned the outside lights on as he crossed the threshold. After handing her a goblet, he sat beside her on the step.

"What in God's name was I thinking?" she asked him. "I just quit my job!"

She was shaky as she took a swallow of the chardonnay, and Wyatt wished he could hear her voice. He had a feeling it would be shrill and tremulous. He chose not to field her question. He knew precisely what she'd been thinking when she turned in her badge, and it was probably a decision long overdue. But she hadn't stopped to think about all the repercussions she would face after she did it.

She suddenly burst into tears. Wyatt couldn't hear her sobs, but he could see every jerk of her slender body. Feeling helpless, he shifted his glass into his left hand and curled his right arm around her shoulders. She pressed her face against his shirt. Each time she spoke, he felt the vibrations, but he couldn't tell what she said.

"Sometimes," he told her, "people make what seem to be snap decisions when they really aren't. They've been thinking about doing something for a long time, then life throws them a curveball, and the next thing they know, they've done it."

She drew back to look up at him. On the surface, Erin was a self-confident woman who had excelled as a law officer. But underneath that no-nonsense layer, she was sensitive and caring in ways that she kept hidden.

"When I became a cop, I believed I could make a big difference in the world. Only I found out right away that I couldn't save even a tiny corner of it. Being a cop in the Seattle area nearly destroyed me. Coming to Mystic Creek gave me a break from the truly awful stuff, but now look what happened to Jen today. Right here in Mystic Creek, where there's supposedly little crime. That is such bullshit. People here live with a false sense of security. It's out there. The evilness and hopelessness is everywhere."

Wyatt reached up to smooth her hair, which had been dented by the brim of her Stetson and come loose from its moorings when she tugged it off and laid it on the porch beside her. He had lived in Mystic Creek for over five years. The crime rate really was pretty low. What had happened to Jenette was an anomaly, perpetrated by a teenage boy who was mentally unstable. He chose not to voice any of those thoughts to Erin. He could tell that she was emotionally exhausted, and it wasn't his place to decide whether or not she should have turned in her badge. If she changed her mind about that in the morning, Sheriff Adams would probably let her go back on duty. Maybe she wasn't a happy cop, but she was a good one.

In the moonlight and shadows cast by the dim porchlight, he struggled to read her lips. She needed to talk, and Wyatt didn't have anywhere to be. Kennedy had texted to tell him he was safe at the ranch and that he'd given Tex his truck keys before he opened a bottle of whiskey. Wyatt didn't mind if his brother drank. He was twenty-two now, and that was his choice to make. Wyatt guessed this was a night when a lot of people felt compelled to drown their sorrows in booze.

Erin rambled as people do when their lives have fallen apart. Wyatt kept her wineglass filled and just listened. She told him about vomiting the first time she saw a gunshot victim. How scared she was when she'd been the one dodging a bullet. How hard it was for her to call Children's Protective Services and just walk away from a little child in need of help.

"It did something to me," she said. "Changed me, somehow."

Wyatt couldn't imagine being a law officer. "I think you made the right decision tonight," he finally said. "When a job is that wrong for a person, maybe it's better to make a quick, clean break." He let her talk. Got her more wine. Over the next two hours, she polished off a full bottle all by herself while Wyatt still hadn't finished his first glass. That was okay. He had drunk himself stupid once or twice, and he understood that sometimes people just needed to tie one on. Erin was no exception, and he knew she wasn't upset only because she'd quit her job. She was a woman, and today she'd seen a girl who had endured one of the worst fates a female could experience.

All of a sudden, Erin stopped talking and pressed a palm to her waist. "I think I'm going to be sick."

Wyatt wasn't surprised. She probably hadn't taken a break that evening to eat, and now she had a bottle of wine sloshing around on an empty stomach. He helped her walk to a flower bed that looked bedraggled and pathetic even in the dark. When she bent over to purge her stomach, she almost pitched forward onto her head. He held her up until the spasms finally passed and then led her into the house, which became a zigzag course because Erin was weaving. Wyatt thought about just picking her up and carrying her. As it was, she led him to the kitchen. He thought maybe the door he'd seen off that room went to her bedroom, but it housed only a guest bathroom.

"Where's your bedroom?" he asked.

She peered owlishly up at him. Normally, her face had a sun-kissed look, but now it was drained of color. "Why? We're only friends, and you stressed the *only*."

Wyatt couldn't help but smile. "I thought you might want to go to bed."

She blinked. "Not with you. Not with anyone, actually."

"I promise not to join you," he assured her. "But I think it's time for you to lie down. Lights out, as the saying goes."

Under her direction, he got her to the bedroom. It was tidy just like the rest of her house. He lowered her to sit on the foot of the bed and rifled through her drawers for a pair of pajamas or a nightgown. All he found were sweatpants and T-shirts. He settled on one of each, led her to the adjoining bathroom, which featured a beautiful garden tub, and got her perched on the toilet seat.

"You think you can manage by yourself?"

"Yup."

Wyatt helped remove her belt, which he thought might be problematic for someone whose fingers were no longer getting the messages from her brain. He left her to figure the rest out by herself and sat on the end of the bed while he waited. He couldn't tell if she was bumping around in the bathroom, and his only reference for the time was his cell phone.

Ten minutes passed, and Wyatt decided maybe she had decided to grab a shower. She'd worked all day. He liked to feel fresh when he hit the sack. Only she still hadn't emerged after five more minutes dragged by. He decided he'd better check on her. To say she was a little drunk would be an understatement. He stepped over to the door and rapped on it. Then he eased it open a crack.

"Erin, are you okay?" *Nothing.* But that was the story of his life. If she'd just cried out that she was bleeding to death, he wouldn't know. Gathering his courage, he stepped into the enclosure, half expecting to find her naked. Instead she still sat on the toilet fully clothed. Well, she'd managed to unbutton her uniform shirt partway down, and he couldn't say she was exactly sitting. She was slumped sideways with her shoulder pressed against the side of the vanity and her chin resting on her chest, which he tried not to look at. "Erin? I thought you were going to get your nightclothes on."

She lifted her head to peer at him from under eyelids at half-mast. "Yup. Only I'm sick again."

Oh, boy. Wyatt stepped over to help her up. Then, holding her upright with one arm, he lifted the commode seat and got her situated on her knees. She propped both arms on the rim of the bowl and hung her head over the water as if the answers to a thousand questions could be found down there. All of a sudden, she snapped erect and only the brace of his hand between her shoulder blades kept her from falling backward.

She turned her face up to him, and he saw that her eyes had opened all the way. "Oh, *God.* I can't puke in there. Toilets are icky. Just the thought makes me sick."

To punctuate that sentence, her body lurched as a wave of nausea struck her. Wyatt grabbed her waste can, which fortunately had a disposable liner, and let her hurl up what remained in her stomach. Then he carried her to the bed and deposited her gently on the mattress, which made her partially unbuttoned shirt gape open. She clutched the front plackets, trying without success to cover herself, but the garment had bunched up behind her back.

"Don't look!"

Wyatt read those two words, but she said more that he couldn't see with her uplifted arms blocking his view. "I'm not looking." That was a lie, but he was trying not to, and that had to count for something. "Just—um—relax."

He didn't want to let her sleep in her clothes, but he needed to get her covered up, not undress her even more. He grabbed a handful of her bedspread and jerked it over her.

"There, honey, you're all covered again."

She hugged the chenille close. "Thank you, Wyatt." He saw her larynx bob, and she grimaced. "Oh, no."

He ran for the bathroom, grabbed the waste receptacle, and made it back to the bed just in time. Afterward, he decided she might need a bucket during the night. "I'll leave the trash can right next to you. Okay?" He saw that her eyes were closed and wasn't sure if she'd heard him. "Erin, look at me. I'm talking to you."

"I'm not deaf, Wyatt. I can hear with my eyes closed."

"Okay. What did I just say?"

"You're leaving the trash can."

"Very good." He couldn't help but smile. "Goodnight, then. Try to sleep it off."

She lifted her lashes as if even that motion took all her concentration. "Thank you. For taking care of me, I mean. I would have slept on the toilet."

Wyatt left her bedroom and scoped out the sofa, which was too short for him. But he'd slept in worse places. He kicked off his boots and sat to text Kennedy. Tell the boss I got held up in town. I'll be on time in the morning. I'm spending the night with a friend.

That made him grin. He hadn't lied. Erin was a friend. He opened the clock function on his phone and set the timer for two hours so he would wake up to check on her. Chances were that she'd be fine, but having been drunk a couple of times himself, he knew how sick a person could get. Unfortunately, he also knew that drunks who woke up still half-lit could do some pretty stupid stuff, like deciding they needed to walk it off and falling into snowbanks. There was no snow on the ground, but Erin's house overlooked the creek. He didn't want her to tumble in and drown.

Grabbing a sofa pillow, he wedged it against the cushioned arm of the couch and lay down. His feet hung out over the end, and his legs might go to sleep. But that was okay as long as the rest of him could grab some shut-eye, too. He slipped the cell into his shirt pocket, confident that the vibration would wake him, and closed his eyes.

Erin woke up before dawn. Her mouth tasted like a science project on a refrigerator shelf, and her head felt twice its normal size. She rolled, sat up, and planted her feet on the floor to keep her balance. *What on earth did I do?* She remembered snatches of last night. Quitting her job. Then Wyatt meeting her here with wine. Wyatt talking with her. But after that, it all got blurry. She staggered to her feet, groaned when she looked in the wastebasket, and made her way into the bathroom, thinking that a shower might clear away the cobwebs in her brain. She stripped off down to her underwear, planning to step under a warm stream of water. But, oh, God, her head hurt. She decided that the sooner she took some ibuprofen, the better. That way, it might start working while she showered.

She was halfway across the living room when she noticed Wyatt sitting on the sofa, his shoulders hunched as he pulled on his boots. She shrieked. He didn't even glance up. She realized that he didn't know she was there. She ran back to her bedroom and slammed the door, one thought pounding inside her aching head. *Thank God he didn't see me.* She stood at the closed door, listening. Pretty soon, she heard him walk outside and close the door behind him. A moment later she heard the rumble of a diesel engine.

Wyatt couldn't get the picture out of his head of Erin wearing only French-cut panties and a skimpy bra. He didn't get why she was so self-conscious about her body, because he thought every inch of her was perfect. Seeing her in the buff might have been even worse, but he doubted it. His imagination was doing a fine job of peeling away what little clothing she'd had on.

Driving to the ranch, he barely noticed the countryside, which was uncommon for him. His brain was stuck on seeing Erin naked. Well, almost naked. And all he could do was pray he didn't remember what she looked like when he was trying to fall asleep at night.

When he parked his truck near the main house, he saw Kennedy hotfooting it across the patchy grass toward him. As he opened his truck door, Kennedy started signing to him in ASL, asking if he knew how Jenette was doing.

Wyatt swung out of the vehicle. "The last I heard, she was still in critical condition. I was hoping to get more updates from Erin, but she quit her job last night."

"She *what?* I thought she planned to work through next winter. What happened to change her mind? She wanted to pay her folks off before quitting."

Wyatt held up his hands. "What happened to Jenette was the straw that broke the camel's back. She's been unhappy with her job for a long while, and this just pushed her over the edge."

Kennedy folded his arms and closed his eyes. "She thinks Jen is going to die, then?"

"I didn't say that. The last I heard, she's still hanging on." Wyatt curled a hand over his brother's shoulder. "Why don't you take the day off and drive to Crystal Falls? Her parents are probably at the hospital in a waiting room. Maybe you can find them, and they'll tell you more. I don't know if anyone at the sheriff's department is being kept in the loop, but if they are, they may not tell us anything because of patient privacy laws."

"But I'm supposed to work. I don't have classes today."

"I'll cover for you. Just go. The boss will understand."

Wyatt watched his brother race to the bunkhouse like the place was on fire and he had the only water bucket. He smiled slightly and shook his head. At twenty-two, Wyatt had still been a virgin, and he had never been in love until now. As difficult as it was for Wyatt to stick to his guns and resist Erin, he was kind of glad of the misery. It helped him to better understand how Kennedy must be feeling. His brother might fall in love a few times before he found his forever lady, and it would be nice to understand the range of emotions he might experience each time.

Wyatt worked all morning, took a break for lunch, and then hit it again. On a ranch, there were always chores, and the two fellows Slade had hired as spring help were still in training. Normally, Wyatt was teaching new guys the ropes when there was still snow in the pastures. Getting married and being blissfully happy for the first time in over forty years had messed with Slade's usual schedule. They weren't technically shorthanded, but right now the new hires still didn't know their asses from holes in the ground.

As a result, Wyatt was tired when he resumed work after lunch. With Kennedy gone, he had to do his brother's chores as well as his own. The spring grass wasn't yet nutrient-rich enough to sustain the herd, so they were still throwing hay. Kennedy often did that, but today it was Wyatt's ball game. He didn't trust the two new guys to do it right. And it was vitally important that the lactating cows got plenty of nourishment. Water troughs also had to be checked, and on a ranch so large, that alone took a couple of hours, because there was often a water leak to fix, and it sometimes took a trained eye to notice something was wrong.

Around two o'clock, judging by the angle of the sun, Wyatt saw Erin's black Honda pull in. He was surprised, because the last time he'd talked to Buck at the Timing Light, he'd been told the car would be out of commission for at least another week. He half expected Erin to walk over in a temper and chew him out for putting the estimate on his credit card. Instead she went straight into the main house. He guessed maybe she'd come to tell her uncle about quitting her job. He figured Slade and Vickie would take it pretty well. Unlike Erin's parents, all they really wanted was for Erin to be happy.

Two hours later, Wyatt was mucking out stalls when he saw Erin finally emerge from the house. She made a beeline for him. He leaned on the pitchfork handle and struggled not to smile. She had *hangover* written all over her. When she drew close, he said, "Looks to me like you need some hair of the dog."

She rolled her pretty blue eyes. "I've sworn off wine forever, amen. First, let me say thank you for paying the repair costs on my car."

"You're welcome."

"Second, you can start holding a portion of my wages back to pay for my half."

Wyatt thought for a moment that he'd misread her lips. "Come again?"

"You read it right. I asked Uncle Slade for a job, and he gave me one. That makes you my boss now, I think. He sent me out here so you can get me lined out."

Wyatt could have groaned. A picture of her in sexy underwear flashed through his head, and the first question that entered his mind was where in the hell she was going to sleep. The bunkhouse wasn't set up for unisex use. There wasn't a privacy screen in the whole place, and except for a spare toilet for emergency use, he and the other men shared a full bathroom.

"You don't look overjoyed to hear that I'll be working under you."

Wyatt wouldn't have minded her working *under* him. Scratch that. He couldn't allow himself to think about things like that. He realized he was scowling and made a herculean effort to relax his forehead. "I'm sorry. I have to admit I'm taken by surprise. I never got the impression that you even *like* horses and cows."

"I like them. From a distance. And, um, I kind of left one part out. Uncle Slade left the final decision to you. About hiring me, I mean."

Wyatt was relieved to hear that. But a fat lot of good it did him. If he nixed the idea, he'd be the Shithead of the Year. Definitely in Erin's eyes, and his boss might not like it all that much, either. "Erin, you can't admire the horses and cows from a distance. You'll be up close and personal with them a dozen times a day, and even well-trained horses and docile cattle can be dangerous." That wasn't a stretch of the truth; it was fact. He didn't want to scare her, but he didn't want her to get hurt, either. "You know next to nothing about livestock."

She looked away and swallowed hard. He had a bad feeling she was battling tears. When she faced him again, two bright spots of color dotted her cheeks. "I need a job, Wyatt. Sheriff Adams called me this morning to tell me I can have my position back, and he even suggested that I take a short, paid vacation before I make a final decision." She swallowed again. "But I'm done. Law enforcement is slowly killing me on the inside, where no one can see."

After talking with her last night, Wyatt figured he understood that better than most people. "I guess it can't hurt to give you a fair shot," he finally said.

She closed her eyes for a moment. Upon lifting her lashes, she said, "Thank you. I promise to work harder than anyone else on the ranch. You won't regret taking a chance on me."

Wyatt already regretted it, but his reasons had nothing to do with Erin's future performance. He just wasn't sure how he would handle being around her all the time. "Where will you sleep? I don't mean to sound sexist, but the bunkhouse is no place for a lady."

"Aunt Vickie says I can have the whole upstairs to myself now that Brody and his family have moved into their own house."

Wyatt nodded. "Okay. Well, that's good."

"You're not happy about this. I can tell. Is it because you're afraid I can't do the work?"

"No, absolutely not. Ranching is hard labor, but a woman can do it as well as a man. This just came as a surprise to me. The first time I met you, you weren't exactly another Calamity Jane. More like just a calamity."

She finally smiled. "A-hole."

He laughed. "Well, you were a calamity, the way I saw it. Making me cut the twine on expensive, certified weed-free hay. Refusing to believe I was deaf. Trying to walk back to the trailhead barefoot. You were awful."

"And you were as well. You didn't like me at first sight. You felt that I'd been neglecting my uncle and didn't love him."

"Guilty as charged." Wyatt picked up the pitchfork and rammed the tines back into the dirt. "I was wrong about all that. But you were wrong about me, too."

Her cheek dimpled in a grin. "I'm glad I was."

Wyatt really, *really* wished she wouldn't smile at him like that. It made him feel like he'd just lassoed the moon for her or something. "I'm glad I was wrong, too. Even though Brody is here now, and Slade's got plenty of family to love, he still holds you in high regard. He'll enjoy having you at the ranch."

And wasn't that just the problem? Wyatt knew he was between a rock and a hard spot about hiring Erin. He'd be damned if he did and damned if he didn't.

CHAPTER ELEVEN

Seemingly oblivious to Wyatt's turmoil, Erin squinted against the sunlight. "So," she said. "Where do I start?"

Again, Wyatt couldn't help but smile. "You can't learn all there is to know in five minutes. But if you'll wait while I finish cleaning stalls, I'll give you a tour."

"I've seen it all before."

"Yes, but as a visitor, not a hired hand."

"Okay," she said. "I'm game."

When Wyatt turned to go back into the barn, she followed him. "Do you have another pitchfork?" She leaned around his arm to look up at him so he could read her lips. "I'd like to help."

Wyatt jabbed a thumb at where another implement hung on the wall, and the next thing he knew, she was in the next stall, throwing manure mixed with straw into a pile in the alley. She had apparently overlooked the fact that he was throwing stuff into the uplifted skidder bucket, which made waste removal a one-throw job. He was pleased by her willingness to work up a sweat, though, especially since he knew her head probably ached, but he also grew concerned, because she was pitching hay faster than he was. To last at ranch work, a person had to pace himself.

He stepped out into the alley. "Whoa! This isn't a race."

She gave him a startled look. "Okay. Trust me when I say that I can work as hard and as fast as any man."

"When you see me busting my ass to be quick, you can. That'll mean something has to be done fast or all hell will rain on our heads. But otherwise pace yourself. Okay?"

She nodded. "Whatever you say, boss."

"I'm your foreman. *Boss* is a title reserved for Slade."

She shrugged. "Okay. What'll I call you, then?"

"*Wyatt* will do. And you aren't supposed to pitch that shit into a pile. It goes in the skidder bucket, the way I'm doing it. Now you'll have to fork it twice. Get it in the bucket. When it's full, we'll run it out to the compost pile, dump it, and then come back for more."

Erin couldn't help but feel excited as she climbed into one of the side-by-sides to take a tour of the ranch with Wyatt. She was actually going to work here, and she couldn't wait to start. Domino almost jumped up to go with them, but he saw Pistol and Four Toes off in the trees and ran to play with them instead.

As they set off, Wyatt hit a rut, and she grabbed a bar of the roll cage. "You okay?" he asked. "Nobody here has been killed in one of these yet."

"I've driven in high-speed chases when I was in training at the academy. Trust me, vehicles don't scare me."

Ten seconds later, she almost wet her pants when the side-by-side hit mud and nearly flipped end over end. Erin was thrown forward. Wyatt let loose with a string of curse words, many of them mispronounced, which was a first.

"Water main leak!" he said. "I told the new hired hands to watch for soggy ground. These pastures are always well drained unless there's a line leaking. It happens all the time." He jumped out of the vehicle and immediately sank into muck almost to mid-shin. He didn't seem to mind mud oozing over into his boots. He grabbed a shovel from the back cargo area. "Come on. If you're going to be a ranch hand, you may as well get friendly with mud."

Erin hoped if she climbed out of the side-by-side and stepped lightly, she wouldn't sink. No such luck. Only unlike Wyatt, she sank almost to her knees. "Oh, God!"

He flashed her a grin that displayed beautiful, white teeth. "Sure you want to work here? Leaks are always muddy. Normally not this bad. I let the new hires check the water troughs this morning, and they must have ignored the soggy ground. When a main line is leaking and left to spew water, it gets bad fast."

Erin held on to the closed door of the vehicle to pry one foot loose from the muck. She wore her commando boots, and it felt as if she had toilet plungers on her feet. A loud sucking sound came from the mud, and bubbles rose to the surface. She watched Wyatt trudge over to an aluminum pipe. She struck off after him. A couple of times, she almost fell. But using all her strength, she managed to reach higher ground and better footing. Then the work began, and Erin became well acquainted with mud.

Two hours later, they had replaced a section of main line, which was large-diameter pipe and heavy to work with. Erin didn't know if she could have done the job by herself, and the thought frightened her. If she couldn't carry her weight at the ranch, she couldn't keep the job, even though her uncle might make exceptions for her. That wouldn't be fair to the other employees.

When she and Wyatt got back into the side-by-side to resume touring the ranch, Wyatt started the engine and smiled at her. "Good job. You were there whenever I needed you. If you ever come across a broken main line when you're out alone, call for help. It requires two people."

Erin wondered whether he was telling the truth or felt she was incapable of doing the job alone. She had little time to worry about that, though. As Wyatt drove her around the ranch, she learned so much she wished she could take notes. One field, which Wyatt called the east pasture, was especially important. It was an area for pregnant cows due to calve late. He explained that Slade's old-school philosophies on impregnating the cows made it difficult to prevent late births.

Erin gazed out at the bovines. "So these cows didn't take when they were supposed to?"

"Exactly."

"Maybe Uncle Slade should consider a March calving season so cows covered during the second bull turnout don't have their babies so late."

He flashed her a grin that made her belly go warm and tingly. "There you go. You're thinking like a rancher."

She returned her attention to the cows, which all looked as if they'd swallowed ginormous bowling balls. "So what do you look for when you're checking these ladies?"

Wyatt crawled out of the vehicle and motioned for her to follow him. When they reached the fence, the cows moved closer. "They think I may feed them, which makes this part easier. A cow's vaginal ligaments loosen up twelve to twenty-four hours prior to giving birth, and her vulva will look swollen and possibly wet with mucus. When we see that, we move her to a calving area and start checking her every couple of hours."

It felt weird to stand beside a man to whom she was wildly attracted and listen to him talk about female body parts. She collected her wayward thoughts.

Just then, Tex rode up on a quad to join them. Erin enjoyed Tex. She could never guess what he might say or do next. He swung off the green four-wheeler as if he were dismounting from a horse, and as he walked toward them, his legs were bowed so badly that it looked as if he had an invisible exercise ball clutched between his knees. He slapped at the legs of his Wrangler jeans and reached up to tug on the grimy bill of his ball cap.

"You showin' this pretty gal all our pregnant ladies?" he asked Wyatt.

Wyatt turned from the fence and smiled. He didn't respond to Tex's question, which told Erin he didn't realize that Tex had asked him anything. She chose to answer for him. "I'm getting a crash course in cattle ranching."

The old Texan flashed her a toothy grin, which creased his weather-worn face with so many lines it resembled a crumpled, brown paper bag. "Yep. I already heard you got hired on. That's why I came out. This young pup thinks he knows ever'thing about calvin', but I got a lot more knowledge stored in my brain than he does."

Erin glanced at Wyatt to see that he was now watching Tex's lips. She wondered how he felt about being called a pup. Wyatt only smiled as Tex took over Erin's indoctrination, essentially telling her most of the same things Wyatt just had, only with his own brand of charm. Pregnant cows were apparently one of his favorite topics.

"The surest sign that a cow's about to drop her calf is when her udder gets swoled up with cholesterol, honey. Wyatt thinks the most sure-fire way is to check her Volvo, but that ain't always an accurate sign."

Erin bit back a grin. She translated Tex's explanation to mean that a cow's udder might look swollen with colostrum shortly before she gave birth, and obviously Tex had mispronounced the word *vulva*. Otherwise Erin would have been peering at a cow's behind, looking for a car. Nevertheless, she would never discount anything Tex told her. He was older and had a lot of experience under his belt.

"That ain't to say that the Volvo ain't important to watch," he went on. "When you see one slickin' up, don't ignore it, no how, no way, cuz some-times the dang cholesterol don't come down until after a calf is born."

Wyatt turned away and began fiddling with a loose fencing wire. Erin suspected he needed something to do to keep from laughing. Tex had his own way of training a new hire, and Erin learned the hard way that he could be long-winded if he thought of a story to tell. As he began to wear down, he leveled a gnarly forefinger at Erin's chest.

"And mind my words, girl. Always carry a cell phone when ye're out in the field. As much as I hate them damn gadgets, you'll need one if you find a cow with a baby comin' out back-asswards. The cow and calf can both die if you don't act fast, and Slade gets a mite upset when that happens."

"I can just imagine," Erin replied. "That's a double whammy on the pocketbook."

"Exac'ly," Tex agreed. "I heard ye're gonna be sleepin' at the main house. I sure hope that don't mean you won't be eatin' supper with us fellas."

Erin hadn't even unpacked yet. She hadn't had time to think about where she would take her meals. Brody and his family were in the process of moving into the new home that had been built for them on the property. They'd already gotten their beds set up, but they hadn't yet gotten the kitchen organized and were still taking their evening meals with Vickie and Slade.

"Is it important that I eat dinner with you?" she asked the old man.

"Not dinner, darlin'. Fer the midday meal, we eat at all different times. That ain't the case at supper. Ever'body is at the table. We all go over our day, and a lot of important information is kicked back and forth. You won't know half of what's happenin' on the ranch if you ain't eatin' supper with us."

Erin tapped her temple. "Note taken. I'll talk with Uncle Slade about it."

"He'll understand the need. Back afore Vickie came along, he ate supper with us in the bunkhouse a lot to keep on top of things."

It didn't sound like stimulating dinner conversation, but Erin took Tex's advice to heart, and she would speak to her uncle as soon as possible about taking her evening meal with her coworkers. To be accepted as one of the crew, she should eat whatever they did and take her turns cooking and cleaning up the kitchen, anyway.

When she and Wyatt got back to the horse barn, Kennedy came out of the stable area to greet them. Though he smiled in welcome, his face looked drawn and a little pale. When Wyatt asked about Jenette's condition, the younger man said, "She's still hangin' on. It's touch-and-go. They gave her transfusions, but they can't get her blood pressure back up. They're running tests tonight to see if she's still bleeding somewhere internally."

Wyatt squeezed his brother's shoulder. "I'm sorry to hear that."

Kennedy shrugged. "She's alive. There's hope. But her folks are going through hell."

Erin guessed they weren't alone. Kennedy was worried about the girl, too. That touched her heart. "I'm sorry she hasn't rallied yet."

"She will. She's got to. Otherwise Sorensen wins."

Erin bent her head, once again feeling a wave of frustration wash through her. She might be an old woman before she stopped feeling partially responsible for what had happened to Jenette.

"Okay," Wyatt said. "Time's flying. Let's hit it." He turned to Erin. "You can tidy up the horse paddocks. Same method as we used in the barn. Fork the manure into the skidder bucket and take it out to the compost pile. Make sure you latch the gates as you go in and out. When a horse gets loose on this ranch, it can run a country mile before we get mounts saddled up to catch it."

Kennedy asked, "What should I do?"

"If you can spare the time from studying, you can help Erin. Then crack open the books."

"Okay. I can do that," Kennedy said.

Erin was relieved to know Kennedy meant to stay with her. She prided herself on her expertise with vehicles, but she'd never handled ranch equipment.

An hour later, Erin decided that ranching wasn't for sissies. She'd never worked so hard. Her back, butt, and legs hurt. Blisters had also popped up on her hands. She consoled herself with the thought that she was working her muscles in a different way than she usually did. Another bright spot was that this kind of labor would probably eliminate the need for her gym membership. She could probably even quit running and doing planks every morning.

Kennedy noticed her hands. "Damn it, you've got blisters."

He disappeared while Erin continued wielding the pitchfork. When he returned, he handed her a pair of oversize leather gloves. "Wear protection from now on. Slade is paranoid about blisters. On a ranch, they get infected. Visits to the ER for work-related injuries jack up his insurance rates. I have student coverage now, which is cheaper, but he still raises hell if he sees me working without gloves."

After finishing the paddocks, Erin had just enough time to grab a shower and talk with Uncle Slade before she walked over to the bunkhouse. Her back and butt were killing her, but she pasted on a smile as she entered the building and then promptly forgot her aches and pains. She'd never seen four men milling around in a kitchen. It was apparently Wyatt's night to cook, because he stood at the stove while the other men repeatedly bumped into each other trying to unload the dishwasher.

"That dad-blasted machine don't work!" Tex complained. "This pot ain't clean!"

"That's because it wasn't scrubbed out before it was put in the rack," Kennedy retorted. "You're the only one who doesn't prewash, so it's probably your fault."

"I'll be damned," Tex blustered. "Don't make no sense at all to wash dishes twice. Like I don't got better things to do?"

"Now you have to wash it twice anyway," Kennedy pointed out.

"It'll be snowin' in hell when you see me washin' anything twice! It's sterile. You told me that's why we have to use that newfangled contraption, cuz it gets rid of all the germs."

"I don't want to eat dried-up old food!" Kennedy protested. "That pot is nasty. You have to wash it."

"You been sniffin' after that girl so much that you ain't been here for supper half the time, anyhow!"

Tex held the pot as if he were thinking about bonking Kennedy over the head with it, and Erin began to feel nervous. She glanced at Wyatt, wondering why he didn't intervene before an actual fight erupted. He seemed unconcerned about the commotion. Then she remembered he couldn't hear, and the combatants were behind him. No wonder he always seemed so calm and unruffled. He missed out on a lot of the unpleasant stuff.

Erin stepped forward. "I'll wash the pot."

For a moment, she half expected Tex to bonk *her.* "Ain't nobody gonna wash this here pot twice!" he bellowed. "It's nothin' but dad-blamed foolishness to go washin' stuff twice when we know it's sterile."

Thinking quickly, Erin said, "Sterile or not, that is organic matter in the pot, and there's nothing to say it won't become contaminated sitting on a shelf. Have you ever had food poisoning?"

He lifted the lower plate of his dentures with his tongue and then sucked it back down over his gums, making a clicking noise. "Yes, missy,

I have. You don't eat buckboard food fer over fifty years without gettin' the heaves and shits a few times."

"Do you want to get food poisoning again?" Erin asked.

"No, I sure don't."

She reached out and wrested the pot handle from his gnarly hand. "In that case, I'll wash it, and this quarrel will be over."

"We ain't quarrelin'," he protested. "We're just discussin'."

Kennedy slipped past Erin to grab more plates from the dishwasher. As he turned to put them in a cupboard, he waggled his golden eyebrows at Erin. "Welcome to suppertime at the O.K. Corral."

Erin hid a smile as she stepped over to the double-wide sink to scrub the pot. Kennedy was right; the inside was nasty. She couldn't believe Tex had been about to stick it in a cupboard.

Wyatt noticed her standing beside him and turned his laser-blue gaze on her. "Slade must have said it's okay for you to eat with us."

She nodded.

"Good. That gives us one more cook and dishwasher, taking us up to six. It suits me fine to cook only once a week. Before you leave, get your name on the duty list. We rotate."

Erin was mildly miffed that Wyatt hadn't welcomed her, but she quickly forgot about that when another quarrel broke out between the two new hires, whom she hadn't met. One of them was folding his laundered clothes on what she presumed was his cot when the other newbie yelled from the kitchen, "Damn it, Wade. You stole my wool socks!"

"I did not! I only borrowed 'em."

"You boys hush it," Tex yelled. "We got a lady on the crew now, and she don't cotton to boisterosity! We gotta start mindin' our manners, goddammit!"

Wade threw the wool socks at his coworker, nailing him on the chest. "There. Keep your stupid socks. I just ran out of clean ones, is all."

And so Erin's first meal in the bunkhouse began. Wyatt had cooked a huge pot of hamburger gravy and two baking sheets full of biscuits. When the food made it to the table, Erin noticed there wasn't a vegetable in sight. She stood behind her chair because all the men did, and she was mildly startled when Wyatt bent his head and folded his hands.

"Dear Lord, please bless this food."

Tex inserted, "And don't let none of us get food poison, if you please."

Kennedy piped in with, "From your bounty, we are nourished. Thank you, Lord."

The two new hires mumbled something Erin couldn't catch, and then it was her turn. She hadn't been raised saying a meal blessing and drew a complete blank. She came up with, "Thank you, Lord, for good company and plenty of food for each of us." In actuality, she wanted to pray that the next supper might include a salad and broccoli. If she had to eat this way for any period of time, she'd get as big as a barn.

"Amen," all the men chorused, and then Tex said, "Three beans fer four of us. Thank God there ain't no more of us. Lay back yer ears and dig in."

And to Erin's amazement, that's exactly what they did. The huge pot was nearly empty before she could blink. By the time she got ahold of the metal spoon handle to serve herself a portion, the men were already shoveling food into their mouths. She deposited a tidy mound of hamburger gravy on her plate and reached for a biscuit, which she planned to eat separately.

Tex relieved her of that notion. "That ain't how you eat shit on shingles. First you butter your biscuit. Then you pile the gravy on top."

Erin froze with a forkful of meat halfway to her mouth. Wyatt spoke up and said, "Tex, let Erin eat her food however she likes. It's none of your concern."

"But it don't taste as good thataway!" Tex objected.

Erin cleared her throat. "I'm not big on butter, Tex."

"You ain't?"

"No, I'm not. It's fattening, and too much of it is bad for the heart."

"Well, I'll be." Tex looked mystified. "I'm skinny as a fence rail, and I been eatin' near on a cube a day most of my life. And so far as I know, my ticker must be well greased, cuz it keeps on goin', kind of like that rabbit in them TV commercials."

Erin took a bite of meat gravy, which was surprisingly good. As she chewed, she realized all five men were staring at her, and she wondered if she had gravy on her chin. There were no napkins on the table. Kennedy said, "We're still hungry. We're just wondering if you'd like more. You haven't taken your share yet."

"Oh!" Erin swallowed. "Please, help yourselves. This will be plenty for me."

Wyatt stood up, grabbed the pot, and began slopping equal measures of gravy on every man's second helping of already-buttered biscuits, including his own. Then he sat down and began eating again. Erin decided Wyatt was like a father figure who rode herd over a bunch of ill-mannered kids.

The other men carried on an animated conversation about their days, mentioning things that baffled her. What did it mean when a certain horse had a hitch in its get-along? That it was lame, possibly? Then Wyatt filled everyone in on the leaking water main; leveled an uncompromising stare at Wade and Richard, the newbies; and told them the next time they ignored soggy ground, they'd be collecting their last paychecks.

"Erin and I worked our asses off out there in mud up to our knees," he added. "When you throw hay, watch for leaks. It's a very simple thing, and it's part of your job."

Tex said, "Number one-sixty-four is cakin' up. I dosed her with antibiotics and put balm on her udder, but it's not lookin' good."

"Do I need to call the vet?" Wyatt asked.

"Not till mornin', when I take another look. Might be the medicine will lessen the swellin'. I'll let you know, cuz we sure as hell don't want her udder to rupture."

Wyatt nodded. Erin felt mildly nauseated.

Kennedy opened one of his college textbooks at the table. Only glancing at his food, he shoveled it into his mouth as he read. The other men didn't seem to mind, and Tex gave his blessing by saying to Erin, "Kennedy's gonna get himself a dee-gree. Not a man amongst us that's got one. We're right proud of him for workin' so hard to get smart."

When the meal was finished, the men carried their plates to the sink and then raided the cupboards for what Tex called "dee-zert." A general complaint arose about Wyatt's failure to go shopping to keep the snack shelf full, but they settled for peanut butter and jelly sandwiches, most of them making two. After they consumed their after-meal sweets, Tex got up to start doing dishes. Erin went over to help. Kennedy resumed reading his book at the table and texting someone on his phone. Wade and Richard sprawled on a well-used leather sofa to watch television with the volume up so loud that it hurt her ears. Wyatt left the bunk-house, and Erin couldn't quite blame him. The place was worse than a frat house.

Erin soon elbowed Tex away from the sink and let him load the dishes into the machine. Kennedy was right. The old man didn't scrub anything, and she didn't want to eat food cooked in dirty pans or served on crusty plates.

By the time she left the bunkhouse, she was exhausted in a way she hadn't been in years. Preparing for the Ironman had been brutal, so she reasoned that if she had grown accustomed to those workouts, she would certainly grow inured to the demands of ranch work.

Twilight had descended when Erin struck off for the main house. As she walked, mentally bellyaching about how sore she was, she glimpsed movement off to her right and saw Wyatt standing at one of the corral fences. She detoured toward him, appreciating how good he looked in a relaxed pose, his arms resting on the top rail and one hip jutting for-ward, his opposite leg extended slightly behind him. He was every inch a cowboy, and after working with him that afternoon, she knew he wasn't a pretender who strutted around dressed for the part. He'd earned every one of those steely muscles that bulged beneath his shirt.

When she stepped up beside him, he jerked. "Sorry," she said. "I didn't mean to startle you."

He relaxed and went back to studying the horse that pranced rather frenetically inside the enclosure. "You're the only person ever who can sneak up on me like that."

He'd said as much to Erin before, and she still didn't get how that could be. When he looked down at her, she said, "Other people must startle you. You can't hear anyone approach."

"No, but I feel them getting close to me. Same goes for animals."

She gave him a wondering study. "You *feel* them? How can that be?"

"Beats me. I only know I can."

Erin believed him. As far as she knew, he wasn't given to lying. "That's amazing."

He shrugged. "It started when I was a little tyke. My grandpa overruled my mother and made me work with horses every day. At first I didn't want to. I was frightened of them. Even more frightened than you are, because they're dangerous animals if you aren't careful around them, and not being able to hear put me at a disadvantage." He glanced back at the horse before returning his attention to her face. "But my grandpa was right to insist on me doing chores out there. Somehow I developed my own fifth sense and knew when a horse was invading my space. Once I got over being scared, having to work with the horses became my favorite thing in the world. They didn't care if I couldn't hear. They didn't care if I could talk. They just accepted me as I was. For me, that was wonderful."

A lump rose in Erin's throat. Wyatt had just shared something with her that came straight from his heart. "And you still love horses to this day."

"I do. Don't get me wrong. I'm cautious around them. You never know when one might swing its head and knock you flat or kick out from behind. It's not because they're mean. They're just big. When a fly lands on them, they'll swing their heads or kick at their bellies. If another horse gets too close, they'll nail it with a hard kick. And you never know when that might happen. If you're in the way, you could end up with a broken femur or even worse. Getting kicked in the head is no small thing, either."

Erin realized this wasn't idle conversation. He was imparting knowledge to her that he felt was important for her to know. "I'll try to be very careful."

"Do that, because you're Slade's niece, and he loves you. If you get hurt, I'll feel like you do right now about Jenette. Like I didn't warn you enough or teach you what you needed to know in order to stay safe. And unfortunately, I can't cover all that in one afternoon."

"Okay. I'm warned. And when you have time to tell me this or that, I'll be a sponge, absorbing all the information."

He smiled slightly. "Just don't get stubborn on me, and you should be all right."

Erin released a tight breath. "I didn't come out to get a lecture on safety, although I appreciate you giving me one."

"Why did you come out here, then?"

"To ask how you think I did today. Honest answer, please."

"You did fine, but the true test will come tomorrow and the next day. If you can still walk in the morning, I'll give you an A for your performance today."

Erin had never heard anything quite so ridiculous. "I'm not a hothouse orchid. I can work as hard and as efficiently as any man you put me up against."

"Whoa. I'm not putting you up against anyone. Get that kind of thinking straight out of your head. I know you pushed yourself too hard today, and that isn't necessary. Ranching isn't a male-dominated field. It never has been. Women have been ranchers as far back as the eighteen hundreds. Probably hundreds of years before that in other countries. They're just as capable as men, but they do have a few physical limitations that men aren't as likely to have."

Erin wanted to tell him that she would show him some physical limitations, but she wouldn't be the one who had them.

"You aren't hearing me," he said softly. "I see that prideful, defiant look in your eyes. Lose it. There's no place for it on this ranch."

She straightened away from the fence and struggled to get rid of the look on her face that he found objectionable. She needed this job. As of last night, she'd said farewell to her career in law enforcement and had no other means of earning money. She'd thought about getting a food-service job, but she feared she'd be lousy at it. If Wyatt sent her packing, she didn't know what she would do.

His mouth quirked up at one corner, which made him look boyish. Only she knew that was deceptive. Wyatt was a hard, unbending man just like her uncle. He'd had to be. At the same time, he seemed to have a good heart. It was an attractive combination.

"You need to slow down," he continued in that same, soft voice. "Pay attention to your body. This isn't the controlled environment of a gym. When you lift weights there, the bars are evenly balanced and you assume a certain stance that protects your skeletal structure and muscles. Out here, you can get hurt in a nanosecond if you try to lift something you shouldn't. Most of it is awkward, dead weight, and just one wrong twist of your hips can injure your back."

"I'll be careful."

"If something is too heavy, get creative with the skidder to move it. We're not in competition with one another. Steady and slow wins every race. All that matters at the end of a day is that the important work is done, and I stress the word *important*. On a ranch, you learn to prioritize. Unexpected work that's important will crop up late in the day, and even if you've paced yourself, you can end up so exhausted you can barely lift your feet. Get the important stuff done as early as you can and then pace yourself as you do other things. At quitting time, the important things are that the animals are safe, fed, and watered. During the growing season, the irrigation schedule is also a top priority. Back off and slow down. A rancher who hurries is a rancher who gets injured."

Erin had never been able to slow down and back off. All her life, she had pushed herself to be as good as, or better than, any man. To impress everyone with her strength, her musculature, and her endurance. Through her sessions with Jonas, she was trying to rid herself of masculine mannerisms, but she couldn't picture herself becoming a limp-wristed sissy like Wyatt was describing. She preferred to be more like Vickie, who wasn't afraid to say she was one hell of a woman and then set out to prove it.

"Thank you for the advice. I'll bear in mind everything you've said as I'm working tomorrow."

His eyes darkened to a steely blue, and his facial muscles tightened. "See that you do. I know you need this job, and I don't want to be put in a position where I'm forced to fire you because you refuse to listen."

Erin was steaming as she walked away. She'd done *fine*? No praise for working her tail off. No recognition for blistering her hands so badly they would probably take two weeks to heal. Instead of a pat on the back for a job well done, he'd lectured her and threatened to fire her. Well, she'd show him. Maybe she'd become the best ranch hand on her uncle's payroll and be promoted to foreman. Wyatt Fitzgerald could take his condescending attitude toward women with him when he crawled home to his grandfather's ranch in Klamath Falls.

CHAPTER TWELVE

When Erin entered the main house, she heard her aunt and uncle talking in the kitchen and she decided she should at least tell them goodnight. As she stepped through the archway, she saw them sitting at the table, both leaning forward with their arms braced on its surface, their faces animated and bearing smiles. In that moment, she envied them, but she quickly shoved that feeling away. The two of them had lived nearly their whole lives separated from each other. They deserved to finally be happy, and if Erin was lucky, maybe she would find true love herself someday.

"Just dropping in to say goodnight. I hope you guys had a great evening with Brody and his family."

In the light, Vickie's curly hair glinted like a copper penny, and her green eyes danced with laughter. "We had a wonderful dinner and wanted them to stay for Yahtzee, but the kids had homework to do."

Slade met Erin's gaze. "We didn't get to talk much earlier. After getting a taste of ranch work, are you still thinking it may be right for you?"

Erin had worked too hard to think overmuch about what was right for her, and in the overall scheme of things, she didn't have a lot of choices, anyway. She had bills to pay. "I learned so much today that I didn't spare much thought for anything else. Ask me again tomorrow night, and I may have more to tell you."

Slade raked a hand through his hair, which was still a dark brown, but was now threaded with silver, particularly at the temples. "Vickie says you're staying in the front upstairs bedroom with the adjoining bath. If there's anything you need, don't hesitate to let us know. We hope you'll be comfortable up there."

"It's perfect. From the window, I have a great view of the ranch and the mountains as well."

"Vickie puts out breakfast stuff early in the morning. She doesn't cook until later. Come down and help yourself to some start-up fuel before you head out to work."

"I'll do that, and thank you both again for opening your home to me."

After bidding them goodnight, Erin started up the stairs, holding the handrail and wincing with every step.

E rin awakened the next morning to butter-yellow sunlight pouring through the windows of her room. The morning songs of birds outside in the surrounding pine trees created muted but beautiful music. She smiled against the crisp pillowcase and breathed in the scent of fresh mountain air emanating from the cotton. Vickie liked to line dry her laundry when the weather allowed.

Erin could tell by the light that it was still early, and no one had told her yesterday what time her day would start, so she couldn't really be late. She decided to stay in bed for a few minutes to relish the wonderful warmth of the down comforter. She'd fallen asleep in this position and didn't think she'd moved all night.

She started to turn over onto her back, and an involuntary whimper of pain erupted from her throat. *Oh, God.* Every part of her body screamed. She lay perfectly still for a moment, remembering Wyatt's lecture. Maybe he knew what he was talking about. *Scratch that.* He'd been condescending, and all her romantic notions about him, sexual or otherwise, had crash-landed inside her heart and formed a knot of disappointment. She'd believed he was about as perfect as a guy could get. When would she learn that nobody was perfect? Especially not guys. After growing up around her father, she should know that.

Her personal feelings and change of heart about Wyatt had no bearing on her present situation, though. She needed to figure out how she could get out of bed. Clenching her teeth against the knifelike torture of moving her legs and arms, she rolled onto her side and inched her feet toward the side of the mattress. Her plan was to sit up with her feet on the floor, all in one smooth motion, using her weight for momentum. Only just as she tried that and cried out again, Vickie cracked open the door.

"Good morning! I brought—" Balancing a tray on the bend of one arm, she stepped fully into the room, her green eyes going wide with alarm. "Oh, honey. You overdid it yesterday, didn't you?" She set the tray atop the dresser. "You stay right there. I've been through this and know exactly what to do. Be right back!"

Erin lay helplessly on her side with tears welling in her eyes. She had *not* overdone it. How could she have? She was in peak physical condition. Could she be sick? Viruses sometimes made people hurt all over.

Vickie burst back into the room. This morning she wore a gray-and-black plaid shirt and jeans. She looked younger than her years and cute as a button. Holding up a bottle, she said, "Horse liniment. When I get sore, this saves me every time."

Erin just lay there. "I've never gotten sore from doing any kind of work."

Vickie laughed. "Well, honey, I think you're unaccustomed to ranch work. You use muscles you don't even know you have."

She set the bottle on the nightstand, jerked back the down comforter and sheet, and then grabbed the ankles of Erin's sweatpants and tugged them off her with one hard pull. "Roll over. I'll get the backs of your legs first."

Erin moaned and almost couldn't roll over without screaming. Nonsensical as it was, she was glad she'd worn panties under the sweats. At least she wasn't bare-butt naked. Vickie sat beside her and began massaging the liniment into the backs of Erin's legs from the edge of her underwear down to her ankles.

"Crap. It burns!"

"Yeah, well, as it absorbs in, it's the best burn you've ever felt," Vickie said. "It does wonders. I've worked alongside men a lot, and I've been so sore a few times that I couldn't move without crying. I know you work out and run. Probably do daily biceps and triceps exercises with weights, heaps of squats, and all that. But at the business end of a pitchfork, you're pushing, lifting, and throwing weight from different angles, sometimes even sideways. Trust me, you're using your muscles differently."

Wyatt had said almost the same thing, and Erin hadn't believed him. Now she did. But that sure didn't mean she would cry uncle and act like a baby about it. It wasn't in her makeup to give up. She would work as fast and as effectively as any man on the payroll, or she'd die trying.

When Vickie had applied liniment to every part of Erin's body except her butt and chest, she drew the covers back over her. "There. Prop some pillows behind your back, honey, and sit up. Stay covered. Let those muscles simmer in the warmth while you're having breakfast. I guarantee you'll feel fifty percent better by the time you get dressed."

The smell of wintergreen was so strong Erin wasn't sure she could stomach any food, but she struggled to a sitting position, leaned back against her pillows, and managed a halfhearted smile as Vickie placed the breakfast tray over her lap.

"Go ahead and pour your coffee," Vickie told her. "I'll wash my hands."

After Vickie disappeared into the adjoining bath, it was all Erin could do to lift the coffee carafe, and her aching arm shook as she poured. When Vickie reappeared, she sighed and shook her head. "I know it's bad right now, but after you've eaten, you can get up and do some stretches and squats. You'll still be sore as the devil, but you shouldn't be incapacitated."

Erin hoped Vickie was correct, because she needed to hit it hard again today. She would not be considered a second-rate worker simply because she was a woman.

Vickie sat on the edge of the bed and lifted her mug of coffee. "Raised by a rancher and hunting guide, I grew up determined to be as good as any man at everything, only in addition to being a female, I was also a tiny one. My parrot mouth overloaded my parakeet ass more times than I can count. I think that's how I got Slade to notice me, way back when. He was always taking up for me when my sassy mouth got me into fixes."

Erin put a cinnamon roll onto one of the plates and settled back against the pillows to enjoy it. "If I continue to eat all this fattening stuff, I'll gain thirty pounds in a blink. Last night, Wyatt fixed hamburger gravy and served it over hot, buttered biscuits."

"Oh, shit on shingles! I haven't had that in ages." Vickie chuckled and shook her head. "Working on a ranch, you'll burn off all the calories and no longer worry about your weight. If you can loosen up your sore muscles enough to work today, that is, and every other day ahead."

"It's true that you aren't a very big person. How on earth did you manage to keep up with all the men when you were younger?"

"The same way I do now, by working smarter instead of harder," Vickie replied. "When you're mucking out stalls, you should lift less weight with each swing of the shovel or fork. When you have to lift stuff, you should use leverage to protect your back or figure out a way to lift things with the skidder bucket. Bottom line, a woman doesn't need to be as strong as a man on a ranch, but she does need to work smart."

In other words, Erin thought, *I'm supposed to wimp out simply because I don't have the same equipment behind the fly of my britches that men do.* That stuck in her craw.

After Vickie left with the tray, Erin swung out of bed and loosened up her muscles as best she could. Then she got dressed and made her way to the bunkhouse where she found only Kennedy, who sat at the table eating a bowl of cereal while he studied.

"Wyatt isn't here," he said. "He and the men were out working at first light. I don't know where they are now. You might check the horse barn. He normally holds a huddle there midmorning to assign the guys their work for the day. The first stuff they do is just routine. Feeding, watering, and letting the horses out into the paddocks. After that's all done, they regroup."

Midmorning? It just turned eight o'clock. Erin wandered outside. She saw the side-by-side and three quads parked in front of the barn and walked that way. She found the men strapping on chaps and grabbing light jackets off wall hooks because the early morning air was still chilly. As Erin followed them outside, Wyatt drove up in Uncle Slade's red pickup, pulling a flatbed trailer loaded four layers high with bales of hay.

"You feeling up to getting those bales under cover?" he asked Erin.

"You bet," she said, even though she wanted to groan.

"Good," he said. "Just remember to work smart. Use the skidder as much as possible for the lifting and stacking, and you should do fine."

Erin watched him stride away. He hadn't even wished her good morning. She guessed he didn't appreciate having her on his crew. He must think Uncle Slade had been foolish to hire her. Erin thought back to when she'd gone to the academy and faced young men who didn't like having a woman in their classes or challenging them on the mat. She hadn't backed down then and wouldn't now. But if she wanted to be able to get out of bed tomorrow morning, she did need to follow Vickie's advice and work smarter today.

Erin tried to use the skidder. No one had shown her how to operate it, but by trial and error she figured it out. Well, she had at least figured out how to run the thing, but operating it efficiently was a different kettle of fish. After she got a hay bale inside the bucket, she invariably dropped it en route to the barn. Then she had to climb out of the skidder to wrestle the bale back onto the blade. She finally decided it would be easier just to pick the things up and carry them over to the hay storage area.

That was how Wyatt found her, struggling to carry bales from the flatbed into the hay barn. Erin's face went hot with embarrassment. The first few bales had been easy enough to lift, but after handling a dozen, her back was giving her fits. Wyatt watched her for a moment, then he climbed into the skidder and made short work of transporting the hay into the barn.

When he'd finished, he joined her at the flatbed and said, "That's how you work smarter."

She could have kicked him. "I *tried* to use the skidder. The bales kept falling out of the bucket. I couldn't move much with it."

He tipped his hat to her and said, "Practice makes perfect. You can't expect to become an expert with your first try. Just keep dropping bales until you get the hang of it."

"I wasn't getting any work done that way."

"And you won't get anything at all done tomorrow if you hurt your back trying to buck that much hay. If you don't learn how to work smarter, you're going to fail."

If Erin had been able to lift one of her aching legs high enough, she would have kicked him on the rump as he walked away.

Over the next few days, Erin grew sick of people telling her to "work smarter." Even Vickie kept yammering about it. Erin wanted so badly to tell them she had learned to hold her own on the mat with any male police officer who challenged her. She'd also become an expert marksman and learned to drive like Mario Andretti. She could take down a Seattle street thug, even when he was armed. She didn't need to work smarter. She just needed to toughen up and get her body conditioned for the work.

Wyatt understood that Erin was in desperate need of a job, but he was also worried about her. The other two new hires had at least some ranching experience. Erin not only worked too hard and tried to get things done too fast, but she was pushing her way into dangerous situations where she might get hurt. She'd never been around horses that much and wasn't careful to avoid getting kicked. Wyatt had known strapping men who'd gotten a femur snapped by a well-aimed hoof.

Finally, Wyatt decided the situation was serious enough that he had to talk to Slade. He found his boss in the tack room at the back of the horse barn. Slade was cleaning and conditioning leather with saddle soap. He sat on a tripod stool. When Wyatt entered the enclosure, he closed the door behind him so their conversation wouldn't be overheard. Then he found a stool for himself and sat facing his boss.

"I need to speak with you about Erin."

Slade gave him a sharp look and then returned his attention to the leather. "I'm listening."

Wyatt told him of his concerns. Slade seemed to be mulling it over, and Wyatt half expected him to lose his temper. Complaining to one's boss about a dearly loved relative in his employ wasn't the smartest move Wyatt had ever made.

Finally, Slade said, "You're the foreman. If Erin is taking foolish risks, she's a liability. You need to get her straightened out or let her go. Just because she's my niece doesn't make her so special she can't be fired."

"I'd prefer not to let her go," Wyatt said. "I just can't get her to listen to me."

Slade nodded. "Vickie has mentioned that, too. She thinks Erin has been emotionally messed up by her father. That she can't accept being bested by a man. That's crazy thinking."

Wyatt ran a hand over his face. "I'll try talking to her one more time, boss."

"Just remember this," Slade said. "I keep no hired hand on the payroll who foolishly puts himself at risk of physical injury. I understand that people will do some dangerous stuff in emergency situations, and I do let that slide, but a person who screws up several times a day is out the door. It doesn't matter to me if the transgressor is a stranger or a relative. This ranch is a business, and I treat it as such. That's been my policy for years, and I'm not going to change it for Erin. I'll still love her. She'll still be welcome to stay with us at the main house until she gets back on her feet. But I won't keep her on the payroll if she puts this ranch at risk. For one, if she gets badly hurt, my insurance rates will shoot through the ceiling. For another, I wouldn't put it past her father to sue me."

"I had her sign a waiver, just like everyone else."

"Might not matter to him. Talk with Erin. Lay down the law to her. Handle it however you would with any other employee."

Wyatt was deep in thought as he left the horse barn and ran into Kennedy, who barreled through the doorway as if his tail were on fire.

"I've been looking everywhere for you, even in here. Tex told me Slade is in the tack room, so I was going to see if he knew where you were."

"Well, you've found me. Is something wrong?"

"Jen's dad just called. They finally got her blood pressure back up to normal, and yesterday they were able to do surgery on her arm. I guess they had to bolt her wrist back together."

"Ouch," Wyatt said. "I'm glad to hear she's doing better, though."

"Yeah, me, too," Kennedy agreed. "I'd really like to go see her, Wyatt. Her dad says she's been asking for me."

Things were ramping up on the ranch. Two of the cows had dropped their calves that morning, and Wyatt fully expected more to follow. In his years of working with cattle, he'd come to believe that one cow giving birth somehow got all the other cows in the mood for birthing. He knew it made no sense and wasn't a proven fact, but it sure seemed that way to him. It wasn't a good time for Kennedy to leave him shorthanded.

"When are you wanting to go?"

"Tomorrow, if that's all right. It's Saturday, and I don't have any classes."

Wyatt saw the yearning in his brother's eyes and didn't have the heart to tell him no. "Okay, but the cows are starting to calve, so I may be busy. I might not be able to do all my work and yours, too. I'll need you to catch up on things when you get home, so don't stay gone too late."

"You're the best!" Kennedy stepped forward to give Wyatt an enthusiastic hug. "And I'll hurry back. I promise."

Wyatt watched his brother walk away. Then he decided to find Erin. He didn't believe in putting off things until tomorrow if he could get them done today. He needed to talk to her, and he'd only stew about it if he waited. But before he could even move his feet, Tex rode into the ranch proper on a red quad and sent dust up in a mushroom cloud as he brought the vehicle to a sliding stop.

"We got a calf comin' breech. We need you out there, ASAP."

Wyatt swung onto the four-wheeler behind Tex and grabbed the bars of the back cargo frame, and they tore off for the pasture.

The following day, Kennedy's absence seemed to kick Erin into an even higher gear. She rushed from one task to the next as if she were being timed by a stopwatch and needed to break a speed record. Wyatt hoped she would eventually wear herself out and slow down, but she continued to lift more weight than she safely could. When she went into the hay barn and came out carrying a hay bale that probably weighed a third as much as she did, he bit down hard on his back teeth. But it was late that afternoon when she finally pulled a stunt stupid enough to make him see red.

He'd taken a gelding into one of the barn stalls to check its frog for stones because the animal was limping. He tied the horse off and had just bent over to get its front hoof turned up and wedged between his knees when Erin entered the stall. Even though he'd warned her several times not to walk up behind a horse without speaking to it and putting a hand on its rump, she did exactly that. Walked in and stood directly behind the animal in its blind spot.

Crouched with his rump pointed toward the barn wall, Wyatt glanced up at her.

"I've finished everything on my list. What should I do next? Everyone else is still working on the chores you told them to do this morning. Should I help them get finished, or do you have something else for me to do?"

He could tell by the gleam in her blue eyes that she felt proud of herself for finishing first, and that pissed him off even more than the fact that she had put her safety at risk. "I'd like you to move out from behind the horse!" Wyatt wasn't sure if he yelled. He only knew his throat had gone tight and it felt like the veins were distended in his neck. "*Now*. Not tomorrow. *Move!*"

She quickly sidestepped and held up her hands. "Oops. Sorry. I forgot."

"If you forget the safety procedures around horses, you're going to get hurt. I know I've told you how to safely approach a horse from behind at least a half dozen times now."

"I know, I know. They have a blind spot, and I need to talk to them and touch their butts. I've got it."

"If you've got it, why did you just do the exact opposite?" Wyatt found a stone in the gelding's frog and dislodged it with his pick. As he lowered the animal's leg back to the ground, he straightened and moved toward Erin. He guessed his face mirrored his anger, because she fell back a step. "I think we need to take a walk."

She blinked. He tried not to notice how cute she looked in a red ball cap with her wealth of dark hair poking out the hole in back. She wore a dingy T-shirt over mud-streaked jeans, and her cheeks were rosy from exercise. He knew she'd been working her tail off, which made him feel even worse about what he had to say to her. *Damn it.* Wyatt cared about Erin. He didn't want to hurt her feelings or fire her, but her determination to outdo everyone had to stop before she ended up hurt or possibly lame for the rest of her life.

"I—um—don't really have time for a walk," she said. "If you have something you need me to do, I will, of course. But otherwise I should help the other guys get their work finished. With Kennedy gone today, there's a lot more for us to do."

Wyatt brushed past her and put his hand on the top rail of the gate, which she'd forgotten to close after she rushed in. He had the horse tethered, so it wasn't that big a deal. This time. But what if the animal hadn't been tethered? Erin might have startled it, and it could have taken off for tall timber.

"I just told you what I want you to do," he said. "We're taking a walk."

"But I—"

"No buts. What I have to say to you shouldn't be overheard by the others."

He waited for her to step through the opening and then secured the barrier. "The next time you enter an occupied stall, close the gate."

He struck off for the wide front opening of the barn, measuring his strides so she could catch up with him. When she didn't, he turned to see what the holdup was. She was just standing there with a mutinous expression on her face, and he had a bad feeling this conversation wouldn't go well.

She finally sighed in defeat. He knew that because he saw her shoulders slump. She took long, slow strides toward him. When she finally reached him, he struck off for the creek.

When they reached the log, Wyatt gestured for her to sit down. She glared at him. "If you're going to talk to me, just spit it out. I didn't come down here with you for a cozy visit."

Wyatt scratched behind his ear, dislodged his Stetson, and almost lost it to the brisk breeze. "Okay. I'll sit. I haven't been off my feet all day." He made himself comfortable on the log. "I'll just lay it out for you, Erin. You clearly have issues. I understand that your father was a jerk when you were growing up. Probably still is, but you're a grown woman now, and I can't cut you slack until you get your head on straight."

"Cut me slack? I've been outworking every man on this ranch!"

"And that right there is part of the problem. You see everything we do as some kind of competition, and you rush through every job as if it's a race for you to get done first. Just now wasn't the only time you've walked up behind horses without letting them know you're there. You're going to get hurt, either because you can't be bothered to follow the rules or because you're so bent on outdoing all the men that you do things without any thought for your own well-being. If you don't get a handle on all that, I'm going to have to let you go. You need to decide right now which it's going to be."

Her chest jerked with laughter, but judging by her expression, it wasn't a jovial sound. "So you're going to fire me? The best worker you've got? Maybe you should ask Uncle Slade how he feels about that."

Wyatt had hoped the conversation wouldn't lead him to this point. He had a feeling Erin had already endured enough heartache. "I've already spoken with Slade."

"Oh? And what did he say? Did he tell you to fire me?"

"Yes. If you can't make some changes. You're a liability." Wyatt swallowed. His throat had gone so dry it burned. "As things stand, you're an accident waiting to happen. He doesn't want you to get hurt because he loves you very much, but he also worries about his insurance premiums going straight through the roof if you're badly injured."

Her face drained of color. "He actually said you have the authority to fire me? Without him even talking to me first?"

Wyatt understood how that must make her feel. Slade was a father figure to her, and once again she had failed to measure up. He wished he knew how to make her see it differently, or that there was a balm to heal wounded hearts. But he had no magic at his disposal. "I'm sorry. I don't know why he didn't talk to you himself. It wasn't my business to ask."

Her eyes flared with anger. "I see. So what did you tell him that made him decide I should be fired?"

"He didn't decide. He left the decision up to me."

Her eyes went bright with tears. "What did you tell him?"

"Nothing but the truth. I don't want to let you go. But I'm going to have to if you can't start listening to me about safety."

Nobody had ever threatened to fire Erin, and for a moment, she questioned her own ears. But the stern set of Wyatt's expression and the fact that he met her gaze with unwavering resolve told her he'd spoken nothing but the unvarnished truth and would let her go if she kept screwing up.

"I know very well that I've accomplished just as much every day as, if not more than, the men I'm up against," she told him.

His eyes darkened with what looked like sadness. "You're not up against anyone. Nobody here wants you to fail. Nobody is trying to make you look bad. You're working on a ranch now. Nobody cares how strong you are or how you go about accomplishing tasks. All anyone here cares about is that you get your share of the work done. Do you get that? I hope so, because if you're so focused on outperforming everyone else that you walk in close behind a horse again, I'll fire you on the spot. Even when we're careful, this is dangerous work, and you're not being careful. This is my first and last official warning to you. Deliberately ignore safety procedures again, and you'll be gone."

After delivering that ultimatum, he turned and strode away. Erin balled her hands into fists and took three steps after him. If he was going to fire her, she'd at least give him a reason. "You're an asshole!" she screamed.

Only Wyatt didn't hear the insult. She stood there, watching his retreating back. He was returning to the ranch proper, where he reigned as the shit-kicker king.

Deflated, she sank down on the log and stared through tears at the creek. *I don't do dumb-ass things,* she assured herself. *And who's to say how much punishment my body can take? No matter how sore I was, I hit the deck every morning and put in a hard day with the men. I haven't backed away from a single job, no matter how disgusting or difficult it was. And yet he threatened to fire me? Why? Is it because I refuse to be girly and do everything the easy way?*

Erin knew she was arguing her case inside her mind, which was a normal thing for people to do. But with bone-chilling alarm, she realized it wasn't her voice she heard. It was her father's. What on earth was that all about? She hugged her waist, shivering as if from the cold, only it was a balmy afternoon. As she began to calm down, some of what Wyatt had said to her began to sink in, and she realized that she actually had been competing with the men. Her therapist, Jonas Sterling, would tell her to back off and regroup. He'd also push her to search within herself to answer questions she might never have thought to ask herself.

With Jonas's help, she'd come a long way. But now she felt as if she were back at square one. Her dad's negative input pounded inside her brain, and her competitiveness had returned, as strong as, if not stronger than, it ever was. Erin wasn't sure how that had happened, but emotionally she felt as if she were trying to row a canoe upstream against white water.

With shaky hands, she drew out her phone and dialed her shrink.

Jonas answered on the third ring, sounding all professional. Over time, he'd become her friend as well as her psychologist, and one of the reasons she trusted him so much was that he gave her a hard time, she gave him one back, and neither of them ever took offense. They both knew that no matter how nasty a comment might sound, or how upset either of them might be for an instant, it meant nothing. Jonas didn't pussyfoot around with her. That worked for Erin. In a clinical environ-

ment with a therapist who was always rigidly polite, she didn't feel relaxed and couldn't share her feelings. With Jonas, there were no holds
barred.

Erin cut right to the chase. "I think I'm backsliding."

"Erin? Is that you?"

Frustration turned her voice thin and reedy. "Of course it's me.
Who else could be backsliding?"

"Everyone in this town in one way or another."

Jonas had a way about him that always soothed her. "I need to see
you. Tonight, if possible. Name any time that works for you. I'll be there
even if it means missing supper. Dinner, I mean."

"Six o'clock works. No need for you to miss supper. I'll order a pizza
from the restaurant downstairs. And I'll grab a couple of beers from my
fridge. We'll eat while we talk."

"Thank you for working me in. I'll see you at six sharp."

As Erin ended the call, it occurred to her that it was Saturday. How
many psychologists made themselves available on the weekend? He'd
probably charge her double. She'd pay whatever rate he came up with
and be glad of it. At this point, she felt as if she'd fallen out of the white-
water canoe and was drowning.

CHAPTER THIRTEEN

Erin finished her workday on the ranch as if she were killing poisonous snakes. At the back of her mind, she knew she was in a fever pitch, and if Wyatt was watching, she was only cementing in his mind all the reasons he'd listed for firing her. But she couldn't make herself stop. She felt like a windup toy being controlled by an invisible someone who wanted to destroy her.

She didn't shower or change clothes before she drove into town. If she went inside the main house, she was afraid she would see her uncle and unload both barrels on him. How could he consider letting her go without giving her warning? Wyatt was the foreman and therefore her boss, but Uncle Slade owned the ranch and outranked everyone. He could have taken her aside and expressed his concerns without using Wyatt as a middleman.

Jonas lived in the apartment above the Straw Hat and also worked with his patients there. As Erin walked through the restaurant, packed with evening diners, she felt so embarrassed she wanted to die. Almost everyone in town recognized her now, even if she didn't always know them. And most people also knew that Jonas Sterling, the hometown shrink, saw all his patients in his upstairs living quarters. Gossip probably already abounded about her turning in her badge. Now she was fueling the fire even more by rushing upstairs as if demons chased at her heels.

Once at the landing, Erin nearly burst through the door without knocking just to get out of sight. At the last minute, she knocked on the panel of wood with more force than she intended, sending lances of pain from her knuckles to her elbow.

Jonas answered Erin's knock and ushered her inside. Grinning broadly, he said, "I was expecting you. You could have just walked in."

"My mother would have a coronary," Erin retorted. "She's a female version of Hitler when it comes to ladylike behavior."

Jonas, often referred to by local women as the epitome of a Greek god, ran a hand over his tawny hair. His hazel eyes filled with sympathy. "Have you ever considered all the mixed signals you got from your parents as a kid? Your mom trying to make you into a perfect little lady and your dad doing his damnedest to have you act like a boy. It boggles my mind, and I didn't live through it."

Erin had never thought of it quite that way. "Mostly, I just realized I'd never please either of them."

"But you've never stopped trying." He didn't state that as a question, and Erin jerked around to meet his gaze instead of taking her usual chair. He shrugged and said, "You knocked instead of walking in. Still trying to make points with Mama?"

"I already know I'm a basket case. That's why I'm here. It doesn't really help to have another person pointing it out to me."

Jonas went into the kitchen at the back of his apartment. She heard the door of his refrigerator open. "Ah, but I'm not just pointing it out. I'm asking you to analyze your screwed-up childhood so you can start to understand *why* you're a basket case. Have you ever studied a basket? It's made from dozens of fibers, all woven together. When you and I start picking at one of the fibers that make you who you are, you start to feel as if you're coming apart. I never promised you therapy would be easy. You're going to hit some rough road."

He returned to the office/living area with two cans of beer that were already developing condensation from the heat of his hands. "Want a glass?"

Erin normally drank her beer straight from the can. *Like a guy.* Her stomach clenched as that thought settled into her brain. And then for no reason she could pinpoint, she burst into tears. Jonas flopped down on his leather castor chair and said, "Take a seat, Erin. Or should I say sit before you fall down?"

Erin plucked six tissues from the box. She'd breathed in a lot of dust that day, and now that she'd started crying, the inside of her nasal passages felt as if a child had been making mud pies in there. She clapped the squares over her nose and honked into it. *Just like a guy.* And that thought only made her cry harder. Jonas just reclined in the chair, propped his feet on the desk, and watched her sob.

"I'm sorry. Your pizza is going to get cold," she told him. A box bearing the Straw Hat logo sat on the blotter in front of him. "José's pizzas are expensive."

"They're also worth the money. Don't worry about that. Just let the pressure off so we can talk. If it gets cold, I've got a microwave."

Erin eventually calmed down and collected her composure. "I'm sorry. I try never to cry."

"Maybe you shouldn't do that. Is that another gift from your father, trying never to cry?"

"That isn't what I'm here to talk about! My uncle told the foreman to fire me. *That's* why I'm here."

"Okay. That's bad news."

"It's total bullshit. I've been outperforming every man on the ranch. Working even when I felt so tired I was about to drop."

"Just relax for a moment, Erin. Have some beer. Enjoy my paintings. Try breathing in and out, slowly."

Erin took two gulps of beer and then stared at a framed canvas over his sofa that depicted a fawn, peeking out through pine boughs. It made her think of Wyatt, who seemed to love wildlife, and that only brought fresh tears to her eyes. Then, through the blur, she saw another oil of a mountain stream lined with clusters of aspen. That made her think of the log down by the creek, where she and Wyatt always seemed to end up having unpleasant conversations.

She leaned back in the chair and faced her therapist. "Can you fix me, Jonas?"

He smiled slightly. "No. I'm sorry. But you're not here to be fixed. You're here to figure out how to fix yourself. Even after all that fixing, you'll never be perfect. None of us are, so that isn't our aim. The goal here is for you to be happy with yourself."

She took a deep breath and released it. "I don't know where to start. My life is such a mess right now. I turned in my badge. Just up and quit a really good job. I didn't even give Sheriff Adams notice. That'll look bad if he's ever called upon to give me a reference. Quitting without warning makes me look flighty."

"I heard that Sheriff Adams offered you vacation time to think it over and said your job would still be waiting for you when you came back."

"It's amazing how efficient the gossip network is in this town. Sheriff Adams did make that offer. But the whole time he was assuring me I could have the job back, I felt claustrophobic. I don't want to go back. I'm done, Jonas. I'm not cut out for the work."

While Jonas ate pizza, Erin ranted about her position at the ranch and how hard she had tried to do a stellar job. While chewing industriously, Jonas occasionally nodded and smiled, but sometimes he also frowned at something she'd said. Erin was accustomed to his low-key manner.

He left half of the pizza for her, settled back with his beer, and asked, "Why did you turn in your badge?"

Erin told him how Jenette's misfortune had driven home to her that she would never be able to protect anyone, with a badge or without one. "It was a climactic event for me. It forced me to accept that I'd gone into my profession for all the wrong reasons. And right before I decided to throw in the towel, I was so disgusted by that kid and so angry with him that I had violent thoughts. A good cop handles his emotions better than that."

"Don't you mean 'handles *her* emotions'?" He pushed aside a pile of paperwork to rest his arms on the desk. "There are a lot of really great female cops."

"I'm not one of them. I excelled at everything I was expected to learn. I think I've done reasonably well at the job. But it was never *my* dream. But you know that already."

"Yes, but I wonder if *you* really know that. You say the words. At some level, you're cognizant of the fact that your father pushed you into being a cop. But judging by what I see, you're very upset for someone who realized she made a mistake and finally rectified it."

"The moment I put my badge on Adams's desk, I felt like such a failure. I worked so hard to become a good cop. And there I stood, throwing away my dream."

"But you just said it was never *your* dream. It was your father's dream *for* you. I worry there's a part of you that doesn't see that."

"I don't know what you mean."

"Remember the basket. How it's made from dozens of fibers and will start to fall apart if we remove any of them? That's you, Erin. And one of your fibers is entitled *Deputy*. You've jerked out an element that was part of who you are."

Erin thought about how frantic she'd been feeling over the last few days. "Oh, God, you're right. Now I'm not sure who or what I am. So it's all-important to establish myself as something else, someone else."

"A rancher," Jonas summarized for her.

"And that's going wonderfully well. I work too *hard*. I work too *fast*. I forget *all* the absurd safety rules. In short, according to my uncle and his foreman, I'm a *liability*."

Jonas merely smiled in his usual, unruffled way. "Keep going. You're on a roll. Do you really want to be a rancher? It's a lot of hard work."

"Not if you work smarter instead of harder," Erin retorted with a sneer. "Or so I've been told at least a dozen times."

Jonas linked his fingers behind his head, looking as relaxed as a man could get. "There's actually something to that saying. I don't know if you're aware of it, but I grew up on a ranch. Not a huge one like Wilder's, but my father owns a large chunk of land. We kids all had daily chores, and my mother often worked at my dad's side. She may not have created that saying, but I sure did see her invent ways to work smarter." His eyes twinkled with humor. "One time when she had to feed animals when there were no hay bales out by the fence, she hauled them out on an old Radio Flyer red wagon. It took her a while, but she got the job done."

Erin tried to smile. "I've met your mom. She's not a large woman."

"And neither are you."

"I competed and placed in the—"

"I know you placed in an Ironman triathlon, Erin. But that doesn't make you large. It only means you're determined and won't quit no matter what."

"I was never allowed to quit," she shot back.

"And who's ruling your world now?"

"Wyatt Fitzgerald."

"Really? You just said he's about to can you because, according to him, you don't follow his rules. So who's actually running your show now, Erin?"

She stared at him with a sinking sensation in her chest. "I know what you want me to say. You're pathetically obvious sometimes even though you think you're being subtle."

"If you know what I want you to say, then you already thought of that person yourself. That means I'm probably on the right track."

"My father," she pushed out. "He's been running my life ever since he noticed I was alive."

"And you're still letting him do it. You're thirty-two years old. You're independent. But you're still letting his expectations run your life."

"Thank you for sharing that illuminating observation. But it's nothing new. Would I be here if I didn't realize I'm a mess?"

He sat forward to rest his bent arms on the desk again. "You might be surprised by how many people in this town don't realize they're a mess and want me to fix everyone else around them." He shook his head. "In that way, you've got a big jump on them. You recognize that you've got issues."

"But I don't know how to fix them."

"How about just letting go of them?" He put more weight on his folded arms and looked her directly in the eye. "How about going back to the ranch with a different perspective? We've talked a lot about when you trained to be a cop. You said you had to learn to drive at recklessly high speeds. How to stop. How to put a vehicle into a slide without rolling it. Where to hit another vehicle to send it careening off a road."

Erin nodded. "That's right. But I don't see how any of that pertains to my problems now."

"Those things pertain because during that driving course, you listened to your instructor."

"Well, of course. My life depended on it."

"And you don't think your life may depend on anything Wyatt tells you?"

Erin slumped her shoulders against the back of her chair. "You don't understand the situation. He isn't briefing me on truly dangerous stuff. He's pissed off because I walk up behind horses and might startle them. Because I lift things *he* believes are too heavy for me. Because I sometimes run instead of walk to get my work done faster."

"I see. So essentially he thinks stupid, trivial stuff is dangerous, so why should you listen to him?"

"You're starting to piss me off."

Jonas smiled. "Am I only just starting to? Damn, I must be slipping."

Erin pushed to her feet and paced in a tight circle. Then she sat back down. "I hate you sometimes."

"I know. You're not an easy nut to crack, and sometimes I have to be a little mean to make you see things without wearing your father-colored glasses. Becoming a police officer was a big deal to you. Wasn't it?"

"I wanted to be good at it, so yes."

"Because that was what your father wanted. Right? So, tell me, Erin. What does your dad think about you turning in your badge and becoming a rancher?"

"Beats me. I haven't told him yet."

"When you do tell him, how do you think he'll react?"

"He'll be furious because I've thrown my life away."

Jonas tapped a pen on the blotter. "Correction. You've thrown away the life *he* wanted you to have. And now you're having issues with ranch work and your supervisor because his complaints about your performance all seem stupid."

Erin clenched her teeth.

"Are you seeing the parallel I'm trying to draw?" Jonas asked.

"Like I said, subtlety isn't your strong suit. You're saying that becoming a good deputy was all-important to me, because that's what my father wanted, and becoming a rancher isn't all-important to me, because that isn't what my father wants."

He nodded. "So the question you need to ask yourself is, do you really want to be a good rancher?"

"I feel at peace doing that kind of work." She hesitated and then backed up mentally. "Well, I did feel at peace. Not so much now."

"Why do you think that is?"

"Because I'm facing a double standard. Every time I turn around, I'm told that I should do this or that differently from the way men are doing it. *Not* because I can't do it the regular way, but because I'm a woman." Erin gestured behind her. "Line up a hundred women and ask them how pissed off they'd be if they were treated that way. I'm not second-rate. I don't need a special set of rules just because I'm a female."

"Do you see any of the men walking up behind a horse without letting it know they're there?"

"No. But none of the horses ever kicks, either. They're wonderful animals. I'm still getting used to them, but I can see myself becoming a big fan of equines with time. I just need to get over being scared of them first."

Jonas turned to his computer and swiveled the monitor so she could see it. He typed something in the search line, clicked the mouse button a couple more times, and images popped up on the screen. Photographs of people with awful bruises and wounds. Erin hadn't seen anything that gory since leaving her law enforcement job up north.

Jonas enlarged an image of a woman with the center of her face mutilated. "Kicked by a horse," he said. Then he clicked on an image of a man that was nearly as awful. "Kicked by a horse."

Erin let him continue until she couldn't bear to see any more. "What is your point?"

Jonas turned his chair to face her again. "That maybe you're seeing a double standard where there isn't one. I grew up with horses. They have monocular vision, which means they do have blind spots. When you stand directly in front of an equine, it can't see you. Well, maybe your shoulders and arms, which might be outside the blind spot, but those parts of you would still be blurry."

"They really can't see me if I'm right in front of their nose?"

"Nope." He smiled slightly. "Have you ever noticed how a horse lifts its head when you stand in front of it? Happens a lot when a horse is in an enclosure. It'll lift its head to get farther away so it can see you better. You'll often see the whites of its eyes. A lot of people think that indicates the horse is mean, but they're wrong. There's another blind spot directly behind a horse, and it can't see you back there. Have you ever been unaware that anyone else was in a room and jumped a foot when they suddenly spoke to you?"

"Well, of course. Hasn't everyone?"

Jonas tapped the pen again. "Horses get startled, too. Only instead of jumping, they're more likely to kick. It's a knee-jerk response. That's why Wyatt yammers at you about safely approaching a horse from behind. If you want to wind up looking like those people"—he jabbed a thumb over his shoulder at the monitor—"just keep ignoring his warnings, and you may get your wish."

Erin almost threw up her hands. "You don't believe me about the double standard."

"I believe you." He turned back to his keyboard and executed another search. "Huh. And it appears that you're right. There is no legal maximum weight that people should lift at work. There's no reason for them to be jumping all over you about dreamed-up weight limits."

"You see?" Erin said. "What's the address of that site? I'll enter it in my phone and show it to Uncle Slade. It proves that Wyatt is being unreasonable."

"Oh, wait. There are recommended weight limitations for both men and women at certain levels of their bodies. And there are also guidelines that say women shouldn't be expected to lift as much weight as men. And get this. It says the suggested guidelines for both sexes change when the work environment requires any lifting that involves twisting or bending, if the manual handling is being carried out in a confined space, or if the lifting activity is being repeated. As I recall, all three of those exceptions occur on a ranch."

Erin stood up. "It appears that my hour will be up in ten minutes. I don't mind paying you for ten measly minutes you didn't actually work."

Jonas chuckled. "You know why I like working with you so much? You never hesitate to let me know when I tick you off."

"You're impossible sometimes."

"Ditto right back at you. I hope you'll think about what I've said, though."

She pushed the pizza box toward him. "Eat the rest of your pizza. I prefer healthier fare."

"Meaning that you're still dieting."

"Nobody on Slade's ranch watches what they eat." She met his gaze. "I don't always like what you have to say, Jonas, but I do always think about it, and most of the time, I try to follow your advice."

"I know," he said, his voice pitched low. "And I'll be here whenever you need to talk. But if you lose that job, let me know. I could really use a good cleaning lady."

Erin rolled her eyes. "You're such an a-hole sometimes. If I meet any cleaning *men*, I'll steer them your way."

As she stepped out onto the landing, Jonas fired a parting shot at her. "Men are probably better cleaners than women!"

When Erin got back to the ranch, she was hungry. Not with regular hunger, but sharp pains in her stomach that made her feel weak and nauseated. If she went to the bunkhouse to find something to eat, she'd encounter Wyatt, and she was still too angry with him to be civil. She guessed she'd just have to go to bed hungry, because she didn't wish to see her uncle yet either. She decided to slip in the front door and hurry upstairs to her room as fast as her sore legs would carry her.

Only when Erin slipped into the main house, wonderful smells drifted to her from the kitchen. Vickie had been baking, and Erin's nose told her that chocolate chip cookies were the treat of the day. She stood on the entryway rug and listened. She heard no one stirring downstairs and determined that Vickie and Slade were probably in their new master suite, watching something on television. She crept from the entryway and made it to the kitchen without making a sound. Then she flipped on a light. She nearly moaned when she spotted at least four dozen of her favorite cookies laid out on sheets of waxed paper.

Erin was about to load up her pockets when her uncle entered the room and startled her by saying, "I'm glad you didn't run straight upstairs. I need to talk to you."

She turned to face him. "About what?"

"I know you're pissed at me."

Erin shook her head. "No. I'm not angry, only hurt. I guess I thought blood was thicker than water."

"Blood is thicker than water, honey. It's just that life can interfere with those bonds sometimes. Let me remind you that while performing your job as a deputy, you didn't hesitate to place me under arrest, slap handcuffs on me as you read me my rights, and stuff me into a cop car."

Erin flinched, feeling as if he'd slapped her. "Having to arrest you was part of what led me to realize I was working in the wrong field."

"You still performed your job."

"Only because I had to."

"I understood then that you had no choice, and admired you for doing what you had to do. Now I'd like you to extend me the same courtesy. This ranch isn't just my livelihood. I have people who depend on me to keep the place operating in the black, and now I also have a family who will inherit the operation when I die. I owe it to my son and his kids to make this place as profitable as it can be."

"I understand that."

"You may understand, but you don't see my expenses. My employee health and accident insurance is already sky-high, because ranching can be dangerous work. People get sick, of course. There's no way for me to mitigate that situation. Anyone who is injured while on the clock is also covered. I absorb the cost of that, and I know my premiums will go up even higher when there's an accident, which is inevitable. But there is a way to mitigate that situation. Employees who don't follow our safety rules are booted off my payroll. It helps to keep my insurance costs down. I can't make an exception for you. You aren't listening to sound advice. You're so bent on excelling that you're taking stupid chances. If you don't change your approach to the job, I told Wyatt to let you go."

Erin's throat had gone so tight that she could barely speak. "So I heard. From a second party. I would have appreciated hearing it straight from you."

Slade raked his fingers through his hair, ruffling the dark strands in such a way that the silver ones caught more of the light. "I know telling Wyatt to threaten you with termination was a chickenshit thing for me to do. I feel bad about that." He smiled slightly. "The night Vickie started that brawl at the bar, you performed your job and arrested me yourself. Instead of doing you the same favor, I sent Wyatt to do the dirty work. I guess I just love you too much. I couldn't do it myself." He released a shaky sigh. "You have more courage than I do. I'll give credit where it's due. But your never-say-die approach to your job here is not what I'm looking for in a ranch hand."

"I saw my therapist tonight. I'm trying, Uncle Slade."

"You'll always have a home here as long as I draw breath. I love you, and you are more than welcome to stay here as long as you like. But that doesn't mean I'll keep you in my employ when you're taking stupid chances."

He turned and left the kitchen. Erin glanced at the cookies, but her appetite for them was gone. She no longer even felt hungry. As she climbed the stairs to her room, she had only one consolation. Her legs were no longer as sore as they had been. Her body was beginning to adjust to the demands of the work.

She showered and put on a pair of clean sweatpants and a T-shirt to sleep in. Then she lay in bed with her face pressed into her pillow and started to cry. For so many years, she'd never allowed herself to shed tears. It was weak, according to her dad. Only lately she couldn't seem to govern her emotions. She felt like a confused, frustrated, and heartbroken child again, wishing she could make her parents love her and not knowing how.

Erin awakened to the bluish light of predawn and swung out of bed to stand at the window and look at the ranch. At this hour, the green fields appeared almost black, and mist wreathed the trees on the mountains, creating what looked like a magical world of lakes and islands. She remembered how peaceful and centered she'd felt after working on fences with Uncle Slade. She'd lost that sense of belonging now and knew she would feel edgy the moment she left the house. Wyatt was right. She truly had turned this job into a race and a constant test of her abilities. She was an emotional mess, and talking with Jonas last night hadn't helped her determine how she could get her head on straight. The need within her to measure up was compulsive, and she couldn't seem to slap a lid on it.

Even worse, her presence here was causing problems for Uncle Slade. Oh, he'd meant it when he said she was welcome in his home. She didn't doubt for a second that he loved her. But that didn't mean she fit seamlessly into the pattern of his life. For his sake, she needed to leave. She should just pack up her personal things, get them into her car, and then say goodbye to her aunt and uncle in such a way that they wouldn't feel terrible as she drove away.

It wasn't an easy decision for Erin to make. She had no idea how she was going to pay her bills, and she was frightened. But no matter how she looked at it, she was causing trouble for the people she loved. Uncle Slade and Vickie were still newlyweds, and this should be the happiest time of their life. By coming here to work, she was ruining that for them. Last night, Uncle Slade must have been sitting in the darkened living room, waiting for her to get home. That meant he hadn't been in the master suite, watching television with his wife. He hadn't been doing anything with her at all.

And Erin knew she was the reason for that. She'd already left one job. Doing it again shouldn't be so hard.

CHAPTER FOURTEEN

After doing his early-morning check on the horses, Wyatt saw Erin loading stuff into the back of her car as he left the barn. His heart felt as if it took a nosedive to the toes of his boots. He hadn't handled his talk with her well yesterday. He'd tried to be a good foreman, being cut-and-dried about his complaints, but in doing that, he'd forgotten the most important thing: to also be her friend.

He'd learned early on with Kennedy to be his brother first and his foreman second, but it was different with Erin, and he was so conflicted about his attraction to her that it was difficult to keep his head on straight. He wished she wouldn't leave. One part of her yearned to be seen as feminine, pretty, and desirable. But the other part of her detested everything she secretly wished for. Her yearning to be something she wasn't troubled him.

Wyatt felt that he understood her in a way others didn't—because he was deaf. He'd been born that way, just as Erin had been born a girl. As far back as Wyatt could remember, the world beyond his grandfather's ranch hadn't seemed to accept him as he was. The way he had perceived it, rightly or wrongly, there was pressure on him at every turn to be as much like a hearing person as he could be. As an adult, Wyatt understood that all those individuals had good intentions. They'd only wanted him to have the tools he would need to thrive in a world that would challenge him at every turn. Only as a little boy and later as a teen, Wyatt had felt like a lesser person. He had been everybody's special project. He'd had to learn his letters. He'd had to learn sign language. He'd had to learn to speak. The demands placed upon him were huge and the pressure relentless.

He told himself he'd put all that behind him, but in a lot of ways, he was just like Erin, still driven and trying to be someone he wasn't. He spent at least a half hour each night at his computer, striving to speak as perfectly as he could. When he'd gotten into trouble with that woman, it hadn't been because he'd intended to do her any harm. It had happened because he went into that bar pretending to be something he wasn't. Erin was so much like him in that way, trying with everything she had to be as strong as a man.

Wyatt didn't want her to quit the ranch. He knew firsthand that working with animals was a great way for most people to heal. Erin was seeing a therapist, and Wyatt was glad about that. But she was overlooking the best psychologists in the world: all the critters on this land. If she stayed, she'd eventually learn to deal with those animals on their terms, not hers. She would also learn they would accept her without condition.

It was with animals that Wyatt had first started to appreciate himself for who he was. It was with animals that he'd stopped feeling like a lesser being. It was with animals that he had discovered his own special talents that set him apart from others. And it was with animals that he'd finally found peace.

He struck off toward her across the common. He had no idea what he might say to change her mind about leaving, but he at least had to try. As he drew to a stop near her, he saw that she was stuffing folded clothing into a duffel bag.

He studied her for a moment, and then he said the first thing that came to his mind. "I didn't have you pegged as a quitter."

Her face flushed scarlet with anger, and he patted himself on the back for challenging her instead of trying to counsel her. It was the best tactic to use.

"I am *not* a quitter!" She slammed the trunk lid closed. "My presence on the ranch is disruptive. I'm leaving because taking this job has put my relationship with my uncle in jeopardy and is messing up his honeymoon time."

The muscles across Wyatt's shoulders and down along each side of his spine knotted. "I call BS. You're quitting because you don't have the guts to stay and learn about ranch work. You don't have the guts to accept your own limitations."

Tears gathered in her eyes, which already looked puffy from crying. "You have no idea how I feel!"

"For years I tried to run from something that was impossible for me to escape: that I am and will always be deaf. Do you really believe you're the only person on earth who's spent their whole life trying to be something they can't be? You need to rethink that, because I'm standing right in front of you, and I did exactly that. You told me once that you originally wanted to work with deaf children. Why? I understand that you thought you'd be helping them, and as an adult deaf man, I know those kids need all the help they can get. But can you step out of your own skin long enough to imagine how those little deaf kids feel when every adult they meet is hell-bent on fixing them? Can you understand that others make them feel broken? That it isn't and never will be okay for them to be deaf in the *real* world?"

"I never thought about it like that."

"Well, start."

"Where are you trying to go with this, Wyatt?"

"I'm trying to make you realize that the only way for you to be happy, really happy, is to accept yourself for who and what you are. Have you ever heard of deaf communities and wondered why deaf people seek them out and live around others like them? I think it's because they've come to accept being deaf and actually like being who they are. And they're happiest living in communities filled with people who are also deaf and happy about it. The pressure is off, and they can celebrate just being. Some things can never be fixed, and at some point, doesn't everyone with a disability need to accept it and be glad of it? I've never visited a deaf community, so my take on them may be off base, but

I know how I feel. I—am—deaf. I'm finished with surgeries to make me hear. I'm finished with gadgets that just complicate my life. For a long time, I'd get my hopes up and think there was a breakthrough that might fix me, but I was always disappointed. And at some point, I became content. Content to be deaf. And once I reached that place, I even started to appreciate deafness as a special gift."

He held up a staying hand so she wouldn't interrupt. "That doesn't mean the broken little boy no longer exists inside of me. I still work my ass off to maintain my speaking abilities. The day I met you, I tried to pass as a hearing person. It's a reflex reaction, so I understand when I see you just reacting. I spent all my youth trying to be like hearing individuals. You spent all of yours trying to be the son your father wanted. Old habits are hard to break. I get that. But I also know that you'll never overcome your automatic responses to pressure by quitting and running."

He swung an arm at their surroundings. "There's no better place for you to be right now. If you stay, this ranch will challenge you at every turn, and eventually it'll teach that little, broken girl inside of you that you aren't really broken at all. That it was the people around you that had it all wrong."

All Erin could do was gape at him. She'd never heard Wyatt Fitzgerald talk for so long. Nor had she ever seen him look quite so passionate about what he was saying. But even more mind-blowing was that what he'd just told her made more sense than anything Jonas had ever said to her in countless counseling sessions. She had heard of deaf communities. She'd also read that the people who lived in them claimed to be happy that they were deaf. She'd never really bought into that, because, in her mind, she hadn't been able to fathom how anyone could embrace a disability and be glad they had it. Only Wyatt was right. Were disabled people supposed to rail against fate all their lives and feel that nature or God had played a dirty trick on them? Why not embrace the difference and celebrate it? What was wrong with a person feeling happy about having a disability and looking at all the positive things that came of it? And even more important to her in that moment was another question:

Why should anyone have to live her life feeling miserable because she was trying to fix something about herself that could never be changed?

Erin felt frozen in place. Now she wasn't sure what she should do.

Wyatt held her gaze. "It all boils down to one question. Are you going to let your father win?"

After saying that, he walked away.

Wyatt was shaking after he spoke with Erin. Not a single word he'd said had come easily for him. He had bared his soul to her and told her things he'd never shared with anyone, not even members of his family. He went to the paddocks on the east side of the horse barn. Just before exiting the stable area, he'd haltered a mare and tied her to the fence. She shrieked and danced sideways when he stepped in close and put his hand on the rope that held her fast. Slade had only recently purchased her and suspected she might have been sedated when he examined her before making an offer. She was anything but calm now. People terrified her.

Choosing not to pull on the lead, he hooked his arms over the top rail of the fence to watch her. She was a beauty, a sorrel with a white star on her forehead and four white stockings. She also had great potential, but her previous owner had apparently mistreated her, and now she had serious issues. In a strange way, she reminded him of Erin, not in looks, but in her behavior.

Not allowing himself to turn around and look, he tried to imagine what Erin was doing. Was she putting even more stuff on the back seat of her car? Had his long rant done nothing to discourage her from leaving? He hadn't noticed any dust billowing up from the tires of her vehicle yet, so he felt fairly confident she hadn't left. But that didn't mean she didn't still have every intention of leaving.

He forced himself to focus on the mare. She was head shy, which told Wyatt that someone had twisted her ears and might even have used a twitch on her or whipped her around the head. When she felt threatened, she reared and kicked out behind, telling Wyatt in horse speak that she could kill him in two seconds flat. Then she pranced around, showing off her muscle, her agility, and her speed. Oh, yeah. So very like Erin, trying to overcome her feelings of inadequacy and vulnerability by blustering and trying to impress everyone with her physical abilities.

And suddenly the lady herself appeared beside him, making him jerk with a start. Wyatt was coming to accept there was something special about her that allowed her to sneak up on him. As she stepped onto the bottom rail to rest her arms over the top of the fence like he was, he noticed that she was wearing work gloves, which were way too large for her. For reasons beyond him, she hadn't replaced them with ones that fit. Slade kept all different sizes. He wondered if she was sensitive about her hands being smaller than a man's, guessed that she probably was, and knew he had his work cut out for him. That thought led him to ask himself why he thought it was his job to help her. He didn't want to deal with that question right now.

The answer ran too deep.

Looking up at him, she asked, "Why are you just standing here, holding that horse's lead, and why is it so spooked?"

"Slade and I suspect that she's been mistreated." He searched her upturned face. "Well, don't keep me in suspense. Are you still leaving?"

Her mouth twisted tremulously. Then she swallowed and said, "I've decided to give it one more day."

Wyatt wanted to ask if she planned to go tomorrow, but he decided it wouldn't be wise to press her right then. "That's great, Erin. I'm really glad."

"Are you? Truly?"

Wyatt couldn't recall the last time he'd been quite so delighted about anything. "I truly am." He didn't want to analyze why he was glad. "I think you've made the right decision."

She went back to staring at the horse for a moment before turning to look up at him again. "So what work do you have lined out for me today?"

"I think you should spend your last day here with this mare. She needs someone who can understand her, and I think you can. You need to figure out what her story is. What happened to her, what frightens her? She can't talk, but she'll eventually answer your questions with her behaviors. Once you understand her, maybe you can help her overcome her fears. For instance, I've noticed that she's afraid whenever I raise a hand toward her head. If I were you, I'd work with her on that first."

Erin looked alarmed. "I'm the least experienced person with horses on the ranch. I'm not sure it's a wise choice to have me work with her."

"I'll be watching while you're with her. I honestly don't think she'll hurt you. She acts all mean, but it's mostly bluster. She's been careful to miss me with her hooves when she acts up."

"I hope you're right."

Wyatt nearly smiled. The last thing he'd ever do was send Erin into a situation where he believed she might get hurt. "If I weren't fairly certain, I wouldn't send you in with her."

"How can I work with her to get her over being afraid to have her head touched?"

He was sorely tempted to map out a plan for Erin, but that wasn't going to help her. He truly believed animals were the best psychologists on earth. While trying to help the mare, Erin might come to understand herself in ways she had never imagined.

"Just keep trying to touch her head. Think of ways to make it interesting for her. I normally use treats."

He handed Erin the lead and forced himself to walk away.

Erin had no idea what to do with this horse. The only thing about equines that was clear in her brain was that she was pretty much scared to death of them. Well, not *all* of them, but the ones that pranced around and acted as if they wanted to kill her made her want to run. Yet here she was, attached by a lead rope to a mare that was showing the whites of her eyes and looking as terrified as Erin felt. *Hello, Mr. Fitzgerald, I don't even like horses all that much.*

She could have walked away. She wanted to, that was for sure. But being challenged to do something was one of her triggers, damn it, and the broken little girl inside of her couldn't wimp out. The next time Jonas asked Erin who was running her show, she'd tell him a sad and frustrated child was in charge.

Keeping a firm grip on the rope, Erin climbed over the fence and dropped to her feet inside the enclosure. *Please, don't kill me,* she mentally pled. *Nice horsey.* Only the horse backed up as far as the length of lead allowed her to go. Erin took a step forward. The mare went sideways. Erin felt like a teenager trying to do a country line dance with an overlarge partner who didn't understand the step pattern.

"It's okay, baby girl," Erin said. Speaking was a mistake. The poor horse flinched as if a high-powered rifle had just gone off and reared up, striking the air within a foot of Erin's face. It scared her so badly that she almost wet her pants. Then her common sense kicked in. If the mare had wanted to make contact, she could have. She was only frightened and trying to warn Erin away. "You're so scared. It's okay to be scared sometimes. All of us are. And if it's any comfort, I'm as afraid of you as you are of me."

Erin had no treats for the horse, so she tied her off to the fence, vaulted over the barrier, and ran to the bunkhouse. Kennedy sat at the table, hunched over a textbook. He glanced up. "Where's the fire?"

Erin went to the cupboards and began opening them. "I need horse treats. Wyatt assigned me to that new horse, the one that's afraid to be touched."

"Oh, fun. Good luck with that." He closed his book. "They like carrots and apples. If you're doing treat rewards, you just cut them up in small pieces and carry them around in sandwich bags." He opened the fridge. "You're in luck. Wyatt's gone shopping." He pulled out a large bag of carrots and tossed it on the counter. "We've got apples, too."

While he dug out apples from a vegetable drawer so stuffed it could have fed a third-world country, Erin began running water over one carrot and went to find the vegetable peeler. Kennedy studied her for a moment after putting four apples on the Formica surface. "Um, Erin. It's a horse."

"Yes, I know."

"I'd get at least six carrots, and it's fine to rinse them and cut off the ends, but you don't need to peel them. The skins have a heap of nutrients."

Erin wrinkled her nose. "The skins have ground-in dirt."

"Yep. Like I said, lots of nutrients."

She gave him a long study. "Please don't tell me you cook with un-peeled carrots and ground-in dirt as a flavor enhancer."

Kennedy laughed. "I scrub them clean with a vegetable brush first. If a tiny bit of dirt gets past me, I don't worry about it."

Following Kennedy's advice, Erin trimmed the butts off the carrots, made sure they were well rinsed, and then began to dice one up.

"Erin, it's a horse."

Pausing with the knife poised in midair, Erin said, "If you remind me one more time that it's a horse, I'm going to say, 'No kidding. I thought it was a pig.'"

"Yeah, well, horses don't do diced stuff. They like big chunks. How would you feel if your treat for being good was the size of a BB?"

"Around here, I'd be so surprised I might faint if someone gave me even a BB-size treat for doing well."

Kennedy's smile faded. "Yeah, well, I'm sorry you're having a rough time adjusting to ranch life."

"I think it's more accurate that the ranch is having a rough time adjusting to me."

He laughed again and shook his head. As they finished cutting the treats, their conversation about her problems continued, with Erin vent-ing and saying most of the things she'd told Jonas last night.

Kennedy began filling sandwich bags with fruit and vegetables. "I know the rule about always letting a horse know you're behind it may seem a little over the top, but after you've come to understand horses, you'll no longer feel that way. I'm sure when you were a cop you took training to handle a variety of guns. If someone was checking the cham-ber for bullets in a rifle and had the barrel pointed straight at your chest, what would you do?"

"I'd tell the person to point the barrel at the ground. Only an idiot points a loaded weapon at someone unless he intends to shoot him. And to be safe, one must consider every gun to be loaded and ready to fire."

"Yep. That's one of the top rules of gun safety, and when you see somebody pointing a gun toward other people, all your alarm bells ring, because you know that person knows very little about guns. It's the same for us guys when we see you around horses."

"I'm trying to learn."

"But you need to practice all the safety protocol until you're more familiar with horses, just like someone who's holding a gun for the first time. Point the gun at someone, and you're bound to get yelled at. Same goes when someone does stupid shit around a horse."

Erin gathered the treats into a mound on the countertop. "I don't know how I'll carry all these bags."

"Make an apron pocket out of your front shirttails. That works for me. And be careful about the bags. I leave them outside an enclosure and load the goodies into my pockets when I'm working with a horse. The crinkling of the plastic can sound frightening."

"Really?" Erin found that bit of information mystifying. "Why?"

"Nobody really knows, but the theory is that crinkly things, especially tinfoil, make a sound similar to a rattlesnake, and most horses are instinctively fearful of them."

Erin tied her shirttails at her waist to form a pouch and began loading up the bags. "I forgot to ask how your visit with Jen went yesterday."

Kennedy's eyes filled with shadows. "She was glad to see me. Her face is all swollen and black and blue, but her blood pressure is remaining stable now, so she's out of the woods. Lots of pain from the surgery on her arm, but the doctor says they got it repaired. She'll have full range of motion and full use of her hand after a lot of physical therapy."

Erin was relieved to hear that. "She's a very lucky girl. I think Rob Sorensen meant to end her life."

"Yeah," Kennedy said in an oddly thick voice. "I hope he's put away and never allowed to be loose again."

Erin knew better. The Rob Sorensens of the world plea-bargained and rarely served enough time in prison. But she didn't need to disillusion Kennedy by sharing that. This was his time in life to believe that justice would always prevail.

"Thanks for the talk about gun safety," she told him. "That's a great parallel. It helps me understand why everyone on this ranch is so quick to criticize me."

"Yep. To them, being unsafe around a horse is like pointing a loaded gun at someone. Only you're pointing the barrel at yourself."

Erin paused long enough on the porch after leaving the bunkhouse to take a deep breath and release it. She wasn't sure if she would leave in the morning or decide to stay another day. But one thing she was certain of: She would have a different perspective now and know men yammering at her about safety wasn't necessarily evidence of a double standard.

When Erin reentered the paddock, she was as nervous as a long-tailed cat in a roomful of loggers wearing cork boots. The horse seemed just as nervous. Erin had dumped the contents of one vegetable bag into the pouch of her shirt. Holding tightly to the lead, she tried to reach up and touch the mare's head. With a shrill whinny, the animal reared high onto her back legs and sliced the air around Erin with her front hooves. Again, Erin nearly wet her pants. But this time, she was quicker to note that the mare had avoided striking her. That made her feel less afraid and a little less nervous as well.

"I get it," she said softly.

The mare snorted and swung her massive head.

"Yes, I really do," she said. "I'm scared, too. Not just of you, but a lot of other things." She held out a chunk of carrot, hoping the mare might take it. But that wasn't going to happen. Erin was the enemy, and any food she offered was suspect. "It's only a carrot. You like carrots. Right? And this is a very tasty carrot. At the rate we're making progress, I may have to eat them for lunch."

Erin remembered seeing Wyatt hunker in front of the frightened gelding last fall, how he'd just assumed a position and remained there, not moving a muscle until the horse grew curious and began sniffing his hat and shirt. She led the mare toward the only tree in the paddock, which was a feat in and of itself, because the animal really didn't want to be led anywhere. But to the mare's credit, she wasn't completely ill-mannered in her protests. She neighed and balked and threw her head, but she didn't wheel away and jerk the rope from Erin's hand. Her behavior made Erin feel sad. When she rebelled against her father, she always tried to be polite about it, too.

Erin sat with her back braced against the tree and rested her open hand holding the carrot on her knee, palm up. She relaxed her shoulders, which took concentration. With a gigantic animal standing over her, she felt vulnerable. And it would be just her luck that she was breaking yet another safety rule Wyatt would yammer at her about. He'd said he would be watching her.

Wyatt stood just inside the new horse's stall, resting his shoulder against the gate frame. Erin might see him if she looked. He would deal with that when it happened. For now, he couldn't focus on other chores. He was too worried about her. What she knew about horses would fit into a thimble with room to spare.

It wasn't long before he was smiling, though. When Erin sat motionless under the tree, he recognized one of his own tactics for working with a frightened horse, and he was proud of Erin for remembering it. When an equine felt frightened, a motionless human quickly became a curiosity, and eventually the horse might step closer to figure out what in the heck was wrong. Equally important, though, was that Erin was trying to think of ways to make the horse connect with her. To succeed required understanding of what frightened the animal.

The mare was getting an A in Psychology 101 as far as Wyatt was concerned. And Erin was following all the safety rules that he'd recited to her so far. He wasn't particularly thrilled that she was sitting at the feet of an equine given to rearing and striking, but he couldn't really scold her for that, because she'd learned that trick from him.

Wyatt was still observing Erin when Kennedy entered the stall behind him. Sensing someone's presence, Wyatt turned and then smiled at his brother. "You got home late last night. We didn't get to talk."

"Jen didn't want me to leave," Kennedy told him. "The attack did some bad stuff to her." He tapped his temple. "She knows Sorensen is still locked up, but the other three guys stood and watched. I think she's afraid they'll come find her. I tried to tell her they weren't really responsible. I think it was more a case of being afraid of Rob and not having the guts to interfere. But Jen wouldn't turn loose of my hand so I could go."

Wyatt sighed. "Ah. You saved her from them once. Now she feels afraid if you're not around."

"I guess that's it. I don't think she'll ever be the same after this."

Wyatt couldn't hear the emotions in Kennedy's voice, but he could see them on his face. His brother was starting to care deeply about Jen. "Nobody can ever be the same after living through something like that. But eventually she'll move beyond it. If you decide to walk beside her as she makes that journey, you'll need to be very patient."

"Yeah. Tomorrow after my last class, I'd like to stop by and see her again. It'll make me about an hour late."

"Erin may leave in the morning. If you're late, we'll be shorthanded. We're in the middle of second calving season. You'll have to do all your work after you get home."

"I can do that."

"All right. Just see that you do."

Kennedy shuffled his boot over the straw under his feet. Then he looked up and said, "I hope Erin doesn't quit. I really like her. A lot."

Wyatt glanced out at Erin. She still sat motionless under the tree. The carrot on her palm hadn't been touched, but the mare had moved a little closer. "Yeah, I like her a lot, too."

"I think you like her a little bit too much," Kennedy observed.

Wyatt felt a flush creep up his neck.

"I've seen the way you look at her," Kennedy added. "You're falling in love with her."

Wyatt wasn't foolish enough to deny the charge. "And that's a dead end for me. You should understand that. I've told you why."

"Yep. And I don't blame you for worrying about that possibly happening again. But love is love, Wyatt. You can't turn it off just because you wish you could."

Kennedy turned and walked away, leaving Wyatt to mull that over.

Erin's spine tingled when the mare moved in close enough to nudge her shoulder and sniff her shirt. Then she smiled. But she kept her head bent. Next the mare sniffed at the carrot. Then she snorted and backed away. She didn't trust easily and that made Erin's heart hurt. But she finally stole the carrot with a quick wiggle of her velvety lips.

Erin pretended not to notice and got out another carrot. It wasn't what Wyatt had told her to do, but how could she try to touch the horse's head when the animal kept the rope stretched tight to put distance between them? Erin remembered when she'd once been that wary. In an entirely different way, of course. She'd never feared that her law enforcement colleagues would do her physical harm, but she guessed, in a way, that being mocked or made to feel inadequate had wounded her just as badly down deep where no one could see.

When the horse nudged Erin again, she murmured nonsensical reassurances and touched the mare's neck, which was damp with sweat. It wasn't a hot morning, so Erin knew the animal's perspiration was caused by nervousness. But she felt a surge of satisfaction at being allowed to make physical contact. She pushed slowly to her feet and stepped in close as she'd once seen Wyatt do with a gelding. The mare didn't object when Erin stroked her neck again. She just made soft, rumbling noises, sounding for all the world as if she were talking. Erin had no idea what the mare was trying to convey, so she tried to think what she might want someone to say if she were afraid.

"I know, I know," Erin murmured back. "Someone was very mean to you. I'm so sorry that happened." And Erin sincerely meant it. That such a large and powerful animal had been brought to this state, fearful of even gentle touches, made her feel sick. "But you don't need to be afraid of me. I'm as messed up as you are, and all I want is to be your friend."

As she stroked the horse's neck, she inched her fingertips higher with every pass until she was almost touching the crown of the horse's head. Then she stopped the advance and offered the mare another carrot, which promptly vanished from her palm. The grinding sound as the equine chewed reminded Erin of how easily the horse could bite her. But so far, the mare didn't seem intent on doing Erin harm. She just wanted to be left alone. Only even as Erin thought that, she knew it was wrong, dead wrong. This horse needed a friend as badly as she did, someone she could trust, someone who would love her no matter what, and someone who understood her. It wasn't much to ask for, and yet Erin knew it was absolutely *everything.* She'd never realized that animals needed love just as much as people did, but spending a couple of hours with this mare had opened her mind to lots of things she'd never stopped to think about until now.

Erin got another carrot from the stash in her shirt, let the mare sniff it, and then began stroking her neck again, inching her fingers closer and closer to the animal's head with every pass. She stiffened when she saw Four Toes approaching the paddock. She didn't want to get trampled if the mare went berserk. But apparently the mare and the bear had already met and established a relationship. Four Toes made a moaning sound as he walked along the paddock fence, and the horse rumbled back at him. Erin likened their exchange to that of two people who didn't speak the same language and settled for making sounds of greeting. The bear continued on its way to the main house.

"So, you're not afraid of Four Toes," Erin observed. "I think that may be amazing. I don't imagine horses normally like bears. But then, Four Toes has been domesticated. Maybe he told you about that." Erin reached the crown of the mare's head and offered her another carrot. "You're a good girl," she whispered. "And maybe tomorrow, you'll let me touch your ears. Domino and Four Toes both love to have their ears scratched."

As Erin spoke, she realized she'd just committed to staying on the ranch one more day. The horse was starting to trust her, and Erin didn't think it was right to befriend the animal and then just walk away. That thought reminded her that it had been too long since she'd talked to Julie. Her friend had tried to contact her a few times, but Erin had let her calls go to voicemail. She'd just quit her job and taken another one at the ranch. She'd known Julie would ask questions, she hadn't known how to answer them then, and she still didn't now. But that didn't matter. She still needed to get in touch and at least assure Julie that she was okay.

For another hour, Erin held a piece of carrot in her loosely closed fist, allowing the mare to smell it, but not letting her have the treat until she'd managed to touch the crown of the horse's head. She was pleased when the mare stopped flinching. And at that point, she decided the mare had been through enough for one day.

She went to find something else she could do and ended up mucking stalls for the rest of the afternoon. This time, she tried to follow Vickie's advice and took smaller bites of the straw and manure with the tines of the pitchfork. She also bypassed using the wheelbarrow and used the skidder to haul stuff away.

CHAPTER FIFTEEN

Erin was drained by quitting time, but today it was a good kind of tired. As she walked toward the bunkhouse to help fix dinner, she decided she definitely wanted to remain on the ranch one more day. She wouldn't unload her car. She'd just get out a set of clean clothes and her toiletries. If things got ugly again tomorrow, she'd be ready to leave when her shift ended. The thought of abandoning the mare to fend for herself made Erin sad, but it wasn't as if Wyatt couldn't take over with the animal and do a better job.

Kennedy and Wyatt were cooking when Erin entered. With only a glance, she could tell they worked well as a team. Kennedy was communicating with American Sign Language and so was Wyatt. Erin followed their exchanges and grinned at their nonsense. It was good to see two brothers who got along, even if they were telling each other to "shove it up your ass" when they disagreed on something.

Erin stepped to the fridge for a cold drink and selected a beer. She almost pulled the tab and drank straight from the can, but then she decided she wanted to try it in a glass instead. In bars, she enjoyed cold beer on tap, which was always served in a glass, and there was no one here who would make fun of her for liking it better that way.

Whatever Wyatt was cooking was soon left to simmer on the stove. Erin sniffed the air and thought it smelled like spaghetti sauce, and she wondered if one of the brothers had made meatballs. She used the frozen kind herself, but that didn't mean she liked them. She'd worked long hours and hadn't wanted to be in the kitchen for hours to make a meal for only one person.

The guys joined her at the table with cans of beer.

Kennedy took a long pull of his drink and told his brother, "I can't believe you put sugar in the marinara sauce!"

"Only two tablespoons. I don't like the acidity of straight tomato sauce and seasonings. A tiny bit of sugar makes it better."

"Where did you learn that?" Kennedy asked.

"Chef Boyardee," Wyatt retorted.

Erin couldn't help it and burst out laughing at the startled expression on Kennedy's face. She got up from the table to taste the sauce. When she turned from the stove, she tossed her spoon in the sink and said, "It's fabulous, Wyatt. But I know your guilty secret."

"What secret?" he asked.

"You stole Sissy's recipe."

He guffawed, throwing back his blond head and closing his eyes. Wyatt rarely laughed, and Erin loved the sound. "Don't I wish?"

Kennedy stepped to the sink to prepare broccoli for steaming. Erin asked how Jen had seemed to be feeling emotionally the previous day. She doubted the girl could emerge from such a devastating attack without at least some psychological issues.

Kennedy cast her a glance over his shoulder, his expression solemn. "She acts as if boogeymen are hiding behind the curtains and under her hospital bed. When it was time for me to leave, she clung to my hand and asked me not to go. I understand why, of course, but it's kind of hard for me to sympathize when she knows nobody's really in her room."

As a female deputy, Erin had been required to take coursework for rape counseling and had been assigned to help several women go through the process of filing charges against their attackers, an action that required humiliating photography sessions and physical exams to procure documented evidence. "Victims of violent crimes often no longer trust in their perception of reality," she told Kennedy. "I helped interview the three boys who were present, so I got the details of what happened to Jen that evening, and the attack pretty much came at her from nowhere. She thought her ex-boyfriend wouldn't bother her again. He'd gotten in big trouble, after all. Jen went to work that day as if it were any other day. Everything went well, just as it did on any other day. She never expected what happened. The boys came in on foot, so she didn't see a car to forewarn her. The ex-boyfriend waited in hiding until she skated within his reach, and he dashed out to grab her arm. He carried her behind the dumpster and threw her to the ground, pissed off because she'd gouged his shins with the roller skates. The fall is what shattered her wrist. At that point, she could fight him off with only one hand. Her day became a nightmare beyond her comprehension. With no warning, a boogeyman leaped out. And now she doesn't know when it may happen again. Rationally, she may know she's being silly, but her fears are real. The unthinkable *can* happen, and once a person lives through that, it's hard to get over it."

Kennedy got the vegetables into the steaming rack inside the pot and then returned to the table. "I guess it'd be kind of like me walking through the woods and getting mauled by a grizzly where a grizzly bear should never be. I'd never feel relaxed in a forest again. It would take me a long time to get over it, anyway."

"Exactly," Erin replied. "When Jen seems irrational, just be patient and try to understand."

"Thanks for talking to me. I guess I might be afraid, too, if I were her."

Erin had become very fond of Kennedy. He was a genuinely nice young man. "Jen will now look at every guy she meets and wonder if he's a grizzly bear disguised as a nice person. It'll take her a while to start trusting again. You also need to realize that, in her eyes, you are the guy who once fought off the grizzlies to protect her. She may be super dependent on you for a while, because with you, she feels safer."

After dinner, Erin teamed up with Tex to clean the kitchen and then walked to the main house. Wyatt, who'd gone out after supper to check on all the animals, intercepted her before she reached the porch.

In the twilight, he was so handsome. The breeze lifted his longish hair beneath the brim of his Stetson, swirling it like strands of silk over his shoulders.

"Would you mind taking a walk with me?" he asked.

Erin was tired after sleeping fitfully the prior night, but he was her boss, and although the invitation was cloaked in civility, she knew it was essentially a demand. "Sure."

Moments later, she was glad that she'd come. Walking with Wyatt at this time of evening was surprisingly pleasant. He even stopped once to admire a doe and her fawn. They ended up down at the log where all their conversations seemed to go badly. She hoped this time would be different.

After they sat down, he shifted to face her, resting one bent leg on the log in front of him. Erin followed his example. It would be easier for him to read her lips if she turned toward him.

"What did you learn about the mare's story today?" he asked.

Surprised by the question, Erin replied, "I didn't really think in those terms as I was working with her, so you've taken me off guard."

"It isn't a test with right or wrong answers, Erin. I'd just like to know what impressions you got."

Erin almost said she hadn't gotten any particular impressions, but the words that came out of her mouth were, "She's afraid. I think she once trusted humans, but then she was betrayed, not once, but many times. Someone did mean things that make her afraid for anyone to touch her head. Today she wanted the treats I had and was afraid to take them."

His eyes filled with a distant look. "I thought the same thing. I think she once had a loving owner and a wonderful life. Then she somehow ended up with someone bad." His gaze snapped to hers. "Sorry. In my estimation, people who abuse animals are rotten to the core."

The passion in his voice made Erin's skin tingle. "I agree."

"Did you notice how careful she was not to strike you with her hooves?"

Erin smiled. "She put on a great act and had me scared to death at first. But then I did notice that. She doesn't want to hurt me. She just wants me to leave her alone."

"That was my take, too. I saw you sitting under the tree with your head bent."

Erin couldn't help but laugh. "I saw you do something similar once, and since I know next to nothing about horses, I copied you."

"Did it work?"

"Yes. I think she thought I was asleep or dead, and she came over to sniff and nudge me. When I didn't respond, she swiped the carrot from my hand. After getting a couple more carrots, she seemed to relax, so I got up and stepped in close to her shoulder like I saw you do that day last fall with the gelding. She let me press against her and allowed me to stroke her neck. I was sneaky about it, inching my hand higher and higher, but I finally got to touch the crown of her head."

His full mouth tipped into a crooked and purely devastating grin. "It's her poll, Erin, not the crown of her head."

"Oh." Erin thought about that. "Why make it complicated by calling it a poll?"

His smile broadened, creasing his lean cheeks to form parenthetical brackets around his mouth. "Because it isn't really the crown of a horse's head. It's technically the base of its skull. I've never researched why it's called a poll when it's actually an occipital protrusion, but I don't argue the point. Poll is a lot easier to say, and since it's important when we're riding, we say it a lot."

"How is it important during riding?"

"We'll get to that if you end up staying. If not, it's a bunch of information you don't really need. I'm more interested in your take on the mare."

"My take is that she's been horribly mistreated. She tried not to flinch when I touched her poll, but the fright reaction has been ingrained so deeply I think it's a mindless response. To overcome it, she'll have to learn to trust me and then make herself react differently. But that will take time."

Wyatt nodded. "A lot of time, and I got the same impression from her." His smile diminished to a slight curve of his lips. "So what did you learn about yourself as you worked with her today?"

The question came out of left field, and Erin gave him a bewildered look.

"You don't need to answer," he told her. "But I hope you'll think about it."

He swung off the log and stood, looking down at her. "Ready to head back?"

Erin got to her feet. "I can't believe it. We finally talked down here without being ugly to each other."

He fell into step beside her. "Will wonders never cease?"

Erin had a cup of decaf with Uncle Slade and Aunt Vickie before she went upstairs to shower and rest. Vickie served a plate of the chocolate chip cookies that she'd made the night before, and Erin, unable to resist them, ate five. Uncle Slade didn't seem upset with Erin, which eased her mind, and she was no longer upset with him. With time to think about it, she understood why he'd appointed Wyatt to do the dirty work for him in regards to firing her, and it certainly hadn't stemmed from a lack of courage. Her uncle loved her and simply hadn't wanted to be the bad guy. He'd been trying to preserve their relationship.

As Erin went upstairs, she felt differently than she had that morning, but she couldn't quite pinpoint the reason. Maybe, she decided, it was all a matter of perspective, and hers had changed over the course of the day.

When she climbed into bed and snuggled under the down comforter, she recalled Wyatt's question. How could she possibly learn anything about herself by working with an abused horse? She had never been physically abused as a kid. She had to give her dad credit for that much, even though he'd hurt her in dozens of other ways.

There were no similarities between her and the mare. While working with the horse, she had deduced that the animal had tried to please her former owner and been punished for doing things she didn't know were wrong. Or she may have done nothing wrong and her owner was just impossible to please.

As that thought meandered through Erin's sleepy brain, she blinked wide awake and sat up in bed, suddenly seeing so many similarities between herself and the mare that she was appalled. Erin's father had been impossible to please. In order to gain his approval, she had struggled to attain perfection at anything he wanted her to master, but once she achieved that goal, he only set her a new one. And though he'd never physically punished her for failing at a new assignment, he'd always acted disappointed in her. For Erin, that had hurt as much as, if not more than, any physical blow ever could. She'd yearned for her dad to tell her how proud he was of her. Only no matter how well she performed, she never got that praise. He just set the bar higher.

Resting her shoulders against the headboard, Erin stared at a patch of moonlight on the bedroom wall and mentally moved forward in time to the present. Now, even as an adult, she was still reacting mindlessly to her father's expectations. She also imagined everyone around her was judging her and being critical of her, just as her father had once been. Even worse, she was slipping into top-performance mode so that nobody could criticize her or look down on her. It wasn't so much that she felt a need to compete with the men on this ranch. She just wanted to show them that she could work as hard as they could. *Correction*. What she wanted had little or nothing to do with it. She *needed* to show them that she was as good as they were, just as she'd always needed to show her dad that she was just as good as any boy.

A memory flashed in Erin's mind of when she'd begun to develop at age twelve. She'd stood in front of a mirror, looking at her budding breasts and crying, because she knew boys didn't have them and her father would therefore hate them. In a twinkling, Erin came face-to-face with so many truths that she'd been avoiding. As a young child, she had started to hate her body because her father had hated it, and now, as an adult, she still felt embarrassed when people saw certain parts of her, like the day she'd removed her shirt and Wyatt had walked up. She'd been ashamed for him to see her shoulders and arms, not because they were feminine, but because she'd worked at the gym to pack them with as much muscle as she could without taking steroids. She'd been afraid he would think she looked too masculine, and yet, at the opposite end of the spectrum, she had dieted and worked out like a fiend to have a muscular physique.

Erin closed her eyes and let her head thump against the carved wood that supported her back. She was so screwed up, and her mind was swimming with revelations she'd never been able to see until now. *Oh, God.* Unlike the mare, she didn't threaten people and prance around to show off her muscle, but she did push herself to perform beyond her ability to impress the men around her. And just like during her childhood, she hadn't gotten the reward she always wanted: praise. Instead she'd gotten advice and criticism, and everyone began setting a new goal for her: to work smarter. No wonder she'd reacted badly to that suggestion. All her life, she'd needed to push herself physically in order to feel good about herself.

Erin finally slipped back down on the bed to lie on her side with her knees drawn to her chest. There truly was a little girl within her who'd been made to feel broken and in need of fixing. And no wonder. She kept remembering what Jonas had said to her last night about her screwed-up parents, her father doing everything he could to turn her into a son and her mother striving to make her into a perfect little lady. Talk about a child getting mixed signals.

Erin drifted off to sleep with that realization circling in her mind.

The next morning, Erin was allowed to work with the mare again. By lunchtime, she felt that she and the mare had made a lot of progress, and that was a heady feeling. After quickly making a sandwich at the bunkhouse, she went out to sit by the mare's paddock fence to eat. The horse nuzzled her ball cap and sniffed her hair, sending a shivery sensation down Erin's spine. When the equine nudged her shoulder, Erin finally gave her the rest of her sandwich bread and ate only what was left of the lunch meat.

After wiping her hands clean on her jeans, she drew out her cell phone and called Julie, who answered on the second ring, bypassing hello to say, "It's been forever since you've been in touch. Do you have any idea how worried I've been?"

"I'm okay," Erin assured her. She gave Julie a quick rundown of what had happened the night she quit her job and how she'd been working on her uncle's ranch ever since. "I'm sorry I ignored your calls and let them go to voicemail. I was too upset to answer questions. It's been a difficult time."

"I imagine it has," Julie said. "I heard about the Johnson girl. What a tragedy. It set everybody in town on their ears, including me. The word is that you turned in your badge because the Sorensen boy threatened to rape that girl and no one at the sheriff's department did a thing to stop him."

Erin sighed. "I'm sad to hear that Sheriff Adams is taking heat over my decision to quit. It really wasn't his fault that nothing was done. The boy was in his father's custody and scheduled to stand before a judge. The sheriff's department couldn't interfere with that process."

"So why did you get so upset you quit?"

Erin really didn't want to talk about that. "I'll fill you in another time. My lunch break is almost over. Enough about me. How are you doing?"

Julie sighed. "I've been doing okay until today. I felt a little off all morning, and now my stomach is rolling. I thought I was hungry and ate some soup, but that just made it worse."

"Uh-oh. Is there a virus going around?"

"Not that I know of. But I'm exposed to dozens of people a day."

Erin frowned. "Maybe you should close up early and go home. Drink fluids, rest, take some aspirin. Now that you mention it, you don't sound like your usual self."

"And I'm going downhill by the moment. Maybe I will go home. It isn't that busy today."

"Do it. Text me so I don't worry. If you're sicker, I can come into town tonight. Make you some soup or go shopping for things you think sound appealing. I always crave different stuff when I'm feeling icky."

After Erin ended the call with Julie, she stood, brushed the dirt off her jeans, and turned to go back in the paddock with the horse. She found Wyatt standing directly in her path. He smiled and swept off his Stetson to blot sweat from his brow with his shirtsleeve.

"Didn't mean to startle you. Just thought I'd see how the morning went."

"At first, we were back to square one, but she remembered the apples and carrots from yesterday. It wasn't long before she wanted a treat worse than she wanted to keep me from touching her." Erin gave him a questioning look. "How many apples and carrots can she safely have?"

He frowned thoughtfully. "I wouldn't worry too much about that. She's a big girl. You cut everything up in chunks. Right? She could probably eat all you have with you and not get sick. If you're worried about it, though, you could go with some grain as well. Change it up each time so she doesn't get too much of the same thing. She might like the variety."

Before Erin could say anything more, he walked away.

Blackie stood in the mall area of the Mystic Creek Menagerie and stared in bewilderment at the CLOSED sign on the front door of the Morning Grind. In his recollection, Julie had never closed her coffee shop prior to five o'clock without first posting a warning to her customers. It worried him that she had left today without giving her patrons a heads-up. He always stopped in during his afternoon walk around three, when she had very few customers trailing in. Their visits had become something he looked forward to.

Blackie closed his own shop a couple of times a day. He just slapped a note on the door saying when he'd be back. But he owned the only pawnshop in town. He didn't need to worry about competition or losing business. When people wanted to hock something, they needed money fast, and he knew they would return to strike a bargain with him later. Julie didn't have that luxury. She was up against every eatery on Main. Why had she left unexpectedly in the middle of the day? Something must have happened.

As Blackie left the mall, he saw Tony Chavez putting out place settings on the tables that peppered the revolving dining platform in the middle of the cavernous hall. Tony grinned and turned to say hello as Blackie drew to a stop.

"The Morning Grind is closed," Blackie told the restauranteur. "Do you happen to know why?"

Tony, wearing a white bib apron smeared with tomato sauce, said, "She got sick. Said she had to go home and lie down. She didn't look too good."

"Sick with what?" Blackie asked.

"Nausea, I think. Her face was pale, and she was woozy. Nothing serious, I don't think. Probably just that stomach virus that's been going around. A few of my customers canceled reservations because they were down with it."

Blackie thanked Tony for the information and left. When he got to his shop, he called Julie on his cell phone, but she didn't answer. That worried him even more, so when five o'clock finally rolled around, he closed his shop an hour early and drove out to the Bearberry Loop golf course. Julie's blue Mazda was out front in the parking area. He exited his car and hurried along the walkway to her front porch. When he knocked, he heard no sounds coming from inside, so he rang the bell. He still got no response. So he tried the doorknob and stiffened in surprise when the carved portal swung open under the pressure of his hand.

He believed Julie always locked up. In fact, she was so cautious that she'd even replaced all her downstairs windows with ones that locked in place if she wanted them slightly open. It wasn't like her not to secure all her doors.

He stepped into the foyer, feeling like a burglar. "Julie?" Blackie wondered if she was lying down. She hadn't given him a complete tour of the house the night he'd come for dinner, so he didn't know where her bedroom was, upstairs or down. "Julie? Where are you?"

He heard a faint sound and followed his nose down a short hallway, which led him past a guest bathroom and then to a room with the door ajar. He peeked in and saw Julie curled up in a fetal position on a king-size bed. Still fully clothed, she lay atop the floral bedspread. Judging by the way she hugged herself, she was cold. He crossed the room and stood gazing down at her.

"Sick," she murmured. "Go. Don't want you to catch it."

Blackie had a strong immune system and rarely caught viruses, but even if it meant he might this time, he couldn't leave Julie when she needed someone to take care of her. He rolled her toward him and then stepped around the bed to draw back the spread and blankets. Then he retraced his steps, lifted her into his arms, and deposited her gently on the mattress so he could pull the covers over her.

"Sick, so sick," she told him. "Can't keep anything down."

He sat beside her and took her hand. "I'll drive back into town and get something that might help settle your stomach. And some 7-Up, too. My mother swore by it."

She struggled to focus her gaze on him. "Don't want to bother you."

Blackie brushed a lock of hair back from her cheek. "Don't be silly. I have little else to do, so bother me all you like."

She smiled wanly and then drifted back to sleep. Blackie took a quick tour of the home to make sure all the exterior doors were locked. Then he fished in her purse to find her house keys. A moment later, he roused her from sleep again.

"I've got to take care of a couple of things at my shop. Then I'll be back. If you feel dizzy, don't get up while I'm gone unless you have to. Is there anything you need before I go?"

She shook her head no. Then he heard a text notification come in on her phone. He fished in her purse again to find the device. When the screen lighted up, he saw that Erin De Laney had messaged her. Normally Blackie wouldn't have read the note, but a part of the first line showed on the screen, reading: I'm worried. Are U OK? That prompted him to swipe the screen so he could write back to Julie's friend.

This is Blackie. I just came to check on Julie, and she's feeling pretty bad. I'm going to stay the night. Don't want to leave her alone. But don't be worried. I'll get in touch if she gets any worse.

Erin texted right back. I can take off from work and come if she needs me. No problem. Really.

Blackie typed: I closed my shop early. I'll let you know if I need backup. It's only a virus, I think, a 24-hour bug.

After returning Julie's phone to her purse, Blackie locked the front door as he left the house. Then he drove back to his shop to put a notice on the door that he would be closed for an undetermined period of time. Then he went to Flagg's Market to pick up a few items. He wasn't sure what foods appealed to Julie when she wasn't feeling well, so he got her his favorite sick-day stuff. He also bought a remedy for nausea. He didn't like seeing her sick. It made him feel off-balance.

As Blackie drove back to Julie's home, one thought took up residence in his mind and refused to be evicted: *I'm in love with her.* Blackie had tried his damnedest to control his feelings for her in case it didn't work out between them. She was too young for him, and he'd known from the start that he needed to guard his heart. But somehow he'd taken the leap, anyway.

The following day Erin once again spent the morning with the abused mare. Because the equine was so wary and shrank from Erin's touch, Erin started calling her Violet, short for Shrinking Violet.

Wyatt laughed when he learned of the horse's new name. "She isn't a purebred with a registered name, so it's probably fine for you to call her whatever you like. Slade says he bought her from a guy who raises parade horses. She's half American Saddlebred and half Morgan, a great mix for elegant carriage and high-stepping."

"I didn't realize horses are raised specifically to be in parades."

"They can be put to other uses in between events, which is probably why Slade bought her. She'll make a good ranch horse if we can get her settled down." He sighed. "Unfortunately, she isn't settling in, and the ending for her won't be good, I'm afraid."

Ending. Erin didn't like the sound of that. "What do you mean, *ending?*"

"Oh, nothing like that. Slade doesn't euthanize problem horses. He just won't keep her, is all. This is a ranch, not a therapy compound for troubled horses, and Violet is a very troubled horse." His expression softened as he gazed at the mare for a moment. "Troubled horses are a liability. I don't think it's her aim, but she may hurt someone when she's acting up. Slade will sell her. And then her new owners probably will, too. She'll never find a good home. Unless, of course, a small miracle happens."

"Such as?"

He shrugged. "If her next owner loves her and works with her, she could snap out of it and become a fabulous horse. Not likely to happen, though. Most people want a rideable horse right off the bat. And they aren't knowledgeable enough to help her, anyway."

Erin's chest went suddenly tight. "If that's the case, why are you letting *me* work with her? I'm the least knowledgeable person there is when it comes to horses. A city girl who never even got to have a dog growing up."

His glanced at Pistol and Domino, playing nearby. "But you care about her. And whether you realize it yet or not, you understand her in ways even I don't. The way I see it, you're the perfect person to help her."

As Wyatt walked away, Erin gazed after him. She was no longer quite as upset with him as she had been, so her attraction to him had resurfaced. *Not good.* No matter what happened, she and Wyatt could only ever be friends. Even so, she liked watching him cover ground, his muscular legs measuring off long strides with each loose and rhythmic shift of his hips. He swung his arms with every step, which set off a display of muscles rippling under the back of his shirt. He moved with incredible grace for such a tall man, never seeming to hurry and yet getting where he wanted to go with impressive speed. When she walked beside him, he made an obvious effort to slow down, which bugged her, but she kept telling herself that was silly. Her legs were shorter than his, and she couldn't change that.

She turned toward the fence and studied Violet. Suddenly, working with her was no longer just something she'd been told to do. Erin couldn't let this animal be sold to someone who wouldn't care about her. The mare was frightened; that was all. A *liability?* Erin had almost been fired for the same reason, and unless she learned to work smarter instead of harder, she still might lose her job.

"Wyatt's right," she told the horse. "You and I have a lot in common. But, you know what, Violet? As broke as I'll soon be, I won't let you become the equine equivalent of a foster child, getting bounced from one bad home to another." A sense of purpose burgeoned in Erin's chest. "If Uncle Slade decides to sell you, I'll be first in line to make an offer. Strike that. I probably need to tell him right now that I want you. He may just make a phone call and strike a deal over the phone. I can't let that happen."

The horse made a deep, rumbling sound. Erin wondered what it was called. It was conversational in tone. Not knowing the proper term for all the noises equines made drove home to Erin how ignorant she was about the species.

"I'm going to learn, though, Violet. For your sake, I'll learn."

Blackie's prediction that Julie probably had a twenty-four-hour bug was way off base. He'd held her head over a plastic bin most of the night and morning, and now as afternoon arrived, she was still hurling. At some point, she'd put on some satin pajamas, but those had become casualties of war at about three a.m. Now she had no more fresh nightwear. All of it was going through a wash cycle.

Lifting Julie's head from the pillow, he pressed the rim of a glass to her colorless lips. "Try just a sip, honey. It's 7-Up and should settle your stomach."

Julie took a dutiful sip and promptly lurched sideways, digging her fingers into the edge of the mattress as she hurled it back up. Blackie grabbed the damp washcloth he'd commandeered from her bathroom and dabbed her lips as she sank back against the pillows again. She'd grown so pale that her face was nearly as white as the pillowcases. *Not a twenty-four-hour bug.* If that were the case, Julie would be sipping fluids at this point and maybe even munching cautiously on toast fingers, which were one of his specialties.

"Just sleep if you can," he told her.

Yesterday she had kept telling him he didn't need to stay, and she'd worried aloud that he might catch whatever she had. But today she was too weak for that. He'd found her a large University of Oregon T-shirt that she said she used for gardening. A pair of black leggings hugged her slender legs. Blackie was glad that she'd had the strength to change clothing by herself, which had allowed him to hide like a coward in the hallway until she was covered again. He didn't think he could handle seeing her naked. Well, he would have handled it. But he had a feeling the view would have gotten chiseled into his memory cells, and he didn't need that.

Just then his cell phone rang. He adjourned to the hallway so he wouldn't keep Julie awake while talking. He wasn't surprised when he saw Erin De Laney's name pop up on the screen. He'd called her with an update on Julie's condition last night, using Julie's phone, and during that conversation, he and Erin had exchanged contact information.

"Hello," Blackie said as he sank onto an ornate, Victorian-style chair sitting next to a table that provided a perch for a landline phone. "Nothing much has changed."

Erin's voice came over the airways. "Man, she must have caught a bad one. Are you sure you don't need me there? I mean, well"—her voice trailed away—"I, um, how do I say this? Is she able to take care of all her personal business without you helping her? I know you two are good friends, but if something more has developed between you, Julie hasn't mentioned it. And she's the modest type."

Blackie couldn't help but smile. He'd noticed Julie's conservative approach to fashion. She always managed to look stylish, but except for that blouse with parts of the sleeves missing, she rarely wore anything that displayed much skin. "She's managed all that by herself so far. But if that changes, I'll definitely call you. For now, though, we're good."

"Are you sure? I'm new at this job, and cows are calving, so everyone's really busy. But I'm positive my uncle would give me a couple of days off. He knows Julie is a dear friend."

Blackie hated to ask Erin to take a day off from work. She probably needed all the hours she could get now that she'd turned in her badge. Blackie would face no financial difficulties from keeping his shop closed. "I've got it for right now. And this can't go on much longer. I'll be taking her to the emergency clinic if it does."

Erin asked him to keep her posted and they concluded their conversation. When Blackie returned to the master suite, he found Julie in the bathroom. She had developed diarrhea, and the makeshift nightwear that he'd found for her had bitten the dust. *Leggings.* What had he been thinking? How would he ever get those damned things off her without seeing parts of her that he shouldn't and didn't wish to see?

He got Julie into the shower fully clothed. She was so weak she leaned against the tiled wall, barely managing to stand by herself. He grabbed the handheld nozzle and sprayed her down, clothing and all. Then he began the torturous job of trying to tug wet, stretchy, clingy nylon knit off her butt and down her legs. He handed Julie a towel to cover herself before he began that task, but she was so sick she didn't have the strength to hold it up. He got an eyeful. There was no avoiding it, and the only bright spot in the otherwise gloomy situation was that Julie was so sick she didn't seem to care.

What really blew Blackie's mind, though, wasn't just seeing Julie naked from the waist down, which was pretty damned mind-blowing for a fifty-three-year-old man who hadn't dipped his oil stick anywhere for over three years. Nope, what really took the wind out of his sails was that Julie was a natural blonde.

A natural blonde? He didn't get it. Women all over Mystic Creek went to beauty shops to become blondes, spending heaps of money to keep their dark roots from showing. Yet Julie, whose down-yonder fuzz tagged her as a honey blonde, dyed her hair such a dark brown it was almost black.

Within minutes, Blackie wouldn't have cared if Julie dyed her hair purple. After he got her dressed in another T-shirt and a pair of men's boxer shorts he'd found in one of her drawers, she was too weak to stand up, let alone walk. He feared she was getting dehydrated and decided she needed something more than occasional swallows of Pepto-Bismol, which she promptly vomited back up.

"Julie, honey, I think you need to go to the ER. I can get your robe off the hook in the bathroom to hide what you're wearing, and I'll carry you. You won't have to walk. Do I have your permission to do that?"

She nodded, and that was the only green light he needed. Four hours later, he was carrying Julie back into her house. She'd been given IV fluids for two hours, and Dr. Blake, an internist who volunteered for duty at the clinic, had given her a shot for nausea. Blackie had also filled a prescription for rectal suppositories that were supposed to control the nausea after the shot wore off. Julie hadn't vomited in over an hour, so Blackie was hopeful that the worst might be over.

"Thank you, Blackie," she whispered when he got her situated in bed. "I feel better."

"I'm glad." That was an understatement. He'd fallen head over heels in love with this young woman, and he'd been truly frightened for her. For the moment, he wouldn't allow himself to think about the age difference between them. He also wouldn't think about that handsome doctor with his caramel-colored hair and fudge-brown eyes, who was undoubtedly a far better prospect than Blackie for a woman Julie's age. Nope. He'd just focus on how relieved he was that she seemed to be on the road to recovery. "You're pretty special to me."

When Julie fell asleep, Blackie went to the kitchen. He'd fixed stuff for Julie, but he hadn't eaten a bite of food himself since yesterday. He hadn't realized how hungry he was until he likened the young doctor's hair and eye color to candies. He made himself a grilled cheese sandwich and opened a can of tomato soup, one of his favorite combos. While he ate, he texted Erin to tell her that he'd taken Julie to the clinic. After giving her the necessary details, he concentrated only on eating. He couldn't care for the love of his life if he fainted from lack of sustenance.

The love of your life? Oh, boy, old man. You're in deep shit. But even as Blackie warned himself to guard his heart, he knew he was already a goner.

CHAPTER SIXTEEN

O ver the next couple of days, Erin called Blackie during her lunch
break and again when her shift ended at night. The news Blackie
reported sounded positive. Julie was eating small amounts of food and
feeling stronger. He predicted she would soon be back to normal, which
eased Erin's mind.

Unfortunately, Erin's own situation had not improved. Each morning when she got up, she told herself she would maintain firm control
over her compulsive urges. She wouldn't hurry through any chore. She
wouldn't worry about whether or not she was getting something done
as fast as a man could. That was easy to do while she spent time with
Violet. While with the horse, Erin felt calm and centered. But the moment she left the paddock to do the afternoon chores Wyatt had assigned to her, she found herself slipping back into what she'd come to
think of as her frenzy mode. She struggled to work slowly and remember all the safety rules.

Erin still hadn't unpacked her car. Being ready to leave the ranch at
a moment's notice gave her a sense of security. If Wyatt fired her, she
would be devastated, not only because she needed the job, but because
she couldn't bear to leave Violet behind. Erin didn't know what she'd do

if she were forced to abandon that horse. However, simply knowing that she could leave the ranch made her feel as if she were more in control of her life.

When her first payday arrived, Erin was thrilled to get a check. She immediately went to the main house, hurried upstairs, and sat on the bed with her checkbook to tally how much money she would have in the bank after she deposited it. The sum wasn't huge, but after deducting her last month's rent for the cottage, which would make her square with the landlady, and paying for her auto insurance, she had plenty left over for her cell phone and fuel expenses. What remained would be around three hundred dollars.

She hurried downstairs to find her uncle, who was in the kitchen kissing his wife. Erin cleared her throat. When Slade raised his head, he flushed, the added color lending his burnished complexion a ruddy glow.

"I'm sorry," Erin said, trying to back out of the room. "I should have hollered or something."

Vickie extricated herself from her husband's arms. "Don't be silly. I've got fresh pecan pies, and we're delighted to have you join us."

Uncle Slade sauntered over to take a chair at the table, then patted the oak surface to indicate Erin should join him. Because Vickie and Slade hadn't been married long, Erin was reluctant to infringe upon their privacy. This was *their* home, after all. But Vickie insisted that she have a piece of pie with them, which was accompanied by coffee. Erin was glad of the distraction. She needed to talk with her uncle, and she wasn't quite sure how to start.

After finishing her pie, Erin just blurted out what was on her mind. "Uncle Slade, I've fallen in love with Violet."

"With who?"

"The mare you recently bought. I nicknamed her Violet, because she's the proverbial shrinking violet."

"Oh!" He nodded and then sighed. "I screwed up buying that mare. I think the former owner drugged her up before I looked at her. She seemed as calm as could be until I had her delivered here. Now I've got an impossible-to-handle horse on my hands."

"No!" Erin cried. Then, after modulating her voice, she said more softly, "She's only frightened. Wyatt and I believe she's been abused."

"You don't say?" Uncle Slade frowned and shrugged. "Well, that's sad. But the bottom line is, I'm not running a horse rescue. I hoped to use her as a ranch horse, and that isn't looking likely."

"Please, don't sell her." Erin's throat went tight. "Well, sell her, yes, but only to me."

Both Slade and Vickie gave Erin a startled look.

"To *you*?" Slade looked mystified. "I didn't think you were into horses all that much."

"Not just any horse. That's true. But Violet is special. I really love her a lot, and I think she's coming to love me."

"Huh." Uncle Slade shook his head. "I can't sell you that horse, honey. What if you never get her settled down?"

"I will. She's a very sweet animal." She told her uncle about all the times Violet had acted up but avoided ever touching Erin with her hooves. How the mare had balked on the lead but still minded her manners. "At some point, I believe she was a fabulous riding horse. Then, for reasons I can't imagine, she was sold and ended up with someone who abused her. She's just frightened of being handled now."

Uncle Slade shook his head again. "Honey, a frightened horse is a dangerous horse. And I love you. I can't sell you an animal that may go berserk and turn on you."

"She'll never do that." Erin truly did feel confident of that. "She's not mean. She's just scared. Talk with Wyatt. He agrees with me, and he's been letting me work with her all morning, every morning. Would he do that if he thought the horse might harm me?"

"He'd better not. I don't want anything happening to you out there."

Vickie spoke up. "Don't immediately say no, Slade. At least talk with Wyatt before you reach a decision."

Erin's uncle nodded. "Okay. I'll talk to Wyatt. But don't get your hopes up, Erin. If you were more experienced with horses, I might consider letting you have her, but as it stands, you've been on a horse only a couple of times. That doesn't make you a horsewoman."

"Maybe with Violet, I'll learn," Erin suggested.

———————

Erin was close to tears during supper at the bunkhouse that night. She tried to converse with the men and laugh at their jokes, but her heart was breaking over the uncertain future Violet faced. Here on the ranch, she had a decent chance to recover from whatever had happened to her. If she was sold, there was no telling what kind of person she'd get as her next owner. If someone grew frustrated with the mare and mistreated her, it would be disastrous. Violet might never trust anyone again.

Erin was washing dishes when Uncle Slade walked into the bunkhouse. "Erin," he said, "I need to speak with you."

His tone sounded serious, and judging by his expression, he wasn't there with good news. Erin dried her hands and followed her uncle outside. He looped an arm around her shoulders and led her across the ranch common. When Erin realized they were walking to Violet's paddock, tension snapped her body taut. Once at the fence, Uncle Slade released his hold on her.

"Get in there. I want to see with my own eyes that she won't hurt you."

Erin was appalled. "But Uncle Slade, that isn't how it works. I have to sit still until Violet decides to let me touch her. She'll just act up and be a pill if I change that part."

"Let her be a pill, then. Wyatt swears up and down she won't strike you. I've been working with horses all my life, and I don't believe it. A frightened horse is a dangerous horse, and there's no way in hell I'm giving you the equivalent of a nail in your coffin."

Erin was shaking as she climbed over the fence to get inside the enclosure with Violet. The mare wouldn't understand that her future depended upon this moment. Erin had never rushed her. Each morning, they took their time, and Violet slowly grew accustomed to Erin's presence. If Erin changed that pattern now, the horse might freak out.

Even so, Erin was no longer afraid of Violet. Even at her worst moments, she'd been careful not to hurt Erin. Uncle Slade would see that for himself, and maybe, just maybe, he would consent to selling Erin the mare.

On trembling legs, Erin walked toward the animal. "Hi, baby girl. Are you going to let me pet you tonight?"

Violet stared at Slade, and all the muscles across her back twitched and rippled.

"She doesn't like that you're here," Erin told him. "Will you back away?"

"Hell, no. In the real world, other people won't back away. Move on in. I want to see her act up."

Erin straightened her shoulders and moved in. Violet made that strange rumbling sound, and she heard Uncle Slade say, "Listen to her talk to you. That's positive."

Erin relaxed a bit and moved closer. "Hi, sweet girl." Erin had no treats with her, and she'd never tried to approach Violet without them. But she had no choice but to do so tonight. She took two more steps. Then another. In a moment, she was close enough to press against the mare's shoulder. Erin wanted to shout with joy, but she didn't dare. Instead, she ran her hand up Violet's neck, just as she always did, to touch her poll.

"I'll be damned," Slade said. "You've made some progress with her. I'll give you that."

Just then Uncle Slade tossed his hat over the fence, and Violet gave a violent start. It made Erin angry. She spun around. "Why did you do that?" she cried. "She's starting to trust me, and now you've frightened her."

"Yep. But she stood fast." Uncle Slade grinned, then said, "Get me my Stetson before she tramples it."

Erin collected his hat and took it to him. He simply accepted the offering and turned to walk away. Erin scaled the fence to run after him. She grabbed his shirt sleeve and drew him to a stop. "Well? Are you going to sell her to me or not? I've only got three hundred to spare right now, but I'll make payments."

"I am not going to sell you that horse."

Erin's heart sank. "But *why*? Please, Uncle Slade. I love her! And I promise, no matter what your asking price is, I'll pay you every dime."

He smiled again. "I didn't say you can't have the horse, honey. Only that I won't sell her to you. She's yours. Only she's a gift."

Erin didn't want Violet as a gift. Her mother had given her things when she was a kid, and then her father had taken them away if she displeased him. "I want to buy her, Uncle Slade. I want it all legal, too, with a bill of sale and a payment plan."

Her uncle squinted through the spring twilight to study her face. "Do you remember when you stayed with me when you were six? You wanted a pony so bad you could taste it, and I told you I'd buy you one."

Erin did remember that. She'd been so angry with her parents for putting a stop to that plan. They'd both refused to let her have a horse even after Uncle Slade said he would pay for all of its expenses until it died. "You never got me one, though. My mom and dad wouldn't allow it."

"That's right. And I felt bad, because you were one brokenhearted child. Now, though, your parents have nothing to say about it. Violet isn't a pony, but she is a horse, and I'm giving her to you." He held up a hand. "And I'll draw up a bill of sale to give you ownership in writing. It'll be 'all legal.' Although I gotta say, that smarts. My word should be enough. I don't renege on an agreement."

Erin realized she had hurt his feelings. "I didn't mean it that way, Uncle Slade."

"Yes, honey, you did. But that's okay. I wasn't blind to what went on when you were a kid, and I understand that your father was a heartless son of a bitch sometimes. I also wasn't blind to the fact that my sister allowed him to be. That sin is on both their heads, but not on yours. I remember once when your mother got you a kitten, and your father took it away for some harebrained reason. Something about chin-ups, as I recall."

Erin remembered that incident in her life with heartbreaking clarity. She'd been unable to lift her body weight, and her father had been furious. As a result, he'd taken her kitty to the pound. The memory brought tears to her eyes, not for the heartbroken little girl she'd been at the time, but because this man still ached for her over the injustice.

She moved in to loop her arms around her uncle's waist. "I'm sorry, Uncle Slade. You're nothing like him. If you give me Violet, I don't need a bill of sale or any other kind of paper to make it official."

He gathered Erin close and pressed his cheek to the top of her head. "I always wished you were my little girl. I'm proud of you for what you're trying to do with Violet. Don't much like that name, to tell you the truth. She's too sassy and assertive to be a violet."

"Only on the surface, Uncle Slade. Underneath all the bluff, some of us are actually scared to death. Reactions to fear get programmed in. You know?"

"Which is exactly why you're the perfect person to turn that horse around. After watching her with you, I think she knows you understand how she feels."

Erin hadn't intended to draw a parallel between herself and the horse, and it startled her for a moment to realize that her uncle had. Only when she really thought about it, she guessed anyone who knew the real Erin De Laney would see the similarities. Until this moment, she'd never considered her father to be abusive, but suddenly, as if a light bulb came on in her brain, she realized he had been in both emotional and physical ways. Being unable to lift her own body weight had not been a crime. It had been a limitation she hadn't yet overcome, and her father had punished her in a cruel way for failing to measure up to his expectations.

Erin had finally mastered chin-ups, just as she'd learned to do everything else her dad had expected of her. And deep within her, she burned with anger now because she'd never been rewarded for any of those accomplishments with another kitten.

After saying goodnight to her uncle, Erin returned to the paddock where Violet stood watching her. The horse made the rumbling sounds again, which made Erin smile. "So you're talking to me. I don't know if I can make those same sounds back to you, sweet girl."

But Erin tried, and Violet reciprocated by grunting more enthusiastically. After hopping over the fence, Erin moved in on the horse, confident now that the mare had "hooked on" with her, as Wyatt called it. Erin no longer needed to sit motionless under the tree in order to touch the mare on her neck and shoulder. Violet still didn't want her head touched, but Erin planned to keep working with her on that. Someday Violet would be the best horse on the ranch.

The following morning, Erin still didn't unpack her car, but opening the trunk to dig around for clothing was starting to feel foolish. Looking at it rationally, Erin knew she'd spent several "last days" on the ranch now, and each one had ended only to become another last day the next morning.

After grabbing a quick shower, Erin filched one of Vickie's cinnamon rolls and ate it as she walked across the ranch common to find Wyatt and ask him what her assignment was for the day. Domino became her canine escort, regal in his carriage as he pranced along in front of her. He led Erin to the office, a small enclosure within the horse barn where Wyatt did paperwork.

When she stepped into the office, he sat with his head bent over paperwork. Erin stood there for a moment, waiting for him to acknowledge her presence, but when he didn't, she realized she had sneaked up on him again. She leaned forward to place her hand on the desk blotter, and he jumped.

"Damn it, Erin. You did it again."

She lifted her hands and shrugged. "I'm sorry. I honestly don't sneak up on you."

He raked a hand through his hair. As it fell in a drift of silky blond strands to his shoulders, she yearned to touch it just once to see if it was fine or coarse. "Not your fault. It's just unsettling when someone gets close to me and I don't sense it." He managed a smile that deepened the creases in his lean cheeks and curved his firm yet full mouth. "What can I do for you?"

"I'm just here to get lined out for the day."

His smile deepened and warmed his blue eyes with twinkling light. "Is this your last day again?"

Erin rolled her eyes and grinned. "I've decided to stay on. Uncle Slade gave me Violet last night. It would have been difficult to leave before without an income. Now, with a horse depending on me, it'd be next to impossible." She rested both hands on the edge of the desk and assumed what she knew was probably a masculine-looking stance, but she tried not to care. "So, no, this isn't another last day. I'll be unpacking my car tonight and settling back into my room."

He nodded. "Glad to have you back on board. Today, you can stick to the same routine. Spend the morning with Violet and the afternoon cleaning stalls, restocking the horse barn with hay, and I'd appreciate it if you'd wash all the water troughs before filling them. After you're done with that, you can help Tex."

"Fair enough," Erin said. "But tomorrow, maybe you shouldn't assign me to work with Violet. Now that she's my horse, it doesn't seem fair for me to be on the clock while I'm with her."

"Violet is on this ranch, and until you get her turned around, she's a liability. I'll keep having you work with her until I feel certain she's coming right."

"Whatever you decide." Erin stood erect. "Thanks for your time. I'm sorry I interrupted your work."

Moments later when Erin circled the horse barn to reach Violet's paddock, the mare shrieked and reared before Erin even climbed the fence. That was disheartening. Erin hoped they were simply getting off to a rough start, but the horse forced her to do a rerun of every other day. But Erin had no intention of giving up. She would repeat the same routine for months if that was what it took.

She spent all morning with Violet and then completed her ranch chores before helping Tex. That night after supper at the bunkhouse, she walked back out to Violet's paddock. Unlike that morning, Violet made her talking noises and allowed Erin to approach right away. Erin had treats tonight, which Violet could smell, but Erin didn't let her have a goody until the mare allowed her to lightly touch her poll.

"You're making great progress with her."

The sound of Wyatt's voice coming from behind her startled Erin. She whirled to face him and then relaxed her body. "Hi. I didn't realize you followed me out."

He sauntered forward in that slow, loose way of his and rested his arms on the top fence rail. "I just wanted to see how she's coming along. I pretty much put my ass on the line last night when Slade asked me if working with her was putting you in danger."

Erin walked over to join him at the barrier. "Thank you for assuring him that I'm safe with her. I truly believe I am."

He smiled slightly. "Just don't forget that even a rock-solid horse can accidentally hurt you. Always be on guard."

It was Erin's turn to smile. "I won't forget. Tonight she's calm and had no problem with me petting her right away, but we'll be back at square one again in the morning."

"Has working with her every day taught you anything?" he asked.

Erin knew he was asking if she had drawn similarities between herself and the troubled equine. "I can definitely see parallels between our reactions to pressure. Before working with her, I knew, in a vague sort of way, that I had been emotionally abused as a child. Now I see that what my dad did to me was deliberate and cruel. I'm also coming to accept that he abused me physically by making demands upon my body that I wasn't physically mature enough to do. I've considered what you told me about feeling broken and in need of fixing when you were a little boy. In his own way, my father made me feel broken, too."

"It's not a good feeling. Is it?"

"No." Erin wished she could lean on the fence as he was doing, but he would be unable to read her lips. "Looking back, I realize now that I constantly tried to fix myself to please my dad. No matter how well I performed, he never praised me, and I became compulsive about pushing even harder to become something I could never be."

"The son he wanted," Wyatt supplied.

"I believe Violet was punished in awful ways for not being what her last owner wanted her to be. When you can never measure up, when you can never please your taskmaster, it sticks with you, and when you're pressured in some way later to perform, you feel panicky and just react. Violet does that, and so do I." Erin gazed off at nothing for a moment and then faced him again. "Unfortunately, seeing the similarities between myself and the horse is only a small victory in a huge battle for me. I did feel broken as a child, and deep down, I still do. Until I began sessions with Jonas, I spent my whole life trying to fix myself in all the wrong ways. I felt that I'd been born in the wrong body. I even felt that my emotional responses to life were wrong. Under Jonas's guidance, I tried to stop acting masculine. I struggled to accept myself as I was. And I was doing pretty well until I switched jobs."

Wyatt shook his head. "You did make some changes, and I'll acknowledge that it took hard work. But the way I see it, the changes were all superficial, and you were motivated to make them only because you still felt broken and in need of fixing. I'd like to see you work toward being glad you're a woman, just as I have come to be glad I'm deaf."

Erin cocked her head a little to give him a questioning look. "Are you truly glad of that?"

He chuckled. "I won't say it isn't difficult to be deaf, Erin. I'm just saying I've accepted it. I'm grateful for all the things that being deaf has taught me. I believe I'm a better person, kinder and more compassionate, than I might have been if I'd been born without the disability. When you work your way up to being able to celebrate who you are, you'll be a better and kinder person, too."

"Am I unkind now?"

His smile faded. "Not intentionally, but in ways I think you're blind to how your behavior affects other people."

Erin's heart caught, because she'd never set out to hurt anyone.

"Take Tex, for instance," Wyatt went on. "He's getting up in years. Physical labor is starting to tax him, and he's struggling to hold his own, fearful that he may be replaced by a younger man. Slade would never do that to him, but Tex worries about it. Have you ever stopped to consider how your fierce determination to hold your own has pushed Tex to work harder than he would if you weren't showing him up?"

"Oh, my God." Erin's stomach knotted. "I really like Tex. I never intended to make him look bad."

"I know that. It's just that you've been so focused on trying to make yourself look good that you've paid little attention to how the people around you feel about that, Tex especially."

As Wyatt walked away, Erin felt as if she'd been turned into a pillar of salt for looking back at something forbidden. He was so right. She'd tried to outdo all the men here and increased Tex's angst about growing old. She'd been angry about being born in a weaker, female body.

And she still was. She needed to work on fixing that, only in the right way this time.

It had been five days since Julie had gotten sick with the flu virus, and she had returned to work that morning, feeling one hundred percent back to normal. When she closed up the Morning Grind at five that afternoon, she decided to walk to Blackie's pawnshop to thank him properly for taking such good care of her while she'd been ill. He'd proven himself to be a good friend, and she hoped to take him out for dinner to show her appreciation.

As she crossed the town center, she saw him out on the sidewalk, locking his shop door. She broke into a scampering run across the circular thoroughfare to the corner, waving her arm. "Hey, Blackie! Hold up a minute!"

He wheeled at the sound of her voice, and his suntanned countenance crinkled into a welcoming smile. "Well, I'll be. You look completely recovered."

A little out of breath, she drew up in front of him and grinned. "I really am, and I wanted to thank you for everything you did for me." Her mind shied away from some of the things he'd done. It was embarrassing when a man saw you at your worst, and she had definitely hit bottom in the throes of that flu. "I honestly don't think I would have lived through it by myself."

He shook his head. "Erin would have come. She was on the phone to check on you several times a day, and the only reason she wasn't there was because I told her I had everything under control."

Julie knew Erin was a fabulous friend, too. But it had been Blackie who'd gone the extra mile for her this time. "I was wondering . . . well, I'd like to do something special by way of a thank-you, and I was thinking maybe I could take you out for dinner and drinks."

He arched a black eyebrow. "Hmm. I'm a little old-fashioned about a lady paying my way, so I'll only say yes if you let me cover the beverages and the tip."

"Deal," Julie said with a laugh.

"As it happens, I've been craving Mexican food for days, and José at the Straw Hat makes a mean margarita." He hooked a thumb over his shoulder. "The restaurant is only a few doors down."

Julie shifted the strap of her handbag on her shoulder. "I, um, wasn't thinking of tonight. I'm not dressed to go out."

He narrowed an eye. "You look fabulous."

"In jeans and a top?"

"You do very nice things for a pair of jeans. And look at me." He glanced down at himself. "I'm not exactly dressed up, either."

He wore creased Dockers and a pressed pinstripe shirt with the long sleeves folded back over his forearms, which were dusted with fine, black hair. "You look amazing to me."

Julie hadn't meant to sound as if she were drooling, but in truth, Blackie was a handsome man who did make her mouth water when she looked at him. He seemed to sense her discomfiture, and his dark blue gaze held hers for a long moment that made her pulse flutter. "Ditto, so let's do dinner together tonight. It's not as if the Straw Hat has a dress code."

"Okay," she said, even though she still felt she wasn't dressed for the occasion. "Lead the way."

He laughed and took her arm. "I prefer to let a lady walk beside me." He released her to step around to her left side. Then he cupped her elbow in his hand again. "On the inside, of course, where I can protect you from careening automobiles if there's a wreck."

Julie giggled. "Do you know how that custom originated?"

"I do, and I understand that there are no buggies or wagons out on the street to put you in danger of being sprayed with mud or trampled by a runaway horse. But a car could go out of control and come up over the curb at us."

Julie pulled her elbow free of his grasp to loop her arm through his. "And what would you do if that happened?"

"I'd try to get you out of harm's way, not to say I could."

She sighed. "It's the thought that counts." She glanced up at him. "I feel very safe."

The hostess led Julie and Blackie to a booth that offered them a little more privacy than sitting at a table. When their server arrived, they both ordered a house margarita. In Julie's opinion, José fixed the best ones she'd ever tasted. The server left them to peruse the menu offerings.

"I already know what I want, enchiladas verde. It's my favorite."

Blackie nodded. "Mine, too."

Over their drinks, they began to chat, and before Julie knew it, she relaxed and hung on every word Blackie said. He was a charming conversationalist, a trait he'd exhibited countless times when he visited her shop in the afternoons. But over dinner, talking with him was different. Her attention wasn't divided between him and the occasional customer who wandered in for coffee and a snack. She also felt no pressure to clean her equipment or dust shelves while she sat in someone else's eatery. It was delightfully liberating.

After they finished their meals, Blackie ordered coffee, and Julie did likewise, because lingering over their steaming cups would give them more time together. She was startled when he reached across the table and curled his hand over hers.

"We've got a small problem," he said.

Julie's mind instantly went to the most humiliating turns of her illness, and her chest went tight with anxiety. She definitely hadn't been at her best when she'd lost control of her body and soiled her black leggings. She couldn't blame Blackie if he no longer found her attractive with that image of her lingering in his mind.

"I've fallen in love with you," he said.

Julie's brain froze. "What?"

"You heard me. I tried not to get serious, Julie. But it was difficult to keep the walls around my heart while I was caring for you. You were so sick, and they just crumbled." His mouth curved into a semblance of a smile. "You're under no obligation to say anything. I don't expect a reciprocal gesture from you. I just thought you should know I may want more from this relationship now than you're prepared to give."

"Oh, Blackie." Julie's throat went so tight she couldn't speak for a second. "I love you, too. It started out as loving you only as a friend. Now it goes much deeper. I'm just not sure if it's the forever kind of love."

He tightened his hold on her hand. "Knowing for sure what kind of love each of us feels is difficult. I think that comes with time. Maybe we should keep treading forward with caution until we're both certain of our feelings."

"Or we can throw caution to the wind," she suggested.

He nodded. "Let's sleep on it. I don't want you to make a mistake you'll regret, and I sure don't want to make one myself."

CHAPTER SEVENTEEN

Julie agreed that both she and Blackie should take some time to think about their feelings before they moved forward with their relationship. When they got up from the table, she linked arms with him to leave the restaurant. Once outside, she took a deep breath of the evening air. Dusk had fallen while they were eating, and the faint scent of flowers in window boxes along both sides of Main created a perfect ending to what had been a fabulous evening together.

As they walked along the sidewalk toward his shop, she said, "Thank you so much for joining me for dinner. I thoroughly enjoyed myself. We should do it again soon."

"Only if I pay."

She chuckled. "You do realize that's a really old-fashioned way of thinking. Dating is more casual now. The younger set takes turns paying for meals."

"Have you looked at me lately? I'm not part of the younger set."

She smiled and hugged his arm. "You aren't exactly old, either. And it won't hurt if you allow me to foot a dinner bill now and again."

"True. But next time is on me."

When she tried to slow their pace at the door of his shop, he gave her a tug to set her feet in motion again. "It's late. I'll walk you back to your shop."

Julie laughed. "Oh, dear. It's barely full dark. I've walked along Main alone at least a hundred times, Blackie. You're being overprotective."

"I'm protective, but I don't think *overprotective* describes me."

"Mystic Creek has such a low crime rate it's boring." Julie secretly liked being with a man who wanted to look after her. She'd never been made to feel by Derek that she was important in any way. "It isn't unsafe for women to walk along Main Street after dark when they're alone."

"Most of the time, it isn't. But don't forget what happened to the Johnson girl."

While she'd been sick, Julie had forgotten about that. "Oh. You're right. I guess bad things do happen here sometimes."

He chuckled. "Yes, but a bad thing won't happen to you. At least not tonight. Not as long as I have breath left in my body, anyway."

As they crossed the town center, all the street lanterns came on to cast nimbuses of golden light against the darkening sky. At the fountain, he drew to a stop, released her to fish in his pants pocket, and drew out a fistful of change. He handed Julie a quarter. "Let's make a wish."

Julie had never thrown a coin into this particular fountain, but she had made countless wishes in others over the years. None of them had ever come true. It was such a beautiful spring evening and not that chilly. It put her in a romantic frame of mind, so before she threw in her quarter, she wished that her relationship with Blackie would become a love to last a lifetime. Regardless of his concerns, she didn't think the age difference between them was great enough to matter if they truly loved each other.

Blackie waited for her and tossed his coin in just as she did. Then he smiled wistfully down at her. "Are you going to tell me what your wish was?"

Julie shook her head. "No. If I tell you, my wish won't come true, and then I won't get to spend the rest of my life with you."

His eyes went dark, and Julie found that she couldn't look away. He leaned closer, and the next instant, his mouth laid claim to hers. It was a tentative kiss at first, but then he deepened it and took control. She felt as if the starch in her spine vanished, and she rested her weight against his, wondering how a simple kiss could make her feel hot, excited, and as if all the bones in her body had melted.

"Wow," he said as he drew back. And then with a moan, he settled his mouth over hers again.

Julie lost it. It had been so long since a man had held her in his arms, so long since she'd felt like a woman. There was something about Blackie that ignited all her nerve endings and made her want him in a way she'd never wanted another man.

He suddenly jerked away from her and grasped her shoulders in his strong hands. "Not here. We're in plain sight."

She realized that she'd jerked his shirttails loose from where they'd been tucked in at his waist, and she'd also unfastened two of his shirt buttons to reveal a mat of glistening black chest hair and bronze skin.

He grasped her hand. "My place or yours?"

"Mine."

He broke into a speed walk that had Julie almost running. He looped an arm around her waist to keep her from falling as they hurried across Main to reach the south side. By the time they hotfooted it to the Mystic Creek Menagerie, she was out of breath and wondered what she'd been thinking when she'd suggested her place. The Morning Grind was a coffee and pastry shop with only a bathroom and a storage area in back. Blackie had a full-on residence above his business.

As they dashed through the mall area, Julie tried not to think about how they looked to all the diners on the revolving platform. Turned on. Unbuttoned and untucked. *Oh, God.* They should have gone to Blackie's. His shop had been much closer, and there would have been a bed, at least.

Julie opened the door of her shop, pulled Blackie inside, and quickly locked up again. "The storage room," she told him. "Hurry. People can see through the front windows."

They ran to the back, and the minute she got the storage room door closed behind them, they were in each other's arms again. Julie had watched plenty of films where a man and woman were so turned on by each other that they ripped away clothing and went after each other in a frenzy. She'd always thought how silly that was. Real people didn't destroy each other's garments. Only with Blackie, it was like that. Their clothing went flying, and the next thing she knew, they were lying on the bank of boxes that held all the different coffees she kept on hand.

A moment of sanity cleared her mind. "What if these boxes collapse?"

"I'll go down a happy man."

He put his mouth over a pulse point in her throat and made a sound that reminded her of a growl. Sanity flew straight out the proverbial window again. His hands ignited her skin. His mouth titillated her nerve endings. She couldn't think and didn't want to think. For the first time in her life, she wanted to just *be*. She wanted to just *feel*. And with Blackie, she did.

Afterward they lay limp in each other's arms. When Blackie regained his breath, he groaned and said, "Sweet lord. I'll never feel quite the same about French roast."

Julie burst out giggling, he joined in, and they laughed until tears trickled down their cheeks. When their mirth subsided, he held her in his arms as if he cherished her, and Julie closed her eyes on a wave of pleasure that ran far deeper than the flesh. No one had ever made her feel as important as Blackie did. He stirred to kiss her hair.

"I love you, Julie Price. I didn't think I'd ever love anyone again, but I do, and the way I feel about you is far more powerful than anything I've ever felt before."

"I love you, too." Tears filled her eyes again, only this time they weren't caused by unbridled mirth. "Oh, Blackie, I love you, too."

Julie always lowered the shop thermostat at night to keep her heating bill down, and even with Blackie's body pressed against her, she soon started to feel cold. He must have felt the chill on her skin.

"Come on. We need to find our clothes. I don't want you to relapse."

They got up to collect garments. It was then that Julie realized Blackie still wore his socks. Otherwise he was completely nude, and she was amazed by his musculature. He looked like a man half his age. A very sexy man. He had a stocky build that lent itself well to showy ripples and bulges. "How on earth do you stay in such great shape?"

"Walking. Hiking. Watching what I eat. I've been lucky, I guess." He handed over her bra. "You're absolutely beautiful. I should have kept my head long enough to tell you that."

Julie felt a blush warm her cheeks. When they were completely dressed, Blackie attempted to tidy her hair. He finally gave up and smiled. "Why do you dye it?"

"How do you know I dye it?"

He laughed. "Honey, the hair on your head doesn't match your down-yonder roots."

"Oh!" The heat in her cheeks intensified. "I dyed it dark after the divorce. I felt as if all the light had gone out in my life. I was so sad and blue all the time. You know? And the dark color with a blue streak just seemed right. I told myself that when my broken heart healed, I would go back to my natural color, but until I met you, I didn't think I'd ever feel happy again."

Blackie drew her into his arms and swayed with her. "I'm sorry he hurt you so deeply, honey. You didn't deserve to be treated like that."

"You didn't deserve what happened in your marriage, either." Julie looked up at him. "I want to make love with you again, Blackie. Slowly this time. Will you come over to my house?"

He looked deeply into her eyes. "I'd love to. Should I bring a tooth-brush and my razor?"

She realized he was asking if he would be welcome to spend the night. "Absolutely. I'm not finished with you yet."

He laughed and let go of her. Then a horrified expression crossed his burnished features. "Oh, *shit*!"

"What?" Julie felt slightly panicked. "What's wrong? What is it?"

"I didn't use any protection. I can't *believe* I was so careless."

Julie knew people practiced safe sex for a variety of reasons, and she applauded the choice. But her and Blackie's forgetfulness this one time didn't strike her as being a catastrophe. "I've been with nobody since my divorce. Because Derek was high risk, I was tested after we split up. There's no danger that I'm carrying an STD, and I'm also on the Pill. Not to keep from getting pregnant, obviously, because until now, I haven't been with anyone else. I take birth control to regulate my periods. We're safe, unless there's something you haven't told me."

He released a slow breath. "No. I haven't been to Crystal Falls for a night on the town in over three years. I know I'm clean. I was just worried about my swimmers finding a friendly little egg."

Julie grinned at him. "Well, you needn't worry about that. I'm ninety-nine-point-nine percent safe."

The following morning, Erin was running late. The alarm on her phone hadn't gone off. She had plugged in the device to charge on her nightstand last night, but she hadn't gotten the charger cord seated properly. Her phone had gone deader than a doornail. She took the fastest shower in history, threw on her clothes, and ran so fast down the stairs that she nearly fell. Once in the kitchen, she grabbed what looked like a blueberry muffin and poured herself a cup of coffee, both of which she carried with her as she hurried from the house.

Once at the paddock fence, she glanced at her watch. It was half past eight. Normally she began working with Violet at seven sharp. They'd lost a precious hour together, and Erin wanted to kick herself for failing to make sure her cell phone was properly plugged in. She took a big bite of the muffin and chased it down with coffee that burned her tongue.

Domino appeared at her side. The dog made a habit of intercepting her when she was wolfing down one of Vickie's creations for breakfast, and Erin knew he had his mouth all set for part of her muffin.

"Okay," she said. "I'm an easy mark this morning, and I think blueberries are safe. I know raisins aren't. That's why Vickie stopped putting them in her cinnamon rolls. Because of you and your mooching habits."

Domino gave an excited bark, and Erin handed him what was left of her meal. The animal wolfed it down and then looked up at her expectantly. Erin couldn't help but grin. "That was it. I'm all out of goodies."

Domino wandered away, hoisting his leg on fence posts all the way to the corner of the barn. Erin turned to regard Violet, who watched her with unmistakable nervousness. "I think we need to add grain to your treat list today. Change it up. Make it more exciting for you. Only I'm not about to carry grain in my pockets, girlfriend. I did that once, forgot it was in there, and washed my jeans. Have you ever seen horse grain when it's become mush? So I'm going to find some kind of container that I can stuff inside my bra."

Erin took off for the bunkhouse. She didn't need anything all that big. She figured she could drag a bag of grain to sit outside the paddock and then she could refill the container when needed. She was about to give up when she saw an empty, shake-out bubble gum container sitting on the table. It was the perfect size for her purposes, and the square hole in the lip was just big enough to let grain fall out into her hand.

An hour later Erin was silently congratulating herself on being brilliant. Violet loved the grain and seemed a lot more excited about it than she was about carrots and apple slices. The horse would actually lower her head to eat from the flat of Erin's hand.

Erin and the mare had a phenomenal couple of hours together, and then Erin lost her hold on the bubble gum shaker as she was measuring out a smidgeon of grain. The plastic container fell to the ground, the grain within it striking its sides upon impact.

Violet went berserk. She reared up, her front hooves high above Erin's head. Erin glimpsed the mare's eyes, and they were wild with fright. Instinct took over, and Erin threw herself away from the horse, rolled across the ground, and then sprang to her feet. She ran to the fence, grabbed a top rung, and with terror lending her strength, managed to vault over the barrier.

Ever since the first morning that Erin had worked with the mare, Wyatt had made it his habit to hang out as much as he could in Violet's stall so he could monitor Erin as she handled the horse. As recently as yesterday, he'd decided that it was no longer necessary. Erin was abiding by all the safety rules now. Given Violet's obvious reluctance to hurt anyone, Wyatt believed Erin was unlikely to be injured by the animal. Why he was still watching over her, he didn't know. Habit, he reasoned.

That was an easier explanation for him to deal with than the real one, namely that he had fallen in love with the woman.

But then the bubble gum container struck the ground, and the mare exploded. Before Wyatt could move, Erin hit the dirt, rolled clear of those lethal hooves, and sprang over the fence. Wyatt almost started across the paddock to join Erin outside the enclosure, but the horse's behavior made him think twice. Instead he left the stall and hurried along the alley to the main doors of the barn. Outside, he found Erin bent forward with her hands on her knees. He lightly touched her shoulder, and she jackknifed erect, her blue eyes so wide they were almost as ringed with white as the mare's.

"Don't tell Uncle Slade," she said. "Please, don't tell him, Wyatt."

"Erin, she could have killed you."

"I dropped the grain container near her front feet. It scared her half to death. I don't know why, but I know that horse. It terrified her."

Wyatt had seen it happen. "Did the container make a loud sound when it hit the ground?"

"What?"

He glanced at the horse. Violet was still bucking and kicking, so he guessed that she was also making a lot of noise. He repeated the question, this time raising his volume, which he'd learned to do only with practice.

"Not really loud," Erin told him. "Little popping sounds as it hit and bounced around."

Something niggled at the back of Wyatt's mind, a memory that was trying to slip forward, only he couldn't for the life of him think what it was. He only knew that he'd seen a horse react just that way once before when something was dropped at its feet.

He touched a hand to Erin's shoulder. "You handled yourself like a pro," he told her. "You've come a long way, and I'm really proud of you."

Her chin came up, and he saw a flare of pride glisten in her eyes. "Thank you. I just reacted and tried to get out of her way."

"You reacted exactly right. When a horse blows up and you don't even have a halter on her yet, the first order of business is to get out of harm's way until you can figure out how to handle the situation."

Still nettled by the memory that wouldn't come to him, Wyatt went to stand at the fence. Violet was busy striking the grain container with a viciousness that made his pulse accelerate. He knew Erin didn't want him to tell Slade. She was afraid her uncle might renege on his word about the horse being hers. But Wyatt knew his boss would never do that. He might try to convince Erin to get rid of Violet, but he'd never go back on a promise. Wyatt almost wished the man would. Erin had become very important to Wyatt, and the thought of her getting hurt or killed made his blood run cold.

Erin came to stand beside him and waved a hand in front of his face to get his attention. When he looked down at her, she asked, "Could Violet ever have been in parades? Think of all the noise"—she broke off and waved her hand again, this time as if she were erasing a blackboard—"parades are really noisy. I realize you've never heard one, but the marching bands play music and pound on drums. The crowds along the sidewalks yell and cheer and throw stuff. An easily startled horse would never work out."

Parades. The moment Wyatt saw Erin say that word, the memory that had been evading him popped into the foreground of his mind. "Oh, my God."

"What?"

Wyatt felt heartsick and went back to studying the frantic horse again. She was finally starting to settle down, but every muscle in her body was knotted with tension. "I worked for a guy once over in Medford. That was the one and only time I ever got fired. I was at that ranch so briefly that I can't remember his name now, but he trained parade horses, and I got so pissed at how he was doing it. We had words, and he told me to get off his land. I was so angry I didn't even collect my pay."

"How was he training the horses to high-step?" she asked.

"He would toss lighted firecrackers at their front feet. I couldn't hear the explosives going off, but I saw them bouncing around and how it frightened the horse." With a heavy feeling in his chest, Wyatt closed his eyes for a moment. "I think that's what happened to Violet. I'm not saying the same man owned her, only that people like that are piss-poor horse trainers, and they're mean to the core. The man I knew had no compunction at all about beating a horse, I can tell you that."

"Did you turn him in after you quit the job?"

Wyatt nodded. "I filed a report with the police and the local humane society. I was told the man would be investigated. I have no idea what came of it."

Erin shifted her tear-filled gaze to the horse. Her mouth started to quiver. "You think Violet had firecrackers thrown at her feet?"

Wyatt nodded.

"No wonder she's traumatized. I could see how constantly touching her poll might get her over being afraid when someone reaches for her head. But firecrackers at her feet? How will I ever get her over that?"

Wyatt took a moment to answer. "Repetition," he finally pushed out. "But before we settle on that idea, we need Slade's input first."

Erin immediately said, "No! You promised not to tell him."

"No, Erin. I never promised that."

"You're wonderful with horses. Why do we need Uncle Slade involved in this?"

"Because he's one of the best horsemen I've ever known. Because I trust his instincts and know what a kind heart he has. He won't make you get rid of the horse. Once he hears about this, he'll be pissed off on behalf of the horse, but otherwise, he'll feel as bad for her as we do."

Uncle Slade's first reaction when Erin and Wyatt approached him about Violet was to say, "That rotten, no-good son of a bitch!"

Vickie came running from the kitchen, her curly hair clamped down over her head with a net. Her blue bib apron had flour and what looked like blood all over the front of it, but Erin suspected it was marinara, judging by the delicious aroma coming from the back of the house. "What on earth? Slade, why are you shouting profanities?"

Uncle Slade closed his eyes for a second. "Vickie, those are *not* profanities. They're bywords. And I'm yelling because that man who sold me the mare was a rotten, abusive son of a bitch!"

When Vickie heard about the firecrackers, she went pale. "How horrible. I've heard of people doing that. Then, during a parade, they dropped fake bombs at the horses' feet to make them prance. All they care about is the showmanship, the horse be damned."

"Was he from Medford?" Wyatt asked.

Uncle Slade gave him a perplexed look. "How did you guess that?"

Wyatt's jaw clenched. "Because I once worked for a man who raised parade horses. He was making big bucks off those horses. Over time, some of them get so used to it they don't go crazy, or so I was told, but the more timid ones are ruined. Or at least that's my opinion. I don't believe in using fright tactics to train anything."

Uncle Slade grabbed his Stetson off the hall tree and stormed out the front door. Wyatt followed him, so Erin did as well. They ended up at Violet's paddock. Uncle Slade just stood there and studied the horse. Then he vaulted over the fence, collected the bubble gum container, and returned to where Wyatt and Erin were still standing.

"The only way I know to get her over being fearful of something dropped at her feet is to do it repeatedly," he finally said. "It won't be fun, and it sure won't be pretty, but if you've got the heart for it, Erin, she'll eventually stop blowing up when it happens."

Erin didn't know if she could do something that she knew would terrify the mare. "Won't that just make her distrust me?"

Uncle Slade sighed. "Maybe at first, but over time, she'll learn that the stuff you toss doesn't explode, and she'll lose her fear of it." He turned the damaged container in his hand. "Don't do it too often the first few days. No point in getting her all riled up and keeping her that way. Just, oh, I don't know, maybe three times a morning."

"Less," Wyatt chimed in. "I saw her blow. She went completely berserk. Once, maybe, to start. Let her get used to the idea that nothing happens before you start conditioning her more often."

Erin swallowed. Her throat felt raw with tension. "I'll try."

Uncle Slade leveled a look at her. "No *try* to it, honey. If you love her and want her to have a good life, you have to get her over her fears. Otherwise, she'll be a danger to anyone who tries to handle her."

"And if she doesn't get over it?" Erin asked. "What'll happen to her, then?"

Uncle Slade met and held her gaze. "That'll be up to you. She's your horse now. The only thing I've got to say is, proceed with caution. Don't be inside the paddock when you toss something at her feet. I saw last night that she doesn't want to hurt you, but a frightened horse is a—"

Erin cut him off with, "A dangerous horse. I know."

Slade nodded. "And don't you ever forget it, sweetheart. She's a big, powerful animal. She could kill you in a blink." He removed his hat and slapped it against his pants leg. "I'll leave you two to cuss and discuss. I've got a phone call to make."

After her uncle walked away, Erin looked up at Wyatt. "Who do you suppose he's going to call?"

"The cops," Wyatt said, his voice pitched low. "Slade already suspected that the Medford man doped the horse before he went to look at her. He couldn't prove anything. But now, if it's the same man I once worked for, he knows there's been at least one complaint filed against him already." Wyatt met her gaze and smiled slightly. "I wasn't much more than a kid back then, and I was pretty much nobody in Medford. The complaints I filed with the authorities may not have been enough to launch a real investigation."

"Uncle Slade is nobody in Medford, too. How likely is it that they'll listen to him?"

"He's made a name for himself. If he files a complaint, it'll catch everyone's attention."

Erin looked down at the container that Uncle Slade had handed to her before he walked away. "What if she gets so wound up that she hurts herself?"

Wyatt planted a hand atop her head with a gentle touch. "Erin, look at me."

His voice compelled her to lift her gaze. He smiled even though the gesture didn't quite reach his eyes. "With horses, you've got to do what you've got to do."

Just then Domino ran up and bumped Wyatt's leg with his nose.

Wyatt released Erin and reached down to stroke the dog's head. "Having an animal is a big responsibility. If you keep working with her, she'll one day be one of your best and most trusted friends. To a point, anyway. Never . . ."

Erin interjected, "Let my guard down with a horse. I know. I've got it."

He flashed a crooked grin. "Yep, I think you finally do."

The next morning, Erin began training with Violet by tossing the bubble gum container over the fence at her feet. Violet shrieked and went totally berserk for at least five minutes and was lathered up by the time she calmed down. Erin waited until then to enter the paddock. She left the container lying on the ground, hoping that the mare would begin to accept that it was just a piece of plastic and couldn't harm her.

As the morning progressed, Erin decided Uncle Slade was right. Violet was a wimpy name for such a spirited horse. Shrinking violets were timid creatures afraid of their own shadows. This mare had good reason to be fearful. She had been abused by a human, who was supposed to be a superior being. Instead he'd been the lowest of the low, beating on an animal and terrifying her until he'd almost ruined her.

When the mare finally decided to take a treat from her palm, Erin got up and moved in close to her shoulder. "From now on, I'm calling you Firecracker," she whispered to the horse while she lightly rubbed her neck. "Firecrackers are a part of your history, and with your beautiful red coat and white markings, you need a name with some pizzazz."

The following morning, Erin tucked a quirt into the waistband of her jeans before she entered Firecracker's paddock. Erin wasn't sure what the man might have used to beat Firecracker, but she guessed his weapon of choice would have been something he always had on hand, and Erin had watched enough movies to know that riders often used quirts. They were a shorter version of a whip. She'd never seen any man on the Wilder Ranch use a quirt, but after searching the tack room, she found one.

The mare snorted and huffed when she saw the riding whip. Then she ran to the opposite side of the paddock, stared at Erin, and stomped her feet. Wyatt had once told Erin she would learn the horse's story from her behavior, and she felt pretty confident she'd just discovered what had been used to punish Firecracker. The quirt had a braided lash, which Erin doubted would cause an equine that much pain unless it was used viciously. Going on a hunch, she drew the quirt from her waistband, grabbed the braided section of leather, and swung the handle in a circular motion.

Sure enough, Firecracker screamed and backed up until her rump was testing the strength of the fence rails behind her. Erin had her answer. The mare had been frightened by only the sight of a quirt, but she was beyond terrified when Erin swung the handle. Erin tucked the device back into her pants. Uncle Slade had said repeated exposure would eventually condition Firecracker to no longer be afraid. If that tactic could work with a bubble gum container, why wouldn't it work with the quirt?

Erin knew she was undoing all the trust she'd built between herself and the mare. That made her sad. But she was determined to get Firecracker back to being the wonderful horse she'd once been. And Erin had no question in her mind that Firecracker had once been an amazing animal. She didn't know how the mare had ended up with her last owner. She only knew Uncle Slade had pegged him correctly. The man was a no-good son of a bitch.

CHAPTER EIGHTEEN

Wyatt stood in the horse's stall and watched Erin with a thoughtful smile. *It's happening*, he thought. Erin was learning something new during every session with the mare. And she had been listening. Slade had given her one example of repetitious exposure to eventually cure a horse of being afraid of something, and Erin had extrapolated that bit of information and moved forward. And Wyatt believed Erin was on the right track. In fact, if he'd been working with Violet, he might have done the same thing.

When Erin left the paddock, Wyatt hurried out into the alley of the barn and pretended to be busy sorting through a bunch of tools that someone had left on a bench. He was aware of Erin's approach this time because he knew she was coming, and as a consequence, he felt her presence in way that boggled his mind.

He glanced up and met her sparkling gaze. "Hey. How are you this morning?"

"Upset. Firecracker has been beaten with the handle of a quirt. What kind of man does such a thing?"

Wyatt straightened. "The kind of man who should never have animals."

"Assuming it's the same man you worked for, why'd he fire you?"

Wyatt wasn't sure he wished to share that story. "I grabbed a lighted firecracker out of his hand and shoved it down the front of his pants."

Erin's eyes went as round as dimes. "Pardon me?" Then she waved her hand. "Never mind. I heard you clearly enough." Then an impish grin curved her mouth and dimpled her cheeks. "That was *evil*."

"Yep. It wasn't one of my best moments, but for a few seconds, it sure was fun to watch him drop his drawers to get the explosive away from his—well, you get the picture."

"I do. I wish I'd been there to see it."

They both laughed. "I know you watch me a lot when I'm working with the horse," Erin said. "You don't say much, so I'm going to ask for feedback. Am I nuts to go in there with a riding quirt when I suspect that was what was used to beat her?"

Wyatt had known for a while that he was in love with Erin De Laney, but in that moment, his feelings for her ran so deep that they made his chest ache. "No, I don't think you're nuts. Gutsy, yes. Taking risks, yes. She'll get a whole lot upset."

She smiled slightly again. "Do you believe she's dangerous?"

"I believe she can be pushed into it. When we're cornered, all of us have the potential to be dangerous. But do I think she's mean? No, I've been around mean horses. They do exist, just like mean people exist. But—is that what you're calling her now, Firecracker?" At Erin's nod, he continued. "If she gets so frightened she can't think, she may do you harm. But she doesn't strike me as being bent on hurting anyone. She just wants nothing to do with people."

"Do you blame her?" she asked.

"No. Do you?"

Erin shook her head. Then she pivoted on her heel and walked away. At the door, she turned and said, "Can you read my lips from there?"

"Well enough to guess what you're saying."

"If you see me doing anything you believe is a disservice to Firecracker, please tell me. She's very important to me, and my aim is to help her get better, not make her worse."

"I can do that," Wyatt replied. "Just be careful, Erin. You're important to a lot of people, too."

Wyatt could have added that when it came to people who cared about her, he stood at the front of the line, but his feelings for Erin had to remain his secret. Only Kennedy had guessed how Wyatt felt about her so far, and Wyatt wanted to keep it that way.

Over the next two weeks, Kennedy seemed to be around the ranch less and less, but he kept up with his work, and as the foreman, Wyatt was grateful for that. If Kennedy had been a flake, Wyatt would have been placed in an untenable position of having divided loyalties, one to his boss and the other to his brother. Wyatt understood Kennedy's feelings about Jen and his need to be with her as she recovered. She had endured one of the worst traumas anyone could experience. *If she recovered.* That was the question that looped continuously through Wyatt's mind, and there was no question that it plagued Kennedy as well. Physically, Jen would heal, but she might be emotionally messed up for the rest of her life.

June descended on the Mystic Creek valley, glorious in her shades of verdant green and patterned with brilliant color. Wildflowers bedecked the fields and woodlands, poking up their delicate faces like tiny maidens emerging in all their beauty from the dark underworld of winter. Wyatt had always loved spring, and it came late in eastern and central Oregon, refusing to be governed by the official date for the season. When summer *officially* arrived, spring would be in her full glory and bowing for an encore, much like a talented actress who refused to leave the stage and remove herself from the limelight. Then, as if it happened overnight, summer would elbow her way in and bring sudden heat that dampened shirts, brought perspiration to foreheads, and created dark sweat rings around the crowns of Stetson hats.

For Wyatt, who was attuned to nature as few people were, it was a glorious time. It was also a season of pressure on a ranch, when the calving was over and the babies were standing steady on spindly legs that often looked incapable of supporting their ever-increasing weight. Wyatt found each morning a challenge as he organized his crew and assigned tasks for the day. Livestock needed to be vaccinated. Bull calves had to be banded. Irrigation lines that had developed weaknesses during the brutal freezes of winter always popped a few gaskets. It was nothing to look out across a field to see five or six geysers spewing from wheel lines, and they had to be fixed, posthaste.

Kennedy aced his spring finals and switched gears from scholar to rancher overnight, but unlike in the past, he grabbed a shower and took off for town when his shift ended. When he had irrigation duty, he returned at six in the evening to move wheel lines and swap out defective sprinkler heads, and he was up the next morning to do it again at six. Slade held to a twelve-hour watering schedule, and Wyatt was proud of his brother for manning up to do his job even when it interfered with his love life.

Erin could no longer while away the mornings with Firecracker. Wyatt needed her to partner up with a crew member and do her share to keep the ranch operating like a well-oiled machine. He assigned her to work with Tex. He'd seen the genuine dismay in her expression when he'd told her that her competitiveness pushed the elderly Texan to work harder than his aging body could handle, and Wyatt hoped that Erin's kind heart would overrule her tendency to outperform everyone when she was with the old man. She had a loving nature and a great capacity to care about others, be they human or animal. Working with Tex would be a constant governor for her, similar to the ones installed in new cars to keep them from reaching dangerous speeds.

Instead of neglecting Firecracker and allowing her to backslide, Erin began working with the horse in the predawn gloom and then again at night after the bunkhouse kitchen was cleaned up. Wyatt admired her for that. While the men did only the required work, Erin was tacking four extra hours onto her day. That told Wyatt more about her than she would ever know. She loved with her whole heart. She was compassionate in a way that many people weren't. When she decided to help someone, in this case a horse, she didn't slack off when the going got rough. He was proud of her, and he couldn't help but wonder what more she'd discovered about herself while working with the mare.

Due to sexual deprivation, Wyatt still struggled to sleep well at night. But the long, fair-weather days taxed his body so much that he eventually fell into an exhausted slumber. He saw Erin dozens of times a day, and each encounter left him aroused. She moved with such grace, the muscles of her body working together like dancers on a stage. He noticed that her figure had grown more streamlined and somehow softer looking since she'd come to work for him. He attributed that to the fact that she no longer haunted the Crash and Burn to lift weights and pump up certain parts of her body. Ranching targeted every muscle, but in a natural, unfocused way that fostered lean strength.

Around the middle of June, Kennedy invited Jen out for a tour of the ranch, and he was so excited about her visit that everyone else seemed to catch the disease. Vickie, whose greatest talents lay in the kitchen, planned an outdoor ranch dinner. Wooden picnic tables were unearthed from the barn. A grocery run into town culminated with the bed of Slade's pickup billowing with bags filled to the brim. Every hand on the place helped Vickie unload, including Wyatt. Even the ranch common got groomed. Of an evening while supper was being cooked in the bunkhouse by one person, the other five were outdoors, picking up, weeding, and raking gravel. Tex even advanced on the lawn around the main house, which brought Vickie racing from her kitchen to protect her flowers from a Texan with a Weed Eater.

Kennedy was nervous the day of Jen's visit. Vickie had even called the girl's parents and invited them, which totally threw a wrench in Kennedy's fan blades. He'd spent a lot of time with Mr. and Mrs. Johnson, but while in their environment, Kennedy minded all his manners, never cussed, and just went with the flow. On the ranch, things never went that smoothly. Tex was given to outbursts of temper at unforeseen moments, and the madder he got, the worse his language became. Wade and Richard, the new hires, who'd turned out to be brothers, were big young men, and they got along like two male cats in a gunnysack. Kennedy didn't worry about Erin. As his mom would say, the lady knew how to comport herself. And Wyatt never changed, no matter what was happening around him. But the way Kennedy saw it, he had three loose cannons he would have to control, and he wasn't sure anyone could keep Tex in line.

The day of Jen's visit, she arrived two hours before her parents to take a tour of the ranch. Kennedy had washed the side-by-side, and he'd put a pillow on the front seat to cushion Jen's right arm when they drove over rough ground. Jen was healing. She had some color back in her cheeks. But she seemed fragile to Kennedy, and she was also easily spooked. She trusted him. He knew that. But she still seemed to expect boogeymen to jump out at her from hidden places, and she grew nervous if she thought Kennedy might kiss her. He understood how she must feel. Her last boyfriend had turned on her, and now she felt vulnerable in a way she never had before.

She dressed appropriately for the ranch in blue jeans, sneakers, and a simple cotton top. Her hair hung loose around her smallish shoulders, because she still couldn't use her right hand to do a French braid. Kennedy liked seeing her hair down, and sometimes he fantasized about how it would slip over his skin like silk if they ever made love. As if *that* could happen any time soon. He guessed he should be glad sex wasn't a part of their relationship. If he got a girl pregnant, it could ruin his whole life. Well, he guessed it wouldn't *ruin* it, but it sure would change his plans for college and a future in wildlife management.

Kennedy had direct orders from Vickie to stop at the main house for a snack basket she'd packed for him and Jen to enjoy during their ride. He left Jen in the side-by-side while he ran in to collect their food. Vickie had to give him a rundown on the basket's contents, of course, and Kennedy had to act appropriately grateful as she told him about each item. She was describing the brownies when Kennedy heard someone scream outside.

"Four Toes!" Vickie cried.

Kennedy dashed through the house, threw open the front door, and dashed out onto the porch. Jen was no longer in the vehicle. She was standing on the roof of the cab. Slade's pet bear had climbed into the cargo area, where he sometimes rode with Kennedy while he moved wheel lines.

"It's okay!" Kennedy cried. "He's not a wild bear!"

Jen was screaming so loudly Kennedy doubted she heard him. He wanted to kick himself for not telling her the story about Slade rescuing Four Toes as a cub. It was a great tale with a happy ending. Only Jen had gotten hurt early on after they met, and their conversations after that had been mainly focused on her injuries, her physical therapy, and her fears.

Vickie ran down the steps, her curly red hair dancing in the breeze. Four Toes had snuggled down in the back of the vehicle, looking like a ginormous marshmallow perfectly roasted to a golden brown. "Get out of there, you big galoot!" Vickie yelled. "You've frightened that poor girl half to death!"

Four Toes moaned. That was the bear's answer to almost everything. Kennedy climbed up onto the roof to kneel beside Jen, who stood upright and was still shrieking. He wrapped both arms around her thighs, afraid she might tumble to the ground and break her arm again. She might never regain the use of her right hand if that happened.

"Jen!" he yelled. "He's a tame bear! A rescue bear, just like the ones you worked with last summer at the shelter. He won't hurt you."

Jen stopped midshriek with her mouth yawning and her big blue eyes bugging. "A rescue bear? But he growled at me! And then he climbed in!"

Kennedy tightened his hold on her. She was wiggling around, and he sure didn't want her to fall. "Listen to me. He's tame. He growls a lot. It's how he talks. He wasn't threatening you." Kennedy glanced around. He had to get Jen down to safety. "We need to get off this thing before you take a tumble."

"Down there? With the bear?"

Vickie let loose with, "You are so spoiled, Four Toes. Get out of that side-by-side."

Kennedy felt Jen go from being as taut as a piano wire to limp as a dishcloth. "Sit down, Jen. Can you do that for me?"

She lowered herself to the roof with Kennedy keeping a firm hold on her all the way down. Then he leaped to the ground and turned to lift his arms to her. "Come on. I'll catch you. Just scoot over and dangle your legs off the side."

Jen did that, and Kennedy caught her as she pushed off into his arms. He'd never held her close, and for a moment, he didn't want to release her because it felt so good. He quickly loosened his hold. Jen turned to stare at Four Toes.

"He's *huge*," she said. "He's bulging out over the sides."

"Yeah, well, he's been well fed all his life. When he was a cub, there was a big conspiracy in town to help Slade feed him. Half the business-people in Mystic Creek contributed stuff. It was the best-kept secret of all time. Sheriff Adams never got wind of it until last September, and now Slade has a special permit to keep Four Toes on the ranch. I'll show you his night compound later. We don't let him wander after we turn in. During the day, we can keep an eye out and make sure he doesn't take off."

Jen cradled her right arm against her midriff, making Kennedy worry that she'd hurt herself. "Why is he in the side-by-side? He doesn't fit."

"Tell him that. He loves to go for rides, and I guess he hasn't been on the scales lately."

Jen giggled, and Kennedy stopped worrying. If she were hurt, she wouldn't be laughing.

"Silly bear." She glanced up at Kennedy. "Why can't he go with us? He's already in, and getting him out may be difficult."

As in almost impossible, Kennedy thought. "You sure you can enjoy yourself with a bear his size resting his chin on your shoulder?"

Jen nodded. "I worked all last summer with rescue bears. I'm not afraid of them. It's the wild ones that frighten me. Not to say that bears aren't dangerous, even if tamed. They can turn cranky in a blink."

Kennedy grinned. "When Four Toes gets in a grump, we just toss him a squeeze bottle of ketchup. That always mellows him out. Slade and Vickie keep a plastic tub of ketchup stocked in the pantry. We probably have forty bottles."

Vickie went back inside and returned a moment later with the picnic basket. "If you let Four Toes eat all these baked goods, you'll never again steal fresh lemon meringue pie from my kitchen," she told Kennedy.

"No, ma'am. I'll guard your baked goods with my life."

The ranch tour went well. Jen used the pillow to cushion her sore arm and seemed to be delighted with all the things Kennedy showed her. It was all old hat to him, but he was glad she enjoyed herself. He ended the drive down at the creek where the old fallen log provided a great place to sit.

"Here's where we'll have our picnic."

"What about dinner?" Jen asked. "If I eat now, I may be full. I don't want to offend Vickie. She seems really nice."

"Yeah, well, around Vickie, you have to eat the goodies *and* the meals."

Kennedy liked how Jen fit into his world. She didn't complain about the mud on her sneakers, and she'd taken a shine to Four Toes as if having a bear as a tour companion was commonplace. Kennedy set their basket between them on the log. He was eating a brownie and drinking Coke from a can, and Jen was nibbling on a cinnamon roll when Four Toes walked up behind them and snatched the picnic basket.

"No, Four Toes!" Kennedy yelled.

But the bear wasn't listening. He was far more interested in pigging out. He punctured a hole in the side of Jen's can of pop and sucked so hard on the aluminum that it imploded as he drank.

"I'll share my Coke with you," Kennedy offered.

Jen giggled. "Are we going to tell Vickie about this?"

Kennedy settled a solemn gaze on her. "I really, *really* love her lemon meringue pies, so I vote for lying by omission." He glanced at the bear. "We each got a taste, at least. I swear, Four Toes eats because he's lonely. We came close to getting a girlfriend for him. Slade's permitted to keep black bears now. But the little female we almost got found a forever home in an observation sanctuary."

Jen sat on the log with her back to the creek so she could watch Four Toes eat. Kennedy decided the basket would never pass Vickie's inspection now. It was ruined, and he'd have to tell her about Four Toes confiscating their picnic treats. "I guess I could try to take it away from him," he mused aloud.

"Mmm. I don't think that'd be smart," Jen observed. "He's really into those brownies."

"I was, too," Kennedy grumped. Then he saw something strange in torn tinfoil and said, "What is *that?*"

Jen's eyebrows lifted. "Does Vickie make jalapeño poppers sometimes?"

"Oh, shit!" Kennedy leaped over the log. "No, Four Toes, don't eat those things! They're not for bears."

But Four Toes was nothing if not an eating machine. He scooped jalapeños from the destroyed aluminum foil, shoved them in his mouth, and chewed. Then he groaned. That was because Vickie made her poppers really *pop*. Four Toes got up, walked down to the creek, and plunged into the water, which was icy from snowmelt.

"How do I explain to a bear that cold water after spicy food only makes the burn worse?" Kennedy asked.

Jen shrugged. "It's kind of like, how do you take a picnic basket away from a bear? I don't think you can. Sugar helps with the burn, though." She looked down at the partially eaten cinnamon roll still in her hand. "Do you think he's full?"

"You're joking, right? He could eat a whole garbage can full of cinnamon rolls and brownies."

"I'll try giving him this."

Jen stood up. Kennedy intercepted her before she took a step. "Oh, no, you won't. *I'll* try giving it to him." Kennedy took the cinnamon roll, walked down to the creek, and waded out almost as high as his boot tops. Four Toes, now a wet and shaggy mess, waddled through the water to reach Kennedy, his eyes fixed on the prize. Kennedy handed him the roll. And then Kennedy lost his footing on the slick rocks and fell in the stream. When he crawled out, he was as wet as the bear, and Jen was laughing so hard she had to cross her legs.

"What is so funny?" Kennedy asked. "This is my only pressed shirt! I wanted to look nice for your parents."

The outdoor dinner went well. Kennedy changed into dry clothes, and even though his shirt wasn't pressed, he thought he looked okay. Tex only cussed once, when he came upon a bowl of gnocchi and asked,

"What the fuck's this?" Vickie and Slade had dressed up. Well, they were dressed up for ranchers, anyway, wearing clean Wrangler jeans, their newer riding boots, and pressed Western shirts. Erin arrived in a white blouse, a denim skirt, and the black commando boots she worked in. Wyatt fed horses at the last minute and showed up in a partially wet shirt, because he'd washed at the bunkhouse before coming over to eat. He looked nice, though, and he'd even brushed the hay out of his hair.

Mr. and Mrs. Johnson seemed to have a lot of fun, and Mrs. Johnson helped with cleanup after the meal was over, while her husband walked around the ranch common with Slade. Jen seemed sad about leaving, and Kennedy wished she didn't have to go. But, as his mom said, all good things had to end.

Kennedy felt kind of blue as he settled in on his bunk that night to read while his coworkers watched television and Wyatt practiced his speech on the computer he'd set up in the laundry room. It wasn't often that Kennedy got a chance to read for pleasure, and he didn't appreciate the interruption when his cell phone rang. He got over his aggravation when he saw it was Jen calling.

"You'll never guess what!" she said with a chortle. "I called my old boss at the bear shelter, and I found a girlfriend for Four Toes!"

Kennedy sat straight up. "For real? Are you sure?"

"They're overloaded with bears right now and are kind of desperate to place them. This little girl is about a year old, but my boss says that's good, because she should bond with Four Toes as if he's her daddy or something. Then when she gets older..." Her voice trailed away. "Well, you know. They'll be best friends. Her name is Ginger. I haven't seen her yet, but I bet she's cute."

"How will that work? Four Toes and Ginger and the best friend part. What if they make babies?"

"Well, babies will happen," Jen said. "The cubs should probably go to a wildlife rehabilitation center. Trained veterinarians and technicians will prepare them to be released into the wild."

"Does that work?"

"Sure, if it's done correctly."

"Maybe Slade should just get Four Toes altered."

Jen cracked up laughing, and Kennedy was glad. She'd laughed a lot that day, and she hadn't done much of that since the attack. It meant she was feeling more positive. And he was delighted by the news about Ginger. Four Toes wouldn't be lonesome for someone of his own kind anymore. He'd have his very own girlfriend. Maybe he'd even stop eating so much and trim down a little.

CHAPTER NINETEEN

On Monday morning, Julie woke up and admired the sunshine coming through all the windows of her house as she walked to the kitchen. Her first order of business each day was always a cup of coffee. Thinking of Blackie, who had spent most nights at her place over the last three weeks and loved his coffee when he hit the floor, she smiled as she took the first sip.

Then the hot liquid hit her stomach. She ran for the bathroom and reached the toilet just in time. She vomited until she was weak and felt just as sick as she'd been with the virus. After getting everything up, which wasn't much, she managed to shower and get ready for work. As she drove into town and parked behind the Menagerie, she felt woozy, and that didn't subside as she entered the building. Was it possible for a person to catch the same thing twice?

By ten o'clock, Julie still felt awful. Last time she'd just gone home, thinking she'd get better. She wouldn't make that mistake twice. She decided to see the same guy who'd taken care of her at the emergency clinic. She knew he had only been volunteering when he'd seen her at the clinic, so she called his office on North Huckleberry Lane. She managed to land an appointment for eleven, which gave her only a few min-

utes to get there. It was a short drive. Even as dizzy as she was, she believed she could stay on the road. After locking up, she hurried out to her car and pushed the speed limit all the way.

Richard Andrew Blake was a nice-looking man with a warm smile. After examining Julie, he sat on a roll-around stool and frowned up at her. "You're not running a fever," he said, "and didn't you say this hit you suddenly this morning when you drank coffee?"

Julie nodded.

"From what I understood, you were nauseated for several hours last time before you began vomiting. I honestly don't think this is the same virus. Is there any possibility you could be pregnant?"

"Absolutely none. I'm on birth control." Julie held up a hand. "And I even took my pills while I was sick."

His frown deepened. "You couldn't keep anything down, Julie. Not even water, as I recall. You were dangerously dehydrated."

"Yes, but—" Julie broke off and stared at him. "I still got the pills down. I took them with 7-Up. I didn't forget, and even if I vomited one of them up, I can't see how missing my dose once could result in pregnancy."

The doctor asked, "Have you engaged in unprotected sex over the last few weeks?"

"Only once."

He looked at her matter-of-factly. "Once is enough. I think we should do a pregnancy test."

Julie had entered the Mystic Creek Internal Medicine building with a virus and walked out pregnant. Still feeling as sick as a dog, she sat in her car with her forehead resting on the steering wheel. *Pregnant.* She didn't *want* a baby, not now, not when she'd fallen in love with a man who didn't want children. And how would she ever tell Blackie? He'd be so upset, and she couldn't blame him. He was fifty-three years old and had bypassed the time in his life for starting a family.

Julie leaned back against the seat and closed her eyes. She had friends who had found themselves in this situation and had considered

all of the options, even ending their pregnancies. She placed a hand over her abdomen and felt a sudden rush of maternal protectiveness. Whether she'd planned on this baby or not, she couldn't contemplate getting rid of it. Not for Blackie. Not even for herself. Only, with a business demanding so much of her time, how on earth would she manage? And if Blackie bailed on her, she'd have to raise the child alone. That wouldn't be a walk in the park, for sure. But she would do it. Her baby would never grow up thinking that he or she was unwanted.

That evening after supper and working with Firecracker, Erin walked down to the log by the creek. She wanted some time to think and sort through her childhood memories, which seemed to be slipping back into her mind with alarming frequency now that she'd been working with Firecracker every day. It wasn't a pleasant turn of the leaf for Erin.

She was startled when Wyatt suddenly swung a leg over the log and sat down beside her. "You need to stop sneaking up on me like that," she said with faux aggravation, hoping to make him laugh. She loved the deep, natural sound when mirth caught him by surprise and he just let go. "I came down here to think."

"Oh, wow," he said with a grin. "Erin, thinking. What did you come down here to contemplate?"

"My childhood," Erin confessed. "You were right, Wyatt. Working with Firecracker has helped me look at things and see them for what they really were instead of the way my father painted them."

"And what are your conclusions?" he asked.

Erin tried not to notice the heat that radiated from his body and warmed her arm. "I've concluded that my father is a male chauvinist pig."

Wyatt chuckled. "Okay. I'm listening. Well, not really. That's a figure of speech. But unload it on me."

Erin took a deep breath. "I don't know why it took me so long to see him for what he is, because the signs have always been there. My mom, for instance. My dad doesn't respect her or appreciate anything she does. I don't know how it is between them behind closed doors, but

outside the bedroom, their relationship is pretty much a dead zone. My mother hyperfocuses on being a housewife. My father couldn't care less how hard she works to keep his world perfect. He reads the paper while he eats, barely speaking to her at the table. Then he watches television. She's a fixture in his life. As a child, I would have been ignored as well if he hadn't decided to turn me into a boy. Remembering those days makes me so angry."

Wyatt looped an arm around her shoulders and drew her snugly against him. Erin wanted to make love with him so badly that a tremor coursed through her body. When he bent his head to kiss her forehead, she knew he felt desire, too.

"You have every right to be angry with your father," he said, his voice gone husky. "What he did was wrong. Eventually, you'll get beyond the anger, though. I was so angry in my late teens and early twenties, but I finally came to realize none of the people in my life who made me feel broken had intentionally done so. They truly were trying to help me."

"My father wasn't trying to help *me*. He was trying to change me into the son he wanted."

"True, and I won't argue with you. He's definitely a misogynist. But at this point in your life, Erin, holding on to anger will get you nowhere. You need to see your father for what he is and realize he was probably raised to have that mind-set. The next thing you should ask yourself is if your father can help being the way he is." When Erin stiffened, Wyatt tightened his arm around her. "Just listen for a minute. I'm not making excuses for the man. But I am pointing out that childhood experiences do play a part in molding us into the adults we become. Look at me. Look at yourself. Do any of us reach adulthood without having some hang-ups? I seriously doubt it. Some people want to wallow in misery and complain about things they endured as kids, but are they ever really happy and content with themselves? That should be our aim as adults, to move forward and create our own lives. If we live in the past, we can't move on."

"I'm not wallowing," she said. "I'm just starting to realize most of this stuff."

"I know, and I'm not trying to rush you into getting past your anger. Eventually you'll come to realize other things as well, such as the fact that your mother did nothing to protect you from your dad. Why was that? I'm guessing she reached adulthood with some hang-ups of her own. What I'm basically saying is you can't change either of them, and you certainly can't go back in time and change your childhood. At some point, you can't allow it to have power over you any longer. Does that make any sense?"

Erin sighed. "Yes. But I want to be pissed off for a while before I get all saintly and forgive either one of them."

At that, he did laugh, and she enjoyed hearing the deep rumble. "Fair enough. Stay mad for a while. Then move on."

"I think my mom saw my dad as her ticket off this ranch. She hated it here. Hated the dust and the mud and the manure. As an adult, she's never liked animals. She let me have a kitten once, but I didn't have it for long. Her marriage to my father gave her the life *she* always wanted, and then she couldn't give him the son *he* wanted. I don't know why she never had another child, but isn't it possible that she lived in fear that he would divorce her and marry another woman who could give him a son?"

"I think that's entirely possible." He straightened and tightened his arm around her. "And you're thinking she sacrificed you to keep him from leaving her."

"Yes, that's exactly it, and I'm furious with her for that. How could she stand aside and let him make me act like a boy? Even worse, whenever I was alone with her, she was constantly riding me for not acting like a lady. I couldn't make her happy, and I couldn't make him happy. And when a child never gets any praise, it becomes all-important. At least it did to me. Only now do I understand what I really wanted was to be loved. Instead they made me feel like a disappointment they'd both been saddled with."

"I am so very sorry that they hurt you so deeply and in so many ways."

The husky timbre of Wyatt's voice caught Erin's attention, and she glanced up to meet his gaze. Her breath caught, and her heart skittered, because she saw tears in his eyes. And there was no doubt in her mind that those tears were for her. He wasn't merely commiserating with her and saying what he felt was expected; he truly felt sad for her.

But that wasn't the only epiphany for Erin. She saw something else in those laser-blue depths that sent a shock wave of emotion through her chest. He *loved* her. She read it in his gaze and the tender expression on his face. How had she missed that? This man was looking at her as if she were the center of his whole world.

For a moment, his features blurred in her vision as he bent his head. She felt his warm breath, scented with coffee and mint, caress her lips. She realized that he intended to kiss her, and every pore of her skin tingled with sudden awareness and yearning. *Yes.* She'd dreamed of this. Longed for it. And finally it was going to happen.

Only just as his mouth brushed hers, the brim of his Stetson poked her on the forehead. He jerked away, held her gaze for a long moment, and righted his hat. Then he stood and smiled sadly down at her. "You definitely have a lot to think about. A lot to work your way through as well. Just don't stay down here too long. It's about to get dark. I don't want you to trip and fall going back."

Erin wished he would stay and enjoy the evening with her for a few more minutes. She also wished that he would throw caution to the wind and kiss her. Apparently he wasn't of the same mind, because after giving her a thumbs-up, he walked away.

Trembling and unsettled, Erin wrapped her arms around her waist and stared at the creek. She nearly jumped out of her skin when Wyatt spoke from somewhere just behind her, his voice once again gravelly with emotion.

"Given your past, I can't just walk away without making sure you know something, Erin, and I hope you never forget it. I think you're the most beautiful and wonderful woman I've ever known."

Hope welling within her, Erin twisted on the log to look over her shoulder at him. The last, lingering rays of sunlight cast his face in shadow, so she couldn't read his expression. Even worse, she couldn't think of a single thing to say.

"If I could see my way clear, I'd wrap both my arms around you and hold on for dear life. I'd go down on bended knee and beg you to marry me. I'd ask you to have at least one of my babies and pray it would be a girl just like you. And you know what else, Erin?"

She could barely speak. "No. What?" she pushed out.

"I'd love that baby girl with every fiber of my being. If she turned out to be a tomboy, I'd support her all the way. If she turned out to be a girly-girl, I'd buy her frilly dresses and pretty little shoes. No matter what, I'd be proud to be her father."

Erin's eyes filled. When she blinked, tears spilled over onto her cheeks. She didn't bother to hide them. Voice shaking, she asked, "Why can't we make that happen, Wyatt? There's something special between us. I feel it, and I know you do, too."

He nodded. "Some things just aren't meant to be. There are things about me you don't know. Things I don't want to talk about, things I never even want you to know. However, I do think you need to know that my reasons for walking away have absolutely nothing to do with you. You're beautiful, and you're special. There isn't a single thing about you that I'd ever try to change." He bent his head and dug at the forest floor with the dusty toe of his boot. "As you move forward and try to heal from the craziness of your childhood, I hope you'll remember that one man in this messed-up old world thinks you're damned near perfect."

When she tried to speak, he held up a hand. "I'm walking away now, and if you ever refer to anything I've just said, I'll pretend I don't know what you're talking about. Friends only, Erin. That's all I can offer you. I know you don't understand why. I know you have questions. All I'll say on that score is that I try never to hurt the people I care about, and you've become one of them."

Erin's whole body shook as she watched him vanish into the charcoal shadows of the forest. She wanted to scream his name. To call him back to her. To tell him she already knew his dark secret. She wished now that she had made that confession weeks ago. Maybe then he might have listened to her and considered how they could make an intimate relationship between them work. Only she'd been afraid to tell him that she'd used her badge to invade his privacy. Of all the wrong things she'd ever done, she regretted her actions that evening the most.

He was one of the most honest and straightforward men she'd ever known, and she had betrayed his trust. If she ran after him now and told him what she'd done, would he still think she was damned near perfect? Erin felt fairly certain that he'd never look at her in quite the same way again.

CHAPTER TWENTY

Julie waited three days before she decided to tell Blackie she was pregnant. He had stopped in at her shop. He'd asked her if she was upset with him about something. She'd tried to reassure him and pretend nothing was wrong, but she'd never been an accomplished liar, and something was very wrong indeed. She'd needed time to think. About the baby. About how much she loved Blackie and how this pregnancy might destroy her relationship with him. And in the end, when she had completely assimilated that she was going to have a child, she was glad she'd waited. It had given her an opportunity to realize she and her baby had become a package deal. If Blackie hated her for that, she would have to accept it. As deeply as she loved the man, she would allow no harm to come to her child if she could possibly prevent it.

She called Blackie from her shop and asked him over for dinner that night. She still wasn't sure how she should broach the subject. She knew it would come as a shock to him. It had certainly come as an unpleasant surprise to her.

She fixed a pot roast and all the trimmings for their meal in her Instant Pot, but she decided that eating outdoors would be silly, even though Blackie loved dining al fresco. Once she dropped this bombshell on him, he might walk out, and then she would have to carry in all the dishes and stuff by herself. Her morning sickness lasted well into the afternoon and sometimes even the evening. She'd also been on her feet for twelve hours. In her condition, she needed to pamper herself just a little and rest as much as she could.

When Blackie arrived, he noted how pale she was and asked if she was sick again. Looking up at his sun-darkened face, Julie's heart broke, because she truly did love this man, and she wished she could be with him the rest of her life. But the child they had created together made that very unlikely.

"I am feeling a little sick," she confessed. And once she'd said that much, she saw no sense in waiting for a perfect moment to tell him the news. No matter how she delivered it, it was what it was. "When it first started three mornings ago, I thought it was the virus coming back and went straight to the doctor. Only it's not a virus. I'm pregnant."

"*What?*"

Julie braced her shoulders as if for a blow. "I'm sorry. Believe me when I say I didn't intend for this to happen, but since it has and I can't do anything to change it, I'm happy about it."

"Julie, I'm too *old* to have a baby. I was honest with you from the very start about that. How could you have been so careless?"

Julie flinched as if she'd struck her. "Careless?"

A flush rose up his neck. "Yes, careless. Unless, of course, you did it intentionally. Is that it? I know you yearned to have children during your marriage. Did you decide to get pregnant with my baby on purpose?"

Insulted by his suspicions, she knotted her hands into tight fists. "Don't be a complete ass, Blackie. Of course I didn't do it on purpose! If you'll recall my bout with the flu, I was unable to hold anything down for two days. The doctor says I undoubtedly vomited up at least one, if not two, birth control pills when I was so sick. And apparently one or two missed doses is all it takes sometimes. I never thought about that or the possible risks. I was just as shocked as you are when I found out." She straightened her spine. "But now that I know, I won't lie to you and say I'm sorry. I'm not. I'll have this baby. If you think you can make this go away, you're wrong. I won't end this pregnancy even though it was an accident and is, in your mind, a disastrous mistake." Julie flung her hand toward the archway that led to the front of her house. "Get out and take your small-minded insults with you."

For a long moment, Blackie just stood and stared at her.

Wanting him out of her sight so she could burst into tears, which she refused to do in front of him, she screamed, "I said get *out*! And I mean *now*! My disastrous mistake and I will be better off without you!"

He took a halting step toward her. "Julie, calm down. It's not good for you to get this upset."

"Then stop upsetting me and get out! I won't come after you for child support. You're free of all responsibility. Now get out of my life!"

By the time Blackie got back to his shop, he was devastated. On the way out of Julie's house, he'd heard her sobbing and knew he'd broken her heart by saying what he had. He'd handled that all wrong. What had he been thinking to accuse her of getting pregnant on purpose? Okay. The thought had crossed his mind. He'd known how much she'd yearned to have children during her marriage. And, if he was honest with himself, he knew his feelings of insecurity in the relationship had probably prompted his suspicions, too. He was so much older than Julie, and sometimes he wondered why a beautiful young woman like her would want anything to do with a man like him. He was twenty years her senior. Fighting a daily battle against the middle-age bulge. Going gray at the temples. Julie could crook her little finger and have her pick of all the young, single guys in town. Why would she settle for an old junk heap with so many miles on him?

Blackie locked the street door of the shop and went upstairs to think. He collapsed on his recliner and closed his eyes. In his mind's eye, he pictured how insane it would be to have a kid at his age. Walking the floors with a crying baby at night. Dirty diapers. Colic. Diaper bags, car seats, baby carriers. He was too damned old for all that.

Or was he? Blackie remembered how panicked he'd felt when Julie had gotten so upset that she was shaking, and he suddenly realized with numbing clarity that his concern had not been only for Julie, a healthy young woman in the early stages of pregnancy. He'd been worried about the safety of their baby, too. Most miscarriages occurred during the first trimester. He worried that Julie getting so angry wouldn't be good for their baby.

Blackie's heart squeezed with concern for the woman he'd come to love so much and for the child she now carried. He remembered how sad he'd often felt during his forties when he'd yearned to be a father and knew he never would be. And Julie. God, she was a dream come true in his life, one of the best things that had ever happened to him. So what if he was fifty-three? It was only a number. He was still active and in good physical shape. His own father was still alive and almost ninety. If longevity was passed down, Blackie should have a lot of good years left in him. And like it or not, he'd finally gotten his wish and was about to be a father. He couldn't let Julie go through this without him. She hadn't gotten pregnant without him, and she shouldn't have to deal with this pregnancy and raising the child alone.

Blackie started to feel excited about the baby. Boy or girl, he would love it with his whole heart and soul. Even now when he saw little girls, he melted and wished he were still young enough to have one of his own. And boys? He yearned to teach a little guy how to throw a ball. He instinctively knew he'd been born to be a dad, the kind who read stories, played with dolls, and wore out the front lawn playing tag football. He still wasn't too old for all that, and if he and Julie had their kids over the next couple of years, he wouldn't be too old when they were teenagers if he worked out and stayed in shape.

Blackie grabbed the jacket he'd tossed over the back of his chair and bolted down the stairs. If he begged and pleaded, Julie would forgive him for what he'd said. She *had* to, because he couldn't contemplate living the rest of his life without her.

Julie lay on her bed in a fetal position, which she thought was fitting since as her baby grew, it would lie within her uterus in the same position. From here on out, it would be just the two of them. The thought brought fresh tears to her eyes, and she started crying again.

She wished Blackie were beside her and holding them both in his arms. But he'd made his choice, and she had to live with it.

The doorbell pealed, the loud musical notes bouncing off the walls of her home and snapping her body taut. With a glance at her watch, she saw it was almost eight o'clock, way too late for solicitors, and she knew it couldn't be Erin, who knew Julie needed to be sound asleep by nine. She groaned and sat up, her heart leaping with hope that it might be Blackie. How stupid was that? He had run with his tail between his legs, and right now he was probably thanking his lucky stars over a beer that she'd let him off the hook.

She finally felt better, at least. No nausea now that it was bedtime. She grabbed her robe and slipped it on as she hurried to the front door. After looking through the peephole, she stood frozen on the entryway rug and hugged herself. It was Blackie.

"I heard you come to the door, Julie. Please, just let me in. *Please.*"

A part of her wanted to tell the man to get lost, but another, more civilized part of her couldn't do that. She took a deep breath and disengaged the dead bolt. As the door swung open, Blackie pressed closer and put his foot on the threshold. In that moment, he looked large, forceful, and so masculine she ached to throw herself into his arms.

"What do you want, Blackie? I have to be at my shop at five in the morning."

He held her gaze. "I want to beg your forgiveness. I know what I said was awful and uncalled-for. I think I knew it when I said it. But there's this other side of me, Julie, a side that can't believe you're truly in love with an old guy like me. You're so young. So beautiful. And, damn it, I don't think I can live the rest of my life without you. Knowing that scares me half to death and makes me feel—I don't know—inadequate, I guess, and insecure. I can't help but ask myself what the hell you can possibly see in me, and for just an instant, it did cross my mind that maybe you used me to get pregnant. I'm so sorry for allowing a thought like that into my head. The words were out before I could stop them. If you'll forgive me, I'll spend the rest of my life making it up to you. I— am—*so*—sorry."

Tears rushed to Julie's eyes again. She hadn't looked in a mirror, but she figured her eyes were already red and swollen. She'd cried over him long enough. "You're forgiven," she said stonily. "Thank you for stopping by to apologize."

When she started to close the door, he pressed the flat of his hand against the exterior side of the portal. "Please. I've been thinking about the baby. About what I said about not wanting it at my age. And then about how scared I was when you got so upset. I was afraid for you. I won't lie about that. But mostly, Julie, my first instinct was to be afraid for our baby. It's got such a fragile grip on life right now."

Julie just stared up at him. She felt so empty inside, so horribly empty.

"I love it already," he said softly. "God only knows how, but the feeling's there, Julie. I told you before that I'd always wanted children. All my adult life, I wished I could meet the right lady and raise a family. You just hit me with it so suddenly. I didn't have time to think it through or absorb what it meant. And I just blurted out my first reaction, that I didn't want a baby at my age. Which was true. In that moment, it was true."

"We're a package deal, Blackie. I'm having this baby, and I'm keeping it."

"I know, and I understand that. I'm just asking you to forgive me for what I said and allow me to be a part of this."

Julie remembered her first reaction when the doctor had asked if she might be pregnant. She'd been appalled at the mere suggestion. And she'd actually thought, *I don't want a baby*. She hadn't said the words aloud, but after the shock wore off and she had a moment alone, she fell in love with the baby. Maybe, she thought with a tiny glimmer of hope, Blackie had, too.

"I'm sorry I dumped it on you the way I did. I planned to tell you after dinner, or maybe during dinner. But I was so afraid of your reaction, and I've felt so sick all day. If you were going to dump me over it, I just wanted to say it and be done with it, no matter what happened."

Blackie passed a hand over his eyes. "Dump you? Julie, you're a dream come true for me. The joy of my life." He turned his palms upward like a supplicant. "I know you can't forget those first words that popped out of my mouth, but I swear to you and before God that I didn't really mean them. In fact, I'm feeling really excited now. About the baby, I mean. And I'm even thinking about more kids. If we have them soon, I'll be young enough when they're teenagers to still be a fairly good father."

Julie placed a hand over her abdomen. More children? She was just getting her mind wrapped around having one. "Maybe you should come in. I need to sit down."

Blackie looked vastly relieved. "Does this mean you really do forgive me?"

"Not necessarily. It mostly means I feel weak from not eating much today, and I need to sit."

She turned and Blackie closed the front door before following her to the living room. Julie chose to sit in one of the recliners. If she took a seat on the sofa, she was afraid he would sit beside her, and she didn't trust herself not to throw herself into his arms.

Blackie sat on the couch and braced his arms on his knees with his hands folded. "I honestly didn't mean what I said. It was my insecurity talking. And . . . well, Julie, the news did take me off guard. It was a bit of a shock. I had no time to think before I spoke." He sighed. "I'm as responsible for this pregnancy as you are. I could've worn a condom. I didn't even ask about protection until after the fact. So where was my head that first night when you told me you were protected? I saw you hurl but didn't consider the possibility that you might have missed doses, and that was as much my responsibility as it was yours." He met and held her gaze. "We did this together and we should deal with it together."

Julie wanted to hug him, not because she intended to resume their relationship, but simply because he was now being a stand-up guy. "Blackie, I appreciate your sense of obligation, but the truth is, you never wanted to be a dad at this stage of your life, and I don't want my baby to be a mistake that you feel obligated to deal with."

He sighed. "I had that coming. I know I didn't react well to the news. But now that I've had time to think about it, I'm excited about becoming a father. I've always wanted kids. Granted, I wouldn't have made this decision for myself or for the baby, but it happened. I can't help but think that maybe it's God's way of taking the decision out of my hands and giving me one of the most beautiful gifts of my life, a wonderful woman to love and a child to raise."

Julie realized she was staring at him through tears, and she was unable to hold them back. The moment her shoulders started to jerk with suppressed sobs, he shot to his feet, pulled her up from the recliner, and enveloped her in his arms. His embrace felt so hard and warm and safe. Unable to resist his solid strength, she sank against him.

He held her until she stopped weeping, and then he continued to hold her. "I love you. I knew that long before you told me about the baby. I even told you before we made love. The baby doesn't change that, not one iota. You need to know you're the most important thing in the world to me, and you need to believe that our baby has also become one of the most important things to me."

"Oh, Blackie," she said in between sniffles. "How could you think I might toss you over for a younger man? You're the man I love. You're the only man I want. And I can't really blame you for how you reacted. When the doctor first suggested I might be pregnant, I was appalled. And then the test came back positive, and I was so terrified of your reaction and of losing you. The thought of an abortion flitted through my mind, and then, in a flash, I felt this rush of love for my baby, and I knew I would have it no matter how upset you were. I was frightened about raising it alone. I won't lie about that. But I also knew, way deep down, that I *could* raise it alone and that I *would*."

He started to sway with her pressed against him. "You won't have to do it alone. Nothing, except death itself, is going to stop me from being a part of our child's life. I swear to you, Julie, I don't see this as an obligation. It's the most wonderful thing that's ever happened to me."

She gave a wet laugh. "I know. Right? I didn't want this baby, either. For all of ten minutes. And then, wham, the reality of it all sank in. A baby, Blackie. It was the last thing I expected, and yet it's the most wonderful thing, too."

He pressed a kiss to the top of her head. "I feel exactly the same way. It's like, *wow*! I'm going to be a daddy."

"Parents, we're going to be parents."

"Big question. Are we going to be parents together?"

She twisted in his arms to look up at him. "Are you absolutely sure you want that?"

He released a breath and smiled. "I've never wanted anything more. I know this is old-fashioned, Julie, and you're always giving me a hard time about that, but I want to do this right. I think we should get married right away. I don't want my kid to grow up believing he was an accident. And kids do that, you know. When they're old enough, they do the math and realize their parents had to get married."

Julie gazed up at him. Her feelings of love for him ran so deeply that they were an ache within her. "Is that a proposal?"

He smiled. "Yes, and I know it's a poor excuse for one, but the circumstances don't allow for me to do it the romantic way. I'm also at a disadvantage when it comes to an engagement ring, because I know you always wanted to wear your grandmother's. Only it doesn't seem right. I should provide the ring. That's the traditional way."

All of Julie's resentment and anger had washed away during their talk, and she smiled shakily up at him. "I guess you can buy it back from me. We shouldn't depart from tradition. It'll always bother you."

"Can I take that to mean you're saying yes?"

"You're the only man in the world for me, Blackie. Of course I'm saying yes."

He grinned. "Good. Because I never cashed the check you made out to me, and now I just won't. All we need now is the ring. You said you were going to wear it, but I've never seen it on you."

"I need to get it resized. I was afraid it might slip from my finger and go down one of the shop drains."

"We'll take it to a jeweler tomorrow. I want a ring on your finger."

Julie went up on her tiptoes to hug his neck. "I never wanted to get married again. Until I fell in love with you. And just so you know, Blackie, I would have married you even without a child factoring into the equation."

"And I would have asked you to marry me, anyway. Like I said, you're a dream come true for me."

She tightened her hold on his neck. "Oh, Blackie, how will we ever manage? My shop keeps me so busy, and you have your own business to run. I don't want our baby to have exhausted, overtaxed parents."

"It won't. I've saved a lot of money over the years. Maybe we can sell our individual businesses, pool our funds, and start up the brewery we've both dreamed of. Then we can take care of the baby while we're working. We'll both be around. And neither of us will be exhausted or overtaxed."

"A brewery? You mean it? That would be so *awesome!*"

He chuckled, set her away from him, and ruffled her hair. "Plans for that have to come later. Right now we need to sort out our lives. I think we should live here with the understanding that I'll pay off the mortgage. I don't want a house payment hanging over our heads. Until I sell my shop, I can rent out my apartment." He grabbed her by the hand and led her upstairs. "While I was taking care of you, I toured the house. I wasn't thinking in terms of a baby at the time, but now that I am, I suggest that we should knock out a wall between two of the bedrooms up here to create a large master suite. Then we can turn one of the other bedrooms into the nursery. That will still give us two spare bedrooms in case we have more kids."

"Put on your brakes, Blackie. Let me get through this pregnancy before you start talking about having more kids."

When they reached the landing, he gathered her into his arms and kissed her. As always, Julie felt as if she were melting into him.

When he came up for air, he smiled down at her. "This is right, you know. We were meant to be together."

Julie couldn't have agreed more. "Let's go look at the bedrooms and choose our baby's nursery."

After dinner, Kennedy helped clean up the kitchen at the bunkhouse, then walked over to the main house to speak with Slade and Vickie. He'd waited to tell them about Ginger, the female bear, until Jen checked into it further and was absolutely certain that an adoption could occur.

Vickie answered the door, narrowed an eye at him, and then grinned. "Your sense of smell is absolutely phenomenal. I made lemon meringue pies today, and now, here you are."

Kennedy couldn't help but laugh. "Actually, I came to talk to you and the boss about something. But a piece of my favorite pie will be a really nice perk."

Vickie led him to the kitchen where Slade sat at the table eating a piece of pie. He smiled when he saw Kennedy. "First come, first serve. At least I've gotten one piece this time."

Vickie stepped over to the work island and served up another slice onto a dessert plate. "Coffee, too, Kennedy?"

"Please." Kennedy sat down across from his boss. "I've got some really awesome news. At least, I hope you'll be excited. Jen worked last summer at a bear shelter, and after meeting Four Toes, she inquired to see if the shelter has a female bear suitable as his life partner. As it happens, the facility is really crowded right now, and they have a one-year-old female the administrator thinks will be perfect for him. Her name is Ginger."

Slade stopped chewing and struggled to swallow. "Are you serious? Is it a sure deal? Last time when we didn't get the bear at the very last minute, Vickie was so upset she cried."

"It's a sure deal," Kennedy said. "They're really strapped for space. All you have to do is call them, prove that you have a permit and adequate facilities to keep a wild animal here, and they'll deliver her here within a week."

"Oh, how *fabulous!*" Vickie cried. "I feel so sorry for Four Toes. We all try to keep him from feeling lonely, but it goes against nature for an animal to have no contact with others of its species."

"I just hope they like each other," Kennedy said after he swallowed a bite of filling. "There's a chance they won't, you know. Female and male black bears don't normally hang out together in the wild. Ginger may not want Four Toes around her until she's ready to breed, and then she may give him the boot." Kennedy really didn't want to say the next part, but he had no choice. "Jen also learned that altering Four Toes may be required for the adoption to occur."

"Altering?" Slade looked none too happy at the suggestion. "I really wouldn't want to do that."

"I know," Kennedy commiserated. "But we have to look at it practically, Boss. If Four Toes is left intact, he'll impregnate Ginger. Your aim isn't to raise black bears. And the shelters won't want you to. Then there's the temperament issue. As Four Toes continues to mature, he'll become more aggressive. If he's altered, he'll be a lot mellower and a better companion for Ginger. They'll just be friends."

Vickie reached down to pat Pistol on the head. "You had Pistol neutered, Slade. Controlling the population of a wild species isn't usually a practice, but due to no fault of his own, Four Toes is no longer wild. He's been habituated to humans and can't be free as God intended. Do you really want him and Ginger to have cubs?"

Slade sighed and pushed away his dessert plate. "You're right. I know you're right." He glanced at Kennedy. "Does it have to be done right away?"

"I don't think so. Ginger won't be old enough to breed for a while, so you'll have some time to get used to the idea. I'm pretty sure the shelter will give you a deadline, though. If you don't get it done by then, there's probably a clause in the adoption papers saying they can take Ginger back."

"Maybe we should just get a male cub," Slade suggested.

Kennedy shook his head. "Nope. Then they'd both have to be altered, because they'll grow aggressive with each other as they get older. Think of it this way. In the wild, a black bear's average life-span is eighteen years. The oldest black bear on record in captivity lived forty-four years. If Four Toes lives even to be thirty, do you really think he'll be as happy as he should be without a companion?"

Slade gave Vickie a long look. "I was there once, and no, I don't think he'll be truly happy if he has to be alone for the rest of his life."

Vickie reached out, took Slade's hand, and dimpled her cheeks with a mischievous smile. "What he never experiences, he won't miss. After the surgical procedure, his desire for that will fade, and as Kennedy said, he'll be mellower. For a bear that lives around humans, that will be a good thing. And I believe with all my heart that it's the responsible thing to do as well. We don't want the two of them to make babies. The only goal is to increase the quality of Four Toes's life and to offer Ginger sanctuary where she'll be happy as well."

The next morning, Wyatt received a text from Slade asking him to come to the main house. Normally the boss sought Wyatt out when they needed to confab so Wyatt wasn't called away from his work. When Wyatt knocked, Vickie greeted him and ushered him to the in-home office where Slade sat behind a massive, cherry desk.

"Have a seat," Slade said, gesturing at the empty castor chair across from him. "I have a special assignment for you."

Wyatt immediately thought of all the things that already topped his list and wondered how he would find time to do anything more. "Okay. What's up?"

"I'm sure Kennedy's told you we're getting a female bear as a companion for Four Toes."

Wyatt nodded. "Yes. We all think it's great." Wyatt met his boss's gaze. "But if you're in one of your frugal moods and think I'm going to band that bear or do surgery on him with a pocketknife, you have another think coming."

Slade threw back his head and laughed. "I'm not quite that frugal. When the time comes, I'll have it done by a vet." He rested his arms on the desk blotter. "What I have in mind will actually be a fun assignment for you. Ginger will arrive in a week and a half, and Vickie is very excited about it. She got the idea of turning the first meet between the two bears into an occasion and wants to invite all the people in Mystic Creek who helped feed Four Toes as a cub."

"That should be nice." Wyatt secretly wondered what would be fun about doing a bunch of yardwork to prepare for another party. "What do you need me to do?"

"Well, Vickie thinks the first meet might go better for Ginger if it doesn't occur on the ranch. I didn't stop to think how frightening it might be for a young bear to arrive here and see horses and cows everywhere when she isn't accustomed to them. But Vickie did, and she feels that a woodland setting will be better. A place where we can leave the cows at home and highline the horses at a distance where Ginger won't feel intimidated."

"That makes sense," Wyatt told him. "Is she being exposed to any of her natural habitat at the shelter?"

"Yes. They have large enclosures in wooded areas, so Ginger should feel more at home in a forest. I'm considering Huckleberry Lake. It's beautiful up there, and as you already know, I've often considered that location as a base camp for guided hunts. I even have a permit for that area already. Last year, I got arrested when we were camped on Strawberry Hill, and people from town never got a chance to go up for the usual campout, so that's a selling point for me as well. If we set up camp at Huckleberry Lake, the guests from town will be invited to stay a couple of nights."

"So you want me to ride up and have a whole camp set up by the lake before the little bear comes?" Wyatt's mind raced. "I'd love to do that, boss. I enjoy setting up camps. Being out in the wilderness is one of my favorite things. But I'm swamped right now. I can't just walk away from all this work."

Slade held up a hand. "Oh, but you can, because I'm going to take over your job for the next week and a half." At Wyatt's surprised look, Slade smiled. "Believe it or not, I do know how to run a ranch. At my age, I prefer not to, but it'll be good for me to get my nose back into the operation for a few days. Since marrying Vickie, I've been a slacker. But I still hold to the idea that a boss should work alongside his crew. I think it keeps him tuned in. It'll be good for me, and I'm looking forward to it."

Wyatt couldn't argue that point. Since Vickie's reappearance in Slade's life, he had backed off on spending time with his hired hands. He relaxed on the chair, feeling as if Slade had just offered him a paid vacation. He could almost smell the campfire smoke and taste the boiled coffee.

"So who'll go along to help me?" Wyatt had to resist rubbing his hands together. "Kennedy?"

"Erin," Slade replied.

"What?" Wyatt wanted to say he couldn't believe his ears, but since he didn't have a pair that worked, he bit back the words. "She's probably never set up a tent in her life."

"She's a quick study, though," Slade countered, "and she's strong. With good direction, she'll be a fine helper."

Again Wyatt had to bite his tongue. He absolutely could *not* tell Slade that he had the hots for his niece and would endure living hell if he had to spend over a week alone with her by an isolated lake. "I'd really prefer someone experienced. Can you call one of the guys who goes up with us every year?"

"I can't really afford to," Slade said. "Erin's already on my payroll, and I'll be covering for you. It's not going to cost me anything extra if I send Erin. She's also our least experienced ranch hand. I need the people who know what to do to stay behind. Her knowledge is still pretty limited."

What had sounded like an awesome break from routine suddenly loomed before Wyatt like a brutal test of his restraint. "I'd really like someone besides Erin to go with me," he said. "She's not an experienced woodsman, and I've been told there are wolves at Huckleberry Lake. What if they come in on the horses?"

"Take an extra rifle. She's probably a better marksman than you are."

Wyatt knew in that moment that he wouldn't change Slade's mind. He made all the right noises during the rest of the meeting and couldn't wait to get out of the main house so he could throw his hat on the ground, kick dirt, and cuss. This whole idea would be a disaster.

After Wyatt left the house, Vickie hurried into the office. "Well? How did it go?"

Slade winked at her. "He's not going to be a happy camper up there, but I don't think he suspects a thing."

Vickie hugged her waist. "It was my idea. If it backfires, are you going to be furious with me?"

Slade rocked back in his chair. "Vickie, my sweet, you prick my temper half a dozen times a day. That's why I love you so much. I never know what you may say or do next." He shrugged. "According to you, Erin's had a thing for him for months, and you think Wyatt has strong feelings for her. What can possibly go wrong?"

"Everything?"

He laughed and shook his head. "If Wyatt loves her—and ever since you said something, I've been watching him and think you're right—we're just forcing him to face it himself and hopefully do something about it. He's a good man. If I could handpick a husband for my niece, he'd be my first choice."

"Yes, but even a good man can fall prey to temptation, Slade. That doesn't mean he's making a lifelong commitment."

"Erin's a grown woman. She understands that. I have to trust in her instincts. I don't think she'll expect chapel bells to ring just because they get a little cozy up there. And pushing Wyatt into giving up his hare-brained plan to go without sex for the rest of his life won't be a bad thing, either."

Vickie came to sit on his knee. Slade looped an arm around her waist. "Have you ever told Wyatt you know about the rape charge?" she asked.

Slade hired a professional detective to do his background checks. As the owner of a ranch, he had to know everything possible about a prospective employee. "Nope. I ordered all the court documents after I had the background check done on him. I saw no point in embarrassing him when I knew for sure what had happened and that he'd been found innocent. It's his secret to keep. If he chooses to tell me about it someday, I'll act surprised."

Vickie rested her head on his shoulder. "And you're positive he was in no way to blame for what happened?"

"Yes. Do you think I'd send my niece up that mountain with him if I weren't?"

Slade took over as foreman the next morning so Wyatt could start shopping and packing for the trip. Wyatt was glad he wasn't preparing for a guided hunt, because that required making huge lists and checking them twice. This trip would easy by comparison. He needed to take up tents, lanterns and fuel, kitchen gear, bedding, an ax, a chainsaw, and the like, but he only had to worry about taking enough food to last him and Erin for a little over a week. Vickie was taking care of all the other campout supplies and would bring them up the day she and Slade arrived with the female bear. Compared to a guided hunt, getting ready for this trip was a piece of cake.

Erin came to him late in the afternoon, and when he saw tears in her eyes, his heart leaped. "What's wrong?" he asked.

"I can't leave Firecracker. I just can't. I'm sorry, Wyatt. I know everyone's counting on me to go with you, and I may lose my job for refusing, but I just can't abandon her."

For what seemed like an endlessly long moment, Wyatt considered taking advantage of her reluctance. It was the perfect out for him. If *she* refused to go, he wouldn't be held to blame by Slade. Only that seemed like a really chickenshit thing to do, and when he thought about it, he decided the boss wouldn't let it slip past him, anyway. In less than a nanosecond, Slade would say the same thing Wyatt was about to say.

"Firecracker can just go with us."

"No!" Erin cried. "She'll be terrified the whole time. I can't do that to her."

Wyatt finished tying off a pack. "She won't be afraid. She's not fearful of other horses. It's people she doesn't like. Once we get a halter and lead rope on her, she'll fall into place with the pack animals and be fine."

"Do you really think so?"

"I know so. It may even be good for her. Horses learn by watching other horses. She'll see we don't beat our animals or throw explosives under their feet. It'll also give her a chance to make friends and hear how they feel about being ranch horses."

She wiped under eyes and sniffed. "Do you really think they talk?"

"I know they talk. We just don't understand their language." To cheer her up, he smiled at her. "Lighten up, Erin. Firecracker will enjoy going. And once we get tents set up for ourselves, plus a cook shack, you can take some time each evening to work with her, pretty much like you are right now. That way, she won't be left alone for days on end and forget everything you've accomplished so far."

Erin saw her trip up the mountain as a brutal test of her willpower. Wyatt Fitzgerald turned her on in every possible way a man could. Even worse, she both admired and respected him. Every time she thought about his decision to live the rest of his life without having sex, especially with her because she mattered to him, her heart melted. He truly cared about that Medford woman and what he'd accidentally done to her. Erin couldn't really blame him for not wanting anything like that to ever happen again. It was a noble stance for him to take, and Erin felt obligated to honor their *friendship-only* agreement. She absolutely could *not* flirt with him.

Erin rode a mule named Barbwire. He was a veteran trail mule that Uncle Slade had chosen for her. Uncle Slade said mules were smarter than horses, especially when it came to their own safety. He claimed horses might panic if they got bunched up on a narrow trail, and it wasn't unheard-of for an entire string to plunge off the side of a mountain. A mule, on the other hand, would back away from the cliff, stand fast, and watch his idiotic cousins kill themselves. According to Uncle Slade, Erin would be as safe as a baby in its mother's arms on Barbwire's back.

Unfortunately, Uncle Slade had forgotten to mention that Barbwire had a stubborn streak, a memory like an elephant, and some set ideas on how he should be handled. Erin, being an inexperienced rider, made mistakes, and when Barbwire got it into his head that she didn't know what she was doing, he stopped. And then he wouldn't move until she figured out what she was doing wrong.

It was frustrating for Erin. She'd chosen to ride behind the pack string, and when Barbwire went on strike, Wyatt had to tie off the lead packhorse and circle back to see what she had done.

"You're holding the reins too tight again," Wyatt told her when

Barbwire decided, for about the umpteenth time, to balk. "To a mule, pulling back on the reins means it should stop. You need to hold the reins in a loose grip and let them rest on his neck."

"But then I have no control," she protested.

"You don't need to have control. Barbwire loves horses. Some mules have an inborn desire to be a horse and be with horses—except when they panic and do stupid stuff. He'll follow the string. It's your job to just go along for the ride. Just loosen your grip, and when I head out again, Barbwire will follow. He won't want the horses to leave him."

Erin loosened her hold on the reins, and when Wyatt got the pack string moving again, Barbwire surged forward with his nose only a few feet from Firecracker's rump. It amused Erin to note that Barbwire seemed to know about the blind spot behind a horse, because he was careful never to get within kicking distance of the mare. As much as it rankled to admit it, Erin learned a few things from Barbwire.

By the time they reached Huckleberry Lake, it was late afternoon and Erin was exhausted. Wyatt was in charge of setting up camp, of course, and his first order of business was to get all the packs off the horses, rub the animals down, and then hobble them on a grassy flat near the water so they could eat and drink. Only Barbwire didn't get a pair of ankle bracelets. If the horses couldn't wander off, the mule wouldn't leave them, so Wyatt said hobbling him was unnecessary.

After doing all that, Erin wanted to crash in the shade for a while to admire the scenery. The lake wasn't large, but it was beautiful beyond description, a jewel of dark blue at the center of a verdant meadow surrounded by old-growth ponderosa and jack pines. Erin had never visited a high-mountain wilderness lake. It called to her, and she wished she could kick off her riding boots to wade in all that azure coolness.

Wyatt had different ideas. The very first thing they needed to do was create a highline where they could tie off the horses at night. When they'd done that, they had to get the packs of hay positioned for supplemental feeding. There was a lot of grass for the horses to graze on, but just in case it was nutritionally insufficient, he wanted to toss the animals a little hay. Then they had to set up their pup tents so they would each have shelter for the night. As they worked, he told Erin they would get the cook shack erected the following day, but for tonight, dinner would be a can of beef stew heated on an open fire. He also had wieners and marshmallows they could roast. Erin was starving and voted for the hot dogs.

They worked until the sun started to go down. Erin wished Wyatt had placed her tent closer to his. Ten feet of distance seemed a little bit much to her. She'd slept alone in a small wall tent at Uncle Slade's base camp on Strawberry Hill last fall, but she'd been surrounded by other people. Up here, she was afraid her only neighbors would be animals with saber teeth.

As Erin unrolled her sleeping bag inside her shelter, she congratulated herself for bringing only what she needed. There wasn't anything electrical in her duffel, only bare necessities. She hadn't thought to bring any makeup, and she'd look like hell all week. *That's okay,* she lectured herself. She hadn't come up here to seduce Wyatt Fitzgerald. She'd promised not to hit on him, and she tried never to break her word.

When she emerged from her tent, Domino bounced around her legs like a black-and-white tennis ball. Apparently he shared his master's love of camping out in wilderness areas and was excited to have her present for the fun. Erin guessed it would be enjoyable during the daytime. The lake was beautiful, and the weather was glorious, sunny but not too hot. She wasn't looking forward to the nights, however. Sleeping on a mountaintop populated by bears, coyotes, and cougars when she had only nylon walls to protect her didn't sound fun.

Wyatt had built a fire ring and gathered wood. He was hunkered down by the circle of rocks to build a fire, and since Erin figured she might have to do that herself before this week and a half was over, she watched everything he did. While growing up, she'd never gone camping.

Erin crouched across the flickering flames from Wyatt and immediately felt bowled over by how he looked—a quintessential cowboy out on the open range. Broad shoulders, well-muscled chest and arms, a narrow waist, and long legs that stretched the denim of his jeans tightly over his thighs. Even his long, straight hair screamed, *Film set*. She almost sighed with a rush of longing, but she squelched it, not because Wyatt could hear her feminine emissions of body-pulsing need, but because she'd promised him and herself that she would never allow her feelings to compromise their friendship.

He glanced up. "Are you hungry? We can eat right away or enjoy this incredible vista over a couple of before-dinner drinks."

Erin had seen Wyatt drink at Vickie and Slade's wedding reception and later over dinner with her at the Cauldron, but otherwise he seemed to be a teetotaler. "I didn't think you drank very much."

"I don't. But I always indulge at night in a wilderness camp. It helps me unwind after a long day and loosens up all my muscles."

Erin could think of another activity that might loosen him up, and she was disgusted with herself for letting her thoughts drift in that direction. *Again*. It was going to be a very long nine days. It didn't help that she knew now that he had deep feelings for her. She rested her hand on Domino's head to fondle his silky ears. "I'm up for a drink or two. Maybe it'll help relax my legs. I'm not used to riding."

"Are you saddle sore?"

"Not yet, and I hope I won't be. But sometimes abused muscles don't scream until the next morning."

He left and went to his tent. When he returned, he held two red Solo cups, a half gallon of Jameson, and a can of Coke. "The pop is for you. I prefer my whiskey straight." He squatted beside her, unloaded everything onto the ground, and poured them each a measure of alcohol. "Mixed or straight?"

Erin had taken her hard liquor straight with colleagues so many times that she no longer even got teary-eyed, but the truth was, she preferred whiskey diluted by something sweet. And she didn't have to be one of the guys with Wyatt. "Mixed, please."

He popped the can tab and sloshed Coke into her liquor.

"Cheers," she said, touching her Solo cup to his.

He resumed his former position across the fire from her. The flames were leaping higher now, and she felt warmth moving over her body. She wasn't sure if the heat came from the burning wood or from looking at

Wyatt. To stop herself from ogling him, she buried her nose in the wide-mouth cup to taste her drink. It was perfect, even without ice, a blend of fiery and sweet.

Wyatt fell quiet and sat cross-legged to gaze across the lake. "Look," he said. "Fawns."

It took Erin a moment to see the babies because of all the trees and tall grass on the opposite shoreline. "Oh, Wyatt, they're so sweet!"

He said nothing, and she was reminded that he didn't know she'd said anything. She sat down, too. Then she joined him in enjoying the natural beauty that abounded nearly everywhere she looked. The silence between them settled over her like a warm blanket on a cold night. Not talking allowed her to listen to sounds she rarely noticed: the soft twitter of birds as they roosted for the night, the soft whisper of a breeze in the trees, and the occasional raucous call of a hawk searching for dinner before dark. It was incredibly perfect, something she'd never experienced with any other person. She just wished that Wyatt could hear the marvelous symphony of nature, too.

After dinner, which for Erin was a roasted wiener on a bun and eight charred marshmallows, they cleaned up their utensils with water from the lake and then had an after-dinner drink.

"Did you remember to bring that solar charger for your phone that you bought last fall?" At her nod, he said, "Well, don't forget to charge your phone tonight. It's important up here to have a communication device in case of an emergency. The charger may not be at its best. Sit it out in the sunlight tomorrow."

Again, she only nodded.

"The reception up here isn't great. My phone shows only two bars. If you need to call out, you may have to find a high place for a better signal. We can text here, though. That requires less signal strength. I already let Slade know that we arrived, and he texted back, so I know my message got through."

The rigors of the day were catching up with Erin. After telling Wyatt goodnight, she rinsed her cup with lake water and took it with her to the tent. Wyatt had given her a tiny, battery-operated lantern, which she turned on while she got ready for bed. It cast a surprisingly bright glow, filling the small area with bluish-white illumination. She'd brought sweatpants and an old T-shirt to sleep in, and she made short work of changing because it was already growing cold. Then she slipped into her sleeping bag and doused the lamp. Absolute darkness dropped over her like a thick, black cloak. For a moment, she couldn't see her hand in front of her face. Then, as her eyes adjusted, she saw the light of the fire playing over the front flap of her tent. That comforted her, and she was so tired she fell asleep almost the instant her head touched the pillow.

Erin had no idea how much time had passed when she awakened with a violent start. For a moment, she couldn't imagine what had jerked her from a sound sleep. Then she heard them. Wolves, howling at the moon. Only she didn't believe for an instant that they were really moon worshipers. She thought they howled to each other as a form of communication, and she felt fairly sure that they were saying, *Here she is, a stupid woman who doesn't even have a gun. She smells really good to eat.*

She was out of the sleeping bag in one second flat. She couldn't count on Wyatt to wake up and save her. Thinking quickly, she bundled her sleeping bag and pillow into her arms, shoved her feet into her boots, and grabbed her lantern. Without turning it on—she didn't want to carry a beacon to guide the wolves straight to her—she plunged through the tent flap into the night and ran to Wyatt's tent. The campfire had gone dead, and she caught the toe of her boot on something and almost fell. When she reached his door flap, she flipped on her lantern so she wouldn't accidentally step on Wyatt when she entered the enclosure.

To her surprise, he was sitting up in bed. He winced and cupped a hand over his eyes at the sudden light. "What are you doing?" he asked.

"There are wolves out there!" she cried.

"Ah. I knew I felt something. Is that what it is?"

"Yes, and they sound hungry. I think I'm on the menu tonight. I don't even have a gun!"

She expected him to smirk. She knew she sounded like an archetypal city girl. Instead he frowned and said, "Slade sent up a rifle and ammunition for you. I'll go get it."

Erin's inner alarm went off. "If you think I'm going back to my tent with only a gun for protection, you're delusional. I've seen wolves in movies. They travel in packs. You may as well send me back with a BB gun for all the good a rifle will do me."

He ran a hand through his hair and then let it fall to his shoulders. "Erin, don't take this personally, but I'm not sharing a tent with you. Besides, if what I felt is wolves, I need to get to the horses."

"I'll help."

He gazed up at her for a long moment. "There's really no reason to be scared. Wolves normally don't go after people. They're just hungry and want an easy dinner. To wolves, those horses look kind of like McDonald's does to us."

Firecracker. Her beautiful horse was out there, tied up and unable to run in order to save herself. Erin dropped everything in her arms and ran from the tent holding her lantern high. Domino gave a shrill bark, as if warning her of danger, but he stayed in the tent with Wyatt. *Smart dog.* Wolves would polish off the horses and have him for dessert.

Erin raced toward the horses. When she reached them, Firecracker rumbled at her. Erin went directly to her, and for once, she didn't have to move in slowly. Firecracker was frightened by the howling and almost pathetically glad to see her. Erin soothed her with long strokes of her hands. Then, still holding her lantern up, she walked the length of the highline they'd strung up between two trees. It wasn't *only* Firecracker she needed to protect until Wyatt got there. All the other horses were important, too. It was just that she loved Firecracker, so saving her had been Erin's first thought.

When Wyatt arrived with his dog, he carried his tent bundled up under one arm and a rifle in his other hand. "What are you doing?"

Erin wondered if that was going to be his question of the night. "I'm protecting the horses."

"With what? You don't even have a gun yet."

"You've never been on a mat with me. Trust me when I say I'm an expert kickboxer."

He smiled and thrust the rifle at her. "Take this. If they come in while I'm gone, fire off a couple of shots. That should scare them off."

"Where are you going?"

"To get the rest of my stuff and your bedding." He glanced down at his dog. "Domino, stay."

Erin stared after Wyatt until he was gobbled up by the darkness. Then she set the lantern on the ground to jack a cartridge into the rifle chamber. After doing that, she paced up and down the highline, Domino right beside her. The lantern helped her see the immediate area, and once she thought she glimpsed eyes glowing in the woods. That totally creeped her out. But she wasn't about to fire the weapon unless she had good reason. Taking potshots was for rookies.

When Wyatt reappeared, he carried his duffel, their bedding, and another rifle. He seemed absolutely calm as he checked on all the horses. She guessed she might feel less agitated, too, if she hadn't heard the wolves.

When he joined her, he asked, "Do you think you can use that light to find rocks to build a fire ring and then collect wood to start a fire?"

Erin felt safer now that she had a weapon. "Yes, I can do that."

"Good. A fire will help hold the wolves at bay. Well, it's supposed to, anyway. To tell the truth, wolves are new to Oregon. I don't have much experience with them."

By the time Erin made a rock circle and managed to build a fire, at least an hour had passed. Wyatt had pitched his tent dead center along the highline and only about six feet from the horses.

"Do you feel them now?" Erin asked. "I haven't heard them howl for a few minutes."

He nodded. "They're still out there. But I'm guessing they're taking stock of the situation and counting their losses. Tied horses are an easy meal. Now that we're here, not so much. Most wolves have a healthy respect for humans and guns."

"How do you know that if you have little experience with them?"

He flashed her a grin. "I read. Ever since I heard wolves had been transplanted in Oregon, I started researching them. I knew it was only a matter of time before they became thick in the wilderness areas." He bent to stroke his dog's head. "Good boy."

Erin suddenly felt exhausted. "Maybe we should sit up all night."

He smiled again. "That won't be necessary. I'll get up every couple of hours to throw wood on the fire. Just know that tomorrow we'll be moving your tent here so you'll have your own sleeping area."

Just then, Erin heard another wolf howl, and she decided, right then and there, that Wyatt Fitzgerald was delusional if he thought she'd sleep alone in this dangerous place. Two people stood a better chance of fighting off wolves.

Wyatt arranged the bedding in the tent, and he'd tried to put space between their sleeping bags, but in a pup tent, all he'd managed was a scant inch of separation. All Erin had to do was kick her boots off before she retired again, but she decided to keep her footwear on all night. A forest floor was covered with prickly stuff, and she didn't want to be gimping around out there while she tried to protect her horse if the wolves came in. She crawled into bed and rolled onto her side. She chose not to zip up her bag. Wyatt lay so close she could have reached out and touched him. For the first time, she noticed he wasn't wearing a shirt. She wondered if he'd been sleeping in the buff when she rushed into his tent earlier and found him sitting up in bed. Now she knew he was at least wearing jeans.

"You going to turn that light off?" he asked.

"Won't it illuminate our tent and be another wolf deterrent?"

He sighed. "Yes. But it also throws our shadows against the walls, letting them know exactly where we are. I prefer an element of surprise. I'll feel them if they come in close again, and hopefully you'll hear them."

Erin thought it odd that he seemed to have more confidence in his acquired fifth sense than he did in her ability to hear. She sighed and doused the lantern. Blackness settled over her.

"About lanterns inside tents," he said. "You should think twice about using a light when you're changing clothes so you don't give anyone else a peep show."

Her face went instantly hot. "You could see me undressing?"

No answer. Wyatt couldn't hear her and he could no longer see her. She snuggled deeper into her sleeping bag. The earth was cold and seeped up through the fill to make her shudder. Her last thought was that it would take forever for her to fall asleep.

Wyatt awakened to a fabulous feeling of heat and softness pressing against him through his sleeping bag. He rolled onto his side to gather it closer, only to come wide awake when he realized Erin had invaded his space. He almost woke her up and asked her to get back on her own side of the tent, but she lay snuggled up against him like a child seeking warmth. And it was cold. Once they got camp set up, they'd each have a small wall tent with cots to sleep on, which would protect them both from the chill of an earthen floor. But for now, he was the only source of heat she had.

He sighed and let his arm relax around her. In her sleep, she burrowed closer, and even through two sleeping bags, he could feel the shape of her. He recalled the shadow dance she'd performed against the wall of her tent and almost groaned. She had a gorgeous silhouette. He'd tried not to look, but anchoring his gaze on something else hadn't been the easiest thing he'd ever done. So, he had looked. Only a couple of peeks, but that had been enough to engrave the sight of her on his brain.

He lay awake for a long while and tried to imagine having the privilege of holding her in his arms every night. As tantalizing as that dream might be, though, Erin was too sweet a person for him to wish himself on her. If he lived to be a hundred, he would never forget that night in Medford with the woman he had violated. When he realized she was trying to get him off of her, he'd leaped from her bed and flipped on the nightstand lamp. She had hugged the sheets to her upper body and shrunk away from him as if he were a monster that might attack her. She'd started crying. Her whole body had been shaking. When she'd grabbed her phone, she messed up dialing 911 three times. He remembered just standing there, knowing she'd called the cops. He could have run. A part of him had wanted to run. But another part of him remembered feeling the vibration of her voice against his chest, and he knew then with dread-filled certainty that she'd asked him to stop and he hadn't.

Wyatt often wondered if she'd ever completely recovered from the experience. He hadn't meant to do her any harm. And yet he had. And he worried that she might never get over it. He couldn't and wouldn't subject Erin to that risk. Wyatt suspected Slade had sent Erin up here with him as part of a matchmaking scheme. He couldn't understand what Slade was thinking. Of course, the boss didn't know about Wyatt's checkered past, so maybe he thought of it as just trying to hook his niece up with the deaf guy who didn't have a love life. It burned Wyatt that he'd possibly become a special project. *Find Wyatt a woman.* Well, Wyatt could find a woman by himself if he wanted to. That wasn't the problem.

The following day Wyatt was weary from lack of sleep and in a grumpy mood. The first thing they needed to do now that they had temporary tents was to set up the cook shack. That was no small task. Just getting the tent erected was a bitch with only Erin to help. As Slade had pointed out, she was a quick study and learned how the frame went together fairly fast, but she wasn't tall enough to hold up ceiling joists without standing on a plastic tub. Wyatt was fearful she might lose her balance and fall. She didn't, but even with compensation for her lack of height, she took longer to help him than a man might. When he needed assistance in seating the joints, she had to hop off her makeshift stepstool, drag it from one side of the tent to the other, and then climb back up to hold the metal tubing. He got cricks in his shoulders from standing with his arms extended above his head to hold the joists up. It was an awkward position. And watching Erin go up on her tiptoes to stretch as tall as she could was sheer torture for him. Every curve of her body was displayed.

When they finally had the tent erected, they had to install the wood floor, which consisted of wooden pallets with sheets of plywood nailed down on top of them. Erin helped as best she could, but recalling her penchant for outdoing men, Wyatt refrained from lifting the long, rectangular pieces of plywood by himself and pretended he needed her to assist him.

By sundown, they had the floor in and the propane stove set up, but they had none of their food or utensils unpacked, and they had no table yet. Wyatt could have kept working, but Erin's shoulders were sagging, and he knew she was done in. They could rifle through the packs again for any flatware they needed.

"You mind roasting hot dogs again tonight?" he asked.

"No, not as long as you do all the marshmallows. All mine caught fire."

He laughed in spite of himself, then handed her a pocketknife. "Go cut us some more roasting sticks while I build us another fire ring and get a good blaze going."

He had decided to move the highline in closer to where he wanted the main camp, a choice he believed Slade would applaud. With wolves in the area, he'd want all the horses near them at night. Normally, they put the horses farther away because of the smell of fresh manure, which drew flies. But Wyatt figured they could clean the highline area each morning.

When Erin returned with their roasting sticks, the dusky gray of twilight had settled over the lake, and it was beautiful beyond measure. A breeze kicked up ripples on the water, and the setting sun, still peeking over the Cascades, sprinkled diamonds on the wavelets. He wanted to sit on the lakeshore and just absorb the grandeur of nature for a while, but he knew Erin was probably starving, so he resisted the urge.

"Let's have a drink first," she suggested. "We can sit by the water and watch to see if the fawns come back tonight."

It went through Wyatt's mind that she was the perfect woman for him. He hadn't voiced his yearning to just sit for a while. It was if she'd read his mind. Only he didn't think that was the case. She seemed to appreciate the beauty around them as much as he did.

When they reached the water, drinks in hand, they sat side by side on the shore with their legs curled partly under them, one arm braced on the earth. He expected Erin to press him for conversation, but instead she just stared across the lake as if mesmerized by everything she saw. He knew how that felt, and he was content to enjoy the moment, too.

Erin elbowed him and pointed. He followed her gaze and saw the fawns that they'd seen the day before. The babies stood together, one a little larger than the other and on slightly higher ground. Their spots gleamed like white polka dots against their reddish-blond fur.

"One's a little girl," he whispered to Erin. Well, he hoped he'd pitched his voice to a whisper, anyway. "Look at how dainty her head is compared to her brother's."

Erin studied the babies. Turning her face toward him, she said, "I don't see their mother. Maybe they're orphaned."

Wyatt considered the possibility. Awful things happened in the wild. Four Toes had been only a tiny cub when his mother had been killed in a rockslide. "Maybe so."

She smiled. "Or maybe they were both orphaned separately. Then they found each other and have become best friends. Someday, after they grow up, she'll love him, and he'll love her, and they'll get married in a deer-style wedding."

Wyatt didn't fantasize much about wildlife, but he guessed the part about the fawns being orphaned and finding each other was possible. He doubted a full-grown buck would confine his arduous pursuits to only one doe, though, and a marriage between two deer was a plot for children's storybooks.

Still, it was fun to imagine that happening, impossibly romantic though it was. But just then, an osprey circled over the lake and made a spectacular dive into the water. Erin grew so excited she grabbed Wyatt's arm, her gaze fixed on the bird. He found himself watching her instead of the raptor.

"She got a fish!" Erin told him. "Watch! She's going to take it back to the nest." She pointed high into a pine tree at the opposite side of the lake. "I can hear the babies cheeping."

Wyatt wished he could hear them. He had no idea what cheeping sounded like and couldn't even imagine it. But Erin turned toward him and said, "Cheep, cheep, cheep," and the quick movement of her lips gave him an inkling. He located the nest high in the trees, saw that it was quite large, and wondered how old it was. Ospreys returned each year to their nesting location, and sometimes generations of them remodeled the same residence year after year. Wyatt had read that ospreys could end up with nests ten to thirteen feet deep and up to six feet wide, large enough for a man to easily sit in. In what he hoped was a low voice, he shared that information with Erin.

"Wow. Really?"

She seemed genuinely interested, so Wyatt shared more with her, ending with, "The osprey parents work together to build the nest and locate it within twelve miles of water where the fish swim close to the surface. Ospreys can dive only three feet down."

"Imagine carrying a fish in your beak for twelve miles," Erin said. "How incredible is that?"

Wyatt gazed at her upturned face and wanted to kiss her so badly that he ached. From the start, he had suspected Erin had been sent with him because Vickie and Slade hoped the two of them might fall for each other. What they didn't know was that Wyatt had already lost his heart to Erin, but he wouldn't ever act on it.

"What are you thinking? You're looking at me oddly."

Thinking fast, Wyatt said, "I'm thinking I'd better feed you before you faint from hunger." He stood, shifted his cup into his left hand, and extended his arm toward her. "Up you go. Let's roast wieners and marshmallows."

For the second time since knowing Wyatt, Erin had seen in his eyes a depth of emotion and yearning that rocked her whole world. Down by the lake, he'd gazed at her as if he were committing every plane of her face to memory. *He cares for me,* she thought. She'd wished that he might return her feelings someday, but she hadn't expected it to ever happen. And now that she knew it had, she felt almost sick with guilt. He had no idea that she'd wrongly used her position as a deputy to invade his privacy. No idea that she'd read all the testimonies that had been given at his trial. No idea that she'd learned his secrets and his worst fears.

The way he had been looking at her told Erin he thought a lot more highly of her than she deserved. She wasn't a perfect person. Julie had argued against Erin ever telling Wyatt what she'd done, but that just didn't seem right. He'd been so honest with her that afternoon when he'd told her about feeling broken and in need of fixing as a little boy, and his willingness to share something so personal and painful had helped her realize that she, too, had been made to feel broken as a child.

While Wyatt whittled bark from their roasting sticks and laid out their food, Erin went to feed the horses at the highline. They'd already drunk their fill from the lake, so she only had to pitch each of them some hay. In the morning, they'd be hobbled in the meadow to graze again. While she worked, her conscience bedeviled her. A part of her wanted to follow Julie's advice and never tell Wyatt what she'd done, but another part of her believed honesty was always the best policy, especially in relationships where feelings ran deep. And she had seen in Wyatt's eyes that he was starting to love her. The thought both excited and terrified her, because if she told him what she'd done, he might walk away from her and never look back.

She remembered her dream about loving Wyatt and watching him walk away. At the time, she had kept assuring herself that she didn't really love him. But she'd been lying to herself that night. She didn't know what it was about him, but she'd been strongly attracted to him on almost every level even then, and those feelings had morphed into something far more meaningful now.

As Erin walked back to camp, she steeled herself to tell him what she'd done. Only how should she start a conversation like that? Their hot dogs were nearly ready to eat when she reached the campfire. Wyatt flashed her one of those crooked grins that always made her feel a little weak in the knees.

"You about ready for a wilderness feast?" he asked.

She forced herself to smile. "Ready? I'm starving." Only that wasn't true. Her stomach was tied in knots, and she wasn't sure she could eat. Wyatt had to be hungry, though, so she decided to wait until after he'd had his meal before she told him what she'd done. "Where are the condiments? I'll run and grab them."

"White cooler," he told her.

When she returned a moment later, Wyatt had assembled their hot dogs on paper plates, four for him and two for her. She set the squeeze bottles of mayo, mustard, ketchup, and relish on a folded plastic table-cloth that he'd laid on the grass. He immediately began drizzling his choice of flavors onto his buns. Erin sat cross-legged opposite him and followed his lead.

Erin's appetite returned the moment she took her first bite. They'd worked hard that day, and her body demanded nourishment. Wyatt reached across their makeshift table to dab at her chin with a paper towel.

She smiled and finished the job with her own napkin. "Sorry. I went overboard with the relish."

He chewed and swallowed. "I'll have mustard all over my face before I'm finished."

They both applied themselves to the meal. After they had disposed of the plates by tossing them into the fire, Wyatt pushed marshmallows onto sticks and stood by the flames to roast them. Erin took advantage of the opportunity to study him while he was unaware of her perusal. He was, without question, one of the handsomest men she'd ever met, but his attractiveness went far beyond the physical. He was also one of the most honest and principled men she'd ever met, and he deserved the same level of integrity from her.

To go with their marshmallow desserts, Wyatt made them each another drink, his straight up, hers mixed with just the right amount of Coke. The marshmallows went fast, and Erin soon found herself with no excuse to keep putting off the inevitable. Maybe she was the biggest fool ever born, but she couldn't lie to this man by omission.

It was nearly dark, but by the light of the fire, Erin could clearly see his face and assumed he could see hers. "Wyatt, there's something I really need to tell you. And I'm afraid you may be very angry with me when I do."

He locked gazes with her. "Okay. Hit me."

"Remember when you told me you had a brush with the law over a woman? It was the day you came to my house while I was throwing away pots of petunias."

He curled both hands around his cup and rested his muscular arms on his bent knees. "I remember."

"Do you also remember the day I was at the ranch and helped Uncle Slade repair fencing?"

"Sure. I remember."

"When I left, you didn't walk back to the ranch proper with me. I thought we had forged a friendship, and I hoped you would leave with me, but you didn't, and it bothered me." Erin's heart squeezed. She was making excuses for herself, and in reality there was no excuse for what she'd done. But she at least wanted him to understand *why* she'd done it. "You're probably going to tell me that my conceit knows no bounds again, but you'd told me that you were attracted to me, and yet you seemed so determined to avoid being around me that I couldn't help but wonder why. If you were *really* attracted to me, why would you avoid being alone with me to that degree? It was broad daylight, and we would have been in plain sight."

"Where are you going with this, Erin?"

An awful ache in her chest moved upward into her throat. "I did something reprehensible that night. I went to the sheriff's department and used my clearance to get on a computer to search all your records. Please know I immediately regretted doing it. I had no right to invade your privacy that way. I read all about the rape charge filed against you and also the trial transcripts."

For what seemed an interminably long while to Erin, Wyatt just stared at her. Finally, he said, "Why did you do that? I told you what I chose to share with you. The rest of it—that's something I've deliberately left in the past. The only people I care about who know are my parents and grandfather. More recently, I finally told Kennedy, but only because I had to disabuse him of the notion that I was gay."

"I'm so sorry, Wyatt. I should never have done it. It was your secret to keep, and I was wrong to dig into your past. In my own defense, it didn't seem wrong to me until I read all the testimony. All court documents are normally public records. Civilians can order the transcripts, but they have to pay for them. I didn't realize until afterward that I had unearthed something that was, to you, very private and painful."

He pushed to his feet and tossed what remained of the liquid in his glass onto the fire. The alcohol flared in the flames like a mini bomb. "Private and painful?" His jaw muscle began to tic. "What happened that night will haunt me until I die. And the trial was the most frightening and humiliating time of my life. Do you think I'm proud of what I did to that poor woman? Do you think I want *anyone* to know?" He crushed the Solo cup with a squeeze of his big hand, and the loud snap of the plastic made Erin jerk. "I wasn't found guilty, but the truth is, I raped her. When a woman says no, she means no, and the man with her should stop. I didn't."

"You couldn't hear her!" Erin cried.

"But I knew I wouldn't be able to hear her. I wanted to score that night. In order to pick up women, I had to pretend I wasn't deaf. And that was all I cared about, *scoring.* Don't you get it? Can't you comprehend how ashamed I am now of my thought process that night? You had no right to read all that shit. If I'd wanted you to know all the awful details, I would have told you, damn it!"

Erin gazed after him as he strode away into the darkness. It was just like in her dream. He had turned his back on her.

"I love you!" she screamed.

Wyatt couldn't hear her and just kept walking.

W yatt was shaking with outrage as he circled the lake. He was furious with Erin, and he needed to walk it off. How could she have dared to dig up his past? He'd never read the court documents, but it was humiliating to think of Erin seeing them. Did those transcripts reveal only the words spoken? Or did they also include the emotional outbursts of the witnesses? He had blubbered like a baby on the stand. And that poor woman. Dear God, she'd grown so upset during cross-examination that she'd fallen apart and the judge had called for a recess. If any man on earth needed to feel guilty for the rest of his life, it was undoubtedly him. He had harmed a woman, all in the name of painting the town red and getting his rocks off.

Wyatt sat on a log on the opposite side of the lake from camp. He could see Erin still sitting by the fire. Domino had been staying with her instead of going with Wyatt ever since he'd ordered the dog to stay with her last night. Erin appeared to be crying, and Domino was trying to lick the tears from her face. Wyatt didn't want to care, but he did. He took a deep breath and tried to tamp down his anger. She'd made a totally crazy reference to the time he'd told her that her conceit knew no bounds. What the hell did *that* have to do with anything?

And then he suddenly got it. He'd been wildly attracted to her and admitted that to her. And yet, when she'd left the men that afternoon, he hadn't made his apologies in order to leave with her. Why wouldn't a guy who was into a woman try his best to be with her whenever he could? If his and Erin's roles had been reversed, he might have wondered the same thing. And the only answer he would have been able to come up with was that some really bad shit had gone down.

Wouldn't he have been curious about what had happened, just as Erin had been? Was he positive that he wouldn't have done a little research on the woman he was interested in? Oh, yeah, he liked to think he was noble, but the reality was that he'd tried to satisfy his own physical needs nearly seven years ago and ended up doing great harm to a woman he hadn't even cared about. She'd meant nothing more to him than a means to an end.

Still staring at Erin, Wyatt saw her suddenly leap to her feet and run off into the darkness. Domino, being the loyal dog he was, ran behind her. Once he stopped to bark. Even though Wyatt couldn't hear the animal, he knew how Dom's front feet left the ground when he grew vocal. Then they were both swallowed up by blackness. A moment later, Erin ran back into the circular illumination cast by their campfire, and she was carrying the rifle. Wyatt sprang to his feet.

And then he felt it. He'd been so upset and lost in his musings that he hadn't been paying attention, but now he realized that all the hair on his body was standing on end—just as it had last night when the wolves had come in close to their camp. He couldn't hear them, but now he felt them, and he knew he was surrounded. He broke into a run to get back around the lake. It probably wasn't the smartest move he'd ever made. Predatory animals grew excited when potential prey ran. But every fiber of his being screamed with fear for Erin's safety. How close were the wolves to her? How many were there? He fleetingly thought of the horses and Domino, which were more likely to be the victims of hungry, wild dogs. He loved his horse and dog. He truly did. But his feelings for them were eclipsed by how deeply he'd come to love Erin De Laney. As she got closer to the fire, he could see her more clearly, and he saw her jack a cartridge into the firing chamber.

As he raced along the lakeshore, his cheeks jiggled with every impact of his boots against the ground. He saw a tree limb that had washed up on the bank and bent to grab it, never breaking stride. *Erin.* She wasn't a rookie who took her weapon off safety for no reason. She definitely wasn't a person who would jack a bullet into the chamber unless she intended to fire.

His lungs began to burn. He couldn't see the ground clearly and tripped on a rock, barely managing to keep his feet. It seemed to him he was running against a headwind. *Erin.* If something happened to her because he'd gotten into a snit and forgotten about the damned wolves, he would never forgive himself.

As he rounded the last curve to get around the body of water, he was about a hundred yards from the campfire, only he didn't see Erin or Domino. Where had they gone? Had the wolves come in? Had Domino run from them? Had Erin gone after him to try and protect him? *Dear God, please, no.* Normally wolves didn't choose humans as a food source, but Wyatt doubted they would hesitate to go for blood if a woman got between them and their next meal.

When Wyatt reached the fire, he screamed Erin's name. But even if she had answered, he wouldn't have been able to hear her. He turned in a circle, yelling with nearly every breath. *This* was why he'd sworn never to love a woman. If the situation wasn't just right, he couldn't protect her, not even from himself.

Just as Wyatt broke into a run to find Erin, Domino came charging up to him. His feet not only left the ground with his barks but cleared the earth by several inches, telling Wyatt the dog was beside himself. Still holding the tree limb, Wyatt whirled in a circle, desperately trying to see Erin, only he couldn't. Domino lunged at Wyatt's leg, sinking his teeth into the denim of his jeans. The tug from the dog was language all of its own. Domino was asking Wyatt to follow him.

"Go!" Wyatt yelled. "Find Erin!"

The border collie mix took off like a shot, and Wyatt fell in behind him. It was all he could do to keep up. And as he ran, he knew exactly where Erin had gone. She was protecting the horses. Fear for her lent Wyatt speed he didn't know he possessed.

When he reached the highline, he saw Erin lying on her belly and facing the forest. She held the butt of the rifle snug against her shoulder. He ran toward her, and she rolled onto her back, throwing up the barrel of the weapon to sight in on him. Then she rolled back onto her stomach and reassumed a firing position. He saw her body jerk and knew she'd pulled the trigger. With a jerk of his gaze, he followed where the weapon was pointed and saw large, gray shapes skulking through the trees.

He jerked the tree limb back level with his shoulder as if it were a baseball bat, and ran toward them, yelling until the muscles along each side of his throat burned. The wolves scattered. Wyatt took a wild swing and hit one of them. Domino charged in like a black-and-white ghost in the darkness and tangled briefly with a wild dog four times his size. It was the wolf that broke away and ran with its tail tucked between its legs. Not Dom. And Wyatt had never felt such a surge of pride in his life.

"Good *boy*!" he cried, running over to the dog with tears in his eyes. He gathered Domino into his arms for a quick hug. "You are *awesome*!"

Then Wyatt remembered Erin and doubled back to eat up the distance between them with strides so long that the muscles of his groin panged. Erin left the rifle lying on the ground and rose to her knees. Wyatt did a home base slide on his own knees as he braked. When their bodies collided, he grabbed her in his arms, locked his muscles tight, and cried, "Are you all right? Did they hurt you? Answer me, damn it!"

Only she couldn't. He felt the vibration of her voice. It moved through his tightly clenched arms and into his chest. But he couldn't hear a word she said. He set her slightly away from him. In the faint moonlight, he could see her precious face, but there wasn't enough illumination for him to read her lips. He began to run his hands over her, feeling for any sign of dampness to indicate she was bleeding. And suddenly she grabbed his wrists, shoved his arms back, and then drew his hands to her chest. He felt her fingers moving. And then she thumped herself between her breasts. He realized she was telling him something in ASL. *"I'm okay."*

Wyatt felt as if all his bones dissolved. He grabbed her again, so relieved that tears came to his eyes.

She pulled away and scrambled to her feet. He followed her to the horses. She moved in on Barbwire. He saw her arm come up and knew that she'd put her hand on the rump of the mule to let him know she was there. For the second time in just as many minutes, Wyatt felt fiercely proud. While he'd been watching her work with Firecracker day after day, she'd become one hell of a horsewoman. He moved forward.

"Erin, did they get to him?" he asked. "Answer me."

She turned and began signing with her hands against his chest. Wyatt couldn't quite get what she was saying. In ASL, the signs weren't confined to only hand and finger movement; they included gestures, and it was next to impossible for him to catch everything in the darkness. In that moment, he felt as impotent as an old man and every bit as useless. Maybe he was *more* useless. Even old men weren't stone deaf. They could at least hear part of what was said to them.

Finally Wyatt was able to interpret Erin's hand motions enough to know that one wolf had gotten to Barbwire and they needed to check him for injuries.

"We need a light," he said, staring down at Erin's face, which shone in the darkness like a gray oval. "Let's go get a lantern. We can't do anything for him without being able to see."

He grabbed her arm and pulled her along beside him as they ran toward their temporary tent. When they got there, Wyatt dove through the loose flap, swatted his palms all over the earthen floor, and found both their lanterns perched side by side at the top of their sleeping bags. He snatched them up and ran hunched over to get back outside. He thrust one lamp at Erin, and together they started back toward the horses. Wyatt made a quick detour to grab the first aid kit. He'd removed it from a pack almost immediately last night, and the white plastic case glowed in the darkness like a bluish-white beacon.

When they reached the horses, Erin held her lantern high so Wyatt could see Barbwire, but the sphere of light allowed him to examine only parts of the mule at a time. Wyatt found one long gash on his right hindquarter. It didn't run deep. The animal was barely bleeding. What had happened was obvious. Barbwire, unable to run because he was tied to the highline, had been attacked. But something had stopped the wolf from doing any more damage.

Wyatt fixed his gaze on Erin. Holding her light high above her head, she was bathed in bluish illumination and resembled a ragtag angel dressed in dirty jeans and a limp T-shirt. Her countenance was an indistinct blur of shadow and gray planes, but Wyatt wasn't frustrated by the darkness. He had memorized every line of her face.

"He's okay," he told her. "We should probably disinfect the wound, though." He glanced toward the trees, which were cloaked in blackness. "Did you shoot any of them?"

"No. I aimed high, hoping to just scare them off. That's what you said to do."

After they flooded the shallow slash on Barbwire's haunch with disinfectant, they walked the highline, checking on every horse. Wyatt talked, but he didn't know if Erin replied. And he suddenly felt like he was five years old again, a little deaf boy who wanted a drink of water or something to eat and had difficulty communicating his needs to the adults around him.

When they finally returned to the campfire, which burned brightly only about fifty feet from the highline, they both collapsed on the ground beside each other, Wyatt from exhaustion after running around half of the lake, and Erin with relief. Erin knew why Wyatt was drained. She assumed he knew her reasons for feeling just as exhausted. Being terrified and trying to fend off a pack of wolves had been one of the most harrowing experiences of her life, far worse than the time a crazy guy in Seattle had held his wife hostage at gunpoint. Every officer on the scene had been afraid the husband might open fire on them at any moment, and Erin had been just as afraid as all her colleagues.

The skirmish with the wolves had been even worse. At least back in King County, Erin had known where the man with the gun was, and she'd been able to determine from what direction a bullet might come. With the wolves, she'd been surrounded, and an attack could have come from any angle.

"You okay?" Wyatt asked.

Firelight illuminating her face, she turned toward him and said, "Just shaken up. It'll be a while before I can relax and go to sleep." She drew her shoulders up in a shrug. "I didn't live near wilderness areas as a kid like you did. I love it up here." She gestured at the darkness that surrounded them like impenetrable walls. "Don't get me wrong. It's beautiful. But the most dangerous dog I ever encountered in King County was a miniature schnauzer with an attitude problem. Those wolves are gigantic, and as regal as they look in photographs, there's nothing inspiring about them when they move in on you drooling with hunger." She lifted her loosely cupped hands. "And I'm still upset about our quarrel. Well, not a quarrel, really. I can't argue that what I did was right. I can only beg for your forgiveness, and I do that tongue in cheek, because I would be furious if you'd done the same thing to me."

W yatt's outrage had been snuffed out the moment he'd seen Erin run back into the firelight with a rifle. Instead of walking off his anger, he'd been forced to run it off. Now, he felt calm, as if all his emotions had been deadened. Well, not all his emotions. He still loved Erin. In fact, he was now aware of how deeply his affection for her ran. When he'd believed she might be injured or even killed, all his peripheral feelings had boiled away like steam from a stewpot, and he was left with only an intense love for someone he could never be with. Not if he truly loved her. And he did.

"Actually, Erin, when I look at it rationally, I have to admit that I might have done the same thing." He took a deep breath. "And now, in retrospect, I'm glad you read the transcripts. You saw for yourself that I'm not a safe bet when it comes to intimacy. And after tonight, you know that when the circumstances aren't just right, I'm unable even to protect you. You need a better man than I am."

"What makes you think I need to be protected?"

"Don't get all bent out of shape and let your father take part in this conversation." He set his jaw and held her gaze. "Away from the fire, there was no light. For a few minutes there, I was both blind and deaf. I had no idea where you were, and if it hadn't been for Domino coming to get me, I would have been tearing around out here, looking for you in all the wrong places. You could have been killed."

"Looking at that rationally, I'm an expert marksman and was just as capable of fending off a pack of wolves as you would have been." She jutted her chin at him. "And my saying that has nothing to do with my former hang-ups about measuring up to or outshining any man, including you. It's a matter of fact."

"Your *former* hang-ups?"

"Yes, *former* hang-ups. I'm almost over that, Wyatt. Being at the ranch—no, being around you and working with Firecracker has changed me. My father no longer has a hold over me. Surely you've noticed the difference." She bent her knees and hugged them to her chest. "I no longer feel a frantic need to prove anything to anyone. Maybe the broken little girl inside me will rear her ugly head every once in a while. I sure do see the broken little boy within you showing his face tonight. But I'll never allow that little girl to control me again."

Wyatt bristled. "What the hell does that mean? My broken little boy grew up and faced reality a long time ago."

"*His* view of reality. Oh, yeah. You faced his version and accepted it. Right? You're so glad to be deaf now that you're feeling giddy. You're not broken anymore. Nothing about you needs to be fixed now. You've come to feel at peace with your disability. The only problem is, by accepting it, you've taken your own measure, found yourself lacking, and are running from life."

"Oh, wow," he said. "The bullshit is getting so deep it's up to my eyebrows."

"Exactly. Who can see clearly through a bunch of bullshit? Only it's bullshit of your own making that's blinding you, not mine." She reached over and tapped his shoulder lightly. "Did you feel that?"

Wyatt didn't understand the point she was trying to make. "Of course I felt it."

"Point made!" She glared up at him. "For a man who's an expert at communicating in ASL, you're incredibly dense when it comes to the possibility of other signs of communication working well for you!" Her chin jutted forward again. "Let's say that a tap on your shoulder means 'Stop!' Nice and easy for you to understand, even in the dark! But your little boy can't go there, because he's still broken, and his brokenness harmed someone. Instead of facing what happened and making sure it can never occur again, you're running from ever being with a woman again."

Wyatt pushed to his feet. "I couldn't set up stupid *tap* signals with that woman because she didn't know I was deaf. And what's that got to do with what happened with the wolves tonight? I was *useless*."

"You *weren't* useless. You grabbed the first weapon you could get your hands on, and when you found me, you charged into a pack of wolves, swinging. And, by the way, I *do* know you're deaf. Tap signals wouldn't be a big deal for us to set up. We could create our own special sign language for when we're making love, but you won't even consider the possibility!"

Wyatt turned and stalked off into the darkness. He needed to get away from Erin, fast. Tap signals? For just a moment, his heart had leaped with wild hope only to crash at his feet when reality sank in again. What did she think, that certain numbers of taps could signify different messages? One for stop. Two for don't touch me. Three for that hurts. Did she think a guy could count when he was having sex? Wyatt had heard of men mentally reciting baseball stats to avoid premature ejaculation or just to perform longer, but that was a tactic to dampen their ardor and deal with a bedroom failing. *Definitely not a pleasure enhancer.* He could almost picture himself staring stupidly into the darkness, trying to remember what the hell three taps were supposed to mean.

And he had to keep his head on straight about what had happened tonight. He'd been upset and hadn't sensed the presence of the wolves until it had been almost too late. He'd made it around the lake in time, but if it hadn't been for Domino, he wouldn't have found Erin soon enough to help drive off the wolves. And even then, the only weapon he'd had was a big stick when anyone with half a brain would have been carrying a rifle.

He felt both exhausted and heartsick when he returned to the fire and found Erin still sitting near the flames as if he'd only taken a break from their conversation. He didn't want to talk anymore. He didn't even want to be near her. Why test his willpower when he didn't have to?

He hunkered by the fire and stared into the flames. One good thing about being deaf was his ability to shut other people out by simply not looking at them. He was still congratulating himself on that when a pine cone hit him on the shoulder. He glanced up to find Erin grinning at him.

"Give me this week," she said. "I'll never ask for anything more, only this week, Wyatt. If I haven't changed your mind by the time we leave this mountain lake, I'll cut my losses and accept that there can never be anything more between us." When he said nothing, she added, "Think of it as a dare. Maybe even a double dare. Throw caution to the wind and just make love with me. If it's awful, the cure for that is simple. We just won't do it again. What do you say?"

"I say you're nuts." She had no idea how badly he wanted to take her up on the proposition. What guy alive could turn his nose up at an offer of a week's vacation in the arms of a beautiful woman, with no strings attached? "And I say, no, thanks. You weren't there that night. It was horrible, and I'll never go there again. I care about you. I want you. Don't think my refusal has anything to do with you or your desirability, because it doesn't. This is only about me."

"No, Wyatt, this is about your fears. The truth is, what happened that night left you bleeding, and you're too chicken to put *yourself* at risk again." She scrambled to her feet and gazed down at him. "I'm going to bed. And just so you know, I'm not about to sleep alone in the other tent. If you try to bed down somewhere else, I'll find you."

"The wolves won't be back tonight. Maybe not ever. As a pack, they pick easy kills, and they know now that the horses are well guarded."

"Tell it to a tree. I'm not going to take any chances."

As she turned to walk away, he couldn't resist saying, "But you're willing to take chances on a guy like me?"

He'd intended it as a dig, but she was smiling as she turned to face him again. "In a heartbeat," she told him.

After she vanished into the darkness, he remained by the fire. He was aware when a lantern came on inside the tent, and he tried his damnedest not to look in that direction, but his eyes felt like refrigerator magnets that couldn't resist the draw of steel. She was undressing. Her silhouette was cast against the nylon wall of the tent. In stark detail, he could see the shape of her breasts, the slope of her ribs, the indentation of her waist, and the sexy flare of her hips. His mouth went as dry as a sun-bleached bone. He'd warned her about not using a light in the tent. It followed that she knew very well she was putting on a show and that he might be watching. The realization infuriated him, and he sprang to his feet.

With both anger and need pushing him, he strode to the tent, swept aside the flap, and stepped inside. He'd intended to make a grand entrance and intimidate the hell out of her, but he'd forgotten this was a pup tent that didn't allow him to stand erect. The space was also tiny, barely large enough for two people to sleep beside each other without spooning. His nose was level with hers, because unlike him, she was short enough to stand upright. She was still stark naked as well, and she made no attempt to cover any part of herself with her hands or arms. Wyatt could remember when she'd been mortified to have him see her in a tank top. He guessed maybe being at the ranch truly had helped her win the war with some of her demons. She definitely didn't look embarrassed now. She stood with her shoulders back, a woman who knew she was beautiful and felt empowered.

It aggravated the hell out of him.

"Are you sure this is what you want? Sex with a bad boy for a whole week? Because I can give you bad, Erin. Just say the word."

"What word would that be? I can think of only three: go for it."

Angry and aroused wasn't a good combination of emotions for a man to have when a woman challenged him to take her. Wyatt snaked out a hand, grabbed her wrist, and jerked her toward him. Stooped over as he was, her breasts were available to him with a mere dip of his head, and he latched onto a nipple. He didn't try to be gentle. He hoped to scare the sand out of her and make her think twice about daring a dangerous man to make love to her.

Only she didn't react as if he'd shocked her. Instead she ran her hands into his hair, made fists, and drew him closer. He felt her body arch toward him, and in that moment, his need of her wiped every shred of reluctance from his mind. *Erin.* She had perspired all day while working with him. Her nipple was as salty as a potato chip and tasted even better. He had to suckle the other one, and he felt the vibrations from her moans of pleasure. At least, he hoped those were moans of pleasure, because she'd pushed him to the snapping point. He couldn't have stopped himself then if he had tried.

Wyatt caught her behind the knees, scooped her into his arms, and all but fell with her onto their bedding, only narrowly missing Domino, who'd taken up squatting rights on his pillow. When he abandoned her breast to kiss her, she caught his face between her hands.

"There are two ground rules," she told him. "One tap means that I want you to stop. Two taps means I enjoy what you're doing and *don't* want you to stop. Are we clear on that?"

Wyatt was so far gone at that point that he no longer cared about her tapping plan. The lantern was still on. As long as he could see her face, he was good. Now that he'd finally gone for the hook and swallowed it, she was stuck with him. He kissed her. It wasn't one of those hello moments reserved for first kisses. He'd already said hello to her in his dreams a dozen times, and holding her in his arms was even more erotic than he had imagined. She opened sweetly for him. He could taste the lingering flavor of marshmallows on her tongue when she intertwined it with his. Passion, hot and fiery, coursed through his body in thought-obliterating waves. His body screamed for release, he went after her breasts again, and she began double-tapping his shoulder, his arms, and his back. That was all the go-ahead he needed.

He wasn't sure how he got rid of his boots and pants. He only knew he felt the jolt when her velvety skin pressed against his. Just as he had imagined that afternoon when he'd watched her digging postholes, he felt the supple strength in her legs and arms as she enveloped his body with sweetness and drew him to her. His shaft found her opening as if it were one of those high-tech, heat-seeking missiles, and he thrust himself into her with everything he had. The incredible, wet heat of her surrounded him, and for the first time in his life, he felt as if he'd finally come home.

He also knew, as only a man can, that he was going to ejaculate too soon. But he couldn't control his body. He tried and just couldn't. Spasms of pleasure rocked his whole frame, and when they subsided, his arms felt as limp and heavy as wet bath towels.

Erin held him close and trailed kisses over his shoulder and up the side of his neck. He clung to her like a child, too spent to pretend she hadn't just rocked his world. *Erin.* He'd dreamed of holding her like this, and now that he had, he didn't know if he could ever let her go. Tears flooded into his eyes and dripped onto his cheeks, and her signal to him wasn't a tap, but a fierce clench of her arms around his neck that nearly choked him but also told him she understood what a life-altering moment this was for him. And maybe for her as well. At least he hoped.

He lifted his head to look down at her precious face, and she gazed up at him with love for him shining in her eyes. That was all he needed to see, and he prayed she saw it in his as well, because he was too exhausted and mentally drained to compose a single word and try to say it.

They fell asleep wrapped in each other's embrace. When Wyatt awakened later, he had no idea how much time had passed, only that they'd left the light on. He lifted his head to gaze down at her face. Her dark lashes fanned over her sun-kissed cheeks. Her full and oh-so-kissable mouth was lax. He could feel Domino snuggled against his back, but he didn't care if the dog got a crash course in sex education. He wanted Erin again, so he kissed her awake, first nibbling at her lips and then moving down to her breasts.

This time when he made love to her, his sole intent was to give her pleasure. He couldn't hear any moans of enjoyment, but he could feel her shivers of delight and the rush of hot wetness at the apex of her beautiful legs. She also double-tapped repeatedly, which meant, *Don't stop.* He took his time and left no part of her unattended. He wanted her to burn for him, just as she'd made him burn for her.

Paybacks were sometimes pure hell. But sometimes they were a man's most carnal fantasy. Something he'd yearned for and never found. A dream that vanished the moment he opened his eyes each morning. A wish that he'd been afraid to ever make.

Trying to cook breakfast over a campfire was an attempt that was aborted before Erin and Wyatt finished their first cup of coffee. They ended up back in the tent again to make love for the third time. For Erin, it was pure bliss. She was with the man she loved, and there was no doubt in her mind that they were meant for each other. Maybe Wyatt still fooled himself into believing this was a temporary departure from normal and their former relationship could be reestablished when they left the lake, but she knew he wouldn't be able to let her go when that time came. Not if he felt about her the way she felt about him. This was forever stuff, and she knew he would come to realize that as the days they had left together wore on.

After making love, Wyatt rolled onto his back and angled an arm over his eyes. "We can't keep doing this. When Slade gets here, he'll expect this camp to be in tip-top condition. How the hell are we going to get anything done?"

Erin snuggled close to him and nipped gently at his nipple. "Well, we'll work—and then we'll play," she said as she reared up so he could see her lips. "What we need to do is establish goals. When we get the cook shack table and shelving set up, we can take an hour break. Then we'll hit it again. How's that for a plan?"

He tweaked her nose. "Do you realize how draining sex is for a guy? I'm not Tex's little bunny that can just keep going. My batteries need to be recharged."

Erin pushed up on her arms to straddle him and lowered the tips of her breasts to almost graze his lips. He groaned and surrendered. When they were both satiated, she asked, "How was that for a recharge?"

After bathing in the lake together, they ate cold wieners for breakfast and worked like dervishes on the interior of the cook shack so they could prepare food. For lunch, they made grilled cheese sandwiches, two for her and four for him.

As they sat at the table together and ate, Wyatt asked, "Where do we go from here, Erin? I'm assuming you're on birth control, because we haven't used any protection, and you don't seem worried."

She gave him an impish smile. "Heck, no. I'm using you to get a baby. Remember me, the lady whose biological clock is ticking?" At his startled look, she laughed and said, "Not really, Wyatt. I'd never do that. Of course I'm on the Pill. And STDs aren't a worry for me. I haven't been with anyone for a long time."

"I haven't been with anyone for almost seven years, so I'm safe. As for birth control, I'm glad you're protected. We need some time to decide what comes next, and babies have a way of calling all the shots."

Erin figured they needed only a week. He loved her just as much as she loved him. In the past, Erin had never felt confident of herself with a man, but with Wyatt, she sensed that she was already his everything. When the moment of realization struck him, he would ask her to marry him. There wasn't a doubt in her mind about that. If she was wrong, she was afraid it would destroy her, because he had become her everything, and for her, there was no turning back.

That afternoon, Erin's phone jangled to notify her of a text message. She saw that it was from Julie and knew her friend wouldn't disturb her on this trip without good reason. She immediately opened the missive, and what she read nearly made her knees buckle. She sank onto a large rock that radiated warmth from the sunshine.

"Oh, my God! Julie's pregnant! Well, she says that she and Blackie are pregnant, but same thing. When she had that flu, she upchucked her birth control pills. And the first time she and Blackie were together, they didn't use protection. Bang! She's preggers."

"They had unprotected sex only once, and she's pregnant? Wow."

Erin sent him a loaded look. "Wyatt, it only takes once. Didn't you learn that in sex education?"

"Of course, and during my brief time as a player, I always wore protection. But I figured the teachers just told kids that to scare the bejesus out of them."

She laughed and shook her head. "Nope. They were telling the truth. It is a pretty scary thought, though. I'll bet Julie was beside herself when she first found out. Blackie is fifty-three, and the last thing he wanted was a baby. Apparently, he's changed his mind. It sounds as if they're over the moon about it now. And get this! They've gotten a marriage license and have a preacher all lined up. They want to get married fast because of the baby. And I don't have to go back down the mountain for the wedding, because they think it'll be romantic and fun to say their vows up here by the lake on the day Four Toes is introduced to his little lady bear. She says most of their favorite townspeople will be up here for the campout, anyway. She won't even have to send invitations."

Wyatt put his hands on his hips and gazed at the lake, which lapped at the grassy shore like molten sapphires. "It sure is beautiful. I can think of worse places to get married. In fact, I think it's a pretty great idea. Out here, surrounded by nature. Does it get any better than that?"

For the rest of the afternoon, Wyatt didn't talk much. Erin worried that he was regretting his snap decision to make love with her, and a chink developed in her newfound armor of confidence. She hadn't asked for forever when she'd propositioned him last night. In fact, she'd double-dared him to have sex with her. She guessed that hadn't been one of her most stellar moments. She'd made this trip out to be a vacation from Wyatt's reality, and she'd made no conditions. All for fun, no ties to bind.

By dinnertime, he still wasn't saying much, and an ache had taken up residence in Erin's chest. She wouldn't be the first woman to love a man with all her heart and not be loved in return.

Over an evening meal of steak and baked potatoes cooked in foil on hot coals, Wyatt asked, "So do you still think ranching is your cup of tea?"

Erin didn't take the question lightly. "I know I still have heaps to learn, but, yes, I still believe the ranch is where I belong. Maybe it's in my blood. My mom came from generations of ranchers, after all. I feel at peace down at Uncle Slade's. I can't explain it, Wyatt, but it feels as if I've been lost all my life and finally came home. I really enjoy the animals. That surprises me. I didn't set out to be a horse enthusiast, but they've grown on me."

She got up to give Domino what remained of her meal. While the dog gobbled the scraps, she washed her eating utensils with lake water they'd collected in a bucket.

"Speaking of horses, I've neglected Firecracker the last two days. I really should work with her tonight. Do you mind?"

"Not at all. I'll be along in a minute."

Erin couldn't determine what was eating Wyatt, and she tried not to let it bother her as she went through the usual routine with her horse. To her surprise, Firecracker seemed almost eager to be petted tonight. It was as if she'd missed getting the attention and treats that Erin always gave her. She did act up when the bubble gum container was dropped at her front feet, but she didn't rear or strike out with her hooves.

True to his word, Wyatt came to lean against a tree and watch. Toward the end of the session, he said, "You've made huge strides with her, Erin. I couldn't do better myself. She's starting to love you."

As of last night, Erin had become convinced Wyatt loved her, too. But she didn't take it as a good sign that he'd been so thoughtful and quiet all day. She had an awful suspicion that she'd done or said something to put him off.

They walked back to camp after she tied Firecracker off to the highline. At the fire, they sat beside each other, shoulder to shoulder, which made it difficult for Wyatt to carry on a conversation.

"Did I ever mention to you that when my grandfather dies, which I hope doesn't happen anytime soon, I will inherit our family ranch?"

"Maybe. I can't really remember if you told me or someone else did."

He resumed staring at the fire. "When I was younger, I dreamed of turning it into something grand, sort of like Slade's place. There's adjoining land that will come available, so I've been saving money since I left home and got my first job. I'd like to buy it. The owner is old, and his kids aren't into taking over the homestead."

"Have you saved enough to buy it?"

"Not quite enough. I'll have to set aside most of the ranch profit for a couple of years to swing a deal. But that's all it'll take to turn my family ranch into a thriving operation. I'll need more land for running larger numbers of cattle."

"As long as you can pay the bills and keep your equipment maintained, saving most of your profit shouldn't be too hard."

He turned and met her gaze. "Would you be interested in working with me to turn that ranch into what it should be?"

Erin couldn't think what to say. "You mean you want me to relocate to Klamath Falls and work for you?"

"I said 'work *with* me,' Erin. Not only as a worker, but as my life partner."

Her eyes burned with tears. "Are you asking me to marry you?"

He frowned. "Well, I'm sure not asking you to live with me out of wedlock. My mother would have a coronary. Not that she and Dad will be around all that much. They're in their fifties now and want to semi-retire when Grandpa passes on. Mom wants to travel a little, and Dad's only goal in life is to make her happy. But it is the family ranch, and they'll still live in the other house when they come home to roost."

Erin felt her mouth curve into such a big smile that her cheeks ached. "Can you, like, maybe, actually say the *words*? I mean, nobody has ever proposed to me, and I really want to hear those words just once."

With the agility and strength that she'd so often admired, he moved in one fluid motion to get on one knee and faced her with his heart shining in his blue eyes. "Erin De Laney, I love you with all my heart. I have for months. Will you please put me out of my misery and do me the great honor of agreeing to become my wife?"

He still hadn't said the words that she'd always dreamed of, but the sincerity behind his request made up for it. Tears spilled over her lower lashes onto her cheeks. He reached up to thumb them away. "I didn't mean to make you cry."

"Happy tears," she said in a squeaky voice. "And my answer is yes. I've been in love with you for a while, too. I just didn't think you'd ever return my feelings."

"I've returned them from day one. Well, no, that's a stretch. I didn't have much use for you that first day, but after that, every time I saw you, my heart dug a deeper hole for me to wallow in. I was so hung up on you that I actually woke up one night in the middle of a wet dream, and Tex and Kennedy were gaping at me. I don't know what I said or did to wake them up, but it was one of the most humiliating moments of my life."

Erin caught his face between her hands. "No more of that! From now on, I won't be a dream. I'll be real, and you won't be sleeping in a bunkhouse with other men."

She started to get up, her mind already on the pleasure awaiting them inside the tent, but Wyatt grabbed her arms and made her sit still. "I'm not finished. Ever since that text came from Julie, I've been thinking that we should make it a double wedding. How do you feel about that?"

Erin thought it sounded heavenly. "But we don't have a marriage license."

"We can go back to town and apply for one. I think we can get the license right away, but we'll have to wait three days before the ceremony, so we need to do it fast. I was thinking that we can just use Julie and Blackie's preacher. Unless you object for religious reasons, that is. If you want another man of the cloth, I'm okay with that, too."

All Erin cared about was being spiritually and legally bound to this wonderful man for the rest of her life. She kissed him to seal their bargain, and they never made it to the tent. They made love on the lush meadow grass by the fire. Afterward, when Erin lay pressed against him and listened to the haunting cry of an osprey as it circled over the lake, she knew that she'd looked in all the wrong places to find where she truly belonged. For her, home was right where she was, in Wyatt Fitzgerald's arms.

EPILOGUE

On the day of their wedding, Erin and Wyatt stood arm in arm as the campout guests from Mystic Creek arrived. Dozens of people had ridden up on horseback. The entire Sterling family had come, even Jonas, the only bachelor remaining in the Sterling brood of four boys and two girls. His brothers showed up with their wives and kids: Jeb with Mandy; their daughter, Chloe; and their son, Jeremiah. Ben was there with his wife, Sissy, and their two little ones. Barney showed up with his adopted daughter, Sara, and his wife, Taffy, six months pregnant with a baby boy. Ma Thomas absolutely couldn't miss what she called "the triple wedding." She viewed Four Toes's introduction to Ginger as a bear version of marriage and refused to think of it as anything less. Jake, who owned the Jake 'n' Bake, came bearing two large tubs of baked goods, one of them filled with day-old stuff that he explained were for the newlywed bears. Tony Chavez, owner of Dizzy's Roundtable, also made an appearance, although he said he could stay only one night. Tanner Richards and his wife, Crystal, came up with their two kids.

The only people who walked up the mountain were Blackie and Julie, because Blackie wouldn't allow the newly pregnant mother of his child to get on a horse. They had hiked most of the previous day, rested overnight at another camp, and then come the rest of the way that morning so they wouldn't be exhausted for the ceremony. Erin's breath caught when she first saw Julie with honey-blond hair. The blue streak had finally vanished, and Erin knew that meant her friend had found love, happiness, and peace in her heart. The preacher, with whom Blackie and Julie had made the ceremony arrangements, arrived on horseback a little later than they did, but that was fine, because the ceremony wouldn't take place until evening after the two bears had been introduced.

When Kennedy showed up, Erin got nervous butterflies in her stomach. Wyatt's parents had ridden up with their younger son, each of them on a separate mount while Kennedy rode double with Jen, who sat behind him and hugged his waist. Apparently she wasn't yet healed enough to ride by herself. Erin was just thankful that Jen looked healthy and happy.

Wyatt led Erin out to meet his folks. Erin wasn't sure what to expect, except that the couple probably still clung to some pretty old-fashioned ideas. She'd deduced that because of Wyatt's prediction that his mother would have a heart attack if he ever lived with a woman out of wedlock.

The moment Erin clapped eyes on Aiden Fitzgerald, she knew where Wyatt and Kennedy had gotten their laser-blue eyes and Norsemen good looks. Aiden stood as tall as his sons and had the same strapping body of a warrior. Jessica, his wife, was of smaller stature, with dark hair and pale blue eyes that were nothing less than stunning.

"So this is the young woman who finally caught my son's eye," Aiden said as he walked a tight circle around Erin and gave her the once-over. When he returned to stand in front of her again, he winked at Wyatt and said, "She'll do." Jessica thumped her husband on the arm, elbowed him aside, and stepped in close to give Erin a big hug. "Ignore the man. He's spent so much of his life staring at cows' butts that he has no manners at all."

When Aiden threw back his blond head and laughed, Erin knew it would be all right. Her future parents-in-law seemed to have accepted the marriage and be delighted for their son. They wouldn't raise any objections at this late hour. She left Wyatt to reunite with them while she showed Jen around camp. The girl had color in her cheeks and looked almost fully recovered.

"I like Kennedy's mom and dad. Don't you?"

"Well, I don't really know them yet, but I figure they must be fine people, because they raised Wyatt and Kennedy. They're pretty special men."

Vickie and Slade appeared last, both of them on horseback and leading heavily laden pack animals behind them. Atop one of the beasts of burden, Ginger traveled inside a wire cage. The crowd of people awaiting her arrival let loose with an appreciative rumble when she first came into view. She was a little, fluffy thing with fur the color of a cinnamon stick, and she had the most adorable face Erin had ever seen. Four Toes had moseyed up the mountain on foot, of course, and it was clear that his interest had been piqued by the presence of another bear.

Erin had become fond of Four Toes during the time she'd been working at the ranch, and she sincerely hoped he fell wildly in love with Ginger. Slade took excellent care of the older bear, and now Ginger would be treated to the same loving environment where she could wander the huge acreage during the day and then retire to the compound with Four Toes at night. Erin knew little about wild bears, but she believed these two would have a wonderful life together.

The "first meet," which had been whispered about on the sidewalks of Mystic Creek for nearly two weeks, didn't go as smoothly as all the humans had hoped. The moment Ginger was on the ground and looked up at the massive Four Toes, she squealed and ran. Slade tried to catch her, but he wasn't fast enough to nab the yearling bear, whose feet had been lent speed by terror. Several of the younger people, Erin included, dashed out into the forest after her, but no one succeeded in apprehending Ginger. Everyone became worried about the little bear's safety.

"Wyatt and I haven't had a chance to mention it, Uncle Slade, but we've had wolves coming in on our camp. Wyatt thinks they're after the horses, but it probably isn't safe for a little bear out here, either."

Slade scowled. "Where did Four Toes get off to?"

Kennedy chimed in. "I didn't see him leave, but I'll bet he's following Ginger. Maybe he'll get her settled down and bring her back."

Slade wasn't content to stand around and wait for his bears to return. "She's used to people. I think I'll go scouting on Bogey to see what I can see. Maybe if I call her, she'll come running. She's never been out in the woods alone, and she must be frightened."

Slade was gone over an hour, and his mission was unsuccessful. "I didn't see hide nor hair of either bear. Damn it! Now I've lost both of them."

His hangdog expression didn't bode well for the double wedding scheduled for that evening. Erin had envisioned herself going to her and Wyatt's wall tent to change into her wedding dress so she could enjoy wearing it over the afternoon. It was a simple, floral sundress with coordinating sandals, exactly like Julie's ensemble. The two of them had decided to be twins for the day. Only Erin couldn't just wander off to do her own thing when both bears had gone missing. She and Wyatt could always get married another day. If they didn't find Four Toes and Ginger, the bears might meet with a bad end, and that had to be her main focus whether it was her wedding day or not. The men were talking about forming a search party on horses before it got any later.

Erin had just whispered to Julie that she feared the weddings couldn't take place until Ginger was found when Four Toes lumbered out of the woods. The three-year-old bear rolled over onto his back as if he wanted to sunbathe. It was then that Erin saw Ginger peeking out through the bright green boughs of a sapling ponderosa. She had clearly followed Four Toes back to camp, but now, whether due to fear of the bigger bear or of people, she mewled and wouldn't come out of the forest.

Four Toes groaned and regained his feet. He lumbered back over to Ginger and lay down in the shade of a towering ponderosa. At that point, the male bear began bellowing for food, as was his habit. Jake grabbed a tub of baked goods and carried it out to Four Toes. Instead of eating, the bear ignored all the goodies and rolled onto his back again, looking silly and harmless, which lured the smaller bear from her hiding place. When Four Toes reached up with a massive front paw to touch Ginger's chin, she scampered away from him, crying in fear as cubs will.

"Well," Slade said, "she's hanging in close, and I know she can smell the food in that tub. Hopefully, Four Toes will convince her to lie down with him."

Erin hoped so. Even though this was supposed to be her and Julie's big day, Erin decided that she would postpone her wedding if the little bear wouldn't settle in with Four Toes before the scheduled time for the nuptials. She didn't want Vickie and Slade to be so worried that they couldn't enjoy the celebration. And she didn't want to be upset, either.

Holding Erin's hand, Wyatt led her around the camp to visit with friends from Mystic Creek who sat on lawn chairs in meager patches of shade. Erin enjoyed catching up with everyone. Even her former boss, Blake Adams, and his wife, Marietta, were in attendance. Over the course of the afternoon, Erin had been poured so many cups of wine or beer that she had to dump the contents behind trees on the sly. The last thing she wanted was to be tipsy as she joined hands in marriage with the wonderful man who walked beside her.

She was delighted to see that Four Toes had finally succeeded in soothing Ginger's fears. The pair of bears ate ravenously from the tub of baked goods and then snuggled up together under the tree to have a nap. Everyone who'd witnessed the bear nuptials was pleased by that outcome. A common refrain around camp was that Ginger now knew where her food would come from, and even if she dashed away again, she probably wouldn't go far. She lay curled up against Four Toes's big belly as if he was now her protector. Erin believed that Four Toes was already wrapped around Ginger's little bear claw and would fight to the death to make sure nothing happened to her.

That evening, Mother Nature worked her magic to create a beautiful wedding venue as the sunset glimmered on the lake in streaks of rose. Wyatt and Erin, and Blackie and Julie, exchanged vows with the preacher officiating. Kennedy stood in as Wyatt's best man. Both brides walked across a short expanse of meadow to reach their grooms, Julie with Tony Chavez, who'd offered to give her away, and Erin with Uncle Slade, who had agreed to stand in as her father. Julie wasn't ready to tell her family that she was pregnant, so she hadn't notified them of her wedding. Erin had chosen not to invite her parents simply because this was her and Wyatt's moment. Her mother would detest the montane scenery, and her father would have kittens over her plans to be a rancher. She wanted to begin her life with Wyatt on a happy and positive note. He understood that and reminded her that her folks would have plenty of opportunity to rain on their parade later.

When the wedding ceremony began, Wyatt watched the preacher intently instead of gazing down at Erin. Erin understood that he was reading the minister's lips, and since she wanted him to remember this wonderful moment for the rest of their lives, she didn't allow herself to feel slighted.

As they had agreed prior to the wedding, Erin and Wyatt made their vows in ASL and then repeated them vocally for all the witnesses. And Erin got plenty of deep, heartfelt attention from Wyatt as he vowed to love and cherish her in sign language for the rest of his life. She knew ASL was Wyatt's first language, liberating him from the effort it took to formulate words in spoken English. Blackie and Julie repeated their vows shortly after Wyatt and Erin did. With the breeze blowing like a kiss across the pristine mountain lake and fading sunlight shimmering on the deep green grass in brushstrokes of pink, it was an incredibly beautiful ceremony.

When the moment came for Wyatt to seal their union with a kiss, Erin could finally feel truly glad that she had been born a girl, because now she could be Wyatt Fitzgerald's woman. She couldn't think of a better way to spend the rest of her life.

Keep reading for an excerpt from

SPRING FORWARD

A Mystic Creek novel by Catherine Anderson
Available now from Jove

Wind whistled into the big black van, whipping Tanner Richards' hair across his forehead as he drove. Squinting at the gravel road through the brown strands drifting over his eyes, he hauled in a deep breath of pine-scented air. Five years ago he'd agonized over his decision to sell his accounting firm and move to Crystal Falls, Oregon. He'd given up a six-figure annual income with no assurance that he could even find a job in this area. Crazy, really. Looking back on it now, though, he was glad that he'd come. Being a deliveryman wasn't as prestigious as working in his former chosen profession, but he made enough money to provide a good life for his kids, and he truly enjoyed the occupation. Having a rural route suited him. He was required to make fewer stops than he would have been in town, which equated to shorter workdays and more time in the evening to be with his children. And he'd made a lot of friends. Folks around here were more congenial than they were in larger towns.

As he rounded a curve in the country road, Tanner saw Tuck Malloy's house. Sadness punched into him. For three years running, he'd often stopped there to visit at the end of his workday, and he'd enjoyed a lot of cold ones on the porch with his elderly friend. Now the windows reflected the darkness of an empty structure. A For Sale sign rode high on the front gate. It had appeared nearly a month ago.

Tanner had considered calling the Realtor to learn what had happened to the property owner after his calls to Tuck went unanswered, but he really didn't want to know. Tuck had been a crusty old codger and eighty years young, as he'd been fond of saying. Unexpected things could happen to people that age. A heart attack, maybe, or a stroke. Tuck liked that piece of ground, and he would never have left voluntarily. He'd said so more than once. Tanner figured the old fellow was dead. Otherwise why would his place be up for sale?

Tanner pulled over and stopped outside the hurricane fence for a moment, a habit he had developed since the home had been vacated. He trailed his gaze over the front porch, now devoid of the comfortable Adirondack chairs where he had once sat with Tuck to chat. Recalling the old man's recalcitrant dog, he smiled. *Rip.* Tanner hoped the blue heeler had found a good home. He'd been a handful and was probably difficult to place.

Damn, he missed them both. With a sigh Tanner eased the van back onto the road. He had only one more delivery before he could call it a day. Maybe he could mow the lawn and do some weeding before his kids got home. Tori, now eight, had dance class after school today, and Michael, eleven and getting gangly, had baseball practice. Since his wife's death, Tanner had been a single dad, and not a day went by that he wasn't grateful for his mom's help. She got his kids off to the bus stop each morning and chauffeured them to most of their activities, which took a huge load of responsibility off his shoulders.

Tanner delivered the last parcel of the day. After he dropped the van off at Courier Express, he needed to pick up some groceries. Milk, for one thing. Tori wouldn't eat breakfast without it. And if he didn't get bread, he'd have no fixings for his lunch tomorrow.

His cell phone, which rode atop a sticky mat on the dash, chimed with a message notification. Tanner grabbed the device and glanced at the screen to make sure the text wasn't from his mother. She never contacted him during work hours unless it was urgent. When he read the name of the sender, his hand froze on the steering wheel. *Tuck Malloy?*

He almost went off the road into a ditch. How could that be? The old coot was dead. Wasn't he?

Tanner pulled over onto a wide spot, shifted into park, and stared at his phone. The message was definitely from Tuck. They had exchanged cell numbers months ago, and Tuck had occasionally texted to ask Tanner to pick up items he needed from the store. It hadn't been a bother for Tanner. There was a mom-and-pop grocery not that far away, and Tuck's house was on the road he always took back to town.

He swiped the screen. A smile curved his lips as he read the message. *"I fell off the damned porch. Busted my arm, some ribs, and had to get a hip replacement. Now I'm doing time in assisted living, and the bitch that runs the place won't let me have my beer or chew. Can you buy me some of both and sneak it in to me? I'll pay you back."*

Tanner had been picturing the old fart in heaven, sitting on an Adirondack chair with a six-pack of Pabst Blue Ribbon and a spittoon within easy reach. It was unsettling to think someone was dead and then receive a text from him.

He tapped out a response. *"I don't mind bringing you things. My kids have activities this afternoon, so I'm not pressed for time. But I don't want to get in trouble for delivering forbidden substances. My job could be on the line."*

Tuck replied, *"No trouble. Just put it inside a box and pretend it's something I ordered. If I get caught, I'll never tell who brought me the stuff. Sorry I can't just call, but these nurses have sharp ears and I got no privacy."*

Tanner grinned. He trusted the old man not to reveal his name if it came down to that. And he truly did sympathize with Tuck's feelings of deprivation. Just because a man was eighty shouldn't mean he no longer had a right to indulge his habits. Staying at an assisted living facility was costly, and in Tanner's estimation, the residents should be able to do whatever they liked in their apartments as long as their physicians didn't object.

He texted, *"Do you have your doctor's permission to drink and chew?"*

Tuck replied, *"Well, he ain't said I shouldn't. I been drinking and chewing my whole life. I'm eighty. What can he say, that my pleasures might kill me?"*

Tanner chuckled. He agreed to deliver the requested items and asked Tuck for the address. He was surprised to learn the facility was in

Mystic Creek. Tanner didn't cover that area, and it was a thirty-minute drive to get there. He mulled over the fact that he would be driving for more than an hour round-trip in a Courier Express van to run a personal errand. He'd also be using company fuel, which didn't seem right, but he supposed he could top off the tank to make up for that. He could also adjust his time sheet so he wouldn't be paid for an hour he hadn't actually worked.

Whistling tunelessly, Tanner made the drive to Mystic Creek. He hadn't yet gotten over this way. The curvy two-lane highway offered beautiful scenery, tree-covered mountain peaks, craggy buttes, and silvery flashes of a river beyond the stands of ponderosa pine. To his surprise, he saw a turnoff to Crystal Falls—the actual waterfall, not the town—and he made a mental note to bring the kids up sometime to see it. They'd get a kick out of that. Maybe they could spread a blanket on the riverbank and have a picnic.

Once in Mystic Creek, a quaint and well-kept little town, he found a grocery store on East Main called Flagg's Market, where he purchased two six-packs of beer and a whole roll of Copenhagen for his elderly friend. In the van he always carried extra box flats. He assembled a medium-size one, stuck what he now thought of as the contraband into it, and taped the flaps closed. With a ballpoint pen, he wrote Tuck's full name, the address, and the apartment number on a Courier Express mailing slip, which he affixed to the cardboard. *Done.* Now he'd just drive to the facility and make the delivery. The rest would be up to Tuck.

Mystic Creek Retirement Living was in a large brick building with two wings that angled out toward the front parking lot. The back of the facility bordered Mystic Creek, which bubbled and chattered cheerfully between banks lined with greenery, weeping willows, and pines. He suspected the residents spent a lot of time on the rear lawns, enjoying the sounds of rushing water and birdsong. If he were living there, that's what he would do.

Striding across the parking area with the box in his arms, Tanner began to feel nervous. What if someone questioned him? Pausing outside the double glass doors, he took a calming breath and then pushed inside. A middle-aged woman with red hair sat at the front desk. She fixed her friendly-looking blue gaze on Tanner's face and smiled.

"You're new," she observed. "Brian usually delivers our Courier Express packages."

Tanner nodded. "Uh, yeah. Just helping out today.

I've got a package for Tucker Malloy, apartment twenty-three."

She pointed to a wide hallway to the left of the counter. "About halfway down on the right."

Tanner circled her workstation and moved past her. When he reached Tuck's room, he knocked on the door and called, "Delivery. Courier Express."

He heard a shuffling sound, and seconds later, Tuck opened the door, flashing a broad grin. "Come in, come in," he said in a booming voice. "Must be those shoes and pants I ordered."

Tanner winked at his old friend as he made his way through the doorway. As he set the box on the living room floor, he noticed that Tuck held a walking cane in his left hand. After closing the door, he walked with a limp as he crossed the tiny kitchen. Tanner guessed the old fellow's hip still pained him. Otherwise he looked the same, tall and lean with slightly stooped shoulders. His blue eyes held the same merry twinkle. Deep smile creases bracketed his mouth. His hair, still thick, was mostly silver, but a few streaks of brown remained to indicate its original color.

"It's good to see you," Tanner told him. "When your place went up for sale, I tried to call you several times and left you voice mails. Then I couldn't get through anymore. I figured you'd passed away and your phone had been retired to a drawer."

"Hell, no. I'm too ornery to kick the bucket just yet. Not to say it's an outlandish thing for you to think. At eighty, I don't buy green bananas anymore. They're a risky investment."

Tanner laughed. Tuck bent to open the box, plucked a can of beer from one six-pack yoke, and offered it up. With regret, Tanner declined. "I can't stay, Tuck. My kids will be getting home in a couple of hours."

Tuck straightened slowly, as if stiffness had settled into his spine. On his right arm he wore a red elbow-high cast that extended down over the back of his hand to his knuckles and encircled his thumb. "That's a shame. I miss our bullshit sessions."

"Me, too," Tanner confessed. "I'll try to come back for a visit when I have more time." He bent to lift the six-packs from the box. "Where you planning to hide these?"

"In my boots and coat pockets. My beer'll be warm, but that's better'n nothin'."

Tanner carried the twelve-ounce containers to the closet, opened the doors, and began slipping cans into the old man's footwear. Tuck hobbled in with the roll of Copenhagen, which Tanner broke open before stuffing the rounds into shirt and jacket pockets. He couldn't help but grin when everything was hidden. With a wink at Tuck, he whispered, "They'll never know."

"Damn, I hope not," Tuck said. "My Pabst Blue Ribbon helps me relax at night. Without it I toss and turn. When I complain, the damned administrator just scowls at me and says to ask my doctor for sleeping pills. Like that'd be any better for my health? Hell, no. I like my beer."

Tanner stared at him. "What are you going to do with the empties?"

Tuck winked. "They got a resident laundry room down the hall with two tall trash cans. I'll sneak 'em down there and bury 'em real deep under other garbage."

"I see no harm in you enjoying your beer of an evening unless your doctor has forbidden it," Tanner said. "You'd tell me if that were the case. Right?"

"Wouldn't have asked you if he had. I don't have a death wish. I just want my damn beers and chew. The doc knows I have three beers a night and he never said nothin'. Of course, it's a different fella here. Their Dr. Fancy Pants might not make allowances for a man's personal pleasures."

"That sucks." Tanner had never stopped to consider how many liberties people could lose when they grew old. "But it's temporary. Right? Once you've healed, you can live somewhere else again." Tanner remembered the real estate sign on Tuck's front gate. "You *do* get to leave here, I hope."

"The doctors are sayin' that I shouldn't live alone again." He shrugged. "At my age, that's how it goes, with other people decidin' what's best for you."

"I'm sorry to hear you can't live alone anymore." Tanner sincerely meant that. "Maybe you can make arrangements for some kind of in-home care. If you can afford that, of course."

"I'm workin' on it. I got plenty of money saved back, so I had Crystal get me another house here in Mystic Creek. She found a nice little place on ten acres just outside town. It's a short drive from her salon, and she's already livin' there. The house was made over for an old lady in a wheelchair, but she passed away. Crystal thinks it'll suit my needs, and she's willin' to stay there to look after me."

Tanner nodded. "That sounds ideal. Ten acres isn't quite as much land as you had in Crystal Falls, but at least you'll still have elbow room." For most of his life, Tuck had been a rancher. Tanner doubted he would be happy living inside the city limits on a small lot. "You're blessed to have a granddaughter who loves you so much."

"I am, for certain. She's a sweet girl."

"Where's Bolt? At the new place?"

"Nope. Crystal has enough to do without fussin' over a horse. I had her find a place to board him. When I'm able, I'll bring him home and take care of him."

Tanner walked back into the living room, stabbing his fingers under his belt to neaten the tuck of his brown uniform shirt. "I sure wish I could stay for a while, but I've got to run."

"I understand. It'll soon be suppertime, and you've got kiddos to feed. Next time we'll enjoy a beer together and get caught up. You drive safe on that curlicue highway gettin' home. You're all your kids have left."

Tanner paused at the door. An urge came over him to hug the old fart goodbye. He wasn't sure when he'd come to care so much about Tuck, but after believing him to be dead for nearly a month, he found the feelings were there inside him. The old man had some crazy notions that Tanner didn't agree with, and sometimes he told stories so far-fetched that no sane person could believe them. But he also had a big heart, an indomitable spirit, and a way of looking at life that brought everything into perspective for Tanner sometimes. Still, Tanner wasn't sure the older man would appreciate being hugged.

"I'll be seeing you," he said.

Then he let himself out and softly closed the door.